SHADOWS ON AN IRON CURTAIN

A Novel of Camaraderie and Intrigue

By

M. J. Brett

Blue Harmony Press

Blue Harmony  **Press**

528 Southern Cross Drive
Colorado Springs, CO 80906

First Printing, June 2005

Dedication

Winston Churchill said that "An Iron Curtain" descended upon world civilization when the Soviet Union sealed off half of Europe after World War II making it an isolated, communist-dominated prison. In 1989, Ronald Reagan told Mr. Gorbachev to "Tear down this Wall." For forty-plus years of Cold War between these two statements, Western democracies faced down the constant Soviet threat to seize the remainder of Western Europe.

While the Berlin *Wall* was certainly the most visible result of this isolation, few realized that the *Border* stretched across the countryside was more volatile, longer, and more difficult to defend. Yet our soldiers manned every wire, responded to every threat, and defended the longest Border in the world, around the clock, for *all* of those years. Both barriers were the target of constant intrigue, spy activity, and serious terrorist threat. But if an incident occurred at the *Wall*, it was front-page news, and strict protocol was observed at cocktail parties between enemy leaders to prevent confrontation. When an all-out threat of Soviet tanks actually lining up against us occurred at the *Border*, it was classified as secret, and the world never knew about it. In fact, even troops at rear echelon military bases in Germany often knew little of what happened at these isolated *Border* outposts.

Had the Soviets breached that *Border*, life expectancy for our military units on that line was estimated at fifteen minutes.

This novel is dedicated to the people who lived the *Border* life--the men who manned it--these unknown heroes who blocked the advance of Soviet communism--their families unafraid to accompany them, and overseas teachers unafraid to go anywhere in the world to provide education for military children—the greatest children—under conditions that Stateside teachers would never understand. These, too, accepted the risks of the *Border* Life.

I hope all of these will feel I've portrayed their lives with as much sensitivity as they lived them.

Chapter 1

An ancient World Airways jet circled over Frankfurt Airport waiting its turn to land in the dense fog of morning. Though most passengers were waking from naps with the aplomb of seasoned overseas military travelers, Megan James had not slept at all. She hated being the only person awake. Isolation brought thoughts of…well…ending things.

Megan's reverie was interrupted as the stewardess greeted each passenger with a hot morning towel. The stewardess paused as Megan pried her fingers loose from her death grip on the armrests and squirmed to ease the ache in her shoulders.

"I've noticed you never got out of your seat," said the stewardess. She smiled at the frightened young woman. "Apparently, you've been holding the plane up single-handedly this whole nine-hour flight from McGuire Air Force Base? You must ache all over."

"I guess it was my vigilance, alone, that's kept this plane safely in the air," Megan tried to joke. "If these sleeping passengers only knew what a debt they owe me."

The stewardess met her satire with a pat on the shoulder. "Good Girl. We're almost there. Here's a magazine to take your mind off landing." She moved to the next passenger.

The date on the magazine was August 1974. Its well-thumbed pages fell open to the controversial cease-fire from the war in Vietnam flanked by photos of student riots and flag burning. Riot mentality sickened Megan, but she didn't want to read about the ashes of Vietnam either. She slid the magazine into the seat pocket. She would learn about military life soon enough, and she wanted to keep an open mind.

What on earth am I doing here? I guess it was either take this job or slit my wrists--maybe both. Put any kind of face on it you want, though, you're still running away. And now there's no going back.

A ho-hum bustle identified the crowd as experienced

travelers--mostly military men with families who moved every three years. Teens exchanged addresses with new friends made on the plane, youngsters played in the aisles, and long-time teachers chatted amiably as they returned for another fall semester. The pilot interrupted tired passengers with his announcement, "We've finally been cleared to land. Please return to your seat, put away carry-on items, and buckle up."

But as the plane dove steeply through the clouds, bumping along with confidence and touching down to the applause of its passengers, Megan, a stranger to those on the plane, to Germany, and to herself, wondered what this new job held in store for her. It had been a long-held dream to do it together, and now... *You can't live a dream alone*, she thought, but she caught herself drifting to the negative side, and forced away the idea for the hundredth time. With the rollout and taxi to the terminal, she noted among her peers a last sigh for an ended vacation, a last primp to the hair, a last stretch to the muscles, and the clicks from seat belts unfastened simultaneously.

Jet-lagged passengers waited to exit the plane and gathered in lines for passport control. Though Megan had no foreign language skill, a picture of a suitcase adorned every sign and passengers were funneled in the same direction as though the plane had been the only one arriving at dawn. Bags began bumping their way around the luggage carousel. Megan strained to see her hot pink Samsonite. The set had been a gift from her mother when she was hired for this overseas job. She'd never had luggage before. In fact, she had never traveled out of her home state of California before, and certainly she'd never before been on a plane.

She felt unsure why she had run away to Germany, and panic was setting in. "What on earth have I gotten myself into?" she whispered to herself. Everyone else seemed so casual about the whole international thing, while she wished there was a plane going right back home. But that would mean flying again--a frightening prospect. And home was no longer waiting for her, anyway. The person who'd made it *home* was gone.

People at the front of the crowd began hooting with laughter, and Megan strained to see what was going on. A pretty young woman was grabbing all her dainty underwear and clothes from a section of misbehaving baggage belt that had mangled one of her suitcases.

Megan gasped, as the blonde dove again and again at the belt, snatching up her belongings and dropping them into her luggage cart. Young men scurried to help, but they could not resist waving the lacy underwear like flags so their fellow soldiers could see.

How awful! How embarrassing for that poor girl! Forgetting her natural shyness, Megan dived into the fray to help. She gathered an armload of sweaters and slacks, dropped them into the blonde's cart, and returned for another load.

When it seemed that most everything had been recovered, the blonde spoke out loudly with a lazy southern drawl, "Now don't any of y'all little soldier boys keep anything for a souvenir. I'll be in this foreign country all year, and I won't be able to shop for more frilly things over here in Germany. Now 'fess up, please do."

She flashed an unembarrassed smile that melted nearby observers. A small group of young GIs conferred, and one was pushed forward, sheepishly handing over a ruffled, lacy pair of panties to the blonde. Thanking him profusely, she kissed him on the cheek, and the crowd roared its approval.

Megan noticed the low cut bodice under the woman's flapping coat. *This person was not at all upset by the attention.* Feeling embarrassed and vulnerable, Megan turned to her own suitcases, snatched them off the baggage belt, and swung them onto her cart. There was a vanity case under one bag. From its color, it could only have come from one place. She hurried with her cart over to the blonde and offered it shyly.

"Why, thanks, honey," the younger woman said. "What a way to greet Germany--by losing my drawers." She laughed and stuck out her hand. "I'm Lila," she announced with husky force that denoted confidence. "What's your name?"

Megan looked around, wondering if anyone would think she knew this brazen woman. But she couldn't ignore the proffered hand without being rude, and that was against her inner need to please others. So, with mixed feelings, she timidly offered her own hand. "Megan," she said. "Do you think you found all your things?" She felt awkward at conversation.

"Most of it." Lila laughed loudly. "I saw one teen-aged kid slip some panties into his coat pocket, but I didn't want to make a fuss and embarrass him. His hormones are raging, and I'll bet he gets more mileage out of those skivvies than I ever will. He'll be the hit of his class with his 'trophy.'"

Megan didn't know what to say. She had never met anyone so open about such private things. She would have died of embarrassment had it been her own lingerie so exposed. Yet this young woman had carried off the disaster with ease and even now was returning the smiles of other amused passengers and patting her blonde curls into place.

Megan felt grudging admiration for one with such confidence, but became uncomfortable again as Lila bumped through customs with her open bag, piles of clothes and a disarming smile, saying, "I think y'all might want to fix that luggage belt thingy next time you get a lil' minute." The customs officials didn't speak English, but it was obvious what had happened as they moved Lila through the line with barely-concealed smirks. They offered a piece of rope. Megan lost sight of the young woman in the forward push of the crowd.

Outside the customs area, through frosted double doors, a mob of military personnel held up names and destinations on cardboard placards. Megan stood still, bewildered, not sure what to do next. After a few moments, she heard someone a few yards away bellow out in a commanding voice, "Anyone else for Bamberg?"

Megan straggled up to a sturdily built female sergeant. "My orders said 'Bamberg,' but my friends at home couldn't find it on the map of Germany. They claimed it must be a typographical error and Hamburg was where I was going. Is there really a Bamberg?"

"Yes Ma'am," said the sergeant, choking back her laughter. "There's a Bamberg all right. Though some folks say there shouldn't be one. It's a small outpost, way out at the end of the food chain, but right at the edge of the Border. Are you my last teacher?"

"I guess so," said Megan. She was engulfed in a bear hug from Lila.

"Why Honey, you didn't tell me you were going to Bamberg too. We're going to have a great ol' time. Kentucky men were rednecks and unadulterated morons, and I've had a steady progression of them. I have much higher hopes for some of those cute officers my mom said would lounge around any military base. I can't wait for them to sweep me off my feet."

Megan cringed, wondering what she should say to such a woman.

An older lady standing by the sergeant laughed and stuck out

her hand to Lila. "I'm Emily Arnold, and I wish you lots of luck."
Nodding at Megan, she added, "I gather you've not done this before?"

Megan nodded and gave her name. A redhead standing nearby
seemed cool, sophisticated, aloof, more poised than Megan could
quite imagine when she shyly offered her hand and smiled tentatively.
To her surprise, the redhead erupted in smiles and freckles. "I'm
Abby Sims, and we're glad to have you both you 'newbies' in the
overseas teaching program."

Lila was still chattering along to bystanders as she stuffed her
clothing back into the ripped suitcase and tied it together with rope
where the latch had broken. *As though this were the most normal
thing on earth,* thought Megan.

Emily chuckled out loud. "At least this trip is starting off with
a good laugh. I always enjoy an unexpected turn of events."

The uniformed woman announced, "I'm Sergeant Hilfiger.
I'm supposed to have four DoDDS teachers and three GI's in my van.
The soldiers are here. I'm assuming you four are my teacher-types."

Emily laughed, the redhead smiled, and Lila roared out, "Is
that what we are now, *teacher-types*?" Turning to the ladies, she
added, "Honey, you three don't look like GI's so you must be teacher-
types like me. Look out Bamberg, here we come!"

The little group dragged in a haphazard gaggle out to the
street and piled into a green Army van. Sergeant Hilfiger swung the
van out of the airport through an astounding maze of swirls and turns,
finally entering onto a freeway of some proportion, heading east. Eyes
grew wide as Mercedes' and BMW's sped by at astronomical speeds,
rocking the van as they passed.

"Don't you worry none," said the sergeant, sensing her
passengers' anxiety. "We just stay in our right lane except to pass,
and then we'd darn well better high-tail it back into our own lane
afterward. Drive with your rear view mirror so you don't pull out in
front of somebody, because they sure won't, and probably can't, slow
down."

"My Gosh," said Emily, "How fast are they going?"

"Oh, 150 to 230 kilometers per hour. For you first timers,
that's about 90-140 miles per hour. There's no speed limit on the
Autobahn unless it's marked, which it usually isn't."

"I don't think I'll be driving my old *Volkswagen* much,"

announced Emily in a firm voice. "I'm hoping to live to retire from DoDDS. Didn't drive in Iceland or Cuba or the Bahamas much either--nowhere to go—all islands."

"I shipped my mom's antique Chevy from Kentucky," said Lila. "The government wouldn't let me bring my foreign sports car. 'U.S. cars only for new hires,' they said."

Megan added, "I left my old clunker behind. Once I get settled, I'll look for another. Friends told me to get a new car's guarantee in case something goes wrong. I'll be alone here."

"I guess we'll all be alone. I'm looking for a new one too," said Abby. "Shall we go car shopping together?"

"Okay. It may keep us both from making mistakes."

"Be sure you get your license first," said the Sergeant. "It's pretty hard, with about a sixty percent failure rate." Megan decided the Sergeant must be mistaken.

One of the GIs piped up, "What's this place *Ausfahrt* on all the freeway signs?"

The sergeant laughed aloud. Then she said formally, as though she had entertained new recruits many times before, "Ladies and gentlemen. I'll save you from being victims of the first joke an American coming to Germany will hear. People will tell you *Ausfahrt* is the 'biggest city in Germany,' and that 'all roads lead to *Ausfahrt.*' Actually, it means 'exit' so you'll see it everywhere on the *Autobahn.* Now you know. You must also avoid anyone who invites you to a party on *Einbahnstrasse.*" It means 'one-way-street,' so you'd walk all over Bamberg and never find any party."

Her passengers laughed, relaxed, and one by one faded into silence as jet lag overtook them. The sergeant showed no surprise when she had to wake the group two hours later as she stopped in front of the billeting office for the GI's to get their barracks assignments. All her passengers were bewildered and not sure where they were.

"Where do *we* go?" asked Lila, when the van drove away leaving the young men behind. "All I can think about is lunch."

"You ladies will be billeted at the Bamberg Officers' Club. They have guest quarters you'll be using until you can find apartments on the economy."

Seeing the puzzled looks from Lila and Megan, Emily answered the unasked question. "'On the economy' means out in the local foreign community."

"Oh, goodness," said Megan with alarm. "My Government orders stated we'd be in BOQ's, Bachelor Officers' Quarters, on Post. They only let me ship a few pounds of household goods, so I'll have no furniture or dishes. Surely they won't send us away from the American base. I speak no German."

"You'll learn," said the sergeant. "Sign up for the Gateway language program. A sponsor will help you find an apartment off Post. Germany doesn't use 'For Rent' signs. You'll put an ad in the German newspaper saying, 'American teacher is looking for rooms near Bamberg *Kaserne*,' and they'll write you if *they* are interested. *You* won't have much choice, as apartments are scarce. Be sure you ask for 'partially furnished' because 'unfurnished' means no sinks, no kitchen cabinets, no light fixtures, no nothing. It can get expensive."

She paused for a moment and then added an explanation. "We did have BOQ space available for you, but female soldiers just this summer became an official part of the Army. Most are in clerking jobs, none in combat units. The Brass didn't want them in the barracks with men. So enlisted women have taken over some officer BOQ's for the time being. We have no idea how long it will take Brigade Headquarters to figure out what to do with us females."

The Sergeant sighed as though this problem seemed insurmountable--or perhaps it was the officers at Brigade Headquarters with whom she had a conflict.

The sergeant pulled through a wooded area and up to a stately, ornate building with over-sized and heavily carved wooden doors, left over from the old German Army--perhaps from the time of Bismarck. She plopped the teachers' luggage on the sidewalk, waved goodbye, and drove away.

Tired, bedraggled, in desperate need of food, a shower, and sleep, the four new teachers assigned to Bamberg American School, courtesy of the Department of Defense, gathered their bags and staggered up the steps into the lobby.

No one was there.

Chapter 2

The women surveyed the deserted foyer, wondering aloud if there had been some mistake. Sheets draped over chairs. Rolls of paper covered carpeting. Scaffolding leaned against high, dirty windows. A phone cord dangled uselessly from newly painted walls.

"This place is either under renovation or under siege," said Emily. "We can't stay here."

"Where else can we go?" Megan bit her lip, wishing her voice hadn't sounded so frantic.

Hammering and banging echoed from a long hallway. While the others slumped in silence, Lila plopped her bundles on the floor and hurried down the hall toward the sound.

She soon returned, chatting amiably with a workman who bore a startling resemblance to Ichabod Crane. The man bowed low with profuse apologies in English, French, and German marked by a Spanish accent. His formal, cosmopolitan manners were impressive.

"Please allow me to introduce myself. I'm Marco, the *maitre'd*. I've been rearranging my kitchen after the painters mangled it. *Mein Gott!* I am so sorry I cannot offer you ladies lunch, but the Officers' Club will be closed for another two weeks. We were not expecting guests. We have nothing in the kitchen but peanut butter and jelly left in the refrigerator by the workmen."

"That'll do just fine, " Lila gushed. "We're starved." The other women were embarrassed by her forwardness, but equally hungry.

With a flick of his wrist, Marco whipped off sheets revealing heavily- brocaded furniture and a marble inlaid table and invited the ladies to be seated. Removing his blue workman's jacket, he hurried to the kitchen.

He soon returned in a white dinner jacket carrying a silver tray on which rested peanut butter on crackers and cheese slices. He slid into a side room, apparently a bar, and emerged with frosted soft drink bottles. "I am so sorry, ladies. This is all I could find. There are not even glasses since all such things have been packed away during the renovation. Please forgive this poor fare and try our dining room once we are back in operation. The officers will be so happy for you to join us."

"We're amazed at your ingenuity, Marco," said Abby, while the others thanked him and dug into the food.

Only the slightest twitch of his dark mustache indicated he was flattered.

Megan shyly pulled at Marco's sleeve. "Mr. Marco, we were told we could stay here--that there were rooms reserved for us. I assumed this was some type of hotel."

"Forgive me, Ma'am," said the man with grave formality almost hiding his amusement. "Please call me 'Marco.' We have rooms upstairs in the Guest Officer Quarters. I'll prepare some for you now. But I'm afraid there will be nothing here for you to eat, and no one else will be here until the renovations are completed."

As the ladies ate their impromptu lunch with gusto, Marco returned several times until all their bags had been carried upstairs. Then he handed out keys.

"These are only to reassure you," he said. "No one locks doors here, so you needn't do so unless you feel insecure." He bowed again and glided out of sight, as effortlessly as a ghost.

"Wow!" said Lila. "Wasn't he something? Now I've seen a *suave* European."

"I'm sure the Department of Defense didn't warn him we were arriving today. We were no doubt a surprise," said Abby. "But he certainly has a striking elegance of speech and manner, doesn't he? Could anyone tell his nationality, or his age?"

"I can't be sure, but he handled our welcome with such poise, in spite of the renovations," said Megan, admiring anyone who could rise gracefully to an unexpected occasion.

Emily spoke up. "I won't be watching Marco in action long. My nephew is stationed here and has asked me to stay with his family in base housing until I find an apartment. I'll just let my nephew know I'm here, and he can come get me after work."

Abby waved her hand at the dangling phone cord.

Emily nodded her understanding. "At least, I'll *try* to call him, somehow, or I'll just stay here until we find a phone. I have no idea where he's living on Post."

"Well, girls," chirped Lila, "I guess that makes us the four musketeers. We'll have a great time hunting for food, transportation, and apartments together."

Megan kept her doubts to herself, but she noticed Abby was silent as well. Perhaps neither of them formed alliances easily, though Megan knew her own reasons stemmed from a new insecurity. She wondered what prompted Abby's. For the time being, though, it looked as though the women would be pretty much on their own. They headed upstairs.

Though each teacher had a private room and adjoining bath, they soon found that hot water was limited. Shrieks rang out down the hall as Lila's thirty-minute shower forced the other three into cold water. No one complained, however. It felt good just to have clean hair and a change of clothing after the long flight.

Megan stretched out on the bed to rest. Dreamless, relaxing sleep had not come for over a year. Doubt quickly assailed her, as it always did. She was frightened to be alone in a strange place, though that had been her original plan—a place where no one would know her, nor care enough about her to be upset when she *checked out*, as she euphemistically called it. Yet, she was terrified at the prospect of moving off Post into the foreign community. She'd never lived alone.

"Oh, God," she cried out, trying to contain her panic. "Is this plan too staggering a change? We wanted to do it together. You ruined our lives. It wasn't fair!" Quiet tears soaked the pillow under her dark hair as she recited her litany of anger toward God.

Of course, God never answered and, once again, Megan felt cheated. "What do I expect, anyway? You aren't even listening anymore." She said the awful words aloud. "I just want it to be a bad dream. I want to wake up with a different ending. Instead, the same nightmare plays itself out night after night until it wakes me, cold and alone." She knew it wasn't logical to talk to herself so much. She must stop. She felt conflicted, incongruous. *I've always been such an incurable optimist. Is there even such a thing as a suicidal optimist?*

As fatigue quieted her feverish despair, the silence in the building made her curious about the others. Were they alone with their thoughts too, or were they napping? After resting a couple of hours, Megan dressed and peeked into the hallway. Lila was listening at Emily's door.

Lila put her finger to her lips. The strains of *Smoke Gets in Your Eyes*, a very old love song, wafted from the room. Lila giggled. "Should we knock?"

Abby came from her room down the hall in time to answer, "Why not? I guess we're all awake. Did you two get some rest? I've traveled too many time zones to relax yet."

"Is this the 'jet lag' I've heard about?" asked Lila. "I simply died in there, then woke up in only an hour, hearing music. Besides, I'm hungry again…already."

Megan knocked on Emily's door. The humming immediately stopped, and Emily opened the door with a smile, beckoning the younger women inside.

"I hoped someone was waking up," she said. "Please sit down and tell me all about yourselves." She indicated the room's chairs as she sat on the bed, drying her hair with a towel.

"Not much to tell," Lila volunteered. "Kentucky schools weren't very progressive, and Kentucky men weren't very committed. I hope Germany will have greener pastures." She studied her red fingernails. "Plus, my mama kept telling me it was high time a Kentucky girl got married and supplied her with grandchildren. The pressure was getting a bit much."

"That's easy to understand," said Emily, tilting her head in frank appraisal.

Megan felt some mysterious aura in Emily of a woman who seemed at ease with herself—one to whom she could perhaps talk with honesty—someday—before….

"You girls are in a battle with your biological clocks," Emily continued, "and if you ever want children, you need to start thinking about settling down and getting married soon. At fifty-five and divorced, I've already decided not to bother breaking in a new husband. In the military system, most men have retired by my age, anyway. I'm not looking for any adventure here."

"Well, I'm 30, and I *am* looking for adventure. Germany is the place," Lila said, nodding with determination.

Abby shifted, looking a bit uncomfortable. Megan was silent.

"I've made a lot of false starts, but I'm beginning to think about the idea of marriage," said Lila, smoothing the wrinkles from her slacks. "Only to *think*. I may not be ready to *do* it."

"Happy hunting," said Emily. "I have four children--all grown. Guess I showed that derelict ex of mine, though—raised them alone. My youngest daughter, Lucy, is about at that settling down point too, though sometimes I wonder if it's the right thing for her. One never knows about young people these days."

"Well, I hope some of these soldiers are single and like to have fun." Lila's impish grin lit up the room. "I may have let my fun-loving side take over my practical side for too long, but I really do *have* a practical side. I just have trouble making it function, except in the classroom."

"What do you teach?" asked Abby.

"Math and science," said Lila.

"Who would a thunk it?" Emily snorted.

Though Lila had often been teased about the incongruent juxtaposition of her 'dumb-blonde' personality and her technical subject fields, she took no offense. "My mom says I have intelligence, but that's different from common sense, of which she claims I have *none*." In her bubbly southern drawl she added, with a staged bow, "Miss Galloway, professor of Mathematics, summa cum laude, at your service. My father never thought I had a brain in my head, so it was a point of pride to prove him wrong with a master's degree. He didn't live long enough for my graduation--but he got the point!" There was an edge of bitterness in her laugh.

Emily did not probe further, but instead turned to the lighter side of teaching. "I'll bet all your junior high boys fall in love with you," she joked.

"Yeah," answered Lila with a shrug, "but I just tell them, 'Get real, Honey. You can't afford me. The man of my dreams will have to sweep me off my feet.' I get them to laugh about it. Usually, their next step is to try to match me up with their uncle"

Emily smiled as she finished drying her hair and combed it.

"What about you, Emily?" asked Megan. "What age group do you teach?"

"I've had first graders for thirty years. The little ones are so open, and the whole world is new to them. My orders said I'd have a first grade classroom at *Muna*--wherever that is."

"Mine said fifth-grade," said Megan, "same as I taught in California. I like them big enough to argue." A smile lit her lips as she thought of all her recent ten-year-olds.

"Why, Megan, that's the first time you've smiled since we got off the plane. You and Abby must be our shy ones." Lila nodded at Abby. "Okay--your turn--what grade for you?"

"Eighth grade Science. I presume we'll find out what's going on Monday at the first faculty meeting. There wasn't much information in the hiring packet they sent me in the Philippines."

Megan sized up the tall, slender Abby, assuming she was about 29. She also noticed the easy, ranging motion of a natural athlete. *Could be a fun person to know, but I don't want to get close to anyone here that might mess up my plan.*

"Wow!" said Lila. "From the Philippines? You must have been on planes for days."

"Yes. I stayed the summer to travel and see it all--so I wouldn't need to go back again. While teaching there I spent almost every weekend biking across the islands--covered the whole set of islands from North to South."

"I heard those islands weren't very safe, what with bandits and warring factions," said Megan, a hint of admiration in her voice. "You did that all alone?"

"My concession to danger was stopping at hotels rather than my preference of camping out. I find both physical exercise and solitude invigorating."

Lila was intrigued. "How exotic. What did you like best about the islands?"

"Tropical rain on a tin roof, the smell of jasmine wafting through open shutters with no glass windows. I loved having a maid and houseboy to do my chores and a dressmaker to whip up new clothes from my own sketches, but three years in Paradise was quite enough."

Megan noted that Abby was not at all unfriendly, but more sophisticated and self-contained than the rest of their group. She did not seem as 'needy' as Megan *felt* when she asked, "We don't have much information to go on about either school or Germany, do we?"

Lila shrugged her acceptance. "It seems no one was expecting us. We'll just have to get through this weekend somehow before we find out anything about surroundings, colleagues, or classrooms. I always love starting classes, but this weekend may be a bummer. Heck, we slept on the van ride. We don't even know where we *are*. Who's ever heard of Bamberg, anyway?"

"The Sergeant said something about Bamberg being an *outpost*," said Megan. "What do you suppose she meant?" All shrugged, not knowing, but they walked down the stairs together with more confidence than any of them felt, perhaps finding strength in their number.

Marco was nowhere in sight, and there were no further hammering sounds from the German workmen. "Perhaps Germans go home early on Friday," speculated Emily.

As they strolled from the front steps, wondering which way they should turn to find the Army Post, or the town, or anything tangible, a jeep sped into the parking lot and screamed to a halt immediately in front of them. A young 'butter bar' second lieutenant jumped from the jeep as though he were a genie fresh out of a bottle.

"Are you the new teachers?" he asked, fidgeting on first one foot and then the other. On being assured that they were, the young man rushed to the jeep and ceremoniously presented each of them with a long-stemmed red rose. "We, that is, the other officers and I, of the 82nd Engineers, want to welcome all new teachers with a formal get-acquainted party tomorrow night at *Seehof* Carriage House."

"Wow! A party…and such a nice invitation." Lila bubbled at the prospect.

The young man looked to be in his very early twenties and was, by now, blushing. I'll come get you at 1800 hours and bring you back when the party's over."

Lila and Megan looked confused until Emily said, "The military and the Germans use 24-hour clocks."

"I'm Lieutenant Fred Fleming. Can I help you with anything?"

The women looked at each other in wonder. It was almost as though Lt. Fleming had read their collective minds and come at the opportune moment.

"Are the 82nd Engineers the *only* unit here, or are they just more organized?" asked Emily.

Lt. Fleming grinned, sheepishly admitting the truth under Emily's level gaze. "Well, not exactly the only one, Ma'am, but we do like to get in favor with the new ladies before 2nd Armored Cavalry gets word they're here. Our Captain Lang knows a man in Transportation who tells him when a new crop of teachers arrives, and when the others return from summer vacation. We meet them all. This party has become an annual event." He drew himself up taller and straightened his uniform. "Don't you worry, 82nd will take good care of you. Captain Lang has contacts everywhere, and he can get you anything from furniture to typing paper. This party will have great food and…and…great company too," he finished with a stammer and a shy smile.

Emily answered before the rest could recover from their shock. "These ladies will be honored to come, Lieutenant. Of course, your captain didn't count on a school teacher of my advanced age, so I'll be glad to bow out."

"And I don't go to parties, but thank you anyway," Megan rushed to add.

"Oh, no, Ma'am--I mean--Ma'ams," blustered the Lieutenant, turning redder than ever. "When Captain Lang says he wants me to round up all the new teachers, he means *all* of them. You wouldn't want me to get in trouble with Captain Lang for failing my very first mission, would you?" He looked genuinely at a loss. "You all must come. Our officers want you there."

"Well, Lt. Fleming, we certainly wouldn't want you to get in trouble with your captain," said Emily. She glanced at the others with steely eyes. "We will *all* be honored to come, and thank you for your wonderful presentation of the roses." Belatedly, the other three women followed Emily's lead and thanked the red-faced young man. Lila beamed.

Not wanting to miss this opportunity—the only real live person in sight, Abby remembered to ask the burning question. "Do you know where we can find a café nearby?"

"The closest place is in Gardenstadt, about two blocks away, Ma'am. There's a snack bar, but they haven't given you ID cards to get on Post yet, have they?"

Abby shook her head.

"Then Gardenstadt is your only option. I'll take you there" He helped each of the four into the jeep, realizing too late that they would be quite crowded. He drove through the small German village to a café. As the teachers climbed down, they noticed the café's garden where they could sit in the late afternoon August sun.

"Shall I wait for you?" asked the Lieutenant.

"Oh no. We'll enjoy the walk back. You've already been most kind," said Emily.

He drove away, smiling and waving.

The women waved, but then fell into laughter as Lila remarked, "I sure hope there are some men in Bamberg older than Lt. Fleming. But wasn't he a cutie?"

Abby sobered as she thought of a slight problem. "Do any of you have German money?"

She received blank stares accompanied by a thoughtful pause.

"Uh-oh," said Megan. "I was told we'd find a bank at the airport as soon as we arrived. But we were so rushed, I forgot to look for one."

"This calls for the old southern charm," announced Lila and she motioned them all to be seated in the garden while she approached the owner. After bright smiles and flamboyant gestures, she returned to the table.

"Eat whatever y'all can point at on the menu," she whispered. "I *think* I just persuaded him to let us pay in American money. We'll eat *first*, then we'll see if he understood my sign language."

They pointed at the strange German words in which 'ice' turned out to be ice cream instead of something to cool their room temperature drinks. They ate something akin to a hot dog, but fatter, with a spicy sauce. Then they held out their American money helplessly for the proprietor to choose whatever he wanted. He selected a few bills and coins, smiling and bowing continuously. They thanked the man and walked back toward the Officers' Club, wondering if they'd handled the situation properly.

"How did you manage persuading him?" Abby asked of Lila.

"Oh, men are a pushover in any language, if y'all just smile and encourage them. His wife wouldn't have been so quick to agree. But I *think* he was saying we could come back any ol' time." Lila laughed out loud and swung down the street ahead of the others.

"Well, at least we had something good to eat, *whatever* it was," said Megan in awe at Lila's self-confidence. "We need to learn the language quickly."

Abby added, "I'm glad we're all together. I hope we can find someplace to get German money tomorrow, or we'll still be in the same predicament for the whole weekend."

"It'll have to be early because the hiring packet they sent me in Iceland said Germans close up everything by noon on Saturday," said Emily.

Lila turned around and grimaced. "I never get up early."

"I wake up early," said Emily. "And I have a purse-sized German dictionary."

Megan raised her hand. "Me too. Maybe Emily and I can go get enough money for everyone in the morning and pick up some breakfast rolls or something."

"That's a deal," said Abby, handing over bills from her wallet.

Lila added her own bills to Emily's growing stack. As they returned, seemingly by common consent, to Emily's room and sat down, she said, "Now, let's think about something *really* important. Like, what are y'all wearing for the party tomorrow night?"

A restful night, morning rolls, and the ladies regaled each other with stories about their hometowns until late afternoon, when they got serious about dressing for the party.

In a pattern that would become the norm, Lila would be ready last. Emily was first to descend the staircase to the O'Club lobby. She wore a blue dress that had served her well over the years for the few formal occasions she had needed it. With her warm smile, one never worried about fashion.

Abby came down next, stunning in a burnt orange, slim-line, ankle length skirt of Thai silk, embroidered, and tied at the waist, with a contrasting umber shirtwaist blouse. Her soft, tailored hair, turned under at the ends, framed a sophisticated, beautifully serene face.

"This is as close to 'formal' as I ever get," said the younger woman. "Normally I prefer slacks and sweaters."

"Wonderful color on you," said Emily. "I would never have thought a redhead could get away with it, but it looks great, and the outfit is so original."

"Courtesy of that Philippine dressmaker I told you about."

"And would you look here!" Emily's jaw dropped as she glanced up the stairs. "Gliding like a shadow, isn't she? And down a staircase yet."

Abby called out, "Hey, Megan. How do you float so smoothly in high heels?"

Megan blushed, which accentuated freckles against her pale skin and dark curly hair. "Childhood necessity, I guess," she answered as she reached the bottom of the stairs. "I had to learn to walk with a glass of water on my head to counteract a limp. I often got drenched while learning." She felt embarrassed to have admitted something so personal.

Emily and Abby agreed they would *still* be wet if they ever tried such a thing.

"I didn't know we needed a formal until that last information packet from DoDDS. This was all I could find in a hurry," said Megan. "The saleslady said it wouldn't wrinkle, even rolled up in a suitcase." She looked down, apprehensively. "But it's plain--too form-fitted, I think."

"Hey, it's great," said Abby, admiring the simple, high-necked, sleeveless sheath in bias-cut, green jersey. "You have the straight-up posture to get away with wearing it."

They stopped chattering when Lila flounced down the stairs in a haze of fluffy, flowered chiffon. Her cocktail dress had low-cut ruffles framing her bejeweled neck and softly-curled blonde hair.

"Wow, Lila!" said Emily. "You sure know how to command a room. None of those young officers will stand a chance." Her low chuckle reflected genuine joy. "Here I am flanked by a blonde, a brunette, and a redhead. Why, I feel like the mother-of-the-bride!"

Lila admired each of the other three ladies, pausing by Megan. "I sure wish I had your measurements. Where were you hiding that Jane Russell bust line when we were at the airport?"

Megan's hands flew to her throat, pulling her arms in to hide her ample bosom. "I can't go to any party." She turned back toward the steps, but Lila grabbed her arm.

"Oh, Honey, I'm sorry. I didn't know you were bashful about your figure. You're just fine, and we either *all* go to the party, or *none* of us goes, right girls?"

"And you know how much Lila and Abby want to go, don't you?" chimed in Emily.

Megan nodded, near tears. "I was flat as a pancake until they removed my tonsils, and overnight I outgrew everything on top. I've worn oversized clothes ever since, because people stare at me if I wear something fitted, like this stupid gown."

Lila hugged her, pleading, "Don't mind my noticing, Megan, please don't. You look perfect." She stepped back, lifting up the flounces from her own dress with an impish grin. "See, I'm just jealous. Why do y'all think I wear so many ruffles to cover me up?"

Even Megan was able to smile as Lila added, "Hey, we're all

the friends we've got. We *have* to take care of each other."

The four drifted across the lobby as they heard a jeep drive up on the stroke of six.

Lt. Fleming sprang through the door and stopped short. "Wow! I mean…you all look wonderful. The guys at *Seehof* are going to be…I mean…we'd better go." However, he was flummoxed when it came to helping four ladies wearing formal dresses into his jeep's tiny seats. He had added a blanket-covered board to create extra space, but still, he lifted here and pushed there and stepped back to check his handiwork. "I sure hope I didn't crush anything."

Lila couldn't help giggling as the four reassured the young man that they were tucked in securely. Then they were whisked off into the countryside. After bouncing over a dirt road, with its passengers holding on tightly, the jeep circled behind an old palace.

"Lt. Fleming, that place is gorgeous," said Abby. "What is it?"

"That's the *Schloss Seehof*, Ma'am. No one lives there anymore, not since the war trapped its Count behind the Iron Curtain. Like most others, once they are over there, it's a case of life and death to ever get back to the West zone. Most never make it.

"The old palace is badly in need of repair, as you can see, but the Bavarian State caretakers can't afford the renovations. Only the former carriage house out back is rented. Captain Lang and Lt. Sizemore share one side of it and a pilot lives in the other apartment." Lt. Fleming pulled up to the carriage house and stopped.

He helped the ladies out of the jeep, and they stood admiring the ancient building.

Lila grabbed Abby and Megan's hands with a tight squeeze, smiling at Emily. "Here we go, ladies, into our new life. Let's make the most of it."

Chapter 3

The carriage house door opened to light and music. The four were ushered into an oversized and noisy room where at least seventy people chatted by a well-stocked bar, grazed at long trestle tables loaded with a colorful buffet, or gathered on the many overstuffed, government-issue sofas and chairs. Dancers moved on a large sunken floor.

"It's right out of King Arthur's palace," squealed Lila, clapping her hands.

A short, stocky young man greeted each of the women with a courtly bow and a kiss on the hand. "Captain Stan Lang, at your service."

Emily gasped. "I thought you'd be a giant ogre from the description of your considerable power." She added. "You've certainly been most gracious to invite us to your party."

The man flashed a most beautiful smile.

"I like to let my men think I'm a tyrant." He lowered his voice. "Actually, I'm a pussy-cat, but don't tell anyone."

The ladies laughed, as Stan introduced them to waiting escorts.

"Look, y'all. Men definitely outnumber women," Lila whispered. She smiled brightly as she and Abby were whisked off to join different groups seated near arched windows looking out on the old palace across the lake. Emily was escorted in another direction, and Megan lost sight of her, though she could hear her throaty laugh. Megan was taken by the arm and steered across the room toward the bar by a willowy tall, Scandinavian-looking young man.

"I'm Vernon--friends call me Vern. I'm really an interloper from 2/78 Artillery, not an Engineer at all, but Stan doesn't care. He just wants you all to have a good time. May I get you a drink?"

Megan nodded. "Do they have a soft drink, preferably Tab?"

"I'm sure they do. They have everything else. What would you like in it?"

"Just plain, with ice cubes, hopefully. I'm out of place at a party. I don't drink."

"That's okay. At a line base, everyone just does his own

thing. No one will care."

Vern introduced Megan to several people, and she listened to them amiably. But she found her mind wandering as she stared around the room in discomfort. *How can I fit into such a huge crowd? I haven't been to even a small party for years--not after I wrapped my whole life around Andy.*

She was unaware how long she had been daydreaming when she felt a tap on her shoulder, and a smooth voice said, "Take me. I'm easy."

She turned to see a blonde young man holding out his arms to her.

"Where should I take you?" Her brow wrinkled. "We're riding back to the guest quarters with Lt. Fleming, but I'm sure he wouldn't mind if you needed a ride, too."

The young man groaned, clapping a hand to his shaking head. "I can see *you're* going to need someone to look after you." He sighed. "I'm that someone. I'm Carl Sheffield."

"I'm very glad to meet you, Carl. Shall I go ask Lt. Fleming now?"

"No, I don't need a ride. I just saw you surveying the room with that faraway look in your eyes, with your chin held high, and a figure like royalty. I thought maybe you were searching just for me." He held out his arms again, smiling expectantly.

"Oh dear," Megan said, overcome again with self-consciousness. She brought her hands to her face, pulling arms in across her chest. "I only had this one dress to wear for a formal party. The other ladies said it would be okay." She was near tears and, to her dismay, she could feel the rush of blood to her cheeks.

Carl sobered quickly, snatched her drink with his own, and set them down on a nearby table. He took both her hands in his, pulled them away from her face and chest, and looked her up and down, appraisingly, as she stood trembling. "You may not realize it, Lady, but your figure and your posture are perfect for that dress, and you have *nothing* to hide. I'm sorry if I said it all wrong. I just meant that I noticed you from across the room and figured you were sizing up the men, like the women usually do."

"I wasn't looking for anyone…honestly…certainly not sizing up any men. Actually, I was wondering what I was doing here, at a party with all these people I don't know."

"Well, now you know me, and I can recognize pain in the eyes better than most." He looked straight into hers as though he could see inside. "What's his name?"

Startled, Megan answered honestly. "Andy, only he's dead, and I guess I'm not ready to be around a crowd."

"Let's go over to the windows where we can watch the night outside, and you can tell me about him." Carl grasped her arm with one hand, picked up the two drinks by their rims with the other, and led Megan to a vacant sofa. Away from the noise, the dark rustle of trees surrounding the alcove seemed to wrap them in a cocoon. He set down the drinks and licked one of his wet fingers, holding it in the air quizzically "Don't you approve of booze, or are you in AA?"

Megan checked to see he was smiling and not mocking her before she answered. "Neither--I only had one drink in my life, on my twenty-first birthday. My husband had to carry me home. I've been afraid to drink anything since. My tolerance for alcohol must be miniscule."

"You were already married at twenty-one?"

"Already married--with two little girls." She smiled, remembering. "We were best friends from the age of ten and got married at eighteen when he went away to the Navy. We never even dated each other, but we found neither of us could survive with the other one gone."

"When did he die?"

"Over a year ago. A blood clot went to his heart. One minute—well--we were laughing, and the next minute, he was gone. I still feel responsible." Tears gathered on her eyelashes.

Carl reached out to touch her arm gently. "Sounds to me like you're beating yourself up over something no one could possibly have helped."

"I don't know why I told you that. Please forget I said anything." She fumbled for a handkerchief in her evening bag, but the young man reached one from his pocket first.

"You must have loved him very much. You're both lucky to have had that for even a little while. Most of us *never* find it. Every girl here will tell you I've *really* tried." He grinned mischievously, then added, "At least every girl except you new ones. Do I have any takers?" Again he held out his arms with a pleading look and, this time, Megan couldn't help laughing.

"You should laugh more," Carl said. "I'll help you do that. Would you like to dance?" He gestured toward the sunken dance floor where couples pranced in the latest disco dance.

"I haven't danced in years. Andy was from a Southern Baptist family so he never learned how. And I've not seen any of these dances before."

Carl grabbed her hand and pulled her toward the floor. "I'll teach you. It's like riding that old proverbial bicycle...you never forget." He whirled her around the dance floor in spins and a quick waltz that didn't fit with the throbbing music. Megan was startled, but Carl said, "Just checking you out. You can follow my lead. This'll be easy." He called out something to the disc jockey and the music changed to something else she had never heard. "It's a new disco line dance called The Hustle," he said, already moving through the opening steps.

By his second set of steps, Megan was in tandem with him, and they completed the full sequence like one body, close, but without ever touching. Carl's grin crinkled his eyes. By that time, Lila bounced out on the floor dragging the lieutenant with whom she'd been talking, and Stan escorted Abby and another teacher, Mary, to the floor behind Carl and Megan.

"Do it again, y'all," said Lila. "We want to learn it, too."

Carl looked at Megan and shrugged. She nodded, and he signaled again to the disc jockey. Soon he and Megan were calling out the steps as they performed them, and the whole crowd was out on the dance floor trying to follow along. Sometimes the two separated to help a guest having a little trouble, then joined again to continue. After several replays, everyone was moving together in the disco line dance, and any leftover ice with the new arrivals was broken.

As the music changed to a Fox, and then a Rumba, Carl whirled Megan around the floor. Finally, he said, "I think we both need that drink we left. I thought you said you hadn't danced for years. Where did you learn to follow like that and to learn new steps so quickly?"

"I started ballet at five to correct crippling from rickets. It helped. I worked my way through high school and college by dancing--until after my second baby girl was born. When Andy came home after two Navy aircraft carrier cruises, we both went back to college to become teachers. Like I said, he didn't dance."

"Well, I'm glad to finally find someone who can do any dance I throw at them. My folks were dancers, so my sisters and I learned young, and I'm the one who loves it most." He added with enthusiasm, "I've been waiting just for you!"

Megan blushed as Carl escorted her back to the couch and their drinks. Across the room, Lila waved, happily surrounded by an animated group of men. Megan waved back, smiling. She looked around for Abby and Emily, seeing Abby talking earnestly to Vern, and Emily sitting with a group of teachers who had been in Bamberg for a while. I guess we're all surviving, Megan thought. The dancing had been fun. She had forgotten how good it felt to let her body respond naturally to music.

Carl interrupted her thoughts. "We throw a lot of parties around here with the single officers and the teachers, and you just found yourself a permanent dance partner. Do you ski?"

"Oh, no! I never learned how. I'd be scared to do it now. I'm *quite* prone to accidents."

"Well, Bamberg folks are breaking away from Nürnberg Ski Club and forming our own. Stan's president, and he says we'll *all* go. I've never skied before either. We can learn together."

"But I don't want to learn," Megan protested, shaking her head emphatically.

"Hey, Stan," Carl called out to their host, ignoring her alarm. "Come over and convince this lady she needs to learn to ski with me."

Stan strolled over, took Megan's hands in his, looked into her eyes and said forcefully, as though it were an order, "You *will* ski! You *will* enjoy!" Then he grinned broadly. "As for getting tangled up with this pilot here, you're on your own. He's broken hearts all over this Post, half of Europe, and half of Vietnam."

Carl bowed his head in mock shame. Megan couldn't help laughing at him.

Abby and Vern approached the group. "We overheard your latest directive on skiing," said Vern. "We're all for it, and we both ski. When can we get started?"

Stan grabbed a huge calendar tacked to one of the room's pillars and said, "Next weekend we'll all be going to *Rhine Aflame* and the following week the Officers' Club reopens. If there are no alerts, we can schedule our first Ski Club party at the O'Club Ballroom after three or four weeks, set up the trips for the year…"

"And the parties too," added Carl.

"Parties, too," said Stan with a smile. "I figure we can try a few practice runs when the nearby *Fränkische Schweiz* Mountains get their first snow, then hit the Austrian Alps. We'll take our first big trip over Thanksgiving, maybe to Lech. How does that sound?"

Stan had raised his voice to draw in other revelers in the room. People were sorting out his proposed schedule, and Megan was wondering about all the unfamiliar terms he used so easily, when the door flew open and a whole new crew of officers burst in.

"Heard you were having a party, Stan, and you *knew* you couldn't get away with keeping the ladies all to yourselves."

"Can't blame us for trying, Brian," said Stan. He threw back his head in laughter. "We wondered how long it would take you Cavalry cowboys to get in from the Border, make yourself presentable, and crash the party. Let's see, took you until ten. But that beats last year's record."

Hearty handshakes and introductions filled the room.

"It's what you call a 'friendly rivalry'," confided Carl to Abby and Megan. "Actually, everyone around here depends on each other. Because of the Border, we all *need* each other. It's just a standing joke that the 82nd tries to beat out the Cav with the ladies. You'll get used to all of them. Any one of them would gladly die for you."

"That's rather extreme," said Abby, with a startled look. "I hope we never need such an heroic sacrifice, but I suppose it's good to know."

"What's this 'Border' you speak of so reverently, and what do you all *do* that you *need* each other so much?" asked Megan, alarmed at Carl's serious tone.

"You'll hear more about it later. You've landed on a Post that has an essential military mission, that's all. Much is classified—secret. Just remember that no matter *what* happens, you gals will be taken care of. We're like family here, and we take care of our own. A Border base is a unique lifestyle for the Army—everyone is really tight. It's nothing at all like the rear echelon troops stationed at Stuttgart, or Nürnberg, or Heidelberg, or wherever."

"It doesn't take the Cavalry long to get acquainted, though."

Abby pointed out where Lila was surrounded by the new crowd of officers. "She's having fun, isn't she?"

"Aren't you?" Carl asked.

"More than I had hoped," said Abby. Megan nodded agreement, and both women smiled.

Carl was ready to dance again, and a crowd followed them to the floor.

As the evening wore on, the women met so many Bamberg officers and teachers they had difficulty remembering all the names. Lila slowed down long enough to point out to Megan and Abby that teachers and single officers seemed to have a special relationship and did most everything together. "It's delightful, don't y'all think?" She gushed out the names of a half dozen guys who'd made dates for the following weeks. "*This Rhine Aflame* trip will be just great?"

Stan gave details. "Someone will come get you ladies next Saturday noon and we'll be back Sunday evening after a stopover for the wine fest at *Bad Dürkheim*. The O'club should open after renovations the following week and we'll be back on our usual routine. I'll sure be glad to get some decent cooking," he said, patting his ample stomach. "Marco takes care of us."

"What's *Rhine Aflame*?" Megan asked Carl quietly. "We'll have started school by then, and be searching for apartments. We won't be able to go away on a trip."

"You worry too much," he answered. "I'll have to help you with *that,* too. *Rhine Aflame* is a tradition, and you'll love it. Everyone goes out together here, and we travel on weekends. It's sort of like a 'gang.' It'll be a good situation for you right now, Megan--to be part of a group of forty, instead of alone or in a pair. Everyone will go who can get away, or who isn't in the field."

"Now you've lost me again. What's the field?"

"As I said, you need someone to watch out for you, and *I'm here*. Don't ever worry."

His serious tone brought Megan to search his eyes for clues. *Was he hiding something?*

Stan and Vern, standing close enough to overhear, roared. Vern said, "Watch out, Megan, Carl has the best set of girl-catching lines in all aviation, infantry, artillery, and cavalry—but he is accurate that we're all going to the river, and that means you, too."

Megan and Abby looked at Carl with eyebrows raised. He

shrugged, hands held up helplessly and said, "I told you, I keep *trying* my lines, but I rarely get any takers." Megan joined in the laughter Carl's protestations of innocence elicited from everyone around him.

"Hey, don't forget I'm one of the good guys. With the club dining room closed, you four ladies must be scrounging for food. I'll pick you up tomorrow at twelve and take you out to my *Gasthaus* for a decent meal." To their surprise, Carl kissed Abby's hand with great gallantry, and kissed Megan on the cheek. Before she could protest, he interrupted, holding up his hands in mock defense. "Try not to miss me too much. I have an early helicopter flight, so I'm bowing out now. Save the next dance for me, Twinkletoes." He waved at several guests as he made his way to the door and disappeared.

Megan stood stunned, not sure what she should think of the evening's events. Her confusion was interrupted when bubbly Lila swished over with a tall Cavalry officer. She introduced him as Brian. "He's going along to *Rhine Aflame* too," she announced. Her smile at the young man was quite seductive, and Brian's grin was ear to ear."

"I'll just bet he is," said Abby with a wink at Megan and Stan.

Lieutenant Fleming dropped the ladies at their quarters at three in the morning. They gathered in a luxurious corner of the lobby Marco had obviously arranged for them and kicked off their shoes.

"I want to sort out my date book," said Lila. "Y'all have to help me put names with faces. Weren't they all wonderful? And what about those Cavalry guys with their cute lil' mustaches? Do y'all think that's part of the Cav uniform, like their black berets?"

"No," answered Abby. "Vern said they wear them to support their Battalion Commander who was ordered by the Brigade Commander to shave his mustache off. He looked so odd without his that every Cav guy grew a big one just like his. The Brigade Commander couldn't very well court-marshal the whole Cavalry. I gather they are a pretty elite and cocky group."

"Well, they're unique at least," observed Megan. "I wonder what their commander is like for them to be so loyal to him." She approved of loyalty, and assumed *everyone* had it.

"It was a delightful evening," said Emily, rambling with enthusiasm. "I met all the teachers returning from home leave and got lots of information. They said Bamberg is the most beautiful city in

Germany. The buildings on Post, even the schoolrooms, except for the new main school, were German cavalry barns in the 1800's, with sloping cobble-stoned gullies outside for easy cleaning. Those are 'sidewalks' now, and we must be careful of sprained ankles. They also said anything we need that the school's supply man can't find, Captain Lang will obtain for us."

"It's wonderful that he's in favor of education," said Megan.

"You're quite naïve, Megan," said Abby while massaging her temples. "These men aren't *only* interested in education. I had a good time, but I'm a bit suspicious of their motives."

"Oh, posh!" Lila exploded. "They're just friendly and ready for adventure. My date book is full for the next several weeks." Her enthusiasm bubbled out to include the women around her.

"You were definitely a hit with all of them, Lila," observed Emily, as she removed her earrings and rubbed her ears. "They buzzed around you like bees. And Megan, that pilot who spent so much time with you was cute, and such a good dancer."

"I don't understand why he thought he needed to 'take care of me,' though. Do I look like I need to be taken care of?"

The three other women glanced sideways at each other.

"What did you say when he approached you? That'll give us a clue," said Abby, suppressing a grin.

When Megan gravely related her first encounter with Carl, the other women broke into uproarious laughter.

Lila, trying to gulp back her giggles, said, "Didn't you realize he was handing out a line. 'Take me, I'm easy' was probably his best? He must have about fainted when you thought he needed a ride."

"Well, how was I to know? I'm not used to parties, or lines. And with so many people, it was confusing." Megan's cheeks burned. "What *should* I have said to him?"

"You should have taken him up on his offer to 'take care of you' and winked at him," goaded Lila, winking broadly at Megan to demonstrate.

"He's too young. He might have thought I was flirting."

"He can't be that much younger, Megan," added Abby, picking up on the teasing. The guys said he's already been to Vietnam and he's already a pilot. If he didn't seem bothered by any age difference, why should you be? And you aren't old, for Pete's sake."

Abby, Emily, and Lila laughed at Megan's embarrassment,

but they stopped abruptly when she answered in an agitated rush.

"I'm 35, and my husband is dead. Life is over for me, and it's just beginning for him. Carl's probably only about 25 or 26, and he's a pilot on top of it, and I'm scared to death of airplanes. I don't want *anyone* to care about me." Megan paused, noting their startled looks. She tried to control her outburst and divert further questions. "Carl was just being nice, don't you think?" She looked at Emily for support. "He couldn't have meant anything by the teasing."

"I'm not so sure he was only teasing," said Abby. "And I'm sorry about your husband, Megan. You hadn't told us about that."

"I wasn't ready to talk about Andy. I shouldn't have mentioned it." *Why do I blurt out things when I'm trying to keep them secret?* "As for Carl, I'd have to avoid him if I thought his comments were serious, and I loved having a chance to dance again."

While the others watched her quizzically, tears ran down her flushed cheeks. "I'm sorry." She mopped at her face with the back of her hands. "I'm really not ready to be interested in anyone, and Carl said Bamberg would be a good place for me because everyone travels in gangs, rather than by twos. I'm not ready for twos." She couldn't explain the private part of her sorrow. Yet she remembered how quickly she had given some things away to Carl, and resolved to be more careful the next time. By an inner source of will, she pulled herself together and changed the subject. "Carl and Stan said we'd all learn to ski. I'm scared of skiing. I'm only coordinated when there's music playing. I walk into walls if the music stops."

"Well, whatever happens, you and Carl dance wonderfully together, and I'm sure he'll be a good friend." Emily patted her hand. She had a calming effect on Megan's serious anxiety.

"Abby, who'd you like?" Lila asked, apparently shifting the conversation away from Megan in a sudden spirit of compassion. "I could be persuaded by almost *any* of them!"

"All the guys were rather young, but they seemed nice." Abby turned partially away--evidently uncomfortable discussing things she felt were personal.

She hesitated so long that Lila dragged out reluctant conversation. "You looked like you enjoyed talking to Vern, that tall guy from the artillery unit. And I saw you with Robert, too. He was certainly handsome. And Stan's smile is wonderful, isn't it? Then there were Frank and Tim, those two other teachers. They talked with you quite a long time."

"Talk is cheap," Abby said and changed the focus abruptly. "I think Frank and Tim teach in your building, Megan? Tim said you'd be next door to his fifth grade classroom."

Abby's attempt hadn't budged Lila from her favorite topic. "I liked Brian best," she sighed. I'm glad he's going with us next weekend to *Rhine Aflame.* By the way, I don't even know where that is. Does anyone else?"

"By the *Rhine River*, one would assume," said Abby. Her drollery was lost on Lila.

"Carl may have a map when he comes to take us to his *Gasthaus*," offered Emily.

"Do you think he meant that about taking us for lunch tomorrow—oops, today? It's really late, isn't it?" Abby looked at her watch. "Are you sure he wasn't kidding about that, also?"

"He seemed quite sure," said Megan. "He'll pick us up at noon after his flight."

"See," said Lila, flipping out a knowing grin. "You already trust what he says."

Before Megan could protest, Emily broke in. "Girls, I just want to say one thing." An unfamiliar urgency permeated her tone. "Some men on a military base play games. I've heard of those who even have a pact with each other over who can go out with a girl first, *and* how far they can go. Some of them may tell lies to get you to go along with their plans."

"Why would anyone want to lie to us?" Megan asked. A lie was outside her parameters.

Emily sighed. "Well, these young men seem sincere, and I assume you can take care of yourselves." She looked straight at Megan. "Just *watch* yourselves. Don't be in any hurry."

Into the silence, Abby quietly added, "Amen." When the others looked at her curiously, she shrugged. "Some men lie. Let's leave it at that. Emily's right. Be careful."

"I think we should get some sleep," announced Emily, "in case Carl is one of the sincere ones." Following her suggestion and stifling yawns, all trundled upstairs to their rooms.

Chapter 4

Sure enough, as noon rolled around, so did Carl, cramming all four ladies into his blue open top *Volkswagen*. It was a crowded ride for those in the back seat, but full of laughter, as Carl constantly joked about his inability to attract permanent females. At least, Megan *assumed* he was joking. Surely no one would talk about such personal failures so openly, otherwise.

When she asked about his earlier flight, he replied, "Can't tell you much, but it was a beautiful morning to fly a helicopter. We had intelligence notices to look for certain people, so it was urgent. I'm back safely, and that's all you need to worry about." He smiled, raising his eyebrows as he glanced sidewise at her.

She ignored his obvious flirtatious manner and asked, "Do you always have to be secretive about where you go and what you're doing?" Megan began to wonder what he *did* for the Army. "Is what you do dangerous?"

"Glad you asked." He grinned broadly. "It shows you care."

Megan could hear the others snickering in the back seat and blushed. She said quietly, "I'm not supposed to ask--is that it?"

"That's right, Twinkletoes." There are some things going on that we're checking out-- nothing to worry about. As for dangerous, I promise I'll always come back to you." He paused long enough to hear her catch her breath, then added, "Don't worry so much about me. People will talk." He shifted gears suddenly and whizzed down a hill, skirting a lake.

Megan was kept busy clutching the armrest, wondering if Carl always dropped such bombshells and then sped away from a response. Had she been doing the same thing? She was silent the rest of the way, while the ladies jammed in the back seat chattered on about the sweeping hills covered with green forests, and the fields of mustard and flax blossoms shining golden yellow. They were thrilled by the lack of litter and the absence of advertising signs. It was not that Megan was antisocial, only that she didn't feel comfortable with the flirty repartee. *I'm way out of my fish tank here,* she thought.

The *Gasthaus* and brewery over which Carl had an apartment was 800 years old. The proprietor and his wife welcomed the ladies, shaking hands all around. *Herr* Berg spoke a smattering of English to make Carl's new lady friends feel comfortable. Megan couldn't tell if *Frau* Berg understood what was said or not, since she only fluttered around them, clasping her hands with obvious joy.

Herr Berg offered the women drinks. Abby and Emily both opted for beer made in the downstairs brewery, and Lila accepted a white wine. Megan demurred when the host asked her preference, and turned raspberry red when he kept insisting, asking her again and again.

"Will you have a beer? A wine? A mixed drink? A *Schnaps*?"

To each, Megan replied, "No, thank you." But the list kept growing, and she didn't know what to say to convince their host she didn't drink. In desperation, she asked for a glass of water.

"Water!" *Herr* Berg thundered. "Water is for washing, not for drinking! It will rust your insides!" He turned to Carl. "The lady hurts my hospitality." With hand to his heart as though in pain, he added, "She will not drink with me."

Carl whispered to *Herr* Berg in German, and the old man suddenly beamed, looking again at Megan. "I'll get *you* something special," he said, and bustled down to the *Keller*, returning with a bottle of cool *Limonade*. "Carl assures me that by next time we meet, you'll be able to drink some of our wonderful Mosel wine. *You* may call me 'Papa.' Let me kiss your hand." To Megan's embarrassment, and Lila's gleeful grin, the old man did so.

"Carl, whatever did you *say* to him?"

"Oh, I just told him that you were a very special lady and my protégée--that I will teach you *everything* you need to know." He leered, for effect.

Everyone except Megan laughed. She blushed, wondering why Carl kept leaving her embarrassed and speechless.

Carl continued, "Papa Berg is delighted I've brought some new ladies. He thought my last lady friend was snooty. She was! He and his wife keep hoping to plan a wedding for me here in the brewery as though I was their son. They're wonderful people."

Fortunately, at that moment, *Frau* Berg appeared with overwhelming helpings of *Schnitzel mit Spatzle*, German veal cutlets and noodles.

The sumptuous meal included warm *Apfel Strudel* topped by vanilla cream sauce.

In response to the ladies' collective 'oohs, and aahs,' Carl whispered, "Mama Berg always makes my favorite dessert whenever I have guests."

After sincere thanks for the Bergs' kind welcome, the ladies followed Carl upstairs to see his apartment. The ancient, high-ceilinged rooms were spacious as a castle, which made his sparse furniture appear even smaller. He pointed out where *Frau* Berg had added several home-like touches to its barren emptiness—a handmade comforter, matching pillows and drapes. "I really lucked out when I found this place. You'll find it's hard to get a two room flat."

"That's not enough room for my furniture," said Abby. "I'll need more than two rooms."

"They don't count kitchen or bathroom. They also don't have closets because they're counted as an extra room for tax purposes. They use these *Shranks* instead. He indicated a few large armoires freestanding around the room." The women nodded.

"The government lends us basic furniture while we're stationed overseas, so everyone's apartment looks almost exactly alike. You can request some once you find an apartment, but they only give you *one* of everything if you're a single person, like this one twin-sized bed. They don't seem to think you'll ever share your bed." He turned an exaggerated wink to the ladies.

Lila giggled and asked, "Is there any way to get a double, or an extra? I might want to invite someone to come visit."

"And I'd accept in a heartbeat, Sugar, but I don't want anyone mad at me." He cast a sideways glance at Megan to see her reaction. He switched to a serious tone and turned back to answer Lila's question. "Not legally, but Stan can arrange it, should you need an extra twin. That guy can do anything. Why, I've seen him order snow for a Christmas party, and get it!"

At Abby's raised eyebrows, Carl added, "Don't worry, Abby, all the girls are impressed by Stan--and he deserves it. A great guy—and brave, too--just ask any of the guys who flew with him in Vietnam. Combat Engineers are his secondary job. He wants to get back to flying, his first love. But he was badly injured getting his crew chief and gunner out of the helicopter when he was shot down." Carl's face suddenly lost all humor. He spoke slowly. "But don't ever ask anyone around here about Vietnam. Nearly all the guys in

Bamberg have been in Vietnam, and they lost too many comrades to discuss it with anyone. You'll see it in their faces. Don't ever ask, unless they bring it up."

The women exchanged glances.

"Then, may I ask about what you're all doing *here,* in Germany? We're supposed to be at peace now, aren't we?" The questions came from an anxious Megan. "Why all the secrecy? What exactly does it mean to 'guard the Border'? Why Border with a capital B?"

"Ladies, I can't tell you everything today, and some things I can't tell you at all. But at least here at the Border, we know what we're expected to do, and we'll do it. This mission is more clear than in Vietnam." There was a long pause before he added, "Much we do here is classified. But the Cav guys will take you out to see the Border soon. Remember that our Cold War enemies, the Soviets, face us on the other side of that Border. They're well armed, they outnumber us, and they'd *like* to invade all of Europe, instead of just half. The rest we'll keep a mystery for now, shall we?"

He paused. "Oh yeah, I forgot to tell you, in addition to the Border, the Field, Alerts, and maneuvers over at *Grafenwohr* Training Base, you'll also see Reforger. His serious tone collapsed into a grin. "Everyone will be gone during Reforger, and you gals will miss us terribly. You'll see." He looked pointedly at Megan, who shifted uncomfortably.

Before anyone could question him further, he grabbed Lila and Emily's hands, pulling them down the hall. "You have to see my throne room."

"Do you really have a throne?" asked Megan, grateful for his swift mood change.

"Right in here, ladies." He threw open the door so all four could peek inside.

"Oh my." It was all Emily could mutter. The women joined in the laughter.

"They didn't have indoor plumbing in the olden days," said Carl, obviously enjoying the ladies' mirth. "When toilets were invented, they used a regular room. With no place to put the pipes, they put in a false floor under the toilet, lifting it to where we must sit on top."

The toilet did, indeed, sit atop a two-foot high throne right in the middle of the room, with four steps leading up to it. Carl offered the ladies an opportunity to try his throne room any time they liked.

"How gallant of you," said Emily, with an elaborate curtsy.

The five rode back to Bamberg in the swift autumn breeze, enjoying Carl's running commentary on the history of tiny villages through which they drove. He stopped to show them how *Fussweg*--walking paths--wandered parallel to farmer's fields and forests, indicating signs which meant anyone could go walking there.

"You make a wonderful tour guide, Carl," said Lila. "Do you hire yourself out?"

"Only for private trips, Lila. Are you offering?"

His mischievous grin caught even Lila by surprise. She choked back her laughter before answering. "Not *this* time. I'm booked up solid for the next few weeks. Perhaps later, *if* you're ever free." She glanced at Megan, apparently to see if there was any reaction.

"I hope I won't be free anytime soon," he said.

Megan began to relax her guard as a glimmer of insight dawned. *Flirting was just the way Carl related to people, sort of a protective coloration,* she thought. *Perhaps he's more vulnerable than he lets on.*

"You can't help liking that guy, can you?" Abby said, as the four women headed upstairs to their rooms above the Officers' Club.

"He comes on pretty strong, but it's obvious he's just bluffing." Lila offered her advice. "Megan, he likes you. I can tell. Now, don't go shoving him away."

Megan was quiet before answering, "I just don't know what to say or do when he bluffs in such a personal way. I've never known anyone so forward. He seems madly in love with every female he sees, and has such a reputation for chasing women. I should be introducing him to a nice girl his own age. He may need more taking care of than I do." She turned toward her door. "He is funny, though. He flirts with everyone, then swears he has no luck with ladies, all innocent with that silly grin."

"Just enjoy his friendship," said Emily as she stopped by her own door. "We all need friends who can make us laugh, perhaps especially in your situation of overcoming grief and loss. I think Carl could be a friend for a lifetime, if anyone ever gets to understand him."

Megan nodded as Emily squeezed her hand.

"Do y'all get the feeling some of these guys do dangerous things in the Army around here?" Lila asked the others.

"Yes," answered Megan. "I'm still not sure what *kind* of a place we've landed in, or how Bamberg is going to affect us. But there's an awful lot of secrecy."

"Do y'all think there's something scary these officers aren't telling us about?"

"I know it doesn't sound good, Lila, because no one seems free to discuss much." Megan put an arm around the younger woman's shoulder, her natural concern for others beginning to show, in spite of her reluctance to get close to anyone. "I'm sure they'll tell us about whatever this 'Border' means once they get to trust us. Besides, I think they've all seen grief in that long Vietnam War that none of us understood. And now, they seem deeply involved in this whole Cold War thing."

"Our first faculty meeting tomorrow, Teachers," interrupted Abby, "and you know I need my sleep. Let's hit the hay and see what daylight brings."

Monday morning, the sleepy-eyed gate guard fumbled through his list until he found names of the four new teachers, handed each a strip map, and pointed them toward the school.

Past a field with heavily tracked vehicles parked in the mud, and a long narrow building at the end of it, the four went through yet another gate. As they entered the main school for their initial faculty meeting, they realized the main building was outside the Post gate.

Frank, a sixth grade teacher, walked over to reintroduce himself. "Welcome to BAS."

When Lila and Megan appeared puzzled, he repeated, "Bamberg American School. You'll get used to acronyms. The military can't exist without them."

A short meeting, a quick tour of the buildings, paperwork for military ID cards, and a hasty lunch at the Snack Bar behind the muddy field took up their morning. Then the new arrivals were carted off with the returning teachers to some mandatory briefing held in a narrow brick building on what was referred to as 'Main Post.'

"We heard the buildings were formerly barns," said Lila. "Those old Germans sure must have had a lot of lil' ol' horses. All the stable buildings look just alike."

"You'll get your bearings after awhile," said Tim, as their bus stopped in front of the main Headquarters building. The teachers trooped inside and settled into chairs.

"This is your bi-annual Non-combatant's Evacuation Order briefing, or NEO," droned the major at the front of the room. An aide handed out lists of supplies. "Each of you must keep items from this list in an NEO suitcase in your POV. In answer to the blank stares of the new teachers, he repeated, "Privately Owned Vehicle." He sighed, as though disgusted with the necessity of briefing newcomers, though that was his job. "We probably will never activate this NEO plan except for occasional drills, but you must be ready at a fifteen minute warning, just *in case* we need to get you civilians and the families of soldiers out of here quickly."

The major continued, puffing up to a self-important grandeur, "We are a Border outpost. Our Cold War enemy, the Soviets and their satellite communist states, often threaten us and our West German allies by rumbling their tanks right up to that Border with intent to invade West Germany. We have no choice but to rumble ours right back to face them." He used his two hands with fingers spread wide and facing each other to demonstrate this potential tank confrontation. "After a few days, the Communists usually back down and return to their own bases. Then we can do likewise." He turned away one hand and then the other, wiggling his fingers as his mythical tank battalions drew apart. He bared his teeth in what was apparently meant to be a smile, as though everyone should think he was making a joke. "NEO is just in case someday, the Soviets keep on rumbling."

Megan and Lila took rapid notes on their lists, awestruck at the major's words, while Abby and Emily gathered the NEO documents and started filling them out. "He sounds like we're right on top of this mysterious Border," whispered Lila, in some alarm.

"We *are*," another teacher whispered back.

Experienced teachers returning to Bamberg from their summer leave yawned and shifted positions frequently, obviously having heard this speech before. At last the briefing was over, and the group spilled out into the sunshine.

"Boy, y'all didn't tell me we'd be so close to the Soviets," said Lila, sliding up alongside Tim, a fifth grade teacher who had been in Bamberg for years. "What's all this about their using three 'gaps' to attack us? What's a gap?"

"Hof, Coberg, and Fulda gaps are the places wide enough the Russians could get their tanks through the mountains, should they decide to attack the West. Fulda is the flattest and, therefore, maybe the most vulnerable, but our sectors of Hof and Coberg would be breached more quickly. The gaps are manned at all times. Combat Engineers have manholes and bridges in all three gaps loaded with explosives, and detonators are in nearby bunkers.

Lila managed a breathless "Wow!"

"What did the Major mean about signs at the Border, at five Kilometers, and one Kilometer? asked Megan. "He said we can't go past the signs, and our commander would be notified if we did? We're civilians. We don't have any commander."

Frank nodded. "The Soviets consider it an act of war if anyone crosses over the Border, even accidentally. They photograph and report anyone getting near it. At a Border Post, civilians are subject to the same rules as the military. No one but German Border Police, the *Grenzshutz*, or American soldiers assigned patrol are allowed within the boundaries of the one K zone, so don't go near the Border, unescorted. Oh, and our 'commander' is the principal."

"The Cav can guide you within the one K zone to see the Border," said Tim, "but even then, you mustn't wave at the other side or make any gestures with a camera--or a finger."

"I suppose we'll need to find the Commissary sometime today so we can buy the supplies they listed for our emergency suitcase," said Megan, addressing a nearby teacher of third grade who had also been in Bamberg for several years.

The woman seemed quite blasé about the whole evacuation thing. "Don't rush yourself, Sweetie," she said. "Just buy cookie mix." She ripped up her list and tossed it into a trashcan.

Stunned by her dismissive action, Megan asked, "Why cookie mix? What do you mean?"

Christy turned to face Megan and said in a bored tone, "This whole NEO thing is impossible because we're already too close to the Border. The Russians would be here before any fifteen-minute warning was activated. They only tell us this stupid stuff at every NEO briefing because they think some of us might panic. They already know they can't get us out."

"How do you know we can't be evacuated? The Major described some pretty elaborate plans." Abby moved closer and cocked her head, waiting for an answer.

"They've tried before--didn't work. The American troops are *all* that's keeping the West Germans from being cut off behind Russian lines like the people in Berlin. Naturally, the Germans don't want to be left behind. They'll clog the roads immediately. There was gridlock before anyone even got to the main roads out of town." Christy sighed in resignation. "There's no way we'd ever get out. But we keep that knowledge from the women and children stationed here to prevent panic, in case we ever have to try this lame idea. We teachers would be using our fifteen minutes to try to get as many kids on buses as we could. On a line base, teachers know pretty much what the officers know. We won't get out. Get used to the idea."

"But why the cookie mix?" Megan persisted.

"Look, if those East Bloc Forces come across that Border, no help will come until Washington, or the Chief of War Plans, approves sending backup troops or nukes. We all know how long *that* will take. So, when all our Bamberg troops are dead trying to defend the Border by holding back the enemy for their *mandatory* forty-eight hours, and we've used our time to send off our children, *our* only option will be to bake cookies and hope the Soviets like 'em." Christy turned and walked back to the bus, leaving the others to gasp in shock.

"She didn't mean that, did she?" Lila's hands were shaking.

"I don't know. She sounded pretty cynical," said Megan. She patted Lila's arm. "Don't worry. We'll ask Carl or Stan when we see them this weekend. I think they'll tell us the truth. But I don't like Christy's summary that NATO would get help to us *only* after all our Border troops were gone. Does she mean all these men would die right there, waiting for additional reinforcements, while Congress gets around to declaring war?"

Abby nodded. "I think that's exactly what she means. No wonder these guys party hard, drink hard, and are so reluctant to talk about their duties at the Border. They're potentially on a suicide mission."

Chapter 5

The rest of Monday afternoon was spent working in classrooms and attending grade level meetings, as the children's first day would be Wednesday. The four new teachers gathered for dinner at the military Snack Bar behind the muddy field to compare all they'd learned about the school and their roles in it.

"I wish I'd brought some of my bulletin boards and lab equipment from Kentucky," said Lila. "I assumed supplies would be available here."

Emily, more experienced with DoDDS, said, "Not usually. Most of us bring a few teaching materials in our suitcases. The rest come in later shipments, or we make our own."

"When my shipment gets here, you can borrow my stuff for science," Abby offered.

"Our fourth, fifth, and sixth grades have *no* science textbooks," Megan said. "The obsolete ones were picked up, and the new ones never arrived. Tim said last time this happened, books were found on a dock in a Korean harbor, eight years later, labeled 'birdseed.' We'll be writing our own curriculum. Isn't that hard to imagine in a school district back home?"

"The first teachers to come over, in the late 40's, had no textbooks, and the classrooms were in Quonset huts and tents," observed Emily. "DoD asked for 'pioneers,' willing to improvise. They've built a few more schools since then, always too small, and supplies are still almost non-existent, so nothing much has changed."

Megan's eyes lit up at the challenge. "This should be fun. I love the academic freedom of DoDDS teachers to set up subjects whichever way we feel is most effective. No one tells you what to do. At our grade level meeting, they said I could even use the individualized math program we designed in California, and they'd tape it for an in-service workshop. It's all very informal, isn't it?"

"I thought that too," said Lila. "Everything's sort of 'in house.' Apparently there's a drug problem among enlisted troops, and the General wants the school to prepare materials for Drug Education. The principal just pointed at *me* to prepare a workshop for officers. I don't have any experience with the drug culture--all those hippies left over from the sixties and such. I just figured they were all lunatics. I didn't have time for that in college, and I thought drug problems were all over with now. But, here this general wants a drug program for 1974. At least the principal said I could have someone help me." She stared pointedly at her three companions.

"I could help, if you'd like," said Megan.

The others looked at her in surprise. Emily said, "But you're our naïve one. What would you know about drugs?"

"Andy and I volunteered as tutors at an experimental school for drug users who got kicked out of regular school. We also coached their sports teams, and a couple of the kids came to live with our family when their parents threw them out, so I've had a bit of experience in drug rehabilitation programs. At least, I know what works, and what doesn't."

"Great! I'll have to learn fast," said Lila. "The military seems to rely on teachers."

"Where's your classroom, in case we need to find you?" asked Abby. "Lila and I are in the main building, with third, fourth, seventh, eighth, and ninth grades."

"You'll have to bring your ID card to visit me," Megan answered with a sigh. "I'm in that old cavalry barn we passed, next to the muddy field and just inside the Post gate. It's been turned into an Annex with six classrooms in one long row—three fifth grades and three sixth. Apparently classrooms are just stuck in wherever an empty building can be found. The playground is a cobble-stoned street, though they *claim* they close up the gates at both ends so the tanks won't drive through during recess. My room still has rings in the wall to tie up horses."

Rubbing a lump on her forehead, she added, "It also has concrete beams slanting out at an angle from the wall, probably supports for the old feed mangers. The kids are short enough they walk under the supports, but I'm taller, and I forget and walk right into them. I told you guys I'm accident prone if there isn't any music!"

Emily added, "You're right about just sticking classrooms anywhere. I didn't know 'til today that *Muna* is short for 'Munitions Dump.' They said we have enough explosives there to blow up half the country, yet our Kindergarten, first, and second grade classrooms are right in the middle of it. Nobody even bats an eye about the ammunition. My classroom is in an old converted slaughterhouse. It has tiled walls and really smells disgusting." She held her nose.

"One of the teachers told me she keeps air spray in her desk drawer and uses it whenever the smell gets noticeable. It's so habitual, she sprays and teaches simultaneously." Emily flashed her most dramatic gestures and postures. "But she once absent-mindedly sprayed the General's wife during a conference, and the woman protested the supposed insult. She's been careful whom she sprays since. You girls must tell me *another* way to make my classroom smell nice."

Megan, Lila, and Abby had discovered the storyteller in Emily, and all appreciated her humor in relating the 'tragedy of the day.'

By the time they'd taught the first week, these classroom oddities had become part of each evening's entertainment among the quartet. "And what happened to you today?" became the signal for their crazy DoDDS stories and peals of laughter. It was a rare day indeed when *any* classroom was normal.

"Teaching for the military overseas is certainly different from teaching back home in Kentucky," summed up Lila.

By Wednesday, the children's first day of school, all four were excited and anxious to meet their children. Though class sizes were large, the children themselves were among the most adaptable and easy-going Megan had ever seen. Even her ten year olds were surprisingly cosmopolitan, having lived in many foreign lands and having picked up foreign cultures, customs, and even smatterings of language. She found them as eager to meet her, as she was eager to meet them. Megan was also impressed that they were relatively 'un-flappable.'

That night at dinner, she reported to her friends that several windows along the 'manger wall' had suddenly shattered, sending glass showering across the room. "My gosh, it was their first day, and I was frantic, thinking someone could be hurt. In California, that would have become a lawsuit. But the children calmly brushed the shards of glass from their desks and clothes as though this happened every day. One raised his hand and said, 'Mrs. James. You have to open windows on the days they're firing tank guns and artillery down at *Muna* Range'.

"I barely managed to say, 'Thank you for telling me. I'll try to remember next time.' Then I rushed into the hall to call the supply man to come repair the windows and clean up the glass." Megan brushed her naturally unruly curls back with one hand.

"I found out that telephone outside my room is an insecure line meant only for four digit military calls either in or out, but today it wouldn't even connect to the main school. Tim, from the classroom next door sauntered out, saying, 'I hope you don't expect that phone to work when you have a *real* emergency. We call it 'Hitler's revenge.' It only works when it pleases. Send one of your kids with a note.' But I noticed his classroom had open windows!"

"Megan's story wins the prize for today," said Abby, wincing as she gestured.

"What did you do to your shoulder?" asked Emily, noticing the favored arm.

Abby moved it gingerly. "Don't know, but it hurts. I didn't hit it on anything."

"Let's walk over to the clinic," said Lila, as she led the way out of the snack bar.

Abby didn't have a chance to argue. Shortly after, she exited the clinic with a cast. "The doctor said it's a joint inflammation. It's my right arm, so it'll be a nuisance." The others agreed they would help her dress and carry her bag, since they wouldn't allow her to skip the upcoming weekend outing to *Rhine Aflame*.

However, the next day, all four were surprised when the obnoxious NEO Major told them that he needed their rooms at the Officers' Club for visiting VIPs. The ladies were ordered to pack during lunch and put their luggage out in the hall. Their protests that they had no place to go didn't move him one iota, so they called Stan's already familiar number at Engineers. He promised he'd find a place for three of them, since Emily said she could stay with her nephew, as she had originally planned. By this time, they already knew Stan could work miracles.

He and the ever-helpful Lt. Fleming, called Freddy by now, arrived after school, loaded up the suitcases, and carted them off to a family housing building with four main floors of twenty-four apartments, and an attic floor above. Originally, the attic had supplied rooms for maids, when military families had enjoyed that luxury right after WWII. There were no longer any maids. "No elevator, either," Stan puffed, as the two officers manhandled the luggage up five flights to a tiny attic room jammed wall to wall with three parallel twin beds.

Chief Lynden had been waiting for them. "I'm sorry this is a tight fit, ladies." He moved across the hall and pointed to the bathroom. "My troops scrubbed and disinfected it, but it's still so old and skuzzy, you'll want to wear these flip-flops in the shower." He held out three pairs, almost standing at attention, waiting expectantly for their reactions.

The three women looked at this kind man who had obviously worked all afternoon to prepare them a place to stay on such short notice. Abby said, "We really do thank you, Chief. We'll be fine here. Don't worry about us."

"It's only a short walk to school," commented Megan. "Thanks so much for everything."

Lila chimed in. "This is super. Sharing a room, we'll get to know each other better, and the Snack Bar is just across the muddy field. We're all set."

The Chief smiled and added, "My family is one floor below you ladies. My daughter is in your class, Mrs. James. She'll be glad to know you're nearby. If you ladies need anything, feel free to ask us." With that, he backed out of the tiny room and strode down the hall, followed closely by the young lieutenant.

Stan smiled. "Thank you, ladies, for being so gracious. The Chief immediately stepped in to provide for you. We'll have everyone looking for apartments, so you won't be here long." His smile broke into a laugh. "It *is* rather a tight fit, isn't it? I hope none of you snores."

Megan shook her head, frowning at the six-inch space between beds. "I don't snore, but I *do* fall out of bed when I have nightmares. I would slide right down between those beds."

"If that happens, you'd have to wake us up to move the beds over. You'll never get back up out of that narrow space again," said Abby. Remembering her cast, she added, "Come to think of it, I'll probably need help, myself, to climb in over the foot of my bed."

"Don't bother trying to wake me," said Lila. Y'all will find I don't wake up easily."

"I'll just pull my blanket down and sleep underneath the bed, quietly," said Megan.

Everyone joined in giggles as they put a few pieces of clothing into the single dresser drawer and shoved the rest of their suitcases under the beds from the foot end.

"The least I can do is buy you ladies dinner," said Stan, as he watched Lila holding one of Megan's sweaters up to her shoulders with a pair of Abby's slacks over her arm.

"Hey, this may be fun, y'all. We can borrow clothes out of each other's suitcases to mix and match. We'll look like we all have extensive wardrobes."

Megan had overcome enough of her shyness to volunteer, "You're welcome to whatever you find, Lila."

Lila slipped on the sweater and admired herself in the mirror. "I don't think I can fill it out enough." She held out the front in two points. "Does anyone have some falsies?"

Stan turned his red face away to save his dignity and stifle his laughter.

"Uh, oh," said Lila. "Only one mirror, too. This could get dicey with three of us."

"If you can cut down your thirty-minute showers," said Abby, "Megan and I can let you have the mirror all to yourself, since we both wear only lipstick. Is it a deal?"

"Deal!" Lila then remembered her constantly growling stomach. "What did you say about taking us out for dinner, Stan?"

"Let's go, girls. I know a great *Gasthaus* in *Memelsdorf*--the *Drei Kronen*. They have wonderful steaks fit for such good sports."

On Saturday, as promised, Stan arrived with a convoy of cars headed for *Rhine Aflame*. Upon arriving at the port town of *Rüdesheim*, the Americans trooped aboard one of perhaps sixty small cruise boats headed down the *Rhine River*, which glowed golden in the sunset. By dark, the boats stopped close enough together one could have walked from deck to deck. All lights were extinguished before the pyrotechnic explosions came from behind shadowy castles on the hillside. The resulting illumination reflected off the water in spectacular fashion. Excited screams greeted each exhibit of fireworks, and it all looked as though the castles really burned.

When the last flames died away, boats turned again upriver

and relit their strings of lights. Oom-pah-pah bands invited people to
dance, sing, and drink in the beauty of a balmy night. The large group
of Bambergers had already slipped into party mode, joining in the
festivities from a central deck table. Lila was nowhere to be seen.

"I saw her with Brian at the fantail," said Stan, tilting back
his favorite German beer.

"Was she okay?" asked Emily. She tended to worry about *her*
three girls.

"More than okay," answered Stan with a grin. "She and Brian
seemed to be having a fine time. I didn't want to bother them. But I
noticed some bearded German guy had brought them drinks and
joined them at their table, so I doubt Brian's too happy at present."

"She and Brian were cuddled in the back of the boat when I
saw them," said Carl, setting his beer by Megan's lemonade. "Shall
we dance our way over and see if they need a rescue?"

"Sure." Megan was already on her feet. As she and Carl
picked up the fast German polka, he steered her around the dance
floor toward the rear table.

"Brian and that man seem to be arguing," Megan whispered.
I hope Lila is all right."

"I have a feeling Lila can take care of herself, but we'll
check."

"*Guten Abend*," Carl said, as he and Megan approached the
trio. "Allow me to introduce my partner, Megan, and I'm Carl." He
pumped the hand of the bewildered German and wedged himself right
in between a surprised Lila and the older, tanned stranger. The man
narrowed his eyes and glared at Carl as though he would like to bore a
hole right through him. Carl ignored the scowl and kept smiling like
some innocent, unaware fool.

Lila took Carl's arm and leaned closer to Brian as well. She
flashed a relieved smile at the two intruders. "Oh Megan, Carl, I'm *so*
glad y'all came over. This is Klaus Berndt. He's from Bamberg, too.
He said Ilse, that German lady at the *Stars and Stripes* Book Store,
told him a big group was coming on this trip. He was kind enough to
bring us drinks." Turning toward the man, she said in a too-bright
voice, "Would you like to go with us to meet the rest of the gang?"

"No, certainly not!" He pulled at his jacket as though to get it
away from Carl, then added, "at least, not now." He turned toward
Lila once more, grabbed her hand across in front of Carl and said, "At

least I know where to find you, lovely lady—at the American School. I'll drop by to see you another time." He rose with a curt bow, turned precisely, and strode toward the front of the boat.

"Hey, girl," said Carl contritely. "Didn't want to intrude, but it looked like that bruiser was on the make. Are you two all right?"

Lila turned to Brian. "I suppose the man didn't mean any harm. He seemed quite charming, and he had a wonderful accent, didn't he? We certainly didn't want to cause any ol' international incident, but we're glad y'all came over, aren't we, Brian?"

"Suppose so," the Cavalry officer replied, "though I had sort of hoped I could keep Lila all to myself. I don't know where that guy came from or why he picked us, but something about him seemed odd. I think I've seen him someplace before."

"If he mentioned the book store," suggested Megan, "perhaps that's where. It's become a hangout for the readers among us. We've explored it several times already this week, and Ilse is helpful in finding just the right book. She seems to know everyone on Post."

"Well, you're hardly invisible with the beautiful blonde on your arm, Brian," said Carl with a grin. "They all envy you. It was just *that* guy—he looked a bit too intense. Gave me a funny feeling." Carl humped up his shoulders and wriggled as though something slimy were crawling down his back before turning to Lila with a big grin. "Do you two want to join us over at our table, or are you okay here? Your call."

"We'll come with you," said Brian. "That guy sort of raised my hackles too."

Lila nodded her acquiescence, and the four Americans moved to their original table.

Soon, they'd forgotten the incident and were caught up in the German singing and beer drinking songs. The ladies quickly learned the words to *Ein, Zwei, Suffa*!

When the boat docked, Stan roared above the crowd, "All Bambergers, stay together, and we'll meet you at the parking lot."

In the rush from the boat, they found out quickly that Germans do *not* wait patiently in lines, as do Americans and the British. They crowd like cattle, pushing and shoving to wedge 40 people in a place for two. Most of the men moved to the front, trying to create a safe path for the ladies. Brian was ahead of Lila, when she was jostled from behind. Megan could see it was the persistent German, Klaus, who caught Lila in his arms. "I'll see you again soon, lovely lady," he said to her. Just as suddenly, he pushed into the crowd and disappeared.

Megan moved ahead to Lila. "You'd better tell Brian or Carl that guy came back."

"I'm afraid they'd take a poke at him, and I don't want any scene." Instead, Lila reached ahead to grab Brian's hand. "Let's go, Brian. I don't want to get left behind."

After being dropped off at the Snack Bar on Sunday evening following a side trip to their first wine fest in *Bad Durkheim*, Lila said to her friends, "The whole thing was crazy! I don't know where that man came from or what he wanted, but he was *quite* charming."

"I still think you should have told one of the guys that he came to you that second time," said an anxious Megan. She was the only one of the four teachers with no hangover since she had stuck to lemonade while the others had sampled the wonderful *Mosel* wines.

"No. If they'd tried to hit him, they would probably have gotten into a brawl, and we'd all be in jail." Lila laughed. "Everyone gets all worked up over nothing. He didn't really *do* anything. He was just trying to be nice to Americans. He was even sorta' cute with that 'lil beard and all." Her natural mischief came out in a smug grin.

"He didn't look at Carl and Brian as though he was trying to be nice," observed Megan. "He looked angry enough to start a fight with them or something."

"How did he know where you worked?" asked Emily, her expression unusually intense.

"I guess I told him when he came over and introduced himself. He brought us drinks and all. I was just trying to be nice."

"Carl seemed to sense something wrong," added Abby. "And Brian seemed glad to be back with the rest of us, though I know he wanted time with you, alone."

"Or maybe he's just jealous." Lila laughed, but she stopped abruptly when she saw the concerned looks on the other teacher's faces. "Don't y'all think?"

"I don't know, Lila. You're probably right," said Emily. She bit her lip. "But please call one of us to your classroom should that guy show up again, just in case."

Chapter 6

The Officers' Club reopened its dining room, ballroom, and bar the following week, and it was crowded every night when the teachers walked over for dinner. The O'Club was the only place meals could be charged on a running tab, and since teachers didn't get paid until well into September, it was a godsend for new and returning ones alike.

The four new teachers were surprised to be so welcomed into the military group. "Actually," said Megan, "this place is cozy, isn't it? Not at all the 'dark den of iniquity' I associated with a *bar*." The formal atmosphere combined with the informality of a communal gathering place eased her mind. "It seems okay for ladies to be here."

"This is everybody's living room," said Robert, an Artillery officer joining a group already forming in the bar after a superb dinner. "The married officers have their own self-contained family unit, but we single folks live in BOQ or off Post in the German community. We have no TV, no phones, no kitchen facilities, so *this* is where we create *our* 'family.' It's much more fun to be together for dinner and entertaining ourselves. You'll live here too," he said, directing his gaze at Abby. "It's a comfortable place."

"Are we still planning for the new Ski Club's opening party?" Abby smoothly deflected his obvious interest.

"Sure. We'll have it here in the Club's ballroom," answered Stan, slipping in behind her with his girlfriend, Mary, and a good-looking man. "Meet Rex 'Top Cop' Carson. He's Provost Marshall, and he runs things around here, at least in law enforcement."

"Yeah, but Rex needs his Military Police to clean up his *own* act," Robert remarked jokingly. "He's the only guy here who lures ladies to his BOQ with a pot of home-made beans."

Rex raised his square shoulders in a gigantic shrug.

"Beans?" Lila laughed, a bit intrigued.

"Yeah," said Rex, with a swagger. "All the girls around here *love* my beans. Come on over and try 'em." His mustache enhanced strong good looks, and his grin showed he knew it.

Lila had walked right into his trap, and she smiled indulgently, with a wink. But she also turned quickly to Stan and

Mary to ask, "Do y'all need any help setting up the party?"

Stan sat down at a large table, whipped out a pocket notebook, and began writing. "We have questions first. Do we want the club to be for everyone or, like Nürnberg's club, just for officers, their families, and teachers? Do we want to keep the trips cheap by contracting our own buses rather than going through a travel agency?"

"Hey, those were our objections to Nürnberg's group. Let's open it to everyone," said Charlie. "Our soldiers need to learn to ski, too." The men all nodded at his words.

"We can take turns with volunteer trip captains," said Vern. "The cheaper we can keep those trips, the more of our guys can go."

"One problem is that while *we* can get away a little early on Fridays, the enlisted troops usually work until at least five," said Rex. "The buses need to leave by four at the latest to get down to Austria. How can we solve that?" His question met silence.

Timidly, Megan spoke up. "Can't someone simply go talk to all the commanders, and ask them to let their guys off earlier on ski trip days?" Her innocent question turned heads.

"I couldn't do that…I'd get court-marshaled," said Robert.

"Can they court-marshal a teacher?" Megan asked.

Everyone laughed at her naiveté, but Stan shushed the laughter. "The lady has a point. The commanders may not listen to us, but they just might listen to teachers who hold their children captive in school." Turning to Megan, he asked, "Would you like to try?"

Goodness, why did I open my big mouth? "I guess so," she answered slowly. "When would you want me to start?"

"ASAP, I think, so the troops can come to the party and get acquainted. There'll be no rank distinctions on ski trips or parties, and we think skiing will be good for our guys."

"You officers talk about your young soldiers about like we teachers talk about our school kids," Abby noted. "Explain to us why you think a ski club would be such a big help."

Several of the men grinned, sheepishly. "Well," said Rex, slowly, "Bamberg has had some difficult problems since McNamara's 100,000 enlistees--many of them school dropouts with no job skills-- joined the Army to fill shortages left by ending the draft. The commanders are under pressure from Headquarters to solve problems. Naturally, *they* move that pressure on to those of us who deal directly with the troops. But they're tough problems—things like race riots,

rapes, suicides, women being assimilated into the regular Army--
there's a lot of anger out there."

"Some guys get into fights, or take long walks out of third
story barracks windows?" added Robert. "Accidents have been
rampant, so morale is low."

"I see," said Megan, thinking about the mission she'd just
undertaken. She remembered how she and Andy had insisted that the
troubled children who moved into their home be involved in sports,
running with the family daily. "When we teachers work with young
people, getting them involved in teamwork is the key to less trouble. I
can see where you guys are coming from with the Ski Club idea."

"Yeah, but sometimes the commanders don't see it the way
we do," said Stan. "Are you up for trying to persuade them, Megan?"

"I think I can do that. Should I invite the commanders too? I
might persuade them faster--like inviting cops to a party so they
won't panic when neighbors complain the music's too loud."

"They probably won't come, but you can try," said Stan.
"What do you guys think?"

Heads nodded approval around her.

Abby, now out of her cast and always organized, said, "You
guys should give Megan a map of the Post *and* provide a ride."

"I can do better than that," Rex said, turning to Megan. "I'll
pick you up after school Tuesday and take you to the HQ's.
Afterward, we can have beans at my place." He grinned. "Just don't
be startled when you're picked up in an MP jeep."

Megan smiled. "I won't worry about the jeep, but no beans!"

Stan smirked at Rex, then said, "Atta girl, Megan," and shook
her hand formally. "Then I guess that's settled. Abby, if you can
design an invitation flyer for her to pass out, I can get several printed
tomorrow. Mary, you and Lila can choose a disc jockey for the
ballroom." Jeff, you can set up the food with Marco, and Charlie, you
can talk to him about drinks. All the rest of us can be called on for
anything else needed. Am I forgetting anything?"

"A date for the opening party," said Mary.

"Two weeks from Saturday," Stan pronounced it like an
order, and everyone nodded.

Lila started laughing. "Boy, things get done fast around here."

Carl came up behind the women. "Well, it sounds like I got

here just late enough to get out of all Stan's job assignments."

"You can lead the dancing and pester the girls," said Stan.

Carl nodded. "Sounds good to me!" As another pilot walked in behind him, Carl introduced Luke to the women as having gone through flight school with him. He whispered conspiratorially, jerking his head toward the new arrival, "You gals have to watch out for the magicians and musicians who frequently take over this bar. These clowns are apt to interpret any reticence on your part as an invitation to saw you in half or start up a sing-along. Sooner or later, everyone takes his turn as entertainers, and that means *you'll* be called on too."

He took Megan and Abby's arms and pulled them up to the bar. "*My* personal talent is to lead drinking games." Grabbing a stack of beer deckles--the cardboard mats stateside Americans call coasters, he placed them on the bar's edge. With a flip of the hand, he turned them in the air and caught them all together expertly. "Care to try it?"

"Remember, I was in the Philippines," Abby said. "The Air Force taught me the deckle tricks already. I can do this even with my bum arm." She did, and passed the stack to Megan.

But when Megan tried, the deckles flew in all directions, much to her surprise and Carl and Abby's amusement. "You lose, Twinkletoes. You'll have to pay the penalty."

"What's the penalty?"

"For tonight, you'll have to buy Abby and me a drink on your tab." He smiled at her. "Next time, I'll have to think of something more dangerous." This time Megan was not surprised by his evil grin, and merely smiled indulgently, shaking her head.

The bartender gave Abby a beer, and Megan ordered a Tab.

"Oh, so *you're* the one who likes Tab Diet Soda? Marco told me to keep a case on hand for you."

"Marco really does take care of everyone, doesn't he?" Megan asked, pleased by the suave *maitre'd's* quiet efficiency. He seemed to know the preferences of every customer.

"Megan," Carl whispered, "I'll order a *Mosel* wine, and you can try one sip."

"Oh, I don't think..."

"One sip, Megan. I promised *Herr* Berg, remember?" He moved his wine glass over, and she wrinkled up her nose at the unfamiliar taste.

"It's not too bad," she said, "just...different."

Carl grinned. "Atta girl. Now try this trick again with the deckles. I'll help you."

The second time, she caught most of them, and the third try was successful with cheers all down the bar. Megan blushed, pleased with herself after all, though she wasn't sure her family at home would be impressed that she'd mastered a drinking game *in a bar*.

She looked around the room, taking in the whole gathering. One group was playing a noisy game called 'Liar's Dice,' some were quietly talking and, at a corner table, were four people seriously involved in a Pinochle game. She wondered how they could concentrate with noise around them, but they seemed oblivious. Lila, Brian, and several Cavalrymen with their girlfriends, mostly teachers, chatted with animation at yet another table. *It really is everybody's living room*, she mused. Her anxiety at being in a bar melted away.

Another aviator joined the group, accompanied by a long-legged, uniformed man with a bushy mustache and silver streaked dark hair. The aviator, Bill, introduced him as "Father Harry."

Abby immediately realized he was a priest, while Megan, her one sip of wine beginning to have woozy effects, innocently asked him, "Whose father are you?"

"Yours, I hope," he answered with a gargantuan smile, "along with everyone else. I'm one of the chaplains." Harry was older than the other officers, but he seemed an integral part of the bar crowd.

"Isn't it unusual for a priest to be in a bar?" Megan whispered, holding her spinning head up with one elbow on the bar. She wondered how one sip of wine could make it feel *so heavy*.

"This is where all my parishioners are, so I guess this is where I need to be," he whispered back. "Wouldn't you agree?"

Even in her slightly dizzy state, Megan recognized the deep brooding in Harry's eyes that marked him as one who had *been there*, in Vietnam. "I guess so. But, I'm not Catholic—more of a dyed in the wool Presbyterian."

Harry roared. "Friends don't let a little dogma get in the way of the stimulation of clashing intellects. And we're to be friends."

"Father Harry even went Airborne--as an old man, of course," offered a young Airborne Infantry captain on the other side of the chaplain. "He jumped out of perfectly good airplanes with us in Vietnam when he could have had a vine-covered white chapel."

"Hey, watch that 'old man' stuff or I'll see you at the end of the bar for confession," retorted the priest. The mutual laughter marked the man as a leader within the group. He spoke softly to Megan, "These guys come in here heavy with the weight of responsibility for their men. They often need a drink before they can talk about their job on the Border. We go where our people go, if we want to help them, right? Do you have a family?"

"I have children in college in the States. My husband died a year ago. I guess I'm sort of at a crossroads, changing careers, leaving home. I'm not sure if I'm trying to learn to live or die by coming to Germany alone." *Gosh,* she wondered, *what has loosened my tongue so?* But intuitively, she knew she could be honest with this man.

"Understood. Alone is hard. These men are my family, and they'll be yours too." He surveyed the room. "Should you want to talk, I'm here most of the time when I'm not in chapel."

"Hey, Father Harry," interrupted Carl. "Don't go trying to save Megan's soul before I get a chance to corrupt her."

"Carl is my favorite sinner," said Father Harry with a chuckle.

Within a week, the engineers found a basement apartment for Megan, only two miles from Bamberg Kaserne. Others she'd seen had a shared bathroom, or hot water only on Saturdays for a *once*-weekly bath. And there were rules. Each renter was required "...to air bedding and clean stairwells every Saturday morning." It wasn't the cleaning that bothered Megan, but the fact it was ordered on her days off. She preferred to do housework voluntarily, before school during the week, in order to have weekends free.

Magically, Stan produced a truck, and he and the school's supply man drove to the furniture warehouse. As Carl had predicted, single teachers were limited to *one* of each item. But, playing dumb, the two pretended to the Americans that they didn't speak English, and to the German workers that they didn't speak German. They just strolled by the angry workers and picked up an extra couch, *two* pint-sized German refrigerators, a desk, and end tables that weren't allowed to singles. There was still only *one* twin bed, but Stan promised he'd find another before Megan's mother came to visit.

"I'm beginning to feel nervous that someone really likes me these days," quipped Stan.

"Why do you say that?"

"There's this big, black BMW that turns up a lot of places I go. Today it followed me from the warehouse to your apartment, stopped for a moment, and then drove away. It's probably some beautiful woman just pining to make a date." Megan couldn't help laughing at the way men on this Border Post thought continually of women.

Alone in her new apartment, Megan could hardly wait to soak in her clean bathtub, with no need for shower shoes. She borrowed a huge 16,000 watt transformer, necessary to cart around like a ball and chain, since all American 110 electrical appliances needed a transformer to operate at 220 volts. Another teacher lent her a clock radio and a tape recorder with tapes of *Fiddler on the Roof, Pat Boone,* and *Barry Manilow.*

Every morning's wake-up alarm on Armed Forces Network (AFN) radio was a medley of military music and the announcement, "It's six o'clock in Central Europe." This was followed by a voice screaming, "Chick--en Ma--an. He's everywhere, he's everywhere!" Chicken Man was a super hero, but he managed to fail in every three-minute episode to save the world. His cape got caught in a revolving door, or he got locked in a dark closet and singed his wings trying to light a match, or someone mistook him for a chicken restaurant advertisement, and he *always* forgot his secret password. This poor hero was totally ineffectual, and laughs were shared over his daily escapades. Megan thought Chicken Man's popularity mirrored the soldier's heroic attempts to guard the Border from a communist superpower, when things always seemed to go wrong. If one couldn't laugh at the snafu difficulties, one couldn't keep doing the job at all.

AFN's radio couldn't advertise products, but its 'commercials' told of PTA meetings, anti-drug programs, and how *not* to get blown up if your German house had a fuel oil heater. Mostly Megan enjoyed old radio comedies and mysteries...The *Shadow* and *Suspense* helped her through lonely nights when she couldn't sleep--her first nights ever being totally alone.

Sometimes she felt tempted to get on the next plane and go home but, young as they were, her kids had their own lives in college, and she couldn't go home and face that living room door, expecting Andy to walk through it any moment. She wanted to die here in a strange land, where her mother and children would think it was accidental, and where no one would miss her. But now, her simple plan was more complicated. She had already made friends she cared about, and her school children relied on her, so she couldn't let them down--at least, not until there was a natural break for a substitute to take over—Christmas perhaps. She had unaccountable flashes of longing for Andy to hold her, almost believing he could. Her personal fog deluded only herself.

But Megan's natural inclination was to worry more about others than her own problems. Concerned that her girlfriends still in the attic had only snack food, she invited them for dinner. They rented bikes and came off Post. Though Abby was athletic, Lila was purely decorative, and riding a bicycle was most dangerous for her.

"Whew," chirped Lila. "That was hard. Thank goodness you live close to Post." Stomping off dust from the trail, she enthusiastically surveyed Megan's tiny kitchen. "It's a *real* apartment! Gosh, I can't wait to find one."

"I couldn't do much with it yet. The transportation department says my measly thousand pounds of baggage is lost somewhere between Bremerhaven and Frankfurt. They didn't sound concerned."

"I shipped mine from the Philippines early," said Abby, "hoping it would be here by the time I found an apartment. But I don't think it will. I heard there's a porcelain factory at *Staffelstein* that sells cheap 'seconds'. We may have to go buy dishes there."

"Well, I can only cook pasta a little at a time in this tiny pot while the sauce simmers in the skillet. Army Community Services (ACS) lends newcomers a few utensils until their shipments come but, as usual, a single person can borrow only two knives, two forks, two spoons, one pot, and one small frying pan." Megan grinned wickedly. "So--who wants to eat spaghetti with a spoon?"

The women ate dinner in stages, giggling each time they had to switch utensils. After dinner they settled down to serious talk. With Lila, that always came around to discussing men.

"They're all liars," Abby announced firmly.

"Not all, surely," soothed Megan. The ones we've met here have seemed helpful."

"That cute Robert has asked you out several times," Lila added, "and so has Vern. They both seem kind, don't y'all think?" She nodded at Megan who took her cue and nodded too.

"Well, I've been burned by others who seemed nice," said

Abby. I learned to live with those gecko lizards in the Philippines that frequently lost their grip on the ceiling and dropped into my bed, but not the two-faced men who tried to do likewise." She raised her head to a defiant angle. "They promise you the moon and then you find they are either married, have a girlfriend in the states, or are only interested in getting you to bed."

Lila giggled. "So, what's wrong with *that*? I don't think y'all can really judge a fellow until you see how considerate he is in bed."

Megan and Abby looked at each other, and then at Lila. But Lila's innocent grin of obvious pleasure cracked them both up, and soon all were laughing.

"Seriously," said Abby. "I don't know who to trust. I feel bitter about how close I've come to loving someone, yet I have trouble believing in anyone now, and I can't quite imagine sharing my solitude and privacy with another man, either." She paused, perhaps sobered by her own revelation. "Here, they seem so intense."

"I think their intensity is related to their job," said Megan. "Life must seem very short and vulnerable with the Soviets threatening from across the Border all the time. Let one take you out. You might be surprised at how sweet he is."

Abby nodded. "You're a great one to talk. We can't get you to accept any of the invitations you've had from males here."

"My situation's different. I don't want anyone, ever, but you're free."

"We'll see." Abby paused, as though not sure she should ask, then she plunged ahead. "Lila, I've noticed you seem to really like Brian, yet that German, Klaus, has shown up again, hasn't he? I saw you two talking outside your classroom Tuesday."

"He's quite charming." Lila reached up unconsciously to pat her mass of blonde curls. "Isn't his beard sophisticated? He was so sweet I didn't feel it necessary to call anyone like Emily said. He asked me to go to the opera with him. Have y'all been to an opera?"

"Once," said Megan. "This soprano, Camille, was supposed to die, but every time we thought she was a goner, she'd flutter up and sing one more aria. Finally, we just wanted her to get it over with."

Lila nodded, laughing. "So, they all die. Hm. More importantly, what will I *wear*?"

Megan and Abby again looked at each other and giggled.

Lila's priorities seemed so far from their own experience, yet their friend was vivacious, sweet, and an unending source of fun.

"Megan, I've peeked at photos of your husband in the living room," admitted Lila. "Andy looked cute in a rugged lumberjack sort of way. Was he nice? I want a good man, or none at all."

Megan sighed. "*So* nice that I've had trouble understanding why God would take Andy and not the wife-beater down the street. It wasn't fair. I feel bitterness I'm still trying to overcome. I miss him dreadfully." Lila instinctively put her arm around Megan.

"That's okay, Honey. You don't have to talk about him until you feel like it. I've heard that when you can laugh about the good things y'all did together, you've come through the grieving process. Isn't it neat the way we've come to understand each other so well?"

"That happens in DoDDS and in the military," said Abby. "You face all the problems together, and you find long-term friends you depend on. Here, so close to the Border, it seems the single officers and teachers feel an extra responsibility for each other, even if they aren't romantically involved. It's different from anyplace Stateside, or on other bases." She shifted her position on the floor to cross her long legs. "I have to admit I was worried at first that Emily might 'mother' me, and that you, Lila, might overpower my better intentions. I knew unusual things would tend to happen wherever you went." Abby laughed. "We make an unlikely foursome, don't we?"

"Okay, I suppose I do get myself into one jam after another," admitted Lila. "But y'all keep me out of trouble most times."

"We try," said Abby. "Maybe I need to break my old pattern of the carefully cultivated, solitary image. Change might be good."

Lila grew thoughtful. "Megan, you seem quietest—I figured you as over-protected--afraid of everything—and *quite* inexperienced. I knew there was a kind streak, though, when you helped me save my underwear at the baggage belt. You didn't even know me yet."

"I was really scared, and you're right about the protected life," Megan admitted slowly. "It wasn't easy leaving home and traveling so far across the world, alone. But I knew I wasn't whole--wasn't myself--without Andy. I *had* to leave, or…or I'd have dragged everyone I loved down with me." It was a painful revelation, and she rallied herself forcefully. "But, I've already come to love teaching our children with no roots--who move with their military parents to a new Post every three years. Teachers become the children's stability. The kids make me feel needed."

"I know," said Abby. "The kids are super. I guess I needed to start a new life too. Perhaps that's my destiny--to forever be starting over with a new transfer and a new group of people?" She laughed with a trace of bitterness that wasn't lost on her companions.

"This isn't a bad place to start over, though," said Megan. "I get a kick out of the military guys who complain that their friends at home think they're 'seeing the world,' and they only get to see Germany from the top of a tank. These are good people, and they like our being here. Robert is right that this Border assignment molds us into a family. There's something to be said for staying with DoDDS like Emily, drifting from place to place, making worldwide friends."

"Emily's able to walk right into a comfort zone with new people. I always seem to hold back and analyze, and analyze, and analyze." Abby tilted her head from side to side to emphasize her slow pace. "Maybe I probe too much instead of enjoying each moment. I wonder if that was what I found wrong with every man I met at Clark Air Force Base? Because one was a liar, did I need to assume all men were? But of course, there was another who should have told me he had a wife in the states instead of waiting until I truly cared about him. He hadn't even worn his wedding ring."

Megan and Lila both measured the pain in Abby's voice.

"No relationship can work without trust," said Megan. "But, I know for a fact that some men are trustworthy. Andy was."

"Can one train oneself to trust again?" Abby looked down, twisting a ring on her finger.

"That question's too hard for me," said Lila. "Why don't y'all give my approach a try? Just have fun and stop worrying about where a relationship might lead. Perhaps they all lead nowhere." They were quiet for a moment, considering Lila's original idea.

"By the way," Megan asked. "What's Emily doing tonight? She nixed the bike ride."

"When I asked her to join us," Abby answered, "she said she had a date with the Ambassador, and not to worry about her."

"Who do y'all think he is?"

"I don't know, but she says he's called or visited her whenever the rest of us go out," said Abby. She laughed and shook her head. "Emily is wonderful. I can't imagine anyone else who could balance our sanity so well." She checked her watch. "It's getting late, Lila. As slow as you are on a bike, we'd better start back to our attic before it's completely dark."

"I know, I know, I'm the un-athletic one. I can't play volleyball like y'all, nor dance like Megan, nor ride a bike and play racquetball like you, Abby. Why, I'll bet even Emily can beat me walking up our five flights of stairs. But I must be made for more important things, don't y'all think?" She struck a sexy pose and had the other two laughing as they bid good night.

"I'll bring hard-boiled eggs by the attic for breakfast," Megan called out. The two waved from their bicycles as Lila wobbled sideways, catching herself against a parked car. Megan went back in to clean up, still smiling from the relaxed afternoon. She sat down to write her mom and her girls. Letters to her family and friends at home helped her keep some sense of sanity.

Abby, Emily, Tim, and an older Captain soon found a brand new house holding four real apartments, not a basement or attic, but they were further from Post.

Lila rented a furnished attic. Ten-inch gold beetles adorned her bedroom wallpaper. The living room had red ladybug wallpaper accented by purple curtains. The hall flaunted six-inch yellow and blue pansies. "How does one even think in here," Lila complained.

But apartments were hard to find, and the West German taste for mixing unrelated bright colors was impossible to ignore. Lila was immediately in trouble when she ignored the sign on her door requiring her to clean the stairwell on Saturday. In the German language, she thought the sign meant to clean her oven, and she couldn't imagine why anyone cared if she cleaned her oven on a Saturday. Stan went to help her straighten out the misunderstanding.

Finally, all four women were settled, and they could visit each other often and share both their fears and their sense of fun. Lila's first visitor at her attic apartment was Klaus. She had *not* given him her address. In spite of her three friend's anxiety, Lila thought it marvelously flattering that he had cared enough to follow her home.

Chapter 7

Emily's vintage red *Volkswagen* arrived and, miraculously, the four friends passed the dreaded German driver's license test. They explored Bamberg's tiny side streets and cobble-stoned courtyards, often accompanied by one of the school's German culture teachers.

Greta was a jolly native of Bamberg. She spoke excellent English and delighted in retelling old legends of the thousand-year-old city untouched by war. In the new teachers, she found a willing audience. They loved stories of the Bamberg Rider—a statue of a mounted Crusader in the Dom, and the adultery trial of Queen Margarete pictured on the huge sarcophagus she shared with her husband, King Heinrich. These stone panels by Tilman Riemanschneider showed the queen successfully walking barefoot on red-hot shovels—a trial *presumed* to prove her innocence. The teachers thought it amusing, though, that in another statue of the queen outside the *Rathaus,* she wore a noticeable smirk, as though to say, "Well, I got away with that one, didn't I?"

"Because there were disagreements a thousand years ago," explained Greta one windy afternoon, "between the Bishops of Bamberg, who built palaces on one side of the Regnitz River, and the *Bürger* who lived in modest homes, fisheries, and breweries on the other side of the River, the *Rathaus,* or seat of power, was built right in the middle of the river, so one group couldn't rule over the other. It was quite an engineering feat for those days."

It seemed that every cobblestone and doorknocker had a story. Greta knew them all. She happily shared them through the brisk outdoor jaunts. Though somewhat interested in the city's history, Lila and Abby seemed even more delighted to find Witt's and Hertie's department stores, where they could search for gifts and warmer clothes. Shopping was another of Lila's passions.

German weather had turned to an early chill and no-one's warm clothing had arrived. In Germany, heat was controlled by the landlord, kept at 65 degrees from the end of October until March 15, and turned off the rest of the year. When Emily begged her landlord to turn on heat during a mid-October snowstorm, he responded, "Ah, but it is not fully winter yet."

Megan bought a Flocati rug and sat on floor pillows one of her daughters had made, with her back pressed against the radiator. Being cold all the time, plus going to work and returning in the dark in this northern latitude, produced an element of depression, which Megan was already fighting. She thought more often about *non-messy* methods of checking out.

Megan found herself in the middle--between teachers who were older and traveled in twos or threes and went out for coffee and cake every Sunday, where Emily quickly fit in--and those teachers and officers who were younger and kept a hectic pace of physical activities and parties where Abby and Lila fit right in. Megan was always invited with the younger group--and began enjoying volleyball games, parties, movies, dances, *Volksmarsches,* and trips. With all the activities, plus events the teachers arranged for their school children, it kept her from thinking about her past, *most* of the time.

Megan didn't mention in letters to her mom her relief to be neither a social fifth wheel, nor to have someone trying to 'match-make' all the time. She was moving in a group of friends, of a new *family* with no pressure for pairing. Sunday mornings, the singles crowd gathered at their O'Club 'living room' for brunch and to read the *Stars and Stripes.* They planned afternoons for when the Club closed at 1400 hours. The day might include a picnic in the mountains of *Fränkische Schweiz,* or an impromptu party at someone's apartment. Everyone kept at least cheese and crackers, beer, wine, and coke on hand and was known for some specialty for potlucks, made from whatever was available in the commissary that particular week.

Megan took pains to hide her deepening depression. In fact, she was barely aware of it, so *busy* she was at *staying* busy. *I don't want anybody to know beforehand,* she thought.

"It's an adventure to find something to fix for a meal," complained Lila at one of the group's impromptu parties. "We never have much to choose from, do we?"

"I started out planning a menu of barbeque ribs with potato salad and chocolate cake," chimed in Megan. "But I ended up with meat loaf, macaroni salad, and jello. It all depends on what's left on the shelves at that teensy renovated stable of a commissary."

"In an outpost like Bamberg, they're mostly empty," added Mary. "There were fifteen cases of Cheerios, but no eggs, all last week. We need creativity and flexibility in menu planning. If you see it, you'd better buy it, because it won't be there later."

Top Cop Rex said, "I guess they don't expect us to need much at a line base. I wonder if I can do something about limited supplies?"

"Like what?" asked Abby.

He put his finger over his lips. "Shh! Military secret."

But a week later, Rex ordered everyone he saw to "Go shopping today!" Bamberg's tiny commissary suddenly had pot roasts, ribs, and fresh vegetables that had not graced the shelves for months. Government issued gallon cans of dried beef or shrimp, suddenly available, could be reconstituted with water to feed a crowd. Commissary customers bought all they could afford and had well-stocked pantries for a change.

When cornered at the Club, Rex admitted with a sheepish grin, "It was easy. The convoy of trucks bound southeast for the 'big PX in the sky--Nürnberg,' came upon a mysterious roadblock where the Frankfurt/Nürnberg *Autobahn* connects with the #505 Bamberg exit. Can't *imagine* where that roadblock came from." His eyes rose innocently to the ceiling.

"You hijacked those trucks?" Stan accused, barely able to speak between bursts of laughter. "Didn't the military convoy drivers ask questions?"

"Heck, it was midnight, and my MP's stood on top of jeeps directing traffic with lighted wands. Those convoy drivers obey MP's. Twenty-six trucks rolled off the *Autobahn* and headed north toward our Border." Rex looked around furtively before his stage whisper, "And don't call it 'hijacking.' Those truckers just 'got confused.'"

"I wouldn't worry," said Mary. "I doubt Nürnberg even noticed. They always have everything. The Army seems to forget they have people way up here in the wilds of Bamberg."

"By the way," said Rex. "Our soldiers have been freezing their tail feathers off at the Border because long johns never came to our PX. I scrounged dozens of boxes labeled 'winter underwear.' Can you aviation types get them out to the guys guarding the Border?"

Carl and Luke grinned at each other, and Luke said, "I think we can make a special 'rescue' flight out there in the morning."

Of course, the Brass never figured out how those trucks got diverted. And Mary was right that the Nürnberg commissary and PX people never even missed them, considering the plenty rear echelon bases always had on their shelves. Everyone appreciated Rex's ingenuity in getting some additional things for neglected Bamberg.

But when the desperate GI's at the Border unpacked the rescued underwear, they found it contained fifty cases of pink tops and yellow bottoms. They didn't care that somewhere in Germany there were yellow tops and pink bottoms, nor did they care that the long johns were designed for women. They were cold enough to stretch them out and wear them anyway.

The following week, however, Carl reported at the O'Club with barely contained glee, "You should have seen General Horst when I flew him out over the Border lines in the early morning. Out of the blue, he started cussing loud enough the Soviets could have heard him. 'Fly me directly to Frankfurt Warehouse,' he said. 'I won't have those Ruskies laughing at my Border troops running around outside their tents looking like God-Damned tooth fairies!'"

"Did he get the long johns?" asked Lila amid the hysterical reaction of the bar patrons.

"Oh, yeah!" Carl said. "He got 'em all right! The regulation off-white long underwear mysteriously appeared, and the general insisted on flying up to deliver them. He ordered everyone to put away their yellow and pink 'jammies.'" Carl paused to wipe tears from his eyes. "Would you believe the long underwear had been sitting in the warehouse since August? That's our military procurement system. Nothing's too good for the Border guys." His ill-concealed sarcasm brought smiles and more pats on the back for Rex Top Cop and the pilots.

A few days later, when no alert was in progress, Cav scheduled a Border trip for the new teachers. Colin, a delightfully handsome young Lieutenant, Big Don, who was a father figure to everyone, and Lila's friend, Brian, treated them to the '...best mess hall in the world' at the Hof outpost, then all climbed aboard jeeps to see the East German and Soviet guard towers at close range. At one spot, they walked to the rim of a hill for a more panoramic view.

"Oh, my God," gasped Emily. She and her companions surveyed the ruin of a divided Germany for the first time. They were silent, trying to take it all in.

"I've seen photos of the Berlin Wall." Abby finally recovered her voice. I guess I thought that was the *only* dangerous division. No one ever talks about this! And this goes all across Europe!"

The ugly scar of naked earth slashed mile upon mile, as far as anyone could see. Behind the high fences were a mine field, rail lines, soldiers patrolling with German Shepherds, manned machine gun positions, and an eerie gray line of Soviet guard towers at close intervals. The American side held only a road, a meandering river, signs marking the *Grenze,* or Border, in both English and German, as though anyone could accidentally stumble across it, and farm cows contentedly chewing their cud as two U.S. soldiers randomly patrolled in a jeep. As they passed, they saluted and said, "*Toujours,*" and the Cavalry officers answered the salute with, "*Pret.*"

"What was that about?" asked Abby.

Big Don grinned. "Tradition of a cavalry unit that goes all the way back to the Civil War--means 'always ready' in French. You'll find the Cav a bit cocky, I suppose. That's because they are on the tip of the sword, and their life expectancy, should the balloon go up, is about thirty minutes. The officers all know it, though I'm not sure the troopers truly understand that fact. But it helps morale to have tradition backing up training. That's why they 'show off' a bit with their sleek black berets and mustaches. The others with berets are the green ones for Special Forces. They're a proud bunch too."

When the women noticed guns, Colin explained, "Their ammo is locked in the jeep, but the Soviets don't know that. Our guys only look fierce. We want no accidental shooting incident within the one Kilometer zone."

"Why do you guys have black electrical tape covering your names?" Megan asked.

"The communists know we use codes that change frequently and randomly and that we know the battle plan," explained Big Don. "Enemy border guards try to photograph our officers when we get close to the border, hoping they can 'snatch' one of us to get the codes. That's also why we need special permission for ski trips, and why we can't travel to Berlin at all."

"Why isn't this more generally known?" asked Abby.

"The Wall gets the publicity," said Colin, "probably because the dividing line between the Soviet zone and the Allied zone in Berlin is more concentrated--more visible. You'd know immediately in a big city if the Soviets crossed over. This Border runs through the countryside. It's almost invisible unless you live on one of the adjacent farms, or see it from the air."

"From the air, you can even see where they built a 'ghost *Autobahn*'," Brian added. "It runs from far inside the communist zone right up to the other side of that fence. It goes nowhere except that fence, so it doesn't take much Military Intelligence to figure out they would use it to bring up their supplies, equipment, and men, should they decide to attack us one day."

Colin added another story. "Once in a snowstorm, an Engineer bulldozer attempting to clear a road for a convoy of vehicles on our side, somehow crossed over that *Autobahn*. He realized his mistake, drove up over the center divider, and the rest of the unsuspecting vehicles followed his u-turn back to our side. Scary. The visibility was so bad the communists probably weren't quite sure what they'd seen until it was too late to respond."

"I don't think people Stateside, or even those stationed elsewhere in Germany, have much idea of this whole Cold War thing," said Big Don. If the Soviets crossed over here in the countryside, it would take awhile before Central Germany knew they'd been invaded, except for those of us here trying to hold them back. It would be much more dangerous for the rest of Europe than an infringement at the Wall in Berlin. That's why we man this area of the Border *all* the time with at least two Cavalry Sheridan platoons. Those can even be dropped by parachute from a C131, if necessary. They're lighter and faster than the Abrams tanks and are designed to 'shoot and scoot' to another area to hit the enemy again. They're supported by Infantry, Mortars, and Engineers, and patrolled by Air Cavalry, to gain aerial platform intelligence. If they see any changes, the pilots radio Brigade to call an alert. Now you know about all we can tell you—not to be discussed, of course."

The new teachers were silent, processing the information.

Seeing their confusion, Brian said, "Let's just say I don't think people *care* to know about this place, as long as things are quiet. But if they take a notion, the Soviets have their tanks poised to cross over that line very suddenly. Then, we must man our side quickly to defend Western Europe against them."

"Are you allowed to tell us what you must do in one of those alerts?" asked Megan.

"We try to persuade the enemy with a show of armor that it would start a devastating World War III for them to cross over so, hopefully, they'll just stay put," answered Colin. "And, if ever that shouldn't work, and they come across anyway, we're tasked to hold them back for at least forty-eight hours." He stopped talking abruptly and looked across at the enemy hillsides where farm cattle sometimes strayed into communist minefields and were blown to pieces.

His hesitation told better than words that he knew they'd all be killed trying to hold the enemy back. "I see," Megan said quietly.

"It's an obscenity!" proclaimed Emily. "How could anyone divide the country and treat the land so? Mines, razor wire--it's against nature."

"The communists built the Border fences and that open strip of mined earth to keep their own people from running away," said Brian. "Their propaganda says that they built it to keep the U.S. from 'invading' them. But, of course, you can *see* which side they put the minefields, fences and towers on. We'd never invade them, and they know it. We wouldn't want to live over there!" He gestured across the ugly line of fortifications.

The teachers were surprised that the Border was not in a straight line, but ran a convoluted, snaky path, bending at the foot of the hill on which they stood. They surveyed the high fence that divided all Europe into an uneasy Cold War truce in silence. This Border radiated an emotional ugliness that was difficult to accept. "The fences look like shadows, remarked Abby, finally breaking the spell. "Like shadows against the whole horrible Iron Curtain."

"We're standing in the rain looking at them, and they're standing there looking back at us," said Megan. She noticed an East German soldier watching them, his guard dog bristling.

"Creepy," Lila said, wiping her dripping face with her scarf.

"Before we get too depressed, we had one good surprise last week, for a change," said Brian. "An East German railroad worker commandeered a truck and managed to avoid the mines, ram it through the Soviet fences, plunge it into the river. Once he swam to our side of the river, we could help him. That's international law."

"Of course, since then," added Colin, gesturing across to the other side, "you can see where the communists have added new barriers on the road, a new killer dog, and they're moving the railroad lines back behind the second barrier. No one will escape at *this* spot again. Can you see it over there?"

"I can see why some would be desperate enough to try a dangerous escape," said Megan.

"It's drab on the other side," said Emily. "No color, no flower boxes on the houses."

"Nothing like the colorful West Germans," said Abby.

As they hiked along the ridgeline in the rain, Brian explained. "Under communism, the government owns everything. There's no incentive to repair things, or to make things look good. It doesn't pay any more than if you just do the minimum. When they build something, they don't landscape or even cart away excess building materials--they just let them rot in the barren yard."

"To tell you how determined they are, though, seven people escaped in a home-made hot air balloon and landed near Bamberg," said Colin. "They had only a flat sheet of metal for a platform, dangling from the balloon, with a rope tied around the outside as a railing. The adults held three small children in the middle between them. How desperate is that?"

Megan wondered if she could have risked such a frightening journey with her children. "I suppose no one ever knows what he'll be able to do until he's forced to try it."

"This is so sad," said Lila, as she moved closer to the fence.

"Stop right there, Lila," said Brian, in an urgent tone. "They'll see you moving their way. They report everything as a threat."

"I'm no threat. And they probably don't see or care what I do. I'm a civilian."

"Turn around slowly and come back to us," Colin commanded. Lila obeyed. "Now, do you see that tower across the wire?" He waved casually off into the rain. "One guard in that tower has you in his binoculars, and the other has you in his gun sights."

"Wow! How do y'all know that?" asked Lila.

"We're Cav and we're elite," boasted Colin, laughing at Lila's naiveté on military matters and relieving his own tension.

"Know why we're so elite?" asked Don, as he escorted Lila back to one of the jeeps. Lila shook her head, giving him a chance to lighten the mood. "Because Cav has its own gate so the quick reaction force can be off Post in ten minutes. On the Border, we sleep in our clothes on our equipment, so we're right there to slow 'em down.

Brigade supports us, but our orders come directly from SACEUR, Supreme Allied Command, Europe." He sobered. "Of course, you understand, we don't discuss this with outsiders, don't you?" Three of the women nodded.

"Forget the secrecy and acronyms," said Lila, laughing. "I'm the dumb blonde, remember? I probably won't even *remember* what all you guys told us."

On the way back to Post, after surveying several positions along the extensive Border, the women expressed sympathy for the Germans who had been trapped on the wrong side of the line by the Yalta and Potsdam Conferences. The Soviet-manned gun towers, the plowed-up death strip, the razor wire in high fences designed to cut off fingers of any escapees getting that far, the automatically firing scatterguns, the vicious dogs--*all* to keep their people from running to the West, had produced a deep appreciation for their own freedom.

"It's depressing, but I'm glad we came," said Abby. "I think we see more clearly now what our military guys are up against."

"It's as though we're seeing it through their eyes, sort of a gun sight view," added Megan. "Now I see why our friends perhaps drink too much, laugh a lot, or get moody sometimes, and they *need* everyone as 'family.' They're just trying to forget about their jobs."

"You know what's odd?" added Abby. "Even people stationed elsewhere in Germany don't know what this Border is all about. I talked to a friend from Frankfurt and he had no idea what our guys do. Most people in the U.S. only know about the Berlin Wall-- nothing about this imminent threat at all. All people should see this."

"I can also see why the German populace near the Border supports the American military being here to protect them," said Emily. "No one wants the Soviets to come here, too. And I didn't realize how outnumbered our men were here."

It was a depressing day, but the women felt a new sense of pride in their military friends. They also had a better understanding of the isolated place in which they had landed, and its implications for their future.

Megan was not sure, however, that Lila understood the necessary secrecy. Her casual, flippant attitude toward security missions would soon become a matter of grave concern.

Chapter 8

After Wednesday's volleyball, Abby, Lila, and Megan returned to the O'Club for a soft drink, only to find it inundated with ten aviators from Stuttgart's 48th Aviation group whose modified UH-1H helicopters had been grounded in Bamberg by bad weather after a night mission to the Border. They knew some of Bamberg's pilots from Vietnam, so they joined the regular crowd. One big, burly officer pulled up a chair by Megan.

"Hello, You," he said, with a grin. "I'm Milt. Where were they hiding you the last time I was stranded in Bamberg?" Megan was accustomed to military transit or TDY officers dropping by the Club by then, and she was now a little more comfortable meeting most new people. This officer seemed quite jovial and easy-going.

"I'm new a new teacher this year," she answered. "What's your job up here?"

"Oh, I'm one of the *expendable* ones who's supposed to sop up any Cav failures at the Border by laying mines to slow down the Soviets." He kept smiling, so Megan took his statement as a joke.

"Our Cav never fails, or at least that's what they *tell* us."

"Well actually, we just like to come up periodically to talk with new school teachers. What are you interested in?"

Before she quite realized it, Megan was into a spirited discussion that ranged from politics, history, and religion, to literature. The Club closed as they discovered they were both interested in just about everything. As the group dispersed to straggle home, Milt announced, "You *will* have dinner with me here tomorrow night, won't you?"

Surprised, Megan couldn't figure how to respond to such a military *order*. "The whole gang has dinner here after Ski Club meeting tomorrow, but you're welcome to join us."

"In case I forgot to tell you, I've never enjoyed talking with anyone more. I feel like I've always known you, Megan," Milt said quietly. "We're going to take this very slowly because we're going to be together a long time. I don't decide this kind of thing easily."

What an odd thing to say to someone you just met, Megan

thought. *Was this another type of line like Carl's infamous 'take me I'm easy?'* She had no idea how to reply to the man.

After a short Ski Club meeting the next evening, Carl waited at the O'Club bar entrance. "Megan, you must be very careful about aviators."

She laughed. "Carl, *you're* an aviator, and I don't need to be careful with you, do I?"

"That's different. Be sure Luke or Stan or I are nearby while you're with this guy."

"Don't worry so much. No guy would be interested in me anyway."

"Why can't I get it through your head about men, Megan? They notice you. And you're *helpless* when guys toss out lines. Heck, even jokes sail right over your head."

"But I always tell them the same thing—that I don't want any men in my life."

"Oh, thanks a lot!"

"Well, you know what I mean. You already said you're different. Don't be such a worrywart. He probably won't even be here tonight, and you guys will be right there with me."

"Milt's already here, and he's expecting you." Carl's forehead glistened. "After dinner, steer him into the bar with us."

Megan wondered what was bothering Carl so. "Okay, but we just enjoyed talking."

"That's a good girl." They walked into the bar, where everyone was waiting expectantly.

Milt approached the two and offered Megan his arm. "Are you ready to come with me to the dining room?"

Megan felt Abby and Lila's eyes on her, as well as the blood running to her cheeks. There was a sudden hush from everyone else. She could barely nod.

They only ordered pizzas, since they were eating less and couldn't seem to stop talking, She felt comfortable with the big man, with none of her usual uneasiness. She invited Milt to join her friends in the bar for a drink, as Carl had suggested, explaining that she was now up to three or four sips of wine without falling under the table.

Milt laughed. "You should keep up the good work. When I

come back, I'll be able to buy a whole bottle of wine with dinner, instead of one Tab diet drink."

When she shook her head, he asked, "What are you saying 'no' to--me, or the wine?"

"You probably won't be coming back up here anyway, and I will *never* be able to drink half a bottle of wine. I'm aiming for just drinking one glass safely."

"Oh, I *will* be back." Milt looked into her eyes with a serious expression. "Someday, we're going to be together."

She averted her gaze, uncomfortably. Was it her own natural reserve, or Carl's warnings, or the fact that Milt seemed almost too easy to talk with--as though she had known him someplace before, and for a long time.

When they entered the bar, their resident alcoholic schizophrenic, Luke, was performing magic tricks. He had wrapped Stan and Lila together in some combination of knots and strings, challenging them to get uncoupled without untying any knots. "You have all night to figure it out," Luke said with a flourish. He leaned against a pillar with his usual sardonic smile.

The bar patrons cheered the pair on and offered suggestions as they twisted and turned, climbed over each other's arms and under each other's legs until they were hopelessly entangled on the floor, exhausted from the effort.

"I think I'll just have to grin and enjoy it," quipped Stan, reaching his arms over his head to embrace the giggly Lila behind him. Rex borrowed scissors from Marco and rescued them.

"Didn't I warn you the magicians among us would get you in trouble?" crowed Carl, as he helped Lila to her feet.

After this performance, Carl said, "Come on, Megan. I'll walk you to your car.

Milt looked at them blankly. "Do you and Sheffield already have something going?"

"What do you mean?" asked Megan, surprised at the question, and not understanding its implication. "Carl always looks out for me."

Milt's laughter exploded. "Sheffield is looking out for you? You *are* in trouble! But I'll be back to see you another time. That's a promise. I get up to the Fulda Border pretty often, and I can drop by Bamberg on occasion…perhaps as often as these Hof Border air jockeys. I'll tell you good bye when I leave tomorrow morning."

"Wieder bye bye," Carl said curtly, taking Megan's arm and moving her toward the door.   "What's that mean?" Milt called out. "That's just Carl's corruption of the German language," said Megan. "It's short for Auf Wiedersehen, but he's got all of us and half the Germans using it." She waved, and Carl walked her outside.

"Megan, did he try anything at dinner."

"Like what? What do you mean? We just talked. He's friendly. Why do you always ask?"

"I told you I'd look out for you, didn't I? Every guy that comes in always notices you right away, and my job of protecting you gets harder all the time. You are so *damned* naïve. You don't seem to understand how or when to protect yourself, and you think everyone is as honest as you are. Be very careful, okay?

"Yes, fairy godfather," she said indulgently. This time, she kissed *him* on the cheek.

About 1000 hours the next morning, though now accustomed to the throbbing, grinding noise of tanks shattering the quiet of her classroom, shaking the ground under the building, or clanking through the meager, cobble-stoned playground on their way in from the field, Megan became aware of a new, and much louder, 'whop whop' noise. It was the flight of Stuttgart helicopters in formation.

"Mrs. James, look how low that helicopter is," shouted one of her boys.

Megan moved to the window to see if there was some danger. The children followed.

As she looked out, one helicopter hovered lower until it seemed almost parallel to the windows. There in the cockpit sat Milt with his huge 'co-pilot' dog, Rusty, resting his muzzle over the man's shoulder. Milt smiled and waved to the kids. Megan blushed fiercely as the helicopter finally rose and roared away to the east.

"That was neat!" The kids were excited. "Do you know that pilot?" "Did you guys see the big dog?" "I'll bet he's a collie or a retriever." "Is that your boyfriend, Mrs. James?"

Flustered, Megan herded the children back to their seats and said, as calmly as she could, "I don't have a boyfriend. That's just a nice pilot saying goodbye—rather dramatically."

What was it about Milt that had seemed so familiar?

"Maybe he reminds you of someone," said Abby, as they dined later at Emily's apartment.

"I want to know why Carl seemed so worried he tried to drive Milt away," said Emily.

"That bothers me too," Megan said. "It's not like Carl to instantly dislike someone."

"It is if he's jealous," proposed Lila.

"Carl wouldn't be jealous," scoffed Megan, surprised her friend would say such a thing. "He's just helping me avoid getting entangled until I feel ready."

"And he hopes you'll never be ready," said Abby. The other three women laughed.

Lila said, "Megan, you're never even aware of it, but men just seem to seek you out for help, or your opinion, even when the rest of us are sitting right under their noses and flirting with them outrageously. They must see *something* different about you."

"Remember the German firemen that surrounded you at that little Fest in the country?" said Emily. "You got flustered, and they never even said 'hello' to the rest of us."

"I remember, all right," said Megan. "There I was, trapped, and you guys just stood back and giggled. You *could* have come to help me!"

"What about that Yugoslavian in our train compartment going to Florence?" said Lila. "He even wrote to 'Megan of Bamberg,' and the letter arrived! And that Nürnberg pilot, Ron, who followed you into Ingolstadt gas station when he thought you were driving Emily's VW erratically--too sleepy to get home safely. He even joined our Ski Club instead of Nürnberg's."

Emily warmed to her subject, punctuating words with dramatic gestures. "It happens *everywhere*--at airports, restaurants, everywhere we go—and *you* never even notice!

"Stop joking you guys? I'm not young and pretty like Abby and Lila, and I never encourage anyone at all. They just sort of appear, and then I have to avoid them. Carl keeps worrying about that too. Why do they talk to me? Can't they *see* I don't want anybody?"

Abby, noting her friend's agitation, said, "Well, whatever you have going for you, the rest of us will just hang around and hope some of it rubs off on us, huh Lila?"

"I think every time Megan goes anywhere, I'll just give her my order," said Lila, tossing her curls. "Like—'bring me back a tall, blonde boyfriend--hopefully with money.'"

She laughed, while Emily added, "Don't worry, Megan. Milton is just one more who finds you *mysteriously* intriguing. I love a mystery, so I think it's quite exciting, myself."

"Milt *is* easy to talk to, sort of like when Andy and I used to sit up half the night, just talking. I miss that good conversation." Images of Andy flooded back to her, of their sitting together, contentedly, shoulder to shoulder, hand in hand, long into the night, discussing some book or political event. She felt tears of longing threaten her perilous equilibrium. She quickly closed her eyes, folded her hands together, and took a deep breath to force back the pain.

Abby's strained voice dragged her back to the discussion at hand. "Milt doesn't look like Andy, does he?" she asked.

"No, of course not!" Megan brought up the vision for comparison. "Well, there are a *few* similarities--dark-hair, big build, strong shoulders, deep eyes. But, Milt's taller." The reminder of those similarities made her uneasy. "Maybe he does remind me of Andy a *little* bit--in feeling easy to be around, I mean."

Lila shook out her curls. "Do you believe in reincarnation?"

Megan jerked her head up sharply with wide eyes. "Don't say something like that!"

"I just mean they resemble each other, and Milt unnerves you. Unusual isn't it?"

Megan fidgeted uncomfortably, her face masked into a frown. "But if I liked talking to him because he reminds me of Andy, it wouldn't be fair to either of them to see Milt again."

"Well, don't let it bother you," said Emily, reaching out to pour the girls another cup of tea. "You had good memories of Andy, so you needn't avoid Milt."

"He probably won't call. But if he does, I don't intend to go out with him." She drew her shoulders up to the rigid, withdrawn stance her friends already knew well. "I'm not going to date anyone. He'll have to understand that and just be a friend, like everyone else."

"But Megan," nagged Lila, "you have a million good friends and *no beaus*."

Ignoring Lila's assessment, Abby suggested, "If he calls, you could let him visit in a group setting when we're all around. Sooner or later, you'll want to start dating again.

Megan shook her head vehemently, dark hair flying.

"I guess that's what I've been doing with Klaus," said Lila, mercifully pulling the speculation away from the discomfited Megan and settling herself back in the chair, "seeing him only when others are around. I'm getting to like him a lot, but when I want to be alone with him, he asks me about my friends, and their lives, and what they do for the Army, instead. I want him to be interested in just me."

"I'm surprised you're still seeing him," remarked Abby. "He didn't seem like your type, and the guys seem uneasy around him."

"Well, if you're talking about Brian," Lila snorted, "he's uneasy that I'm even dating anyone else at all. He wants me to go exclusively with him, and I haven't even seen all the men around here yet. I want more freedom than that." She bounced across the room to Megan. "You just go ahead and scope out Milt. I thought he was sorta' cute, for an older man."

"Older, being about 38," said Emily, with a wry grin. "That leaves me in the *antique* category, so I'll have to stick with the Ambassador." All the girls laughed along with her. She turned to Megan. "Just go easy and enjoy all your friends. There's no rush. It will be a while before men are on your mind again. Give yourself the time you need."

Megan smiled politely, though she knew her friends would never understand her reluctance or her reasons for avoiding involvement completely.

Chapter 9

The lump sat on the inside of her left breast like an ugly, predatory animal.

"Why didn't I notice this before?" said Megan to her reflection in the mirror. But she had never really looked at herself. She touched the other breast tentatively, wondering if there was a lump there to match the first. No, it was only on one side. That might be ominous, she thought, since breast cancer had taken her grandmother and afflicted her mother.

She thought through her options. Should she see a doctor? But she'd been praying to die and join Andy. Perhaps this lump was God's answer to her prayer. Of course, cancer was a painful death, and it took a long time. She'd prefer something instantaneous. Still, she didn't really care. After this year alone, she believed that physical pain would be *nothing* compared to her searing emotional pain. She decided to ignore the lump and see if nature would take its course. There was nowhere for her to go in any hurry, anyway.

Having made her decision, Megan calmly finished dressing, ran a brush thorough her unruly hair, and grabbed her book bag on the way outside to meet Stan. Each day, she waited on the curb for him and tried greeting her new German neighbors with a cheery 'Grüss Gott—Greetings to God,' the standard Bavarian courtesy. None of them ever returned her greeting. Perhaps they wait for a formal introduction here, Megan thought, as she watched an old man walk his dog across the street to avoid her.

It was raining again when Stan picked her up in his white Mercedes. As he leaned across to open her door, he said, "The radio weatherman said he just saw a submarine periscope go by in the parking lot, if that tells you anything about our next few days."

Megan laughed. "I don't notice bad weather slowing any of us down" After the short drive, she jumped out of the car at the school Annex, her absorption with her students already pushing away thoughts of the lump that perhaps could grant her wish to die.

Megan and Abby went car shopping after school. Each ordered a Fiat. German sales offices had no cars, no test drive, and no returns. Instead, customers picked out the color and model from a catalogue, agreeing to take delivery six weeks later, after the cars were made to order at the factory.

"I don't like this much," said Abby, as a fellow teacher drove them back to Post. "I wanted a test drive before making a down payment, and to pick colors we could first see."

"It's hard to tell anything from an order book," said Megan. "And I hate making decisions alone." Her mind raced to the last car she and Andy had chosen together. *It would be wonderful to be with him again, wouldn't it, if this really is cancer and it takes me away?*

"I'm wondering how those colors will look," Abby continued on, unaware that Megan's mind had drifted away. "And we're stuck once the cars are delivered, whether we like them or not. But I guess this keeps the dealer from end of the year sales. When in Rome..."

Megan was surprised that the words she had intended to keep secret jumped out of her mind and onto her tongue. "Do you think a lump in the breast means anything?"

Abby's reaction was immediate. "You have a lump? When did you discover this?"

"This morning."

"Megan, you're going to the doctor at Post clinic—right now. Jenny, drop us there, would you? We'll get a ride with Stan later."

Megan immediately regretted mentioning the lump. *Why didn't I keep my big mouth shut*, she lamented, as the two entered the clinic to wait.

"How big?" Abby brooked no nonsense, taking Megan's arm as though she feared Megan would run away.

"Oh, maybe six inches long and sort of bulky, but I don't want to see the doctor. It'll probably just go away. I don't even know why I blurted that out to you. Besides, if I get a lump, I just get the lump. It may be a blessing in disguise, since I sort of wanted an easy way out." She slumped in a chair, looking away from her friend.

"Out of what?" Abby was shocked. "You can't go around ignoring a lump that might be cancerous. That's suicidal, and you need to be seen right away."

"Let's just go home. It's probably nothing. They'll laugh at me for coming in. I feel fine."

Megan's lack of alarm scared Abby. "No! We're waiting."

When the nurse called Megan's name, she chastised herself

again for mentioning anything to her friend. But the doctor, a bulky, bespectacled man who exuded a business-like air, immediately called Nürnberg hospital and set up surgery for the following week. "It's large, Mrs. James. It's attached, and it's solid. I can't imagine that you didn't see it or feel it sooner."

"I guess I just don't think about such things," she said lamely, still trying to take in his diagnosis. *I should have known. There's that ugly family history of cancer. But, if he's confirming it might be serious, it could still achieve my purpose, couldn't it?*

"I won't want you driving afterward," said the doctor, automatically assuming she would accept having surgery. She would learn that if you worked for the military, any medical emergency would cause an *order*. A patient wouldn't have a choice in the matter.

"Should the tumor be benign, we'll simply remove it Thursday, and you can go home the next day," he continued. "You'll be in some pain and you'll have to keep ice on it at all times. Should the tumor be malignant, we'll have no choice but to remove the whole left breast. Either way, you'll need to stay with someone afterward."

"If it's malignant, can't you just take them both off and sort of even things up?"

The doctor jerked back sharply, and demanded, "Why on earth would you want to remove both breasts when one may be perfectly healthy?"

Megan was learning it was better not to argue, knowing no one would understand anyway. "No reason, I guess."

Abby scolded Megan all the way to the O'Club, where Megan noticed her speaking to Lila and Emily. "Please don't tell everyone. I told you in confidence."

"My aunt had cancer and tried to keep it a secret too. We should have seen that she got to the hospital sooner." Abby assumed her stance of quiet determination. "It's all set. I called the principal. You'll have a substitute teacher for at least Thursday and Friday. We'll drive you down to the hospital after school Wednesday. I'll cover your Drug Conference on Friday, and Lila will take care of your kid's entries for Saturday's Science Fair. You'll stay with me after you get out. If they do the radical surgery, we'll take turns staying with you."

As Megan shook her head, Abby continued, "Don't argue,

Megan, it's done. Only us four will know if that's how you want it."

"Okay, but I want no fuss. I'll have to do lesson plans" *Long range ones*, she thought, already searching for another alternative.

Wednesday came sooner than Megan could have imagined. After school, the friends piled into Emily's VW, driving an hour to Nürnberg Military Hospital. Megan checked in to Pre-Op, then the four talked in her room until eight o'clock, when visiting hours were over. Abby had promised to meet Robert at the O'Club.

Megan turned out the bed light and lay in the dark, pondering what her feelings were at that moment. Of course, she had written her mom and her daughters that she was having only a routine procedure. But now that she was alone in a hospital room, she prayed God she would not wake up from surgery. She spoke aloud, looking up to the ceiling, "Surely there's a way. It would be so easy--just go to sleep, and not wake up." She could envision Andy, waiting.

Her reverie was interrupted by a soft voice. She turned to find a woman in a volunteer's uniform sitting down at the bedside.

"Mrs. James? I'm Mona," the woman said. "Dr. Farley thought I might help you face up to the idea of your surgery in the morning."

Megan's peaceful feeling slipped away, and Andy's familiar image disappeared.

"I'm okay, Mona, but thank you." Megan hoped the woman would leave, so she could go back to her reverie. That didn't happen.

"But, should the mastectomy be necessary," the woman insisted, "you need to know about prostheses that can make you look normal afterward. They have lots of options now. For instance, I'm wearing a prosthesis, and you can't even tell." She turned sideways. "My mastectomy was six months ago, and I've been counseling women facing surgery ever since."

"You're talking about falsies, aren't you?" Megan tried to keep her voice steady, but she felt herself bristle. "My husband would never accept that. He doesn't approve of anything false." She rose almost to a sitting position, trying in vain to control her sudden tears.

"It says on your records that you're a widow."

"Andy may be dead, but he wouldn't approve of my wearing even false eyelashes. Please leave me alone. Thank you for trying to be kind, but I can't think about this now." Megan turned her face to the wall and pulled the covers over her shaking body.

"I'm sorry, Mrs. James. Most women *want* to hear how to cope after a mastectomy. The prostheses fits right into the bra. You can't even tell. And you don't want your breasts looking different, one side from the other."

"Please, please, just leave me alone now. I'd rather just not wake up, but even if I do, no falsies!" Hot tears scalded her cheeks.

The woman left the room while Megan chastised herself for losing control. "Andy, you must be doing a whirling dervish in your grave about now. I promise you, nothing false."

"Hello, Mrs. James." A lower voice rumbled from behind her. As she turned over to see who was accosting her again with foreign ideas, she noticed the black collar and lay quiet.

"Mona told me you were a bit hysterical about your surgery," the man said in a voice designed for four-year-olds. "I came to see if there was anything I could do to make you feel better." The priest stood tall in the shadows, outlined against the light from the corridor.

"Thank you, Father, but I'm not Catholic, and I'm not hysterical. I'm sorry if I upset Mona, but I'll not wear anything false because my husband wouldn't approve. I can't discuss such a thing."

The priest shifted from one foot to another, probably trying to broach the subject of her husband's being already dead.

Megan intervened, "Please Father, I'm not delusional. And I'm not frightened, either, because if I die, it's no great loss. I'm all right. I just want to be alone for now--please."

"Yes, Daughter. But we won't let you die. Do you mind if I say a prayer for you?"

"Of course not." She tried to smile, but the effort was feeble.

The priest clasped her hand with his cold one, and said the Lord's Prayer, a rather shallow, singsong version. Megan didn't pull away as she had done with the woman, but she felt no particular comfort from his words. They were empty and devoid of feeling. "Thank you, Father," she said in an equally wooden tone.

"I'll leave you to get some sleep now."

With that, the man was gone and Megan was relieved to again imagine how it would feel to see Andy. If there was fear, it was the fear of possibly waking up and having to face her loneliness again. She had deliberately not told the doctor about her tendency to hemorrhage, so she hoped there was at least a chance she could drift away before the surgeon noticed.

She remembered the birth of her second daughter, when she'd been pronounced dead of just such a hemorrhage by the medical team. It had been so easy to relinquish pain. Only the high-pitched alarm from the heart monitor screamed. She had wanted to ask someone to shut the annoying thing off, but no words came. When they did shut it off, it had been peaceful. All pain had stopped as she listened absent-mindedly to the frantic yells of the doctors. She drifted lazily above everything, watching as they fussed over her vacant shell of a body, then reluctantly left her to work over her new baby, who was not yet breathing. She had believed God would save her baby, and she heard the cry and saw the child wriggling in the doctor's arms below.

A golden glow in the distance had beckoned. It was beautiful and soothing. A young intern had laid his head beside her hand on the delivery table, crying at having lost his very first patient. The other team members kept calling him. "Come away, Fitz. She's gone. You can't do anything there." She had drifted toward the light, but then a foreign voice seemed to tell her from inside somewhere, that it wasn't yet time--that Andy couldn't raise the children alone. She had attempted to reach out and pat Dr. Fitz' head to comfort him, as she felt pity for the distraught young man. But bedlam broke loose as Dr. Fitz saw her hand move and screamed. The other doctors came running back. The equipment was reattached. The pain returned.

When she had returned to consciousness the next day, her doctors could scarcely believe she had heard and watched them working over her 'dead' body, until she had told them, word for word, everything they had said and done. Only a couple of years later, another woman had described a near death experience in a book that had made millions. *I should have written it down,* she mused, giggling that she could think of such a thing at a time like this.

That time, it had been thinking of her darling Andy trying to raise two little girls all alone that had finally made her fight to come back. This time, however, there was no reason to fight her way back. Andy's arms would be waiting on the to envelop her when she just let go. Yes, she decided--dying during surgery would be exactly the blessing she would pray for this night. She wouldn't fight it—just let a hemorrhage take her away. "God, if You are out there, please answer my prayer this time, and take me, too." It never occurred to her that she would have no control over whether or not her chosen scenario took place, nor did she know that breast tissue did not have the heavy blood flow of other tissues of the body. She didn't know whether or not incisions would be deep enough for hemorrhage. She had simply *willed* it so. Surely, God would help her, *this* time.

When the sun broke across the horizon, Megan woke and stretched. Today's the day, she thought, relieved. No more nights of reliving Andy's death. The nightmare had tormented her long enough. "Please, God, let me be with Andy. I'm so alone."

Dr. Farley looked in to find her crying softly. Believing her tears were an indication of anxiety, he squeezed her hand. "The nurse gave you a shot to make you drowsy. You mustn't be nervous now. We'll take good care of you." Gentle hands lifted her onto a gurney and the medics rolled her down the hall.

Why is it that the view of a ceiling flowing by on the way to surgery is such a disorientating process? It's all in slow motion somehow, as though one is turning and moving dizzily in answer to another's will—completely out of one's own control. Megan felt tears soak the pillow, but she couldn't imagine they were her own. Were they for her loneliness, for her family, for the unknown? What?

Above the soft squeak of the gurney's wheels, she heard a dissonant clomp, clomp, clomp of someone running down the hall. The sound jolted her from her thoughts. Skidding to a halt at her side was Carl, flushed and out of breath. "I'm glad I got here in time, Megan. I almost dumped the General out of the helicopter, so I could leave him at Headquarters and get over here. How are you feeling?"

"I don't really know what they're going to do yet. How did you know I was here?"

"The girls dropped by the Club last night. When you weren't with them, I asked."

"No one was supposed to know, but I'm glad to see you anyway," she said drowsily.

"Megan, listen to me." He grabbed her shoulders and almost shook her. He seemed so intense, so urgent, that she was forced to listen. "I *know* what's in your mind--you just want to let everything go--but you mustn't do that! Here, give me your hand."

Dazedly, she lifted her right hand, which he clasped palm to palm with his left, curling his fingers around hers.

"Megan, I'm giving all my strength to you, right here through my hand to yours. You have to remember to *fight*, no matter what happens. You're a survivor. You're meant to do something *more* with your life, and someday you'll find out what it is. You need to know that right this minute!"

"Carl," she whispered, "some woman came to talk to me about falsies, and I don't want any of those." To her dazed embarrassment, tears began again to roll down her cheeks.

"Listen to me now, Megan. I have a theory about this." He leaned over the railing of her gurney with a conspiratorial whisper. "Even if they have to remove that whole left breast, you won't need anything false. According to my theory, if one breast is gone, all the hormones will shift, making the remaining breast *the* sweetest, *the* most luscious, and *the* most gorgeous breast in the whole world, just *waiting* to be caressed."

Her eyes opened wide in disbelief. What was he saying? Was this some kind of hallucination? This whole scene had to be a result of the anesthetic playing games with her mind.

Then Carl leaned closer over her face. "And after this is all over, how about letting me come over and *prove* my theory?" He leered and wiggled his eyebrows in Groucho Marx style.

Megan's jaw dropped, "What?" She couldn't believe what she was hearing. Was the crazy young pilot in her dream actually propositioning someone her age at a time like this? It was impossibly out of whack. But her fear was replaced by incredulous wonder when she looked into his face. The apparition was grinning broadly.

"It's okay, Twinkletoes. Just keep my theory in mind while you're in there dreaming about me. Everything is going to be okay…believe me…" He clasped her hand harder. "Remember, my strength to you."

With that, the nurses wheeled her into the operating room and she could vaguely hear Carl's flight boots clumping away down the hall. She had a fit of giggles, wondering if it was part of the medication taking hold--the fact that she could hallucinate so wildly.

"Boy," said Dr. Farley as the nurses lifted her to the operating table. "You're certainly in a better mood than you were earlier. What did that pilot say to you?"

Oh my. If the doctor saw him too, he was no apparition—he

had been real! She tried to focus her hazy thoughts to answer the doctor's question. "Nothing much...just a private joke...really. I have a fairy godfather who can make me laugh...no...matter...what." She smiled as she drifted away under the bright lights.

"Wake up, Megan. I have great news."

She struggled up through foggy layers of sleep to see Dr. Farley's face above her. The afternoon sun streamed in the windows, and its brightness forced her to close her eyes again.

"The tumor was large and deeply embedded, covering much of the inside left breast, but it was benign, so we could cut it away without removing the breast. You'll be fine in a few days and you'll probably not be able to tell the difference--only a tiny scar."

The doctor frowned then, looking down over his glasses and shaking his finger at her. "Why didn't you tell me that you hemorrhaged easily? You *know* you are a new teacher this year, and we had no records on you. We had a hard time stopping the bleeding when we got in deeper under the mass. You should have told us."

Megan looked down at her chest, a mass of bandages that she touched gingerly. She didn't know how to answer his question. "Is it really all there? I can't feel anything."

"Yep, it's all there--a clean surgery. And you giggled in your sleep the whole time. It must have been a good joke. Care to tell me?"

"No, I don't think so." She smiled at the memory. Never in a million years could she tell anyone what Carl had said to her.

But suddenly, her hand flew to her mouth as she realized Carl had come to sabotage her willingness to die...to make her fight to live...he had been trying to save her with his strength. He had wanted her to believe...*what*...that being alive, alone, wouldn't be so bad?

She struggled to bring her thoughts back to the doctor standing quietly beside her and to gain some control. "What happens now?" she asked, finally.

"You can go home tomorrow, providing you keep that breast packed in ice to prevent further swelling and take these pills to prevent infection. You'll have to go easy with no work or strain for a few days. Next week I can remove the stitches and drainage tubes. One of your girlfriends said you could stay at her apartment until you're ready to go back to school." The doctor wrote something on her chart. "That pilot called and said he'd be by to collect you tomorrow afternoon after two." He hung up her chart and turned toward the door. "Does that sound all right to you?"

"Yes, thank you. Everything sounds fine…and thanks for all you did."

"Except for the hemorrhage, it was easy. You're in good physical shape, and you were in *great* spirits in the operating room. Attitude is everything!" He turned and was gone.

"Andy," she whispered softly. "Perhaps I'm not meant to be with you yet. Please help me know what to do until we can be together."

She sat on her bed, dressed in wool slacks and a too large sweater that covered the tubes and bandages. Abby's idea—but a good one. Flowers had appeared after the surgery, with a card signed by the school gang. Her tears came in appreciation for their care.

In the afternoon, Carl entered with a handful of wildflowers, obviously picked on his way in, and thrust them in her hand as he kissed her on the cheek. "Are you ready?"

She nodded, and he threw her overnight bag over his shoulder. The nurses loaded Megan and her flowers into a wheelchair for the trip down to Carl's car.

"Really, I'm all right. I'd rather walk under my own steam."

"Not this time," said the smiling nurse. "I'm responsible, and I don't want you getting weak and messing up my hospital floor."

Megan nodded, and the procession wound down the halls and elevators. Carl had brought a blanket that he tucked around her in the front seat of his car.

"Are you taking me to Abby's now?"

"I promised everyone I'd bring you by the Club for this evening's Happy Hour first."

"But they said I had to pack it in ice." She felt tired and shaky, and she wasn't sure she could face a crowd. "Besides, this is sort of a personal thing, and I really don't want everyone to know about the surgery, and…"

"Number one: everyone already knows and we're tickled to death the tumor was benign. We're all family here, and we take care of our own. Number two: I already told Abby to meet us at the O'Club as always, and I'll take you both to her place afterward.

Number three: I don't think you should change your usual routine beyond getting enough rest. As for the ice, leave that to me. I have it all figured out. Now, quit worrying and relax."

He reached out his hand and gently grasped hers. "Didn't I tell you it would be all right? I don't go around giving my strength to just *anybody*. Why, I was so weak yesterday, I could hardly pull pitch on the helicopter controls." His husky chuckle made her smile.

"You were worried!" Surprise rang in her voice.

"Maybe a little bit. After all, I've waited a long time for a dance partner. I didn't want to risk losing her." His smile faded as he gazed across the seat, the question burning in his eyes.

She suddenly realized that Carl had known—everything. She dropped her eyes to the floorboards. "How did you know what I was feeling?"

His ears turned red, and apparently he wasn't sure how to say what he'd been thinking. "I was pretty sure you were just looking for a way to die, Megan. I couldn't let you go into surgery thinking like that. I wanted you to think positively—about fighting back."

"I didn't know it showed." She locked her fingers together in her lap. "Hemorrhaging during surgery seemed the perfect opportunity to check out gracefully, and my children would never suspect. I didn't ever want them to feel I left them on purpose, but I just hoped..." She turned her head away.

"I know." He focused ahead and was silent for a moment while the road spun away under them. "I'm going to ask you right out, Megan, and I want a straight answer. "Are you over this idea now? We aren't going to need to watch you around guns or drugs or anything, are we?"

"I'm probably too much afraid of botching the job and winding up a burden to somebody," she answered slowly, and as honestly as she could. "And I'm afraid of weapons, anyway. I couldn't use such an obvious way. A friend of mine never recovered from her husband's shooting himself. I couldn't do that to my mom and kids." She sighed with resignation. "I promise you that I'll only *pray* to die. I won't do anything wild."

"I'll hope for a day you won't even pray for it, but we can go one step at a time. Surely you know you're needed here, too. We'd...I'd...be devastated to lose you."

Megan was surprised at the break in his voice, and looked quickly over at his face.

He shook his head, trying to erase the smile that revealed he'd stumbled into a rare emotional statement. He couldn't, and simply grinned at her and shrugged. "Must be some ashes or something in the air," he said, wiping his eyes with the back of one hand.

She thought over what they'd said--and left unsaid. Looking out across the deep forest that whizzed by, knowing it led up 505 Highway into the outskirts of Bamberg, she felt a soft sense of release, recognizing where she was in a supposedly strange country. Bamberg and its military people really *were* becoming her family. She realized their dangerous jobs at the Border made their position much more precarious than her own, and yet they kept going bravely day after day in spite of their fear or loneliness. Her situation was certainly no more frightening than theirs. Perhaps that realization had snuck up on her. Realizing it now, she closed her eyes and smiled. Good people were waiting for her at the Club, and she did feel she belonged there.

She turned slightly to look at Carl. "You know, I thought I had only imagined your coming to me in the hospital." She chuckled. "But I remembered what you said anyway, and you were right. Maybe there *is* something I'm meant to do. If I'm not going to be with Andy for awhile, I need to figure out what to do with my life."

"Atta' girl."

When he smiled, she added, "I guess Bamberg is home to me now, for better or worse."

"I'm glad, Meg. I meant it…whenever you feel shaky, reach for my hand." He stretched his right hand out to her. "I'll always give my strength to you. I'll come whenever and wherever you need me."

She squeezed his hand back. "Thank you. I guess I needed more support than I thought. I appreciate that you came and offered it. The doctor said my 'positive attitude' helped them take care of my bleeding. He said I laughed about your joke all through my surgery."

Carl grinned. "Who was joking? I thought it a perfectly rational theory."

She smiled indulgently. "Well, it made me laugh, and I needed to be able to laugh again."

"I'll only promise you one thing, Megan. I'll never check out my 'theories' until *you* tell me you're ready." He looked at her with raised eyebrows again, and wiggled them.

She smiled, knowing Carl was younger and such thoughts about her were just part of his teasing manner. "That's never going to happen, my friend, but I appreciate the thought."

"Shucks, Megan, you just ruined my daydreams and night sweats."

She smacked his shoulder, forgetting her left side was restricted, and felt a sharp stab of pain fly up her arm to the offending breast. "Ow," she squealed, grasping her chest and bending over. "The pain killers must be wearing off. That hurt!"

Carl smiled and shook his head as he pulled up to the O'Club door. "See, I always say that you should never resist a true lover, and never say 'never.' You'll only hurt yourself."

With that, he jumped out, helped her from the car, kicked the door shut, and steered her up the front steps. Steadying her with his arm around her waist, Carl escorted her into the Club's bar amid cheers and hugs from her friends waiting there.

After seating her in a comfortable chair, Carl signaled Marco, who brought a huge beer glass ten inches high, packed to the brim with chipped ice. He swept out two cans of Tab and, with a flourish, filled the glass to the top, tucked a straw into it, and handed it to Carl.

Looking left and right, Carl moved Megan's arms out of the way and placed the glass gently against the inside of her left breast. He took her hand and folded it around the glass. "Here you go," he whispered. "Just hold it against the bandages between sips, gracefully, and no one will ever be able to tell you're using an improvised ice pack." He gathered up a beer of his own and sat beside her at the table. "You look perfectly natural to me." A grin flooded his face, as he silently toasted her with his beer glass.

Megan realized that Carl had understood completely, both her embarrassment, and her reluctance to be seen in public with an ice bag in a normally private place. She smiled to let him know she appreciated his thoughtfulness in thinking how to make her feel comfortable.

Others drifted over to sit and talk. Megan realized, in that moment, that she was glad to be alive, and she was grateful for such concerned and loving friends.

Chapter 10

Abby's airy apartment, with pastoral view of farmers' fields and forests, and her lovely, exotic furnishings that had finally arrived from the Far East was a comfortable place to recuperate. Megan lounged in an oriental Papasan chair, an iced drink glass serving as ice bag for her bruises. She was feeling much less pain. Emily brought over a peach pie, and the ladies waited for dinner to get done.

"I wish I'd brought some things from home to decorate my apartment," Megan said. "Mine looks pretty bare, especially compared to yours."

"It won't for long," said Abby. "You've already bought your Greek Flocati rug, and you'll find lovely things when you've been overseas awhile. As for me, I wish I could cook like you. I had a maid and a houseboy in the Philippines, so I never learned."

"I'll help you. You can do lots of cooking in the year I'm here."

"I didn't think you could come for only one year," said Abby, shaking her head. "We have a two-year commitment to DoDDS for teaching in Germany."

"They won't ship you or your baggage home if you quit after one year," added Emily. There are only a few one-year areas--Iceland and Cuba, for instance. Germany's two years."

"Oops! I told my California school district and my family I'd be gone only a year.

"You'd best tell them right away that you can't come home yet," said Emily.

Emily and Abby were experienced with DoDDs, so Megan took their words at face value. *Just one more surprise.* Somehow, she didn't feel as distressed to remain in Europe, as she would have only a few days ago. Her girls could come visit. She could get a flight home for summer.

"If your California superintendent won't give you the extra year's leave of absence, you can always quit and stay overseas forever as a 'DoDDS dolly,' like me," said Emily.

"It's not at all what I expected when I came here. But look at how we've all accepted our alerts, dangers and our non-evacuatable status, and now we even find humor in it. Life here at a Border Post is geared more toward single folks, and everyone accepts the responsibility for everyone else. At home, I felt like an extra half of a person after Andy died. Here, it's much easier with a friendly gang, and everyone feels a part of the group."

"It's a more active and flexible lifestyle," said Abby, shrugging her shoulders. "We singles are the ones able to transfer with the program, hop planes for weekends in foreign places, attend two-day professional seminars, coach kids' sports, or stay after school to watch them during military alerts without worrying about running home to take care of someone."

Megan nodded. "Makes me think of your single neighbor, Abby. Have you met the mysterious Captain yet--the one who took the apartment downstairs?"

"Yes. Holt's taken me out a few times, and he's nice. But I think he'll remain mysterious. He doesn't hang out with the gang-- seems sort of a loner, and rather intense."

"Maybe he's just shy," offered Megan.

"Or he doesn't realize what charming ladies he has as house mates," said Emily, as she reached for a second helping of salad. "What about you, Megan. Has Milt, the Stuttgart pilot, called you?"

Megan looked at the drink in her hand. "He's called on that military phone outside my classroom a few times. And he came to help me bake cookies once. He's fun to talk to, and we both like Barry Manilow." But I don't want him to think of me as a date. He keeps making these *predictions* of some permanent relationship, of a future together, while I'm only ready for friendship." She changed the subject, suddenly. "Where's Lila?"

"Hot date with Brian," answered Emily. "She was by earlier, but you were asleep. She didn't want to wake you. They were going to a party down at the Katterbach 'rubber room.' She said First Cavalry aviators hang out there when not assigned to Bamberg."

"Stan said the Katterbach pilots want our ski bus to stop at Feucht *Autobahn* gas station so they can join us instead of Nürnberg's club. They fly with our guys at the Border anyway."

"When is that first ski trip?" asked Emily.

"Over Thanksgiving," said Megan. "The Battalion

Commanders who've agreed to let their enlisted troops off work early for ski trips expect to see some improvement in discipline from their involvement. I guess that means I'm committed to learning to ski to help out, whether I'm any good at it or not."

"What were they like?' asked Abby. "The Battalion Commanders, I mean."

"Overworked, I think, and tired--overburdened with so much responsibility. Yet I liked their idealism. They *believe* in their soldiers like we believe in our kids. But they work late into the night, and they seem frustrated with their Brigade Commander's 'unreasonable' orders for their men." She wrinkled her brow, thinking of her encounters with the officers in charge.

"They seem to have trouble with their marriages, too, except for Lt. Col. Wheeler, who's already divorced. I think they put all their energy into their battalion duties and have little time left for their families. I felt like a 'shrink' when they started confiding in me, as though they thought I should be able to help them solve their marital problems. One also asked me to help him rewrite a map-reading test at a fifth grade level so his 'McNamara men' could show the colonel some progress." Megan juggled the ice in her glass. "However, when I told them we hoped to help with a few of their soldiers' discipline problems by getting them involved productively, they grabbed onto the ski trip as eagerly as a drowning man grabs a life ring."

"Well everyone comes to talk to you about their problems, Megan, even *us*," said Abby. So you shouldn't be surprised the commanders made you feel like a shrink. But if we can get those young troops past the first clumsy day of skiing, they'll love flying down the mountain with arms spread wide. It's fun to watch beginners take to the sport. You'll love it too, with the breeze in your hair. The view from the top is spectacular." It was obvious Abby was way past that first 'clumsy' part.

"Gee, Abby, you almost make me want to ski," Emily said. "But at my age, I don't try anything that might break something important. I'm going off for my annual London reunion with fellow teachers from Iceland, Cuba, and the Bahamas."

"Didn't you say that we were celebrating Thanksgiving a week early because everyone would be gone over the four day holiday? That's soon, isn't it?"

"Yes, we planned it while you were in the hospital," answered

Abby. "It'll be here at my apartment next Sunday. The guys are bringing drinks and mystery meat from the Commissary to bar-b-que. The gals will pot-luck it with side dishes and desserts. And I still can't cook!"

"Never mind, Abby," soothed Megan. "You just keep on making those great salads."

A day later, Lila looked as if she were choking on a secret. She finally worked up her courage and blurted out to Megan, "I set you up with a blind date Saturday with Klaus and me." When Megan looked up sharply and shook her head, Lila hurried on. "It's just this nice man in Stan's unit who got a 'Dear John' letter from his wife last year. His divorce is in the works now. We can all go to dinner. Then we can take in the production of *Sound of Music* at that lil' old theater on Post. It'll be fun, and I'll be right there with you the whole time."

"I appreciate the thought, Lila, but I really don't want to date anyone. I'd be accepting invitations from Milt or Ron or Big Don, if I were interested in dating. I'm not!"

Lila plopped on the couch and took Megan's hands in hers. "We really would like to see you find some interesting men. It's time to move on, and this man is lonely too. Don't you see? This'll be fun. It'll be formal and all. I can hardly wait to get all dressed up."

Megan was still shaking her head when Abby and Emily set about convincing her to go. Megan finally gave in. "All right--but just this *once*, since you've already told the man. But please never do this again. I'm serious when I tell you I'm not looking for anyone."

"Okay, just this once, I *promise*." Lila gave the A-OK signal to Emily and Abby.

On Saturday, Carl and Luke coached Megan's class for their Saturday trampoline workout all morning, and she, in turn, invited the two for lunch at her apartment. Luke begged off, saying he had a hot date with his German girlfriend.

Carl always went where the food was, so he came right over to share Megan's homemade potato soup and ham sandwiches. "Luke doesn't know it yet, but that girl he's been dating is strange," volunteered Carl.

"Strange, how?" asked Megan, pouring Carl and herself

another glass of Tab on ice.

"I really think she's ac/dc." Carl munched contentedly on his sandwich.

Megan raised her eyebrows quizzically. "What's that?"

"You've never heard the term before? You've been *quite* sheltered, Megan."

"I know alternating current and direct current in electronics. I used to help Andy fix radios for the guys on his Navy base. But a girl isn't electronic, so you must mean something else?"

"I think she likes both women and men," he explained. "She looks bi-sexual to me. She was dancing with another girl downtown at a nightclub when I took Monica there for a drink."

"But all these German ladies do that. It might be a holdover from so many men being killed in World War II. It seems culturally acceptable for women to dance together in Germany. It's weird to us Americans, but the Germans don't seem to mean anything by it."

"Not the way those two were dancing. If Luke finds out, he'll be a *bear* to live with. He probably will be embarrassed and not speak to anyone, or disappear like he usually does when he's mad or upset. I've been wondering all week if I should say something to him about it. I've no proof...just suspicion."

"Well, if you aren't sure, perhaps you should wait awhile. But, on the other hand, it would be terrible if Luke really gets serious about her, if you're right. That's a tough decision."

"Luke *never* gets serious. He, Rex, Danny and I used to have this pact about who could get to every girl on Post first, so I guess I'll just let his current fling run its course."

"Used to?" Her eyebrows arched in an honest stare.

Carl grinned. "I bowed out of the pact after Stan's year-opening party." He paused, looking straight at Megan. "What about your blind date tonight? Are you okay with it?"

"Not really," she said, not returning his glance. "How does everyone always know *everything* around here? Lila was so insistent, and she already told this guy I'd go. I don't want to go, but then I don't want to hurt his feelings either."

"But you do like theater, and a nice dinner can't hurt you. I think you'll be all right."

"It's formal, so I suppose I should get out that green gown." She left the kitchen, returning with the dress on a hanger. "I must have spilled something on it." She showed a spot on the skirt to Carl. "This is a good excuse not to go, don't you think?"

He shook his head. "You're not getting out of it that easily." He put the spotted part of the dress under the kitchen faucet and rubbed it with liquid dish soap. "Get me your hair dryer."

When Megan returned with the dryer, Carl hung the dress above him on the door molding, pulled up a chair, and stuck the plug into a socket of the transformer. Then he moved the hair dryer up and down over the soggy gown.

"This is going to be a long evening," said Megan.

"I have this under control. You go take your bath and get all gussied up. It'll be ready by the time you're done." He shoved her out of the kitchen. When she returned in her bulky bathrobe, with dark hair piled on top of her head, the dress was passably dry.

"Take off the robe," Carl ordered.

Megan balked, startled, wide-eyed.

Carl removed the dress from the hanger and held it up in the air. "I grew up with sisters. I said, take off the robe! How can you get this on without mussing your hair unless I help you?"

Megan let the robe fall and stood shivering with embarrassment, even though her long slip revealed even less than would a sundress. Carl dropped the dress around her head, being careful not to wrinkle it or touch her hair-do. His matter-of-fact attitude quieted her discomfort.

Oh well, it's only Carl.

"Does your breast still hurt?"

"Not too bad. There is a tiny little scar about a half inch long, but not much else."

He nodded, "We'll just call that scar all my fault, so it's *mine*, okay?" He grinned, and she began to relax again.

He helped her get her arms through the sleeveless openings, spun her around, and pulled up the long zipper. "There!" he pronounced, turning her around to face him again. "You look just as exciting as the first night I saw you. This guy..."

"Larry."

"This guy, Larry, will be as knocked off his feet as I was. Why I feel jealous just thinking about you spending the evening with him instead of me." He was smiling.

Megan clasped a large pendant behind her neck.

"Now, for gosh sake, what's that for?" Carl frowned and wrinkled up his nose.

"I hoped to draw attention away from...you know." She hung her head, embarrassed.

"Lose it, Megan!" he said, pulling the pendant off and tossing it on the table. "There's *nothing* that's going to draw attention away from your bust line, even when you normally insist on wearing clothes that fit like a gunny sack, so give it up! You need some new clothes that fit like this dress. There is *nothing* wrong with you, just as you are, and I never want to see you raise those arms to cover yourself again, or wear some stupid pendant, either."

At her quick intake of breath to argue, Carl simply waltzed her around the dining room and reminded her it was almost six, time for her to leave to meet the others.

"Do you have plans, Carl--another date with Monica?"

He shook his head and wrinkled up his nose. "She wasn't a 'keeper.'"

"You can come along with us. We can get more tickets."

"No, Megan." He admired his handiwork by holding out her arms and looking her up and down. "I've got a lot of homework for my grad school history class. I'll do it here, where it's quiet, eat some more of your cookies, and go home later. Besides, you need to do this alone. I, your fairy godfather, have helped all I can." He smiled, waving his imaginary wand. "It's time for you to step out there to that pumpkin carriage you borrowed from Emily, and jump in full tilt."

Megan noticed that he swallowed hard when she kissed him on the cheek.

"Go get 'em, Tiger," he whispered, turning away.

Promptly at nine, Megan was banging frantically on Abby's door. She knew Abby retired early, but she couldn't face going home alone, and had been surprised to find herself driving the road to Amlingstadt. She'd been vaguely aware of silver reflectors at the side of the road churning by at high speed. When Abby sleepily opened the door, she found Megan disoriented and hysterical.

"What happened?" Abby demanded, pulling Megan into the living room and to the couch. "I thought you had that blind date. What did he do?"

"He didn't do anything. It was me. I was terrible to him, and I couldn't even explain."

"Tell me what happened...from the beginning." Abby automatically turned on the heat under the teapot before circling Megan and herself around to the divan.

"We went to dinner, and he was gentlemanly--though a cold man...a trained killer. Did you know he was one of the killers of Che Guevara while a Green Beret?"

"Megan, they're *all* trained to kill when they have to. We're talking about the Army."

"Yes, I know, but he seemed to be glad of it. At the play..." Megan began blubbering.

"What about the play?" Abby produced the tissue box.

"Lila and Klaus were three rows up from Larry and I. *Sound of Music* was lovely until they started to sing together...in the gazebo. Larry reached over and took my hand...and I bolted. It was terrible."

"What do you mean, 'you bolted?'" Abby didn't understand.

"I don't know. I just got all scared. I felt sort of like I was being adulterous when I only wanted Andy, and this man took my hand. I tried to leave, but there were people on both the right and the left, so I..." Her agitation made her breathless.

"You tried to leave him *there?*" Abby looked shocked.

"Yes, I had to get away, don't you see? I didn't want anyone else to touch me, and he did, so I climbed over the back of the seat to the aisle and ran away."

"Over the back of the seat...you mean in an evening gown and high heels?" Abby pointed at Megan's long dress in disbelief. "I can't even imagine your being able to do that."

"I guess I must have hiked up the skirt. I don't remember. I just ran from the theater back to my car. I broke off one of my heels in those ugly cobblestones--I was clumsy. It was awful."

Megan mopped her eyes with one tissue and grabbed another. "He caught up with me just as I was getting into the car and held the door. He kept saying, 'I'm so sorry. What did I do to offend you? Please come back with me.' I just couldn't explain--I only wanted to get away, so I gunned the motor and left him standing there. I feel so stupid! The poor man doesn't have a clue what was wrong with me."

"Megan, it's okay. Calm down. You can explain to him some

other time." Abby rose and grabbed cups for their tea, and Megan automatically followed her into the kitchen, still talking.

"I'd be too embarrassed to ever see him again. Besides, how could I explain anyway? I can't very well say, 'Gee, I'm sorry, but I thought I was committing adultery against my dead husband if I let you hold my hand.' Good grief, he'll only see me as terribly rude and probably crazy, too." She couldn't stop sobbing.

"I'm stupid, stupid, stupid. I hurt that poor man's feelings because of my own fears…my own hang-ups. How could I think I was being adulterous in a crowded theater, with Lila and her date there too? I feel so awful. No one will ever understand."

"What was it about his taking your hand that made you feel so bad?" Abby asked.

"I just wanted Andy to be there with me, and no one else should ever be touching me. It felt all wrong and ugly, and it scared me. Now, I just feel stupid, because he'll probably think I'm a nut case or something. Maybe I am. I just didn't want to be touched." Her whole body shuddered, as though she'd felt the hand of an ogre.

Abby chuckled softly as she carried the two steaming cups back to the low, rattan table. "Megan, you touch other men all the time when you're dancing, or you sometimes unconsciously lay your hand on their arm while listening intently to their problems. Carl dances you around the floor without ever letting you go, and he kisses you on the cheek all the time."

"I know. Carl was over this evening to help me get dressed to go out on this date with Larry, too. But that's different."

"In what way is it different? If Carl can spend as time with you like he does, why can't some other man? Try to figure out what made you so scared you had to run away from Larry."

"I don't know. It's just that Carl is…so safe. I don't feel any threat with him, in spite of his teasing me all the time."

"Oh, boy!" Abby took a deep breath, letting it out in a rush. "I'll bet that makes Carl feel *really* good, being called 'safe,' or that you still consider all his propositions as 'teasing.' Look, Megan, it's perfectly okay not to want to hold someone's hand or not to be with him, if you don't want to be. It's quite all right not to go out with just anyone. It will be *your* choice if you ever want to date again. There was nothing wrong with your feelings, only with being so…well…hysterical about them. I'm sure Larry will understand. He may be a good guy, one you could eventually trust the way you trust Carl, Luke, Stan, and Milt--as one of your friends."

"I'm sure he's nice, but I never want to see him again. I was awful, and I could never in a million years explain this to him."

"It's okay, Megan. We rushed you into this. You weren't ready to be around a man in whom you hadn't already developed trust. That's all. Don't feel bad. The time will come when you'll feel okay about being with another man, holding hands, perhaps even making love with him, or marrying him. For now, drink your tea."

Megan shook her head fiercely, watching her fingers in her lap folding and unfolding.

Abby quickly added, "I'm being purely hypothetical. It's nothing to worry about, and it's obviously a long way in the future. Don't even think about it now. You'll know when the time is right. And it won't be adultery then, because you're no longer a wife…you're a widow…and I don't for a moment believe Andy would want you to be alone forever."

Megan started, "But…I don't want…"

"Drink your tea, Megan!" Abby ordered. "All of this will turn out all right. *Drink!*"

Megan began to relax, drinking the warm beverage and listening to Abby's soothing voice. "Give yourself time, Megan. It was our fault for rushing you. It's all right to take your time—to wait until you feel ready."

Finally, Abby removed the cup from Megan's hands, as the distraught young woman's head dropped on the couch pillow, sound asleep with tears still streaked over her cheeks.

When Megan woke the next morning, it took a moment to realize she was on the couch at Abby's apartment instead of in her own bed. She was covered with a hand-crocheted afghan. Glancing in the mirror, she saw last night's upswept hairdo disheveled and curling down around her face. The smell of bacon and toast emanated from the kitchen. Megan followed the aroma."

"How do you like your eggs? I'm not too bad at cooking eggs." Abby stood at the stove, bundled in a green chenille bathrobe for warmth. In her no-nonsense fashion, she threw an extra blue one from a nearby chair to Megan, who *was* a bit chilly in her rumpled, sleeveless gown.

"Scrambled, please." Megan sat at the table. "I'm sorry I barged in on you last night. I must have been practically incoherent."

"Practically," Abby agreed. "But, that's what friends are for."

"I guess I fell asleep on your couch. Did I make you terribly late getting to bed?"

"Terribly," said Abby with a laugh. "But I'll admit, I spiked your tea heavily with Jim Beam. You dropped like a rock once I could get you to calm down and *drink* the stuff."

"No wonder I slept so hard, and I'm all wrinkled this morning. I feel so dumb," said Megan. But Abby was laughing.

"What's so funny?"

"Thinking of it all in retrospect, I'm imagining you with your fairy godfather, as you call Carl, getting ready to go out. Then running out of the theater and losing your heel with Larry chasing you down a cobble-stoned street--like Cinderella escaping the ball."

Megan paused, remembering the scene, met Abby's eyes, and they both broke into uncontrollable giggles.

Megan made a quick trip home to change clothes and bake beans for the afternoon's pre-Thanksgiving potluck. She would be returning Emily's VW to the party and Stan would drive her home. Over thirty people jammed Abby's apartment. Though it was snowing, the guys tended the bar-b-que out on the balcony while bragging about their favorite sauces and marinating skills. The ladies worked in the kitchen, but they couldn't resist running out into the yard occasionally to pelt the chefs on the balcony with snowballs. After dinner, Charlie proposed that the guys do the dishes while the gals prepared games for entertainment.

Being militarily efficient, the men soon formed an assembly line with the senior officer present, Top Cop Rex, directing. Each dish and fork was handed forward from scrape, wash, rinse, dry, to put away, accompanied by cadence calls of "Sound Off." Some military marching lyrics, best not repeated, drifted into the living room.

Abby kept peeking nervously at the guys tossing her mother's wedding plates from hand to hand, but there were no crashes. Afterward, since the snow showed no signs of letting up, the topics for Charades became wackier as the afternoon progressed, and partiers collapsed into laughter and good talk, sitting around the living room floor on the ever-present throw pillows.

It was almost 1600 hours when Lila and her German friend, Klaus, arrived. In spite of the uneasiness of her friends, she had dated the man frequently, proclaiming him 'charming and suave, with none of the teasing demeanor of her American boyfriends.' In fact, Megan had wondered if Klaus *even owned* a sense of humor. Abby greeted Klaus, but her cool tone showed it was only for Lila's sake.

Conversation about the recent alerts continued at first, as officers from 1/52 Battalion described a freak accident with a tank that had severed a young soldier's feet. "Luke flew him down to Nürnberg hospital, feet and all, but they couldn't reattach anything...his feet were too chewed up," said Charlie, shaking his head sadly. "There've been too many accidents lately."

"That helicopter incident Thursday was depressing, too," commented Luke. "Bill knew the pilots and he and I had to pick up the pieces—tragic to bring back those body bags from a remote crash site. Bill just couldn't come along today because he's still feeling so battered. He'll probably be over later to talk and play guitar music with you, Megan, because he's still not straight with it, and we know music is how Bill copes."

Megan nodded, knowing Luke was probably right about Bill. She made a mental note to dig out some new sheet music and her guitar once she got home. Her unofficial talk sessions with her young friends when they were under pressure had multiplied until Father Harry frequently teased that the 'church's counseling annex was in Lichteneiche, at Megan's apartment.'

Luke said, "The rotor flexed down--sliced right through the cockpit. The bird exploded in the air...must have hit the fuel lines."

"It's only on the 'down' slope in NOE (nap of the earth) flying that these canopy strikes happen," said Carl. "We've got to find out why OH 58's don't handle the downward inclines better before we fly them again. They'll be grounded, for sure."

Klaus suddenly perked up with interest. "I heard about that accident. Up at the Border, wasn't it? What model exploded?"

There was silence as the officers realized who had asked the question. "Oh, I don't remember," said Carl all too casually, raising his hand, apparently in a warning motion that finished in a slow scratch of his head.

Everyone got the message except Lila. "Carl, you didn't answer Klaus' question."

"Just old stuff," Carl said, trying to joke lamely. "Helicopters really aren't supposed to be able to fly anyway."

Stan jumped up to propose another round of drinks, simultaneously with Colin proposing another round of games. The interruptions by these two swiftly changed the taboo subject, though most guests noticed Klaus' sullen look at Carl.

At dinner the next evening Lila asked her three friends pointedly, "Why doesn't anyone seem to like Klaus?"

The women looked back and forth, each waiting for someone else to speak.

"He asks a lot of questions, Lila." Megan said, "but then, I don't really know him."

"And he only seems to show up when you'll be partying with the officers," added Abby. "He doesn't come around when it's just us girls, like our other friends do."

"The guys all act like he's an enemy or something." Lila pouted. "He's a nice guy."

"I'm sure he is, Lila," soothed Emily. "The other men just don't talk about tactical problems around a stranger. They're used to having only Americans around. They forget."

"Why should accidents be so secret, anyway?" asked Lila, still not getting the point.

"You know Americans near the Border have been pressured," said Megan. "We've been on alert more than we've been off this year. Even the green glow-in-the-dark license plates on our cars may be easy to follow to the nearest Post when we get lost in a strange city, but they make us vulnerable because anyone can see, even from a distance, that we're Americans. Didn't you read about those Americans who were targeted from bridges along the *Autobahn*?"

"What's that got to do with Klaus?" insisted Lila.

Megan shifted her position, stalling to think of a way to make Lila understand. "Nothing. But our guys have been trained to be wary of anyone who could be an enemy working undercover. We *are* in a war, you know, even though the military is trying to make sure it stays a *cold* one. It's always simmering just under the surface. What if someone from the East zone, or from a terrorist organization, should find out weaknesses in our aircraft, or our tactics, or when a particular aircraft is grounded? They could use that information to sabotage our soldiers' equipment, or pass it on to those who could. The whole long Border is a hotbed of intrigue, with spies on both sides trying to get information. Carl and Stan explained some of that stuff to me."

"Probably Klaus is perfectly fine," added Abby, "but we don't know who else he might talk to about what he hears from our people, or from you. The guys would be nervous with anyone, if they were discussing something classified around a stranger--and accidents are classified. The guys at the party changed subjects quickly, so there was probably no harm done."

"Well, I just don't know why everyone thinks of Klaus as a 'stranger'," said Lila, obviously with hurt feelings. "He knows lots of other people on Post, too, and we've gone out together lots of times. He's always been a perfect gentleman. I trust him."

"It's okay, Lila," said Emily, trying to calm her friend. "People will get used to him if you like him. But just don't expect them to talk about their work around him, and our gang loves to talk about their work. That's why Klaus makes them uncomfortable—plus the fact that he seems to have diverted your attention away from the Cav fellows." She smiled at Lila.

"I still like Brian, but he's been cold lately. I thought having Klaus at the party would make him jealous."

"It's not fair for us to play games with these men, Lila," cautioned Abby, "You'll get hurt."

"I've already been hurt," Lila cried. "Brian said if I wanted this German guy, I could just count him out." She sobbed loudly. "I do like Brian, but he doesn't want me now."

"I'm sorry, Lila," said Abby. "But no one else is exactly headed for any altar, either. Robert has been distracted lately, and Holt, downstairs, seems so pushy, he almost scares me. Someone told me Jonas Litzfeld likes me, but he's so shy, I'll be 85 before he gets up the courage to ask me out, so I'm between dates too."

"And even if I were interested in dating, which I'm not," said Megan, jabbing her finger in the air for emphasis, "look at the options. I'm still in love with my husband who's dead. The nice pilot of Stuttgart reminds me so much of Andy that he scares me, plus he's sort of secretive. I'm deadly at blind dates. And the one living male who really, truly understands me, is at least a decade too young!"

"Maybe it's time for a girls-only weekend after your ski trip," proposed Emily, laughing at her love-lorn friends. "We'll just have fun and forget all about men."

"But Emily, you'll miss seeing the Ambassador if you go away with us," said Abby with a sly grin.

Emily sighed deeply and replied with a flare of one hand to her forehead, ala Jean Harlow, "We'll simply have to suffer through one weekend apart, for the sake of you girls. The Ambassador will have to understand."

"Who is the Ambassador, really?" asked Megan. "He must be a romantic fellow."

Emily nodded. "Oh, he is...he's very attentive."

"Why haven't we ever met him?" Lila dried her eyes.

Emily smiled coyly. "He's very private, and he's very busy. I never know when he'll come. So far, he's only managed to come while you girls are on dates or out with the gang."

Megan was intrigued. "Will we ever meet him?" All three sat at Emily's feet.

"Oh, I don't know." Emily sighed and extended her arms in a dramatic pose. "Perhaps one of these days the world will be a safer place, and he won't have so much to do to keep the peace. In the meantime, he remains incognito so he can come and go unseen." She folded one hand behind her head with the other on her hip.

"Oh," said the girls in unison, realizing from Emily's mellow-dramatic voice that the Ambassador probably existed only in her 'persona.'

Even Lila was smiling. "So *that's* why we haven't seen him."

Chapter 11

Wednesday afternoon forty-four people loaded equipment onto the German bus for the first Bamberg Ski Club trip over the four-day Thanksgiving weekend. Eight enlisted troops came along to learn to ski. Though still skeptical about any answers to their discipline problems, the Battalion Commanders kept their promise to allow the men to leave early. The young soldiers milled around, nervously uncertain. Stan rounded them up and reassured them, welcoming each aboard, "Okay skiers. We're all in this together."

Well-provisioned with food and paper cups, everyone shared dinner items they'd brought on board, and the wine passed freely. Megan had a few sips from Carl's cup, and slept awhile on his shoulder, only vaguely aware of the party rambling up and down the bus. When she woke an hour later, she felt energized, ready to join those dancing in the aisle.

"That's two sips more this week, Megan, and you only slept a little while," Carl said proudly. "That's better than last week. You're almost ready to go back out to Papa's."

Lila and Brian had reconciled yet again. They leaned over the seat to congratulate Megan on learning to drink, even a little bit more. "It's better than quietly sliding under the table," said Brian, teasing her, "like you did the *last* time you had one sip too many."

One of the married couples brought along Chris, their three-year-old son. When Stan fixed him a paper cup of Shirley Temple, made of 7-Up, Chris stood up on a seat, holding his cup aloft and proclaiming loudly that, "...he had a drinking problem just like all the *other* Ski Club members." The crowd roared with laughter.

Megan felt a moment of concern that even a small child could see how many of these men drank too much. Were there alcoholics in the making? Typically, alcohol seemed an escape from their heavy responsibilities in the close proximity of the Border. But the dark thought was fleeting, as little Chris had forgotten it already. He ran down the aisles climbing in one lap after another. Carl and Megan taught him to rub noses in an Eskimo kiss. He would visit a few people, then return to give each of the two yet another "Skimo kiss."

Seeing Carl with the little boy, Megan was acutely aware that he should have a family of his own. When he caught her watching him, he grinned. "I know what you're thinking. I do like kids, but I don't need to have any."

"For now," she muttered quietly, and smiled. Surely, he'd meet the right girl someday, especially if she could persuade him to be a little less forward with 'lines' that scared them off.

The Alpine mountain passes soon became treacherous. Heavily snow-laden trees hung precariously over the circuitous, narrow roads, which were already packed with snow and ice. Visibility was limited by starkly falling flakes. Ledges of snow hung on mountain crags above each curve. The bus driver inched along slowly to avoid vibrating the ledges into an avalanche. But most of his passengers had fallen asleep and never noticed. A groggy crowd, stretching and yawning, spilled off the bus at 0200 hours into the thick snowstorm of Lech, Austria.

"Okay, everyone," Stan said into the microphone up front. "Lech is booked up a year ahead, so we'll be scattered a room here and a room there—a short walk apart. Listen up, and I'll call out names so you can find your *Pension*, bed and breakfast. The owners will be waiting up for you tonight only. We'll meet at 0830 hours tomorrow morning at the main Lech lift."

Abby, Lila, Megan, and another teacher, Cindi, were to share a room at a brand new *Pension* in the outlying village of Zug. The room had hand-carved wooden beds painted with *Bauren*, or farmer's, painted flowers.

"Abby," asked Lila, as everyone settled into bed for the night, "What happens if it doesn't stop snowing? It'll be cold outside, and I'm scared of skiing if the snow's falling."

"Snow doesn't bother you. The beginners take lessons in the morning, so you'll be fine. We'll meet at dinner to swap war stories. Once you learn how to snowplow turn and stop, we can take you to upper slopes where you can ski hard enough to keep a lot warmer."

"It's that *stop* that has me worried," said Megan. "What happens when you can't stop?"

"Don't think about it, now," yawned Abby. "I need some sleep. Good night."

Sunshine brought reflections from crinkly ice crystals drifting above the mountains. Cannons blasted snow accumulations threatening avalanche. The night's snowstorm had left several feet of fresh powder, the sight of which sent the experienced skiers into raptures, as they took off in pairs up the main chairlift. Most wore cowboy hats. 'Major America,' Gary, jokingly sported his red, white and blue cape, and all were whooping and yodeling.

The new recruits helped each other into boots and skis and stumbled their way over to the 'bunny' slope. It looked long and steep, from a beginners' eye view. Snowplows had dug through the deep powder to scrape down to a solid base, leaving high snow walls on either side.

"It's like being in a canyon," said Lila, staring at the straight walls of snow at least a dozen feet high on each side of their tight corridor of packed base. "I'm intimidated already."

Their Austrian ski teacher sent the beginners up a tiny puma lift, lining them up like children at the top. The three women, and Carl, two dentists from the dispensary, a couple of enlisted medics, plus six other enlisted infantry soldiers constituted the beginner's class. Megan was delighted to see the young enlisted men, as their fate was becoming her pet project. All had 'butterflies' and wobbled uncertainly, since even staying still in line required effort and balance.

The instructor demonstrated the snowplow stop, and drew diagrams in the snow with his ski pole to demonstrate the slope and its 'fall line.' As best they could figure out from his broken English, they were to control their speed by using this fall line, *somehow.* They began trying, one at a time. It was a slow process and, after two trips down, Carl was impatient.

"I can't stand this slow stuff," he whispered to Megan. "I'm going up the main lift and try it on my own. How hard can it be? Everyone else is doing it. Come with me?"

"I'd better not, Carl. We don't know enough yet. Why don't you stick around at least 'til lunch time, and then I'll go with you, if we're doing better at stopping by then."

"I can't, Meg--this waiting is driving me crazy. Tell you what--you get the technique down, and I'll go scope out the regular runs, and we can exchange information at lunch, okay?"

"If you're sure you can do it...be careful, though. Flying on Monday when you get back could be difficult, wearing a cast."

"Yeah, yeah, yeah. How hard can it be? See ya' later."

With that, he swooped around the group and down the hill, his green jacket flapping behind him, stopping only when he picked himself up from a pile of snow at the base of the slope. He waved to show he was all right and wobbled into the regular chair lift line.

"What was that all about?" Lila slid back into line.

"Mr. Impatience had to go it alone. If he survives, we'll see him at lunch."

"I'm having a terrible time turning," said Lila, "and I'm really getting cold. I may quit after lunch and go find a place to be a ski bunny. I've heard they can always lap up sympathy."

"Those nineteen-year-old troopers are doing pretty well. Must be the exuberance of youth," puffed Cindi. "At thirty, I'm old enough to be scared. My skis refuse to do as I say."

"The young soldiers are so funny," said Lila, as Megan came back up into the line. "Each seems to be trying to outdo the others. They slip and slide, crash and burn, get right up and do it over again. I sit down at the first excuse, so I won't fall hard. Carl should have stayed with us."

"Probably, but he's a natural athlete. If anyone can figure it out for himself, it'd be him."

Cindi answered Megan with a roll of her eyes. "He thinks he's invincible. We'll see if he's still in one piece tonight."

Megan started down again, pleased at four fairly good turns, parallel to the perpendicular walls. But with the fifth turn, she lost her balance and couldn't turn away from the steep wall of snow. She went right through it, buried into its unplowed depths.

Lila saw Megan disappear and screamed for the instructor, but he was nowhere to be found. The corpsmen and dentists sidestepped back up to where Lila was pointing.

"She just went right in there with her arms out," said Cindi, trying not to laugh. "Look! There's a life-sized imprint through the snow wall, like some cartoon character."

"How far in did she go?" one dentist asked, while trying to stay balanced sideways before he fell over. He crawled to peer into the hole. "I don't even see her anywhere."

Two more beginners skidded down the slope as fast as they dared, joining the group hovered around the imprint into which Megan had disappeared.

"Are you okay in there?" called Lila.

"I think so," came a quavering, far-away answer. "But the more I lean my hand on the snow trying to get up, the deeper I sink in, and snow keeps falling on my head."

One dentist braced himself with his poles, feet planted in a shaky snowplow stance, while the other leaned against his back to keep from falling. The leaning one poked around in the hole with his ski pole...nothing. "Boy," he commented, "if we aren't the blind leading the blind..."

"How far are you in there?" asked one of the medics.

"I don't know. I can't see anything. It's all white. Please...keep talking to me."

"Can you crawl out backwards?" Cindi suggested her idea.

"I'm not sure where backwards is anymore. It all looks alike in here. I can't get to my ski bindings, and I can't seem to move with skis on. I'm stuck, and...there's hardly any room."

Lila's voice rose to a panicky screech. "What should we do?"

A young medic and an artillery trooper half skied, half rolled to the bottom to get help, while Cindi and Lila kept shouting encouragement to Megan. The remaining men struggled to get off their skis so they could dig her out. One dentist got only one ski off when the other ski went out from under him. He slid down the hill on his back. The other dentist took over and leaned on Lila to get his skis off. "God, we beginners must look like the *Keystone Cops*," he said as he started digging. "Keep talking, Megan, so we can find you."

The life-sized hole she had imprinted in the wall collapsed as soon as the digging began.

"It's hard to breathe in here," she called out. There was no answer. "Hey, guys, where are you?" Still no answer. "Stop that! Calm down!" Her own voice sounded distant. Can I reach my ski binding? If I can get one ski off, maybe I can use it to dig a bigger hole and have more air.

Cascading snow closed around her. Claustrophobia made her breath come in little pants, and she tried to remember not to hyperventilate. She thought she might be upside down as she used one hand to dig for her buried right boot and ski, but the sensation of body position was gone. She finally touched one ski, but no longer had the strength to release the binding. She removed a glove to try grasping the release. "Where are you guys?" she called out. No answer.

The snow seemed packed around her more tightly, and it was impossible to see anything in such close quarters. *How odd that the texture of snow on my bare hands and face is grainy, rather than cold.* The ache, and then tingling feelings in her hands and feet gave way to numbness--almost an absence of sensation. Fear gradually drifted away. A fleeting realization that this, too, would be a peaceful way to die made her pause, yearning to sleep...relax. *Much too relaxed!* She forced herself to dig again, though her numb fingers could barely move. Something in her kept fighting. *I did promise someone I wouldn't do anything stupid, didn't I?*

The crew of people outside had finally managed to get their skis off, and they dug frantically with their hands where the wall had collapsed. The instructor whipped in with a plume of flying snow and two other ski rescue members. He began directing their digging, and finally, with Lila crying, and the men exhausted, the ski patrolmen uncovered one end of a ski and dragged Megan out. She was upside down, without her hat or poles, and had enough powdery snow stuffed up her jacket to add three dress sizes.

Disoriented, Megan saw Lila's white face and asked, "Are you all right?" Lila knelt to hug her and said, "Isn't that just like you, worrying about me? I'm fine! It's *you* that's in trouble." Once Cindi and Lila had clawed most of the snow from up Megan's back, they found she was still shaking, her teeth chattered, and the skin under her fingernails was blue.

"Her pulse rate is way down," said one of the dentists, as he felt her wrist.

Megan heard her own frozen words as though from a long distance away. "It felt like I was turning around and around. The snow just kept closing in--I couldn't move." She was helped to her feet and stood wobbling between two sets of arms, embarrassed by the fuss. "Thanks everybody. I was getting scared in there." Body parts seemed unresponsive.

Observing her clumsy movements, the ski patrolmen decided Megan was hypothermic. At their order, the group moved slowly down toward the hospital, carrying their skis, and trying to steer Megan, whose legs kept collapsing.

Suddenly, Charlie and Carl appeared at the bottom of the slope, stuck their skis in the snow, and quickly climbed uphill to the beginner group. Charlie arrived first, whisked Megan up into his arms and began running back down toward the clinic. Carl ripped off his jacket and tucked it around her shoulders, while stumbling alongside Charlie in his yet unfamiliar ski boots.

Upon their breathless and noisy arrival at the emergency room, the nurses made Megan sit first in a tub of cold water, then tepid, and finally, one at room temperature. Cindi and Lila dried Megan's clothes over a radiator in the waiting room. Soon Stan and Luke came looking for them. The story had spread because the returning dentists had told the rest of the group at lunch.

"I should have stayed with you," said Carl. "It's lucky I ran into Charlie at the bottom of that slope, or we wouldn't have known you needed us."

"I'd like to get that ski instructor," said Stan. "He shouldn't have left beginners alone."

"Forget it, guys," Megan said, wrapped tightly in a hospital blanket. She still shook a bit. "I'm warmed up now and, soon as my clothes are dry, I'll go back out and try it again. My turns were getting better. I just have to work on that stopping business." She forced a laugh. "You guys go on out and have a good time. Just tell us where to meet you for dinner."

Stan gave directions for the evening *Gasthaus* to Lila. But Lila was having none of the 'go back out' pep talk. "I'm not a skier. I'm a snow bunny. I *know* that now," she said. Cindi nodded her agreement. Lila crowed her laughter to the guys. "Imagine getting your rear end frostbit on the first trip. Y'all should have seen her sitting in water so it would thaw."

"You just wait," threatened Megan, good-naturedly. "I'll get something on you, too. The least you can do is call it 'derriere' so it doesn't sound so bad." She was feeling a little warmer. "Stan, hasn't this ever happened to anyone else? Surely I can't be the *only* one?"

Stan grinned mischievously and scratched his head, pretending to think hard. "Can't say as I remember this happening before, but I guarantee it'll be in our Ski Club folklore for a long time to come. You've just made this ski trip one to remember, girl."

Chapter 12

The party-mood at dinner revolved around the chief topic of discussion--teasing about Megan's frozen bottom. However, she managed to take it with a wan smile.

Later, Charlie leaned over to whisper to her, "Look at my troopers sitting down the table on your left. Last week they were trying to kill each other, and now they're giving each other tips on how to ski better tomorrow…with bragging rights too, I'll wager." He smiled. "This was a great idea to get the commanders to see skiing as a problem-solving tool."

"It always worked with troubled teens at home. If you can keep 'em active enough in an exciting sport, they'll have better things to do than to get in trouble. These young soldiers of yours aren't much older or any different. Word will spread. We'll get even more of the young guys out on the next trip," Megan said. She sincerely hoped she could learn to ski well enough to be of more help with these troops on future trips.

"I can't wait to tell my Battalion Commander how well this works--at least here."

After a jovial walk through the starlit night, the group began evening entertainment--a band at the local *Gasthaus* in Zug--with dancing, and a good bit of drinking. When Abby, Lila, and Cindi returned to their room down the road, Luke, Carl, Mary, and Stan were still going strong and wanted Megan to stay a bit longer to dance. The bit turned into a couple of hours.

When Mary and Stan retired upstairs together, Megan looked shocked, but Carl took her hand and led her toward the door. He whispered, "They've been an item for two years, don't look so surprised. They'll probably be getting married when Stan goes back to the states."

"But…shouldn't they…"

"No 'buts' Megan. Help me with Luke. He has, as usual, consumed a detrimental amount of alcohol." Megan and Carl started across the road to the two men's quarters first, with Luke leaning heavily between them.

"Remember to come wake me up if I'm not out on the street in the morning," Luke mumbled almost incoherently to Megan. "We're in room number five, just up the stairs."

"I will, Luke. Go along with Carl, now. Get some sleep."

"You won't forget, will you? I can't count on Carl, and I'm hard to wake up."

She could barely understand his slurred speech. "I promise, Luke. Now go."

"Thanks, Megan," said Carl at the door. "I can get him up from here. Can you get to your *Pension* across the street okay?"

"I'm fine. Just get Sleeping Beauty up the stairs. Good night."

Carl threw Luke over his shoulder and carried him into the house with an athletic strength, even though he was shorter and stockier than Luke. Megan crossed to the new *Pension* where her roommates would be waiting. She assumed she could slip in quietly without waking them, but the outer door to the building was locked. The building was so new that it only had wires sticking out where the doorbell would eventually be.

"Wow, what do I do now?" She knocked and called out, but all bedrooms were upstairs where no one could hear. "I can figure this out," she told herself, fighting down momentary alarm. The house backed up against a cliff and was ringed on three sides by a mountain of snow. The line of snow drifted upward, ending on the balcony outside where her friends were sleeping.

Having never been out of Southern California, Megan tried climbing up the snowdrift's ridge to the third floor balcony. Of course, she immediately broke through the crust and was buried to her armpits in powder. "Well, that won't work," she told herself, digging out with something akin to breaststroke swimming movements. She made a snowball and tossed it gently at the third floor windows to wake someone. A second, a third, and a fourth all hit the balcony roof and fell harmlessly back down. "Another wipeout."

Snow began again to fall, and Megan stretched back to look above her where the snowflakes fell hypnotically on her face. She closed her eyes. *Beautiful. Peaceful. Easy. Tempting.* Rousing herself forcibly, she remembered that she couldn't stay. She'd promised Carl. She retraced her steps to the *Gasthaus* where they'd danced. It was locked. The streetlights went out.

She turned toward the house where Carl and Luke were staying, hoping it was still open. Perhaps Carl would know what she could do to get into her room.

The outer door handle turned, and she climbed the stairs in the dark, one step at a time. On the landing, she found three doors. Luke had said room five. She ran her hand over the metal numbers on each door and knocked softly when she felt the five. No answer.

She knocked again and opened the door a crack.

"Carl?" "Luke?" She whispered their names and waited. Still no response, but she could hear Luke's drunken snore. She stepped inside and followed the sound. In the dark, she reached Luke's side of the huge German style bed--actually two oversized beds shoved together, each with its own set of bedclothes and down comforters. Luke was hanging partway over the edge. She shook him. "Luke. Can you hear me? It's Megan."

"Huh?"

"I'm locked out. Do you think you can come help me get in?"

Luke rolled off onto the floor with a thud, and mumbled, "Take my bed." He was immediately asleep again, and shaking him produced no further signs of life.

Carl roused when he heard her voice. "That you, Megan?"

"Yes, it's me. I'm locked out of the other building. Can you help me get in?"

"Absolutely not. Most places in Austria lock up early, and you can't get in until morning." He rose up on his elbow and chuckled. "This could *only* happen to *you,* Megan—no one else. Lie down and get some sleep. Luke will never know he's on the floor "

"I can't sleep here!" she sputtered, offended at the suggestion of staying with two men.

"Megan," Carl said in his sleepy, excessively patient, voice, "You need sleep. I need sleep. You're standing by an unoccupied bed. Lie down!"

She sat gingerly on the edge, but the bed's creaking startled her to her feet again.

From the pillow came Carl's gravelly voice, "And take off your wet clothes, for Pete's sake! You'll get the bed all wet and freeze your derriere again." He didn't suppress his snicker.

She laid down carefully in her long johns and sweater, at least three feet away from her friend on the other bed. Her mind raced, wondering how she might have avoided this catastrophe. As she stared wide-eyed at the ceiling, she felt a hand cover her eyes.

"You'll never go to sleep that way, Megan, and neither can I. Close your doggone eyes! They're reflecting in the moonlight."

"What can I tell the others in the morning?"

"Tell them nothing."

"They'll never understand my being here alone with you two. I don't even understand it." She shifted her position even more toward the far edge of the bed.

"No one but *you* ever thinks about things like that. We live in a different world from when you were last single, Megan. This is the seventies, and you must have missed the discovery of birth control, free love, and a nasty war. It's nobody else's business these days where you are, *or* with whom. Now quit worrying and go to sleep! I want you to ski with me tomorrow so I can watch out for you better." He kissed her on the cheek and turned back over onto his own bed.

She shut her eyes tightly, but hot tears rolled down her cheeks. *How can he say this doesn't matter? All my life I've been told one never sleeps with anyone but one's husband. Here I am in a room with two guys, and he says it's no one else's business. Where I come from, it would be the whole town's business!*

She imagined explaining to her friends across the road what had happened. Lila and Abby would understand, but Cindi wouldn't, and Cindi would be out telling everyone else about her all night escapade. Still worrying, she finally drifted off, having at some point reached down and pulled up the comforter.

"Wake up, Twinkletoes. You need to get back to your own *Pension* to get breakfast. They won't feed you anyplace else."

She stretched and yawned lazily, then her eyes flew open, and she sat bolt upright, hugging the comforter to her chest. Luke was still crashed on the floor. "Oh, dear, I forgot. Can you turn your back so I can get my slacks and jacket."

"What do you have on now?" asked Carl, in a slyly insinuating tone, as he dutifully put his fingers over his eyes.

"My long johns."

"Darn! No use peeking, long johns are no fun." His smile was just as warm in the morning light.

Megan pulled on her outer clothes and started for the door. "Can you get Luke up okay?"

"Yeah. Standard procedure is to grab him by the ankles and pull him off the bed so his head hits the floor, but since he's already on the floor, I'll just pour cold water on him."

"He looks like a dead person when he's been drinking."

"He almost is…something in his metabolism slows him down--no pulse, no discernable breathing. People have even called the medics before, but he *is* alive--barely."

They heard footsteps in the hall. Megan's hand recoiled from the door handle as though it were burning. Eyes wide, she turned to her friend. "There's someone out there. What can I say to them?"

"Say 'good morning.'" Carl smiled and demonstrated, dipping his head as though he were greeting the person himself. And that's *all* you need to say--to *anyone*. For Pete's sake *don't* try to explain. With *you*, it only gets worse. Now get going. I'll meet you at the chair lift."

Megan walked out to the stair landing. A maid glanced at her without recognition. Megan forced herself to say, "Good morning," then fled down the steps, out the door, and across to her own building. As Carl had predicted, the door was now open.

"Please, let them still be asleep." Her whispered prayer was barely audible as she tiptoed up the stairs to the third floor and opened the door softly.

"Where have you been all night?" demanded Cindi.

"Well, I tried…good morning…I mean I was…"

"If you're going to sleep with someone else, the least you could do is let us know, so we don't worry." Cindi's strident voice sent quivers up Megan's spine.

She fumbled with her jacket. "I'm sorry, I didn't mean to…"

"Just what we need, someone out 'tom-cattin' all night when the rest of us need sleep."

"But I wasn't, I mean…" The tears that had been trembling on her eyelashes ran down her cheeks.

Abby moved across the floor to Megan, and Lila stormed out of the bathroom. "Enough, Cindi," said Abby. "I'm sure Megan had a good reason for not being here, and whatever it is, *you* don't need to hear it." She stood staunchly in front of Megan.

"Lay off, Cindi," added Lila. "If Megan wants to tell us what happened, she will. If she doesn't, it's *nobody's* business." She put her arm around the quaking Megan and pushed her toward the bathroom. "Get cleaned up, Honey. You can have my make-up time."

Megan could hear Cindi continuing to fuss until Lila said loudly, "Cindi, take your lil' ol' self down to breakfast and wait for us there. If I hear one lil' word about this coming from your mouth, I'll take care of you later." The door slammed.

When Megan emerged, her friends were waiting. They sat on their beds, Lila swinging her legs back and forth. "Do you need anything, Honey, like anything personal?"

"For what?" came the puzzled reply.

Lila and Abby exchanged knowing glances and smiled.

Megan said quietly, "I need to tell you what happened."

"You don't have to," said Abby.

"I want to. Carl said not to try to explain because I'd only make it worse, but Cindi will blab this all over like she did about my frostbite." She took a deep breath. "I waited too late to come home from dancing, and the *Pension's* door was locked. Then the *Gasthaus* was closed, too. I couldn't climb up that snow pile to the third floor because I kept sinking in deeper and getting wetter and colder."

Abby, from Wisconsin, was horrified. "You tried to climb up that snow bank outside? You could have died in another snowdrift, and we wouldn't have found you 'til spring."

"Yeah, I got sort of scared, so I went to Luke and Carl's *Pension* and their door was open. Carl made me stay there with them. He said I'd freeze outside and there was no way to get in my own *Pension* until they opened up this morning. He said I had no choice."

"That was the right thing, Honey. Don't you worry about Cindi--I'll take care of her."

"What's everyone going to think of me, sleeping with those guys?" Megan sobbed.

"Anyone who knows *you*, knows nothing happened," said Abby. "Don't give it another thought. And if you ever decide the time is right to *let* something happen, no one will think anything of that either. Now relax. She handed Megan a tissue to dry her eyes.

Megan got her sobs controlled to a sniffle, and reached out to join hands with her two friends. "Thank you," she whispered.

"Come on down to breakfast," said Abby, "and just act normal. We'll have a good day of skiing. And this time, try not to get buried in any snow holes, okay?" Abby winked at Lila as she steered Megan toward the door.

Megan and Carl skied together for the day--a bit awkwardly and slowly. The first time they reached the top of a ski lift, they were compelled to stop and rediscover the universe from a new vantage point--the top of the mountain. "I can see all the way to eternity," said Megan, breathing in the cold air. "It's so peaceful."

Carl turned to each direction, as though trying to drink in the beauty. "God must live at the top of a mountain."

"Like it's just you, me, and...God." For a brief moment, the first in a long time, Megan almost did feel His presence. "All other trouble seems so far away."

Finally, breaking the spell, Carl said, "I suppose we have to go down to meet the others."

"I suppose so, though I hate to. I'll follow you down. Don't do anything too fancy."

Abby and Luke swooped in behind them to bring up the rear. "We came to check on you --in case we need to scoop up any bodies," explained Abby.

All went well until suddenly, just a few feet ahead of her, Megan heard Carl say, "Oh, sh**!" and disappear. She immediately sat down in a panic stop at the edge of a precipice. Carl never said anything off color around ladies, so she *knew* he was in trouble.

"Oh, God no!" She screamed. "Not losing another..." Unwillingly, she remembered her pilot friends saying those were always the last two words on any crashed airplane's black box voice recorder. "Pilots may *sound* calm on those recordings because they're absolutely sure they can still save the aircraft," Carl had told her once. "It's only at the last moment of life, when the pilot finally realizes there's nothing else he can do to rescue the plane, that he says those two words of frustration." So Megan knew Carl's situation had to be serious. She peered fearfully over the edge where he had disappeared.

"Oh my goodness! He's flying," she shouted. "Look, his jacket is open and he's sailing like some kind of bat. It's gonna' hurt when he lands. We've got to get down there." She scrambled to her feet and approached the edge to follow after her friend.

Luke grabbed the back of her jacket, pulling her from the edge. "No, you don't!" he said gruffly. He and Abby approached the edge and looked over. Luke started laughing.

"Anyone else would have killed themselves going off a cliff like that. Looks like Carl landed with both feet under him, like it was nothing. No form--just guts. He's a natural!"

"It must be something in the helicopter pilot syndrome," said Abby, "just hurtling down the slope on sheer energy alone."

Luke and Abby looked eager to follow Carl over the cliff's edge, but Luke remembered their accident-prone beginner and said, "Megan, we'll go to the right where there's actually a trail. Don't worry, we'll find him waiting for us at the bottom." And they did.

The road home to Bamberg Sunday night went through snowy passes, both narrow and treacherous, with deep ravines on the side. Sleeping passengers were rudely awakened when the bus driver hurled expletives in German and screamed. The bus lurched sidewise, noisily skidding along the mountain road, as its passengers were jolted out of their seats, holding on to each other to protect against injury. All they could see was a torrent of sparks trailing by the windows.

When they finally crunched to a halt, Stan called out, "Anybody hurt?"

Passengers got out to inspect the damage. The bus had thrown a rear wheel and its chain and had dragged along the highway into a snow bank. Lila calmly remarked, "It's good we hit the snow bank rather than skidding off the other edge, huh?"

The German bus driver yelled and cursed, throwing his hat onto the snow in his fit of temper. He apparently was concerned about the necessity of calling an expensive tow truck.

But the engineers, who had experience getting disabled tanks out of ditches under combat conditions, quietly went to work.

"Nothing phases these guys, does it?" remarked Abby.

"It's the Border," said Megan. "They know about difficulty and danger. It's no big deal to them. Guess it isn't to us, either."

In no time, the men gathered wood, built supports under the frame, and jacked up the bus to replace the wheel. Stan called out, "All aboard," and the bus was again on the road. The bus driver was still blustering, while his American military passengers, not even mildly surprised by the incident, had already gone back to sleep.

Chapter 13

Learning to live in a milieu of European idiosyncrasies and military snafus, often *equally* foreign, was a double challenge for new teachers. When the four traveled to France the following weekend, Megan drove her new Fiat. Though Abby and Megan had chosen the same color from the catalogue, Abby's arrived golden in color, while Megan's was a horrible yellowy-green, baby-puke color. The guys called it something even worse. She suspected the car had serious problems when the front window shattered before she even got it home. She had taken it back to the dealer, but the mechanic hadn't seemed surprised. The Fiat necessitated Megan's learning to handle a car's problems--just one more new adjustment, alone.

In no time, everyone on Post knew that Fiat! A gregarious Italian car that purred wonderfully along the *Autobahn,* it apparently hated to be left alone for more than an hour or two, and required battery jumper cables whenever she returned to a parking lot. Fiats were jokingly referred to by another acronym—Fix It Again, Tony. Now, instead of being greeted by friends with, "Hi, Megan, how are you?" it was now, "Hi, Megan. How's the Fiat?"

Not to change its image overnight, when the four women showed their passports to the French officials near Strasbourg, the Fiat coughed and died. The French officers fussed and wiggled wires and finally pushed the car to a start, saying a genial good-bye. The car strangled and stopped again. By the fourth repetition of this scene, everyone acted like old friends, and Lila had given her address to a particularly cute French border guard. Once they were finally able to wave good-bye for the last time, all were laughing hysterically.

Lila patted the dashboard and said, "What a sweet lil' ol' car you are! Y'all stayed there just long enough for me to make a new friend."

"I hope you don't see anyone *else* you like, Lila," said Megan, winking at Emily, "because I want this car to behave until we get home." Within two miles, however, there was a loud clank. The tail pipe had broken away from the muffler and dragging in the street.

Megan opened the back hatch and stripped slacks from a clothes hanger. She bent the hanger deftly into a loop, stuck the business end of the tail pipe back into the protruding muffler, wrapped the hanger loop under it, and hooked it over the back bumper. As the other women watched in amazement, she dusted off her hands and ordered everyone back into the car.

"Where'd you learn to do *that*?" said Abby, as they purred down the French highway.

"We had old used cars at home in California, and with a car full of kids on the way to play their championship ball game, you'd *better* learn to improvise. This'll get us home." Megan suddenly realized that something from her past had helped her cope with her present. It was a startling discovery. *What else can I learn to do? Andy would be proud of me.*

The women explored marvelous old cobbled paths along the Canals and tributaries of the Rhine River that rambled through Strasbourg. They noticed at least one cat luxuriating in every sunny window like a city trademark. They went shopping at pottery factories they could ill afford, mugged for the camera, and talked out all their latest frustrations. Dan, the dentist, had proved less than honest about a previous girlfriend, so Abby was the one with hurt feelings this week, but the others listened and sympathized. These four variant personalities had blended their lives, becoming more independent by laughing and problem solving with each other, as a team.

"Nothing like some girlfriend fun and fine dining to keep us from thinking about men," said Lila, prodding Abby and Megan ahead of her up the steps to a famous restaurant on the main square. The two exchanged amused glances, knowing Lila's mind was never far from men--*or* food.

Emily brought up the rear as the practical guide, collecting tourist brochures. "This looks like fun," she said, while Lila poured over the menu to appease her ever-present hunger.

The three women started ragging on Emily first, reminding her they had heard about her 'wild behavior' on the London bus as the passengers waited an additional six hours before embarking on the channel ferry because of a terrible storm over Thanksgiving weekend.

"Who, me?" said Emily with arched eyebrows. "I would never engage in wild behavior."

"Then what was Betty talking about when she said you entertained everyone on the bus by singing *Smoke Gets in Your Eyes* and doing a striptease?" It was Abby who asked. Lila and Megan pricked up their ears and smiled.

"Oh, *that!*" said Emily, placing one hand on her hip and stretching the other one out straight before her. "It was nothing--just that everyone was so bored with waiting and so scared of the wind rocking our whole bus, and we couldn't get off, so somebody had to do *something* to calm them all down."

Megan was shocked. "Then Betty told the truth, you really *did* do it?"

"One can always create an illusion." Emily slowly removed an imaginary long evening glove and twirled it around. "An illusion of removing clothing can become true if you can convince your audience to *believe* it's true." She gracefully tossed the glove away. "One can always believe what one wants to believe, and if it helped pass the time when people were frightened of a storm, why not?"

By this time, Emily was deep into her performance, and the other three women were looking at each other curiously, with slowly spreading grins.

"Did she or didn't she?" asked Lila. The other two shrugged. Emily smiled slyly and said, "I'll never tell."

A running batch of jokes and chatter soon had Abby back to her old smiling self. "What do I care how many others he's gone out with. I'm not in the market right now. I'm resting."

"That's great," bubbled Lila. "What do any of us need with men, anyway? I'm through with them all--especially Brian and Klaus--except maybe Charlie. He's sort of nice, and maybe if that cute lil' French guard writes me…"

Abby shook her head with a laugh. "You gotta love her, don't ya? That's our Lila."

As she had predicted, Megan's coat hanger fix-it job did get the quartet back home. The Fiat dealer had become quite friendly with his American customer since within a few weeks electric wiring, headlights, carburetor, and non-functioning locks were replaced— almost everything except motor and transmission. She had no doubt those would come later.

As Megan entered the shop, a jovial explosion greeted her. "*Frau* James. What happened to you this time?" But as they walked behind the car, the agency owner's smile turned to a groan at the sight of the wire hangar hooked over her bumper. "*Frau* James, what did you do?"

At her simple explanation, the man turned white. "You cannot do something so strange to your car! A good, civilized German would have gone immediately to a garage for welding."

Struggling to control her frustration, Megan said, "Well, I didn't want to spend our only French weekend in some foreign garage, and this worked fine to get me back to your garage."

The man raised his eyes and hands to Heaven in a desperate plea, "*Only* an American would do such a thing! You Americans are crazy!"

"We call it 'Yankee ingenuity.' It's a good thing to have. We just solve the problem whatever way that works, and drive right on to the next challenge."

"No *wonder* you Americans won the war--you never know when to decently quit!"

Megan couldn't help laughing at his loss of composure, but she decided to ask, "Would you say, as often as you see me here, that this car is a lemon?"

He faced her with a blank look. "What is a lemon?" She explained in her halting German, since it was obvious he had never before heard the term. He cocked his head to one side. When he finally understood her explanation, he nodded vigorously, and said, with no particular alarm or surprise, "*Yah, es ist eine Zitrone.*"

She found she could laugh about it. It meant she had taken giant steps toward learning to survive in a foreign environment. *Yankee ingenuity? Perhaps I have more of it than I thought.*

The next snafu was for the Military Police. A young dependent wife married to a recently arrived GI claimed she'd been raped while her husband was out in the field. This started the desperate month-long search by Top Cop Rex and his MP's for the 'mad rapist.' The Commanding General demanded Rex find the man, calling him on the carpet daily for an update on the search. But Rex investigated everyone on Post with even a slight resemblance to the young woman's description, which seemed to change daily. There was not a single shred of evidence such a man existed. By the time the woman admitted she had made up the story, the supposed 'mad rapist' was the joke of the whole Post, and Rex was constantly bombarded with shrill voices crying, "Yoo hoo. Did you catch the 'mad rapist' yet?" Rex gritted his teeth and scowled.

Because of their interest in Bamberg's history, Emily and Megan found wonderful places to take visitors. Soon, they had become the resident experts and were in frequent demand to do the 'fifty-cent tour' of the old city.

The two women enjoyed exposing newcomers to the historic city everyone called "...the best kept secret in Europe." But one evening a TDY colonel asked Stan who could show him the city while he was there. Stan immediately indicated Megan, and she agreed to give the colonel the "Lights of Bamberg" tour.

But at each stop through the city, as she pointed out the historic Dom with its four towers, and St. Michelsberg with its ceiling painted with herbs used by monks in Bamberg's first hospital, the Colonel's silent stare made her uncomfortable. Finally, they reached Megan's favorite spot of all--the walk to the fortress Altenburg. It sat atop the highest hill, where one could stroll along a moat containing an ancient, egg-loving bear named Poldi, instead of water. From the fortress wall, one could see the best views of the whole city.

As Megan pointed out some of the buildings below and told their legends, the man suddenly turned all paws, and made a grab for her. Shocked, she stepped away, but he grabbed her again. She found herself being tugged from behind while she hung onto the top of the wall, screaming and trying to wrest herself away from this madman. For someone who had always believed the best of everyone, she felt a devastating sense of betrayal.

"Why are you fighting me?" The man huffed and grunted like some rutting animal.

Struggling and kicking at him with her boots, Megan tried to find breath to answer, "No one should...behave like this. What's wrong with you?"

"You must have...wanted me too, or you wouldn't have come...out here in the dark with me." He yanked at her clothing as he finished huffing, "...to this desolate place."

"I don't want *anybody*," she screamed. "You said you wanted to see Bamberg." Megan jerked herself away from the man, but he grabbed the belt of her slacks with one hand and was tearing at her jacket with the other. "Get away from me!" She kicked at him again, but was yanked off her feet. She hit the icy ground--hard. *God, he's so heavy. I've never seen ...I don't know what to do. Did both Stan and I miss some sign, some signal? What would Andy or Carl tell me to do in this situation?* She knew that answer, at least. *Keep fighting!*

Finally, in desperation, she shouted in her best imitation of command voice, "Colonel, you are a disgrace! Get off me. Stop immediately, or I'll report you to your Commander." It suddenly occurred to her that might have been a dangerous thing to say. If it didn't bring him to his senses, he could just as easily kill her to keep her from reporting him. She felt very alone.

But her determined voice must have awakened the specter of losing his next promotion, because he stopped abruptly, stood up, and straightened his clothing. He offered her his hand to rise, but she rolled over and crawled up by herself, not wanting him to touch her.

Megan said coldly, determined not to let this man see her cry, "You have two options. If you can behave yourself, I will give you a ride back to your quarters over the Officers' Club, but don't attempt to reenter the Club with my friends, or I'll have your career! Your other choice is to find your way back as best you can."

The man opted for the ride back to base. The atmosphere in the car was frigid as Megan dropped him at the outside staircase. "I'm terribly sorry," he said sheepishly, and fled upstairs.

Megan stopped at the restroom to wash the cold sweat from her face and try to get the brick and dirty snow stains out of her clothing. Her hands shook, and her fingernails were bleeding where she had torn them on the fortress wall. After several deep breaths, staring into the mirror, she tried to figure out how this had really happened. Finally, she rejoined her friends, struggling to regain her composure. The group immediately welcomed her back and asked after the colonel. "Don't ever ask me to show anyone the 'Lights of Bamberg' again, unless you know him."

The group stared at her bleeding hands in stunned silence. Marco disappeared, and returned quickly with hot poultices. Stan gently bandaged her hands.

"Are you all right? I mean, *really*?"

She nodded, tears in her eyes. "I think so. I never knew *anyone* would act like that!"

"I'm so sorry, Megan. I thought he'd be as trustworthy as the rest of our visitors."

"Well, he wasn't. I don't ever want to see him again. Do any of you know this guy's name or his unit?" No one did.

"From now on, we'll check out anyone who comes here, regardless of the guest's rank," promised Vern, shaking his head. "Let's call Rex Top Cop so you can make a statement?"

Megan shook her head. "I'd be embarrassed. He said I shouldn't have gone to such a dark place. I hadn't even given it a thought. Was this *my* fault? I've shown *lots* of people that hilltop and this never happened before. What could he have been thinking?"

"It wasn't your fault, Megan," said Stan, comforting her with an arm around her shoulders. "We were all too trusting, and you always trust *everyone*. We should have remembered that you were too naïve to know what to do if someone acted badly. The Colonel took advantage of his guest status."

"He'd better hope none of us sees him again, said Charlie. "He's just darned lucky Carl and Luke are out flying."

Marco returned in a few moments and addressed the group, "The colonel is gone. I called a taxi and informed him he wasn't welcome at this Club ever again. Please don't worry."

A week later, several teachers were invited to a military ball down at Ansbach/Katterbach Officers' Club with friends from the Air Cavalry. It was a formal occasion, so the guys wore their dress blue uniforms, topped by Vietnam Air Cavalry Stetson hats which, though not exactly regulation, were tolerated for the war vets. They also wore their sabers, slung from the hip. Carl told Megan, privately, he worried that he would probably skewer himself on his.

The Cav pilots and their wives or friends sat at one large table. After dinner, the ladies excused themselves to go to the powder room. As Megan rounded the corner at her usual quick pace, she collided violently with a colonel in full dress uniform. She would have been knocked to the ground had the colonel not caught her in an almost prone position a few inches from the floor. Only then did they get a clear look at each other. The colonel immediately froze as he saw the recognition in Megan's face.

From her reclining position, Megan could see a militant-looking woman and a teen-aged girl standing beside the man. He stammered out a stupid imitation of an introduction while he still held her near the floor. "This is Megan of Bamberg. Megan, this is my wife and daughter."

His wife responded with glacial authority, "Don't you think you should help the lady up instead of holding her in that silly position?" The colonel lifted a stunned Megan to her feet, while apologizing profusely. Megan merely nodded at his family members, excused herself, and fled to the safety of her comrades' table.

Twenty minutes later, Megan saw the man stand up, surveying the room. She ducked to minimize her chance of being seen. *Too late.* The colonel approached the table and, though there were twenty others there, he addressed his comments only to Megan.

"How nice to see you again. Will you be here long? What brings you to Ansbach?"

She answered, in an icily polite tone, her eyes focused studiously on the saltshaker, "I'm here with my friends for this banquet, and I'll return to Bamberg tomorrow."

"Oh." The colonel inquired archly to the group, "Are you *all* down here from Bamberg?"

There was an audible gasp from the group before Luke rose and said something dangerously close to insubordination. "Colonel, we're in Air Cav, and many of us work here in Katterbach...*for you.* It's odd you're unable to recognize your own men."

The startled colonel mumbled something under his breath, turned, and stalked off.

The laughter was immediate, as Megan blushed beet-red. The truth suddenly dawned on the aviators, and Luke burst out, "I'll lay odds he's the 'Lights of Bamberg,' isn't he?"

She nodded, and joined in the mutual hilarity as the story went up and down the table.

"I'd like a word with that man," said Carl, rising to his feet.

Megan grabbed his arm and held tightly. "No, Carl. That mean looking 'first sergeant' wife of his will take care of him. His behavior was *so* idiotic, I'm quite sure she realized something had happened. I'll bet he's already in hot water!"

"You're probably right. I'm proud of you, Megan. You're growing stronger every day."

Chapter 14

Having a curious nature, and perhaps a little more interest in international affairs than some of their friends, Megan and Abby enjoyed observing the intrigues surrounding the Border. When a delegation arriving at the O'Club introduced themselves as scientists from White Sands, New Mexico, 'just visiting' for several days, they knew international intelligence operatives from *both* sides would be aware of their presence. All roads ended at the Border, so *no one* 'just visited' Bamberg unless ordered for tactical purposes. These scientists would have had a nuclear reason for coming, but the women knew to welcome the visitors, but ignore their actions and not ask questions. Certainly, they knew not to discuss their speculations with Lila.

Brian's Cavalry had defended against five alerts in one month, so Lila had been seeing far too much of Klaus.

"I'm worried about her," commented Emily. "Why can't she see for herself that that man is strange?"

"She told me Klaus wanted her to find out when air worthiness tests would reinstate helicopters of the type that crashed," said Abby. "Now *why* would he need to know that? Lila wouldn't even *remember* that without asking our pilots. I told her *not* to ask."

The others agreed. They couldn't *wait* to get Lila safely on a plane to Kentucky for the holidays. In the meantime, they tried to distract her through a glorious beginning of the Christmas Season in Germany, which they all enjoyed. Fests in every little village and Christmas Markets in larger cities made the smell of spiced wine, *Gluhwein,* and *Lebkuchen,* gingerbread, an antidote for cold weather.

Beautiful hand carved ornaments that had been a cottage industry for centuries graced every outdoor shop, and the women purchased wildly for their families back home. Megan's ski accidents had become *legendary*, and all her friends found comic ornaments for her that showed skiers upside down, or wrapped around trees with caps over their eyes. They became her most treasured possessions.

But it was the children's carols one heard everywhere that brought a lump to Megan's throat, and set her thinking of past Christmas concerts when her own children had sung or played in the orchestra, or when she and Andy had harmonized on their favorite

Christmas carols. She couldn't help whispering, "I'm trying, Andy, I'm really trying to learn to live alone. How am I doing?"

Life as the holidays approached was not without good fun. The appearance of an Annex teacher on the front page of *Stars and Stripes* with the headline "Fifth graders ask Santa for a boyfriend for their teacher," surprised the whole staff.

"It was a contest for the best letters to Santa," cried Kelly, trying to figure out why her children would do such a thing to her as *advertise* for a boyfriend. "The bike offered as prize was incentive enough for ten-year-olds to become *believers.* But when I suggested they ask for a gift for someone other than themselves, I figured they'd ask Santa for World Peace or something. They just stuffed all their letters in a manila envelope and mailed it. I can't *believe* those kids would do such a thing. I thought they liked me."

"They do," said Tim, hiding a smirk. "That's why they want to find you a boyfriend."

An agitated Kelly was in Megan's classroom where the six teachers of the Annex often met for lunch.

"How many letters have come thus far?" asked Megan.

"Hundreds." Kelly didn't see anything funny about the situation. "I'm making the kids answer every blasted letter themselves. They started this whole thing." She toyed with the sandwich Frank had handed her. "I'm so embarrassed. Vern came to ask me to a party this morning, and I hadn't seen the paper yet…He knew about this. Now I'll have to cancel the date."

"Why?" asked Tim. "Maybe he just needed to know you were available--now he knows." The others tried not to laugh, but giggles burst out. Finally, Kelly was able to join in.

"They probably just envisioned Santa bringing you Prince Charming," said Megan. "Thank the kids for thinking of you, and forget it. It'll die down in a few days."

About that time, Christy and Lila dropped by from the main building. "Hey, Kelly, we came over to see if we can have your rejects," Christy said. "I'm frankly looking for a boyfriend, and my third graders didn't think to help me out."

"What fun," said Lila. "I'll bet you'll have more offers than you can possibly handle. We're here to help you take care of them."

"So you think it's okay to go to the party with Vern, and this will all go away?"

"Sure," came the unanimous answer.

But, they hadn't counted on the usually strict Brigade Commander who thought the whole affair funny, and had arranged a stag party as a *surprise* for Kelly. He brought all the single guys in from the field so Kelly's students could interview them and pick a beau for her. 'Santa Claus' came, and the *Stars and Stripes* photographers arrived. After conducting their own interrogations of all the men who came to the party, the children chose Vern. The 'rejects' laughingly assumed Vern had paid off the kids, as they moved the party over to the O'Club for dancing afterward.

"All us 'rejects' must be back out in the field by 0600 tomorrow," said Carl, as he swung Megan around the dance floor.

"Why did you think you'd be a reject?"

Carl laughed. "The kids specifically asked for 'tall, dark and handsome.' That already lets me out. I'm short, blonde, and only my mother thinks I'm handsome."

Megan laughed. "I agree with your mom, and girls love you."

"Gee, that's great! I'd never have known it from the responses I get. Does that mean you've altered your opinion of me, too?"

"Behave, Carl," Megan said with an indulgent grin.

"It was funny because Kelly is so shy and sweet," said Lila, when they rejoined her at the table and all were laughing about the stag party. "If she'd been obvious like me, no one would have even noticed if she needed a boyfriend or not."

Abby gave what she thought were malt balls to her Junior High class, and they turned out to be rum balls, a common phenomenon in Germany where almost every dessert was laced with some type of liquor. When the class became tipsy, the incident was dubbed the "great rum ball caper."

"It's funny when sophisticated Abby gets herself in as much trouble as the rest of us," said Emily. "You may have some explaining to do with parents, my friend." Abby blushed.

The four took a walk in the snowy countryside after school to help Abby forget about the incident. Christmas season in a foreign country was full of surprises. They stumbled across an old Bavarian shepherd in the snow, leaning on his staff, watching his flock of sheep. His black dog rounded up any stray with a mere whistle. A feather-tufted hat and a forest green cape hanging over his high leather boots seemed like a photo from a travel folder.

"It's almost Biblical, isn't it?" whispered Emily.

"It's so quiet with the snow falling. I feel especially calm right now," said Abby.

"Sometimes it's hard," said Megan, "being so far away from my mom and kids for the first time in my life. But right this second, I wouldn't change places with anyone."

"It's y'all and our friendship that make this place so great," announced Lila.

Abby reached out her hand to the center, and one by one they slid their hands into the pile, accepting Lila's assessment silently.

The storms deepened, ice skaters filled every pond, and driving conditions became red, which, in Germany, meant one couldn't drive except in an emergency. By late afternoon the last school day, the storm had interrupted power on the Post, so the children were sent home early.

The teachers negotiated treacherously icy, cobble-stoned sidewalks over to the O'Club for the holiday dance, wondering if it could still take place. Marco, ever the innovator, had hired a small German band, since a disc jockey couldn't work without electricity. He'd bar-b-qued hams on the outdoor charcoal grill, and sliced them by hand. The man was a wizard. The rooms were lit with candles in antique wall sconces. Once the dancing started, the cold no longer mattered. Marco beamed, watching *his* Americans have a good time.

"A great send-off for all you teacher-types going home or on trips without us," remarked Stan, as he helped Mary with her coat.

"I hate it that you guys can't go along," said Abby.

"We hate it too," said Luke, "but accidents need investigation. You gals just have a great time and come home to us safely."

"How are you getting to Frankfurt airport?" asked Carl.

"By train. Brenda's Air Force friend will take us to the train station. He can't be gone from Post more than fifteen minutes, so he'll drop us and run. I didn't know anyone around here was on *that* tight of schedule, though having those White Sands scientists visit here made me realize they're hiding *something* out there in Muna."

"That's another thing you probably shouldn't mention to anyone," Carl said with a low chuckle. "I'll tell you what I can about it, later." He reached out his palm in the now familiar gesture and said, "My strength for the airplane rides. Have fun."

"It's strange. I feel sadness along with the excitement to see Spain. This is the first time I'll be without my family at Christmas."

"But I'm glad you're not going home to California," Carl said. "I'd be afraid you'd stay there and not come back to us. You're needed here. We're your family now, too."

Returning from her two-week Christmas vacation in Spain Megan gathered with the gang at the O'Club, sharing all the good stories on everyone's trips. Abby and Lila had enjoyed family time in the states, while Emily had joined several other teachers for a trip to Vienna, Austria to see the opera and the Lippizaner stallions.

Two of the more sedate teachers, however, told of their frightening tour to Egypt--from ptomaine poisoning to airlines that refused to honor their tickets. The pair had drunk coke from their plastic hair spray lids because the glasses in hotels were so dirty. Three other tour members were held hostage, and the PLO had fired guns next to their heads to terrorize them. One lady from Wiesbaden was raped on the street. Thankfully, Bamberg's two teachers had arrived home scared, but safe. They reported the incidents to the American Embassy, but the Ambassador laughed, saying, "We've had a lot of complaints about such things lately." Nothing was done.

It was the feeling of those in heated discussions at the O'Club, where all political ideas were hashed out, that the U.S. government would do nothing to anger Arab countries. "Mustn't make terrorists mad, now must we?" said Rex, his tone dripping with sarcasm.

Old Middle Eastern nations were in disarray with new infusions of PLO and other terrorist cells, drawing them closer to anarchy. Terror campaigns and kidnappings against Americans and other foreigners were becoming frequent and more violent. No one seemed ready with any answers to the escalating terrorist behavior.

To lighten the mood, Megan told about her surprise when her German neighbors, upon her return from vacation, had suddenly become friendly. "They said they were afraid I'd gone home to stay, and they welcomed me back to the neighborhood like a lost cousin."

"That's odd," said Abby, "particularly when they wouldn't

even respond to your morning greetings all these months."

"Maybe they missed my persistence," said Megan. "Now, they call me *their* American, and I have *neighbors.*"

Post Chaplain Father Harry had received a new assignment to Berchtesgaden, and everyone ribbed him about being stationed so close to Heaven. He was obviously delighted. He'd have a house too large for a single Lt. Colonel, including a gigantic room with ten beds. Being gregarious, Harry invited everyone down to stay in his 'dormitory.' He repeated a native Berchtesgadeners' remark that '...it would be a long, cold winter because the bees left the Alps.' "Whatever that means," he added, shrugging.

Abby, ever the most practical, said, "It probably means we'd better go shopping in Nürnberg to get more heavy clothing."

Carl entered late, still in his flight suit and looking particularly tired. By January, Megan was up to ten sips of his wine, and she jokingly asked if he wanted his usual Mosel.

"Not tonight, Twinkletoes, but I'm glad you're back. Missed you. Your flights weren't so bad, now, were they?"

"Oh, no...not at all," she replied with arch innocence. "I drew blood on Tim's knee on the first takeoff, so he refused to sit next to me anymore. I got John's arm on the second. We were searched for weapons in Zurich because Brenda and John tried to carry on decorative damascene swords. A delay for 'repairs,' scared me to death. Then some big guard tried to pat me down and I hit her when she touched me where she shouldn't. It sort of caused a ruckus with the Swiss armed guards, but we *finally* got to get on the plane. But even Brenda wouldn't sit by me on the flight back to Frankfurt."

Carl shook his head, laughing. "I was hoping you'd get over your fear, so you'd let me take you flying one of these days."

"We enjoyed Spain, but I hate landings and takeoffs." She paused. "You never mentioned you flew anything except helicopters."

"In Ft. Rucker, I rent a plane or fly for a local charter company. I've had my pilot's license since I was nineteen, and I'll buy a plane soon. My sailboat is shrink wrapped there too."

"How could you take me up, if you only fly in the states?"

He smiled, toasting her with his cola glass. "I'm still assuming ours is a long term relationship. One day you'll get used to me and follow me home."

"Carl, there you go again. Now, be good."

"I *am* good! You just won't let me to prove it to you, *yet*." He tipped up the glass of cola and drained it. "I only came by to welcome you home. I have to leave again, right away."

Father Harry turned to the aviator and asked, "Have you found the swimmers?"

"Not yet. Bill's out there now. I dropped by here while my crew chief is refueling the bird. We won't be in until we find them."

"What are you talking about?" Megan asked. Several others moved closer to listen.

Father Harry answered her question. "A rubber raft collapsed with four infantry troops from 1/52 on a night river crossing exercise on the upper Regnitz River. One kid made it to shore. The helicopter pilots have been searching for the other three all evening."

"We have to find those guys, *now*. The water's freezing cold." At Megan's worried expression, he added, "We're hoping they just floated downstream, and we'll find them holed up at some local *Gasthaus*, drinking a beer." He tried an encouraging smile that fell flat. "It'll have to be tonight for rescue, or it'll be a recovery operation by tomorrow!"

Marco entered with a packet of food, and Carl scrunched the bundle under one arm.

"Wait up," called Father Harry. "Can you use a navigator?"

"Sure, I'll drop you off in a couple of hours on the next refueling stop. I can use the company and the holy support."

The two men strode out to the hall and disappeared.

Quiet descended on the crowd, as they contemplated the possible loss of three of their own. The crowd quickly dispersed.

"What are you thinking, Megan?" Abby asked, as they walked to their cars.

"About those poor men flailing around in an icy river, hoping someone will find them. But I'm worried for the pilots flying in the dark looking for them, too. Won't they have to fly dangerously low to pick out signs of people in the water or on the banks?"

"You care for him, don't you?"

"Not in the way you're thinking. But he's my friend and especially understanding. I couldn't bear anything happening to him."

"That's a good sign of progress, Megan. You're beginning to truly care about people again. We'll send out special prayers tonight."

Chapter 15

Three days went by without word from 1/52 or Air Cav. The mood on Post was somber. Even the school children had heard about the accident. Friday evening, the usual crowd gathered for dinner at the Club, but no one felt like dancing, so most went home early.

Megan bathed and curled up in bed, using her loneliest, sleepless time to write her mom. Usually, her mother and children received wrinkled, squashed letters where she had fallen asleep on top of them, but it didn't matter. It seemed the only way she could get to sleep at all. The other teachers teased her about the large amount of mail she received at the APO mailroom.

Toward midnight, she heard pounding at her door. Grabbing her warm robe, she padded barefoot through the entry hall as the knocking came again, louder.

"Who is it?"

"It's me, Megan."

She opened the door to find Carl leaning against the wall in a dirty flight suit and aviator's jacket, unshaven and shivering.

"My God, Carl. Get in here and warm up. You look terrible. Are you all right?"

He stepped into the hall, dripping dirt on the linoleum and apologizing for waking her.

"We found them...all dead...four days in the water...bloated up like balloons...it was awful!" His voice broke in a way she recognized. She'd known that wrenching pain, too.

"Oh, Carl. I'm so sorry." She quickly wrapped her arms around him as he bent his tousled head to her shoulder.

"My crew chief and I spotted them this evening. We radioed the MP's for a boat. They pulled them out while we landed on the bank. Two were tangled in the reeds, and one was under a mud shelf. God, it was horrible. Their skin had even changed color. I couldn't..."

"Get those dirty clothes off while I run a hot tub of water for you. You'll get pneumonia."

When Carl seemed confused and didn't respond, Megan unzipped his jacket and peeled it off. He slid down the wall to sit bedraggled on the floor. She pulled off his boots, helped him back to his feet, and led him to the bathroom. As hot water streamed into the tub, she added her favorite bubble bath. "Can you manage to get in, while I go fix you some hot cocoa?"

"I guess so." He sniffed at his arm. "I smell disgusting. We had to manhandle the corpses onto the shore and into body bags. They stunk so bad we both threw up after pulling them into the helicopter. They must have weighed three hundred pounds apiece...all swelled up." Telltale streaks marked his smudged face. "No one should have to die like that. No one."

"I know, Carl. I know." She fought back tears of her own as she unzipped his one-piece flight suit and pulled it down over his shoulders. As he roused himself enough to finish undressing, she laid several large bath towels nearby. "Get into the water and warm up. I'll bring you some hot chocolate, and then we'll talk, if you want to."

Carl nodded dully, fumbling with the rest of his clothing as she stepped out and closed the door behind her.

Minutes later, with two steaming cups of cocoa on a tray, she knocked.

"Come on in, Megan. Your bubble bath seems to have covered me quite decently."

She stepped into the steamy room, placed the tray on the flat end of the tub, and brought a cup up to his lips. "Are you a little warmer? Try this."

Taking the cup, he sipped it. "Thanks, it's good. Listen, I'm sorry. I shouldn't have come to you like this. My crew chief went home to his wife, but I just couldn't face the thought of going home alone, and I didn't know where to go." The words tumbled out uncontrolled, troubled, huskily. "There's no one else I could talk to."

"Shh. It's okay. You shouldn't be alone. We'll get you warm, and you can get some sleep on my Flocati rug the rest of the night. Have you eaten anything?"

"No, but I'm not hungry. Just feel cold and...I don't know...helpless, I guess."

"You've been out there for days. You did the best you could."

"We should have found them sooner. We just didn't see any sign--no sign at all, until I thought I saw something flashing in the reeds. It was one guy's belt buckle. They must have tried to stay together. Another was face down nearby. It took some time to find the third one under an overhanging bank. It was harder to get him untangled. We didn't want to wait until morning. If we brought one home, we needed to bring them all home…" His voice choked.

"Shh, Carl, don't torture yourself so." She reached into the water and massaged his shoulders, splashing the warm water over his head and face. With her shampoo, she gently washed his matted hair, soothing him into silence.

"You can go on doing that all day," he finally said, trying much too hard to joke.

"You must be feeling better." She teasingly turned the hand shower to cooler water as she rinsed his hair. "You'd better get out of that tub before the mud in the bottom gets you dirty all over again." She held up a huge towel in front of him, turning her face away as he stood up and wrapped it around himself. "This is a lady's razor, but they're probably all the same," she said, laying a purple one from a cellophane package on the sink. "A shave might feel good to you, but you'd better be careful while your hands are shaking like that." Holding out a new toothbrush as well, she inquired softly, "Can you manage?" At his tentative nod, she closed the door behind her.

"Thanks, Megan," he called out.

While he shaved off his three-day stubble, Megan pulled out sheets and a blanket and made a pallet on the thick Flokati rug. She opened the German *Rolladen* blinds a smidgen so that a shaft of morning sun would wake him in case he had to fly the next day.

He finally emerged with a dry towel wrapped around his waist, and another on his wet head. Jerking his thumb over his shoulder, he said, "I left my clothes in your bathtub to soak. Hope you don't mind. I couldn't bear to put them back on, stinking like that."

"What time do you have to be back at the airfield?"

"No particular time." The words were almost unintelligible, lost between a sigh and a long yawn. "We radioed ahead for the military coroner to meet us when we landed. He took the bodies and said he'd notify the families. I just have to get the bird cleaned up and back in by evening. I suppose we can always do the 'old hair dryer trick,' if the flight suit doesn't dry in time." He yawned again, allowing himself to be led to the pallet.

"Here you go, my friend. Don't think about anything except sleep." She covered him with the blanket and heard him sigh deeply.

"Thanks, Meggie," he mumbled. "I didn't know I could be this tired and still fly the bird." He yawned once more and, exhausted, sleep caught up with him.

Returning to her bedroom, Megan felt relieved he hadn't gone home alone after such a harrowing experience. It was hard to be alone...she knew it...he knew it too. She dozed off, only to be awakened an hour later by shouts and groans. She hit the floor, running for the living room. Carl was thrashing and fighting the covers, obviously in the middle of a terrible nightmare.

Kneeling beside him, Megan put her arm over his shoulder and held him tightly. "It's okay, Carl. Wake up. You're not alone."

He struggled awake, confused and pale. "It was awful." He put his arms around her kneeling figure and buried his head into the folds of her long flannel granny gown.

"It was only a nightmare." Megan stroked his damp head. "It's understandable after the ordeal you've had. Try to relax." She noticed he was shaking all over. "You're really cold. Let me get another blanket." She disentangled herself and returned to cover him more heavily, tucking it around him. He stared straight ahead. "Turn over and let me rub your shoulders. You're tense and exhausted." Even as he obeyed, his whole body quivered.

"I could see their faces, Meg." The words came out slowly, as though his brain cortex was not functioning normally. "They were so unnatural... blue-white, mushy...and so cold...the feel of their skin was..." His voice broke. "I've never seen anyone who drowned before. It was different from war. When we struggled to get them into the body bags, you could see where fish had been nibbling..."

Megan continued rubbing his neck and shoulders quietly, with a growing awareness that he was *not* becoming more relaxed, and though his body temperature seemed unnaturally low, he was bathed in a cold sweat. *Something was not right, but it couldn't be physical shock—it had to be from the trauma. I don't think I can get him up the steps and into the car by myself, to go to the emergency room? I hate not having a phone!*

Carl continued talking through chattering teeth. "I dreamed I was diving again and again to free one guy's foot so we could pull him out. It was as though his arms were waving over me and pulling me under." Brushing a hand across his face, he said, "I'm sorry, I can't stop this stupid shaking. I feel so bad that we didn't find them in time." He rolled to his side, away from her, and covered his face.

His shaky voice was lost in emotion, and his skin--cold,

clammy to the touch--was this a delayed traumatic shock? *But what can I do to help him? I can only remember something about warming and calming—I can't think of anything else.* She hesitated no longer, but peeled off her gown, slid in behind him, and encircled his cold, shaking body with her own warm one. *My strength to you this time.* She rubbed his arms vigorously and wrapped her legs around his, holding him still. He sighed, nestling his back against her stomach until her arms were worn out, and his shaking had subsided.

Warmed and exhausted, they drifted off to sleep. At some point, Carl turned to her, snuggled the covers around them both, and laid his head on her shoulder. Drowsily, she wrapped her arms around his shoulders and did not wake enough to move away.

Megan woke with shards of sunlight falling across her face, allowing her eyes to drift shut, lazily, luxuriating in the contentment of having slept peacefully, without her nightly dream. Relaxed, she realized she hadn't stirred. Her legs were still draped over his, which were bent under hers as he lay on his side, pressed tightly against her. His arm lay relaxed across her waist. She felt his rumpled hair against her cheek, and gently kissed the beloved forehead.

Suddenly she stiffened, her eyes flew open, and the peaceful moment between sleeping and waking was shattered. The man in her arms was not Andy!

"Easy, Meggie," Carl murmured as he raised his head to see her face. He tightened his hold on her waist as she struggled and pulled her arms away. "You're okay. It's only me."

The finality of her sudden realization sickened her. "Andy's really gone!" she whispered, shaking her head to be rid of the image inside it. "He's never coming back, is he?"

"Meggie, he can't come back, though I know he'd want to." He stroked her face. "Somewhere inside, you know it's no use waiting for him any longer. But you're alive, and the love you had with Andy will never go away."

She wasn't hearing him.

"Talk to me, Megan. What is it?"

"It's just that...that when I woke, we were all wrapped together like Andy and I used to be and, for a moment, I thought it was him. But when I kissed you, I realized it wasn't." She lost her battle with the tears. "It was so final, somehow." She sobbed deeply, from the core of her body. "When I kissed you, I knew—I knew he was really dead." She covered her eyes with one hand. "All this time, was I deluding myself that it was just a bad dream?"

She didn't wait for an answer. "I relived our last night together every time I slept, right down to the love-making, the ambulance, and my still being wrapped in his old bathrobe at the hospital. I feared if I took it off, he'd be gone forever, but then the doctor said he was gone anyway. I didn't want to believe him." Her hand slid from her eyes down over her mouth to stop the awful words.

Carl waited, holding her gently, letting her tell it her own way, his own trauma forgotten in his anxiety for hers.

"I think I expected him to come back to me so we could go on together, if I just waited patiently enough--you know, like when he was overseas. Now, I know he's never coming back. He didn't even come in the dream last night." She leaned her head against Carl's chest and cried in gut-wrenching sobs. His own eyes misted.

He spoke quietly, wrapping his arms around her more tightly. "It's normal, Megan, denial--what you wanted to believe. I've felt all along that you hadn't yet believed he was dead. It's what helped you carry on bravely, but it's also probably what made you uncomfortable with other men." He paused, apparently trying to frame his words carefully. "As hard as it is to accept that he's gone, maybe if you can face the truth of it, the truth will help you get past this milestone. It helps to accept what's *real*. You need to let him go in peace, Megan, and get on with the grieving you've avoided all this time."

"Oh, Carl, it hurts so. If he's gone, what do I do now?"

"Shh, it's okay. Let it all go. You've held it in far too long." Carl rocked her back and forth in his arms as her breath came in wrenching gasps, and sobs tore at her body.

"Why didn't God take me with Andy when I begged him so?"

Holding her protectively, Carl swept one hand over her face, wiping tears and smoothing back her hair, speaking soft words into her anguished gasps. "It wasn't your time, Meggie. It was *his* time."

After what seemed an eternity, she lay quietly in his arms, breathing hard, exhausted emotionally and empty spiritually. Her tears, and his own, lapsed into a shared fatigue.

"Let's just rest awhile, Meggie. Emotions are pretty ragged right now...for both of us. Just relax and catch your breath. Don't try to think it all out yet. We have plenty of time." Carl held her quite still until he felt her shift her position, trying to pull up the covers under her arms when she remembered she hadn't her nightgown on.

"Don't worry, Megan," he said, tucking the covers around her carefully. "This comes under the category of helping each other make it through the night. Neither of us needs to feel uncomfortable with the other. You've wanted to die, and I felt helpless last night too, yet here we are both alive. We've survived crisis somehow, together. That's special, isn't it--sort of an important turning point in a trusted friendship, don't you think?"

She nodded, eyes wide, as she looked into his for answers.

"I know you've come to trust me, Megan, and you know I'd never hurt you." He tried to make her smile. "I hope you realize I've been wanting to hold you in my arms for months now, and what do I do when I finally have you under the covers with me? I fall asleep!" He gestured wildly for emphasis. "What is this going to do to my reputation as a true lover?"

He finally got her wan smile. He even got an out-loud giggle.

"I guess we just won't tell anybody. I certainly wouldn't want to ruin your reputation."

"I promised you I'd wait until you said you were ready."

"I know," she said quietly.

"There's always now." He flashed her his best, wicked grin.

She looked straight at him. "I care about you too much for that. You'd die!"

"That's crazy!" But from her look, he knew she was serious.

"Andy did. I killed him." The frozen words escaped from her throat. "We had just finished making love when he died. It must have been too stressful--all my fault!" She could feel herself verging on hysteria. She had never revealed this secret fear before…to anyone.

"Meggie, no." Carl was shocked. "It doesn't work like that."

"If I hadn't made love with him that night, he'd still be alive now. I should've told him 'no,' or pleaded a headache. We were both always so wild, and he'd never even been sick." She looked away for a moment, reliving the painful moment her husband had died in her arms. "It happened so fast. Now, night after night, I dream it all again, play it through my mind, and it was my fault. I'll never want sex again because--I'd kill someone else." She blurted out the words.

Carl caressed her contorted face, pulling his palm under her chin to force her attention. "Andy was your first and only lover?"

She nodded.

"Had you ever told him 'no' before that?"

"Oh no! Never! We were so young when we married. We thought we'd discovered making love all by ourselves, like it was our own special gift from God. I'll admit we both liked it--a lot." She put her hand over her mouth and sighed, embarrassed she'd blurted out yet another secret thing. "But I should have sensed something wrong, and I should have said 'no' *that* time. I should have..." Her voice rose hysterically. "I'm far too scared of killing someone else to ever think of...even if I wanted to, which I don't." She sounded dorky, and she knew it, but she felt the need to get the awful words confessed. "Nothing can happen, ever. I couldn't face losing someone I cared about ever again. Her normal contralto had reached soprano pitch.

"Stop it, Meggie, and listen to me." Carl massaged her shoulder gently as he spoke. "If Andy was meant to die that night, he would have died no matter *what* you'd done--or not done. You'd have felt worse if that had been the one time in his life you had pushed him away, and he died anyway?" He took a deep breath into her silence.

"Look, he died in your arms, content and happy. Most of us would give up a lifetime for that opportunity, and most people never find the contentment you're talking about. He had the best you had to give. I'm sure he died a happy man. It doesn't get better than that."

A wan smile played around her lips. "He would always *say* something like that-- afterward—'Wow, I could die happy.' I always thought he was just being funny. I certainly never dreamed he would die that way. It was so fast. I've felt like the 'black widow' ever since." She lay deadly quiet.

"Look at me, Meggie, and get this through your thick head. *You* didn't kill him! A blood clot moves whenever it wants. You could neither have predicted it, nor protected him from it. We could die right now, and it would be no one's fault. Are you hearing me?"

She nodded. "You don't think our having been too eager to make love killed him?"

"Heck no, Megan. Every time I climb into a helicopter and fly the Border, I'm aware I could die. If the Communists come across the Border, that would be our mission--to hold them back at all costs. But I just might be helping to keep us out of a war by maintaining a balance of power, too, so that makes it okay. I'd never stop flying because it *might* be dangerous. Or you could keel over in a classroom from a sudden heart attack, but that *possibility* would never keep you away from your class of kids, now would it?" She was listening.

"None of us knows when our time will come. But, believe me right now, if God ever gave me a *choice* of the time I wanted to die, it would be in the arms of someone I loved." His strained face exploded into a wicked grin. "After great sex, of course."

"That sort of makes sense," she said, wiping her tears, and finally smiling quietly.

"Megan, you'll get through this, I promise, just as you made me believe last night that I could get through not finding those men in time. We both have some type of survivor's guilt--why them, and not us. We have to help each other get over our losses."

She could tell he was going to say something she wouldn't want to hear by the way he paused and gathered a deep breath.

"Andy would want you to heal the pain and start living again. Someday, you'll be ready to love someone, in a completely different way, and make love to him, and maybe marry him."

She shook her head, even as she remembered Abby had told her something very similar.

"Not right away, but someday--when you're ready. Of course, if you need further *proof* you won't kill someone by making love, a guinea pig to practice on, I'm willing to take on that terribly dangerous risk--*any* time—even right now!"

He leered and wiggled his eyebrows until she attacked his middle, tickling him into helplessness. He scrambled out of the covers, and she chased him with his towel.

"A guinea pig, indeed," she finally was able to gasp out. "You're hopeless."

"I know." He grinned at her. "And so are you. I'm willing to wait until you *beg* me." He expected the attack with the towel, and almost ducked in time.

After rescuing their dignity and finding two sets of Megan's running suits that worked equally well for a man or a woman, they talked the morning away over breakfast, facing their most terrible fears amid growing confidence they could draw strength from each other.

"I'll tell you something," Carl said, as though confessing a great secret. "I've never before fallen asleep in a woman's arms."

"Goodness, I'm quite sure I'm not the only woman you've ever been near."

"No, I've been with women. A few even said, 'thank you.'" He grinned with his usual leer. "They never seemed important--more just opportunity of the moment, I guess. But I always felt incomplete, or disgusted, or just sorry I flirted in the first place. Is that weird?"

"No wonder you say you have no luck with the ladies despite using 'your best lines.' Holding someone you love through the night is the most wonderful expression of tenderness." She paused for a moment and then added, with a drop of her chin, "I think that's what I've missed most since Andy died--just being held when I'm lonely or scared. You were very gentle with me. You could be with someone else, if you'd just try."

"I feel natural with you. No games, no pretense. I guess men need to be held sometimes too, though I'm not sure any of us would admit it. I'm not really sure what I was feeling last night, except the need to have someone I cared about talk me through a horrible crisis. I needed you. And this morning, you needed me. We both had heavy things on our minds."

"I feel safe with you, Carl. I've already figured out that your lines and your clowning, are a front--a pretense to keep yourself from caring too much and getting hurt. You aren't nearly so predatory and confident as you'd like others to think."

Carl chuckled. "Think you're so smart, don't ya?" Pausing a moment, he said, "I guess you're right. How did you know I'm afraid to be in love? I've been in *lust* lots of times." He looked away. "You see right through me, and that's scary. But I know a secret about you, as well." He bit his lip, then said, "You won't hit me now, will you?"

She looked across the table at him with curiosity.

"I'm glad you've been so busy fighting men off, misunderstanding their lines, and running away from everybody, because you've been ripe for someone to take advantage of you, and you didn't even know it, yourself." He actually blushed. "At least, I wouldn't do that."

She gasped. "Whatever makes you think I was..." She was indignant at the suggestion.

"You drop things a lot--get jumpy and accident-prone. When you walk into a room, a guy can feel some kind of...vibration." He wobbled his hand to emphasize this odd phenomenon. "You've been alone over a year, and you liked sex before, with Andy. What *else* would I think?"

"Honestly, I've not thought about why I felt restless." she said. "Andy always said I started sneezing and my eyes changed color when I was feeling sexy, but I don't let anyone close enough to look at my eyes now, though I guess I am still sneezing."

"I've noticed that," Carl said, with a grin.

But nothing can come of my having such feelings. I'll just go right on dropping things." *How can Carl make such an assessment? Am I 'ripe' for disaster, as he said?*

"I'll be here any time you decide you want to do something about it." He grinned.

"You're too eager," she said, laughing at his persistence. "*And* too young."

"Hell, Meggie, you may be a decade older than me in calendar years, but you're a decade younger than me in experience and in knowledge of ways of the modern world. I think that makes us *even*."

She took a deep breath, blowing it out through pursed lips. "I want you to have a life and love and a family of your own."

"I'm not really interested in anyone now. And you don't want anyone. We're both accidents waiting to happen. I'm afraid someone will eventually take advantage of you, and I'm always making mistakes and picking the wrong women."

He shifted position, folding his hands in his lap. "Look, I know I can't ever meet *all* your needs. You need Luke to take you to symphonies, Milt for those intellectual history discussions, Bill to sing with you, Stan to create a lively social life. Heck, it would take an army of men to fill Andy's shoes. Plus you have all your female friends. But until you find the guy who can be everything to you, I know I'm the one who understands you best and cares about you most." He lowered his voice as though some invisible spy were listening. "I worry about your being alone, and I don't want to be alone, either."

She nodded, touched that he understood her so well.

He inhaled deeply and sped on. "We trust each other. We'd be good to each other and…I don't want you running around out there alone, getting hurt." He grinned as he reached over to take her hand. "I'll come to you in a heartbeat, and we won't have to worry about making dangerous choices with anyone else until we're darned good and ready." He hurried on before she could intervene. "And, should you ever find a guy you'll accept, I'll check him out first, to be sure he's a good guy. But then I'll dance at your wedding, if that's what you want. I promise."

She couldn't help laughing at his unusual idea. Carl could always be trusted to challenge one's preconceived notions.

"We live so close to the edge here, so involved in our Border existence, our accidents, our spies, our mission, it influences our relationships. It's hard *not* to get in a hurry. Everyone just sort of takes care of each other. But you've come from such a protected lifestyle, it probably seems odd to you--the cultural changes—from the rigidity of the fifties, the loose 'anything goes' of the sixties, and the live and let live attitude of sex in the seventies. There may be something else in the eighties. I promised myself I'd never rush you until you told me you were ready." He kissed her gently on the cheek, and misquoted, "In the midst of death we are in life."

"I do feel better able to think ahead today, Carl. Thank you for talking me through all this negative stuff. I guess I've been carrying it around in my head for a long time."

"Don't forget, we talked *each other* through the negative stuff. I think you've crossed a Border of your own today, probably as treacherous as the one we defend across Europe. We *are* glad to be alive, now, *aren't we?*" He elbowed her in the arm with a grin.

She couldn't resist the laughter in his voice, and nodded. "I'm even beginning to wonder what comes next."

"It's a decision to live, Meggie. Accept that as fact, for both of our sakes. If you find the man you'll accept, I suppose he'll be some grumpy old guy who'll never be able to keep up with you." He pouted for effect until she laughed and hugged him. "Some day, you'll see I'm right. I can wait. And didn't I tell you that Flocati rug should be used for something better than writing letters?"

Chapter 16

Reforger soon took all the guys away, as had the all-too-frequent alerts. Reforger--short for 'Return of Forces to Germany,' was a yearly war game to practice dispersing troops and deterring aggression, and 12,000 stateside troops arrived in waves. A 1968 crisis in Soviet-controlled Czechoslovakia had sparked a U.S. pledge to deploy ten divisions within ten days to defend Western Europe from the communists. This year's exercise included the Canadian, German, Dutch, and Norwegian units from NATO bases also, all to prepare for a wartime scenario of a Soviet armored assault to seize the West that everyone *hoped* would never take place.

The tiny Bamberg Army Airfield, which normally had only a scattering of helicopters at facilities shared with a German Glider Club, suddenly was handling more than 300 flights a day, mostly helicopters, but including a few old propeller-driven troop carriers from less well-equipped NATO allies. Carlson, the Airfield Manager, single–handedly manned his 'control tower' around the clock, equipped only with one microphone attached to an antique radio, a pair of binoculars, and a fairly short runway. The officers talked about an accident looking for a time and place to happen, and they worried.

Early on, Milt of Stuttgart had an emergency landing when hydraulic lines iced up in a blizzard. He had given everyone a scare since, once he disappeared from Carlson's radio, no transmissions came through, and weather clearance wasn't good enough for a search and rescue mission. Those expecting him at the O'Club had waited most of the night for word that Milt, his dog Rusty, and his crew and cargo had been found.

Two days later, when Milt returned, he told the group that the helicopter had precious little time or maneuverability, and *no* visibility, to get down safely. He couldn't do a standard running landing since the snow could hide obstacles. He had no choice but to plop down hard in the powder, which they could see from the chin bubble was quite deep. He had almost completely buried the bird. Opening the door brought in piles of loose snow. Leaving the co-pilot and two crew members to guard the 'box,' the big man and his dog set out to find the nearest German village to call the airfield, since he needed both chase planes and ground troops to safeguard his mysterious cargo of euphemistically called 'special weapons' so near the Border. The mission would have to be rescued by a Chinook cargo helicopter when the storm let up, provided the Chinook could spot the smaller, wrecked helicopter in the deep powder.

Milt's journey with Rusty became a near-death experience when he couldn't find a road. After an hour, he realized Rusty was not behind him and heard the dog barking through the blinding snow. Determined to find his dog, he struggled toward the noise. He then realized he'd been circling in a field, making no headway at all, while *Rusty* had found the road. But which way might be a village?

Milt chose a direction and he and Rusty trudged miles in zero-zero visibility until Milt resembled the Abominable Snowman and Rusty's paws were bleeding. There was no choice but to go on, since the crew and box needed rescue, Milt could not have carried the big dog, and there was no shelter. When he finally saw a light and stumbled into a village's pub, the only building open so late at night, the men of the *Stammtisch,* the German 'regulars,' quickly filled both Milt and Rusty with *Schnaps* to warm them, and fed Rusty their steak bones, since they considered the dog a hero—soon a *drunk* one.

"Just *try* calling a military number from a German civilian phone without the secret access numbers," the big man joked. "I'll memorize the dang things next time! I finally convinced the operator it was an emergency, and she got Bamberg tower. I knew they couldn't find my bird until daybreak, but it was almost daybreak already, and I wasn't sure I could find it again, myself. We just had to hope our enemies couldn't find it either!"

Milt could joke about the incident once his crew, his bird and the 'box' were safe, but whether the cargo was simulated or real, even the pilot would not know, because all such cargos were treated with the same protocol. If the irony that the 'box' might have been empty, merely a dummy, occurred to the big man, he would have denied that he could have done anything else except take the risks of a blinding snowstorm to protect it *anyway*. Such was the rule of the Border.

The jovial man visited Bamberg often for a time, and was always good fun, but he seemed to have some secret side to his life. They never knew if it was related to his work, or something in his personal life. But mysteries aside, his crash landing and trek in the blizzard had been a *near* thing that all pilots could appreciate.

From her classroom window, Megan could see tanks clanking and groaning their way out of muddy staging areas, heading for the 'war-zone' site for this year's exercise near Rattelsdorf. Small boys pelted the moving tanks with snowballs in a mock war, and good-natured soldiers threw them back. The snowball fights took everyone's mind off the mass exodus of troops, and the type of scenario under which it might ever have to be used—for real.

Military equipment was heard all hours of the day and night rumbling around in the surrounding villages, with blank machine-gun fire for good measure. "Don't the Germans dislike all the noise?" Lila asked Frank, as they all shared an impromptu teacher's luncheon.

"Even if they did, they wouldn't say much. They know our troops are all that's standing between them and the communists. They *want* us to be successful if the Russians cross that Border." He chuckled. "Of course, once in awhile a tank wipes out the corner of a house when it negotiates a tight turn in thousand year old villages, and the U.S. government pays for damages."

Tim added, "Big Don said German farmers actually *hope* the Americans will track through their field because our government must then pay them for this year's crop, next year's crop that would have come from the seed, then the seed of the seed from the following year. It's sort of a 'racket.' They even let their chickens out of the coop when they hear tanks coming."

"And heaven help the Cavalry if they run over a chicken," added Frank. "You can imagine…the fee is for the chicken, all the eggs it would have laid in its charmed life, plus all the eggs that would have come from its offspring, and…"

"I get the picture," said Abby.

"I'd still hate to be on the enemy side," commented Lila. "Our guys look impressive."

"So do theirs," Frank said quickly. "Don't get complacent. They outnumber us."

"My sweet, wealthy German friend, Klaus, asked about the convoys," said Lila with a grin. "He's an exciting man, and he buys me lovely gifts. He wants to know who's in charge. Who calls the shots for the international troop movements?"

Frank looked sharply at Lila. "He doesn't need to know that!"

Tim changed the subject quickly to a safer topic. "Tell Klaus to get behind a convoy on the road, if he wants some excitement. Unless it's actually an alert, the tanks only go as fast as a ground guide can walk in front them to prevent accidents. The drivers can't see out well. And it's illegal to pass the convoy, so you just have to bumble along until the tanks get back to Post."

Lila nodded, seemingly oblivious to their gentle reminder of military security. The other teachers exchanged shrugs. *Why does she keep seeing that man?* thought Megan. *I have a bad feeling about this.*

With all the troops gone, things were too quiet on Post. Once in awhile a unit could come in to make repairs on heavy equipment and collect additional supplies. But the men had little time to socialize. They were gone again within hours. The average time away from Post for 2/2 Cavalry was around 340 days of 365...not a good thing for those with families.

One weekend the Engineers were in, they planned to help teachers repaint hopscotch lines on the cobblestone playground, but it rained so hard the group sought other activities--an impromptu indoor picnic, followed by a movie, *Young Frankenstein*. As the group swelled in number, they went downtown for pizza. When they returned to their cars, *every* car with shiny green American military plates had parking tickets, yet fourteen German plated cars, parked in the same area, had none. Stan had counted them.

Coincidence? Of course not! Harassment of Americans? Probably. But the officers going back out to Reforger had enjoyed a companionable day, ticket or no ticket. They'd be leaving again by 0500 hours to practice rubber raft landings and fake bridge blow ups.

The next thing they knew, however, Charlie was back. Megan and Abby came upon him unexpectedly, sitting on the outside steps of the deserted O'Club. He was disconsolate, having lost one of his young privates.

"The kid was driving a damned ten-ton flatbed truck with a bulldozer chained down to the back on a 12% downgrade, and the damned truck got away from him. He was a damned good soldier and a damned good driver, and I *know* he wouldn't have made any damned mistake, yet the Brass is trying to call it 'operator error.' I brought my platoon in so we can investigate, ourselves. I know the Commander won't. He says we have no time for investigation, and the truck cab was such a twisted wreck we'll probably never know anyway. I think the damned brakes failed, yet I know my guys checked them before the accident. That's the only thing that would…" He threw up his hands in helpless fury, his face contorted.

Megan and Abby had never heard Charlie use so many 'damns' since they'd met him, so they recognized his anguish over the tragedy. The women sat with him on the steps while he vented his frustration. "If we lose so many guys to accidents just practicing, in case the Soviets come across that damned Border," he said, "imagine what we'd lose in a real war?"

Abby and Megan comforted Charlie as best they could, knowing he was right. There had been just too many accidents lately, with no logical explanation for any of them.

When Reforger was finally over, after three rainy, miserable weeks, it was good to hear male voices around the O'Club again. All had come back unshaven, tired, and hungry. The young lieutenant who had been so excitedly looking forward to his first Reforger, returned disillusioned. He said that all he could think about while watching his tent float away in the rain and snow was playing volleyball with the gang again on Wednesday nights.

He didn't get to do so, however. Reforger was followed by yet another alert. This time, the women were lucky enough to see a whole squadron of helicopters take off at once and move out in close formation. Megan had a terrible lump in her throat—proud of them all—praying for them all. The four watched in awe as the flight filled up the sky with power and their unique whop, whop noise, moving off together toward the northeast. The last helicopter had disappeared before anyone could speak. It was an experience none could forget.

Megan suddenly had an insight into an Infantry commander she had heard describe a flight of helicopters in Vietnam. He had said, "When your men are wounded, surrounded, and out of ammunition, angels don't come with a soft whirr of delicate wings. They arrive with the whop, whop, whop of an Army helicopter pilot and crew."

Megan's calendar showed they'd been on alert more than they'd been off for the year.

One evening during the alert, the four women descended on the O'Club for dinner, though they knew they'd probably be the only ones there. But four strangers entered, obviously of military bearing, but wearing civilian clothes. Marco seemed to know them, and he seated them at a nearby table. Marco asked the women if they would play hostess. Bamberg tradition was to be friendly to strangers, so they acquiesced. Marco told the men, "If you want a drink, the ladies know where everything is located. My bartender is a soldier by day, an office clerk, and she must stay at HQ for the duration of the alert."

Lila and Abby stepped behind the bar and brought back the beers requested by the visitors and cokes for the ladies, and all settled into comfortable lounge chairs. They seemed to split naturally into conversational pairs, the older, taller gentleman getting into a discussion with Megan about the present crisis. The other three men seemed almost interchangeable in their uniformity—young, sturdily built, constantly searching the perimeter as though they did not trust the O'Club to be safe.

When Megan wondered aloud how long the alert might last, the tall man answered, "Until the Soviets back down and, according to our latest signal intercepts, that could be quite awhile this time."

"Is this one so serious, then?"

"I suppose so, but we always hope an all-out confrontation can be avoided." He waved a hand, taking in the three younger men who by this time were in deep conversation with Abby, Lila, and Emily across the room, and said quietly, "Our mission to inspect weapons should last about two days. Marco quartered us upstairs in the guest rooms. Do you ladies live nearby?"

"I'm close by, in Lichteneiche, Lila is a little further in Memmelsdorf, and the other two live in the opposite direction, way out in Amlingstadt, but we hang out together most times." She asked again about his mission. "What is it that you do as an inspector?"

He changed the subject abruptly. "I've heard Bamberg now has a Ski Club of its own, and good things are being said about it."

Megan beamed, not at first picking up on his variation of topic. "Yes, it's great. We weren't sure how to get it started, but so far we've had several weekend trips. We're trying to get young soldiers involved, too, because they need something constructive to do with their energy. We even told the General he'd have to schedule his field problems so they wouldn't conflict with our ski trips." She laughed. "Of course, that was a joke, but he took it well. Do you ski?"

"I go with the Stuttgart's Patch Club when I can, or with my friend, Pete, but traveling around so much, I usually wind up just going to Garmisch, alone."

His direct eyes bored into hers, almost demanding her

attention. He struck her as a loner, one who would be willing to ski, or perhaps do almost anything else, alone.

His voice softened. "And I'd heard about your lower discipline incidents from some commanders who seemed happy with your Ski Club as well. When's your next trip?"

"In a couple of weeks," answered Megan, "provided the alert is over by then. I'm still at a basic level, but I love it. As the resident 'klutz,' though, I hurt myself a lot." She remembered her 'orders' from her ski buddies and giggled. "My friends demand that I hum a waltz as I ski, so that I have music. They tell me I'm graceful with music, but I'm quite accident-prone if the music stops."

The big man chuckled. "Perhaps I could coach you into a more advanced level."

"Are you around here that often?" *Perhaps I overestimated his solitary style.*

"My job takes me back and forth, so it's hard to say with any degree of certainty when, but yes, I'll be here pretty often, as well as several other line bases." He stuck out a huge hand to shake her slender one. "By the way, I'm Ed O'Brien, and my friends call me 'Big Ed.'" He leaned forward to whisper, "My sister calls me 'Baldy.' Can't imagine why?" He grinned widely as he ran a hand over his close-cropped head. He waited for her name.

"I'm Megan James and we're all teachers at the school." Megan found herself intrigued by Ed's almost contagious grin.

"And you aren't afraid to be here during an alert instead of safely at home?"

"We've already decided we're staying, in case we can help in some way. No NEO evacuation for us. All our friends are out there." She jerked her head in the direction of the Border. "And we know their mission." Ed nodded.

Megan was still curious about the man's purpose in Bamberg. "What kind of weapons are you inspecting? I assumed most of our weaponry went out to the Border with our troops."

Ed lowered his voice and said, "Not all. Some special weapons aren't meant for firing at such close range. And we have a few problems we're trying to work out here on Post."

Megan thought that statement over for a moment and then matched his quiet voice, "You guys aren't checking out something nuclear, are you?"

"What on earth makes you think that?" The man's voice betrayed no emotion.

"Because we have Air Force officers down at Muna, six actually, three shifts of two, that can never stay long at our Ski Club parties. Two of them at a time are always on duty. They can never be further from each other than ten minutes. I'm assuming half of each of those three teams has half of the launch codes, and they have to be close enough to join up quickly. And then there's the fact that during alerts the gang can only get together at *Seehof,* or at my little apartment, because I'm within the ten minute limit."

"And how, may I ask, did you decide this?" Ed arched his eyebrows. "Have you been reading too many science fiction novels?"

"I guess you could call me an observer. I listen, I see things, and I analyze them. It's fun to 'read' people. And I know there are low-yield things available to Cav and Engineers to destroy bridges and roadblocks, and the Artillery has some extra weapons they're pretty quiet about. And we have a Stuttgart helicopter pilot friend who is awfully mysterious about the 'boxes' he carries around and where he goes. Also, some scientists from White Sands were here a while back, and it seemed odd they'd come to Bamberg since we're pretty low on the food chain. But I don't talk about it--except to you, because you seem to know more about this whole thing than most."

"And what if I were an enemy spy?" A smile twitched behind his conspiratorial whisper.

Her eyes flashed. "Marco would *never* have ushered you in during an alert unless he already knew you belonged here. Marco knows everyone, so he knows if someone is without proper credentials. He brought you right in to us, and he looks out *very* carefully for us. So I know that you're one of the good guys. Also, he doesn't billet anyone upstairs unless they have orders, so I know you're here on something official. The guards outside during an alert are really thorough at checking ID, as well." She tried to decide if her curiosity was too outspoken. "Why don't you travel in uniform?"

"The better to keep young ladies like you from asking too many questions, my dear." He shook his head and laughed. "You intrigue me with your analysis. I'm glad you have such an inquiring mind. Perhaps you'll be included in our next round of NATO war planning. For now, could we agree that you'll have dinner here with me tomorrow night and we can talk about skiing?"

Megan knew she had guessed right, or nearly right, and he had confirmed her suspicions. But Ed took her curiosity with good grace, without admitting anything. She looked carefully at his eyes, since she'd always believed them to be mirror of the soul. Though they'd seemed cold earlier, they now had a friendly warmth. His face, and yes—the top of his head as well—was bronzed from the sun, so she knew he spent much time outdoors. With his slight southern drawl, and his obvious intelligence, she found herself quite comfortable with this man. Feeling completely unthreatened, she nodded. "Why not?"

"About five? I should be done with my inspections by then. And no, I can't tell you about them until I know you much better." He flashed a mischievous grin. "But I'd *like* to know you much better."

Ed motioned to the other three men. All rose simultaneously, made courteous farewells, and walked upstairs, almost as one unit.

"How nice they were," said Emily. "They must be important to be here when all the rest of the guys are out at the Border."

"It's obvious Megan gets all the rank--again," said Abby, grinning at Emily.

"Why do you think that? They were all dressed in civvies."

"When he rose, the other three snapped up and followed. They wouldn't do that if they were all of equal rank. And that military bearing would mark him an officer from a mile off. You really need to start noticing these things, Megan."

"I notice other things, but rank doesn't mean anything to me. For instance, I noticed that Ed is fun to talk to, he has a contagious smile, and we're interested in some of the same things."

"Like what?" Lila asked.

"Like skiing. He offered to work me up to intermediate level." Megan deliberately circumvented conversation of her other suspicions about the genial man's job.

"Already! Y'all work fast. I was hoping that blonde guy would ask me out."

"What about Brian?" asked Emily.

"Well, Brian isn't here, Klaus can't come on Post during an alert, and this guy, Ralph, is right here!" She grinned until they all started laughing.

"Well, at least you got his name this time," said Abby, shaking her head.

The following evening, Megan finished her lesson plans, and waited for mothers to pick up their children—standard procedure during an alert. At the O'Club entrance, a staff car pulled up precisely at five. All four officers were resplendent in three-piece dark business suits, ties, and sunglasses. As soon as Ed saw Megan, he hurried to her side. "Would you mind having a drink with my colleagues while I go change into something more comfortable?"

It might as well have been an order, because the other three officers immediately walked Megan into the deserted bar. She got each of the men a beer from the 'fridge back of the bar, since she knew nothing about making mixed drinks. They talked about frivolous things for a few minutes until Big Ed returned in casual slacks and a soft, gray turtleneck sweater. He towered over her and the other officers, but his warm grin seemed to make all else unimportant. He thanked the men, and escorted Megan into the private fireside dining room.

Marco suggested his prime rib. "It's prepared, Colonel, for a special occasion."

Ed looked across at Megan and smiled. "Yes, Marco, I can see that this is a special occasion, and we'll take your prime rib."

Suave Marco actually winked at Megan as he hustled away to get their wine.

Megan was a bit shy at first, as she had never seen Marco so attentive, even to the local commanding General and his party.

"Well, Megan. How was your day? Were your little darlings all behaving appropriately?"

Megan nodded and told him how some were upset by alerts, and two had started acting out a bit by fighting.

"And what does one do with a pair of battling ten-year-olds?"

"Oh, I have a system. I simply wear them out until they have no strength left to fight. I started them with ten pushups, but one still wanted to fight, so I made his penalty twenty. Then he tried pulling rank on me."

She bristled up her shoulders in imitation of William. "'*My* dad is a Major and you can't make me do pushups.' That upped his ante to thirty. 'But my dad will come over here, and he outranks you.'

I told him to 'bring on' his dad because I didn't think he'd appreciate his son using rank not his own. I made the penalty forty." Megan brushed a strand of her long hair back from where it had fallen over her eyes. "By this time the other kid had finished his ten pushups, and was back out playing. Still William started again, 'My dad…' So I just told him, 'Your dad earned his rank, and you've done nothing yet to earn yours. Make it fifty.'"

Ed's laugh was a huge, warm rumble. "I'd hate to have had you for a first sergeant. Did William do the pushups?"

"He gave up at thirty-three, but I don't think he'll try that stupid rank thing again."

"I love the way you grow so animated when talking about your school children. Are all DoDDS teachers so dedicated?

"All of them *I* know."

With wine, they were exchanging backgrounds. With salad, they were making plans for future activities on the ski slope. By the entrée, they were as comfortable as old friends. Soon Marco was at their table to see what else he could do to make the meal festive.

"Marco tells me you're the one who knows the history of this town and all the good places to see," Ed said, as he glanced at the headwaiter.

Megan had a flash of insight that Marco was promoting this friendship, and she couldn't help wondering why. "Marco seems to talk a lot," she said with a chuckle. "Is this a hint that you'd like to see Bamberg?"

"Oh, would you show me?" Ed asked with mock surprise, giving Marco a staged wink.

"I suppose so," she said slowly, still hesitating, looking at Marco tentatively. He nodded, signaling that *this* man was safe. "Since you two seem to have already decided for me," she concluded. We'll take my car, so your staff car won't be seen during an alert."

Ed first excused himself a moment and spoke with one of the other officers in the bar. She saw them synchronize watches, then Ed returned to her, beaming.

"I don't always get away easily, but my aides know when to expect me. This won't take longer than a couple of hours, will it?"

"We'll do the two hour, fifty-cent tour, just to meet your deadline." *Funny, I can't seem to avoid smiling at this man. His grin just begs to be returned.*

　　While they explored the town, Ed asked questions about Bamberg's history, its music, and the surrounding area. He seemed genuinely interested in her ideas, her school, her friends, the Ski Club--a plethora of topics. When she mentioned that a Bamberg restaurant was famous for its smoked beer, he asked if they could spend an evening in the famous *Schlenkerle*. "When I come back," he said. "And I *will* come back," he added, "...if you'll let me."

　　Megan found herself agreeing. She had thoroughly enjoyed the evening with the big man and his even bigger smile. It seemed strange, though, that Marco seemed to want her to go out with Ed. It also nagged at her thoughts that Ed seemed to have a time limit. He was nice though. Megan felt comfortable with him, and she was sure Carl and Abby would be proud of her. This time, she hadn't run away.

　　With the alert seeming endless, the teachers drove down to Berchesgaden to pester Father Harry at his dormitory. Harry enjoyed having company from Bamberg and made everyone feel welcome. He got along wonderfully with the Southern Bavarians and "schussed" his way through conversations as though he knew the dialect. But the Bavarians loved him as much as did the Bambergers.

　　From first arrival, he would open all guests a beer and put the bottle cap in his kitchen drawer with a reminder that everyone at his house was only drinking "for the orphans." Apparently the Bavarians, heavy beer drinkers themselves, had a charity that accepted beer caps and, in return, donated money to the Bavarian orphan asylum. Harry wanted everyone to "do his share," so mandatory beer drinking was part of every visit. The drawer was always full.

　　On this visit, Father Harry took the four teachers to his favorite restaurant, *Im Vino Veritas*, and asked after dinner for the host to bring out *Flaumen Schnaps*, or *Prunau*, as the locals called it. Megan refused the drink as she had already had her one 'safe' glass of wine, but the others ordered the drink. A little flag skewered a prune in each glass. No one else liked prunes, so Megan volunteered to eat their prunes. By the time she had eaten four prunes, Father Harry had to carry her out of the restaurant and back to the car. It seemed that *Flaumen Schnaps* is made from steeping prunes in alcohol for months, so the lonely little prunes probably had more alcohol in them than the drinks themselves. Harry made it a point to tell his Bavarian friends that Megan was the only teacher he had ever seen that could get falling down drunk on four little prunes. The proprietors never saw Megan after that without asking if she wanted a prune from the *Schnaps* vat. Their big grins warmed her with the private joke.

The teachers had more time to enjoy downtown Bamberg as well. The whole inner city was one big historic district, and while owners could modernize the inside of their buildings, they were forced by law to leave the outside in its historic condition.

Walking the deeply worn steps of the *Dom Platz*, Megan could almost *feel* centuries of footsteps. She was finding it comforting to be a part of history--to be carrying it on in some small way. However, thinking of this always forced her to wonder just what her small part would be, now that she would be doing it alone. Her imagination allowed her, in a quiet moment, to faintly hear the conversations of a thousand years. But then her reveries would be interrupted at noon every day when all twenty-nine of the city's churches pealed out their bells in mutual cacophony. Of course, twenty-nine breweries lined the river to complement the churches, as well--the mark of a well-balanced city, Lila claimed.

Field trips, from map-reading exercises to shopping expeditions at the open-air market created downtown adventures. Megan and Tim took their fifth graders down to the old *Rathaus* Bridge one rare, sunny day. The children used the wide bridge railings as easels to sketch scenes along the river where fishermen's nets dried in the wind. German pedestrians offered suggestions, so the children practiced their conversational language skills. The teachers stood by, amused, while an old man pointed out something to a ten-year old. When he didn't understand, the old man got frustrated, grabbed the pastel chalk from the boy's hand, and drew the feature in, himself. Both the old man and the child smiled at the result.

In addition to seeing the German culture first hand, the children also learned to use the city's buses. After taking them on each trip, Megan's homework assignment was for the children to take a parent downtown on the bus and get them home again without getting lost. "So many of these young mothers are fearful of going out onto the foreign economy," Megan told her friends later.

"I wish they would take advantage of learning more about the

German culture while they're stationed here," echoed Emily. "It's the chance of a lifetime they'll probably never be able to afford once they go home. Twenty years from now they'll break the bank for a two-week European vacation, and wonder why they hadn't learned more German while they had the chance."

Megan felt a certain pride in overcoming her fear of moving comfortably in a foreign country and sharing the joy with her class.

Tim, Kelly, and Megan decided to take their three fifth grade classes on a *Volksmarsch* one Saturday when no alert was in progress. Tim explained, "It's a 10 to 20 kilometer hike followed by a fest with music and food. You'll get a medal picturing a local landmark, and you can collect medals from seeing Germany literally foot by foot." The ten-year-olds were as eager as their teachers.

This walking route was where Coberg Castle, an old fortress, overlooked the communist zone. It was slushy, rainy, snowy, and the ninety ten-year-olds and three teachers slipped in the mud, frequently able to make progress up the steep slopes only by forming a human chain between trees. No one was in any mood for the news they received once over the hill and back down. It seemed the tenth Kilometer of the route went inside the one-Kilometer zone that was off-limits to Americans. A *Volksmarsch* official suggested they return the way they had come, back up and over the slippery castle hill, and he'd give the children their medals at the starting line.

Tim stared at the man. "I'm not going back up that hill."

Kelly wiped her skinned knee through her torn jeans and long johns, and echoed his comment, "Neither am I."

"I really don't think the kids can do it again," said Megan. "Let's ask them."

Unanimously, the children vetoed re-climbing the muddy hill for nine Kilometers when they were within one level Kilometer of the end. They were too tired, too cold, too wet, and the teachers already feared there'd be a zillion colds at the end of this outing.

So, marching proudly, and humming along with the oom-pah band they could already hear coming from the tent at the end of the *Volksmarsch* route, the group finished their trek alongside the hated, fortified fence of the Border zone, under the watchful binoculars of Soviet communist guards. "Don't you dare speak English," Tim whispered to the children, not wanting the guards, or the passing West Germans, to document that they had violated the regulations.

Megan had a vague sensation of being watched. In peripheral vision, she noticed a man standing near the path seemed familiar in some way—something about the way he slouched. She had noticed him a couple of places along the trail, and she looked again, trying to place the man. But he turned his back, pulled down his hat brim, and walked a few feet into the woods. She shook her head and ushered her young children into the warm Fest Tent. But she saw the man again in the parking lot where she and the other teachers loaded the children aboard the school bus. When she looked his way, he climbed hurriedly into a dark car and drove away, with his wheels spinning on the gravel. *Must have been imagining all that. No one would have reason to follow my kids. Megan, my girl, you are getting paranoid.*

Of course, their principal had the report of their entering the One K zone on his desk before their busses even arrived home. Protocol demanded he call the three teachers on the carpet and scold them, but when he heard the circumstances, and what their alternative would have been--three more hours uphill in the mud, he agreed they had done what he would have done as well, so the dressing down they had expected went no further up the chain of command.

Then, in a climate of increased military accidents, even the school had one. A bus with junior high kids on their way to Ansbach to compete in a drama festival lost control, slid, and turned on its side on the slippery road. One child got a broken wrist, but she would probably have lost her hand, or worse, had not Gus, the bus driver, grabbed her and flung her backwards when she started to fall through the exit stairwell. The door had inexplicably opened.

It was a frightening accident, but thankfully, there were no more serious injuries, and another 'tin can military bus' went to pick up the kids. They put on their play after all, with assorted bumps and bruises, having learned that "...the show must go on."

Afterward, Gus complained that the fluid line in the steering system had broken, but he had inspected it only minutes before they started. He also felt it highly suspicious that the door should have opened upon impact when it was designed to stay sturdily closed. He demanded of Rex Top Cop to have some answers once the accident was investigated, but, mysteriously, no cause could be found.

Chapter 17

In March, the officers were on edge over news events soon to have devastating effects upon the Cold War Border—the last military groups leaving Vietnam, plus new CIA Congressional Investigations. Veterans of the Vietnam conflict believed Nixon and Kissinger's pullout of troops was a 'sell-out.' Stan was especially upset.

"That so-called truce and dividing line they negotiated," he said, "was all phony--a ploy to save face for the administration."

"Saigon can't hold out long—a month at most," said Charlie. "It's my guess that Nixon kept our troops there long enough so Saigon wouldn't fall before his reelection. Now, all of a sudden we are 'friends' with China, and we don't even send help, when the Thais, Cambodians, South Vietnamese, and the Montagnard fighters we trained are wiped out by the communists.

"It makes me mad," continued Stan, "that before the truce, we were ordered to hold the highlands at all costs, even though my men had no equipment, food, or medicine for days, and several friends were killed. Then these same big wigs evacuated the highlands, and tried to handle everything from the coastal lowlands.' They knew they couldn't do it, even then!"

"In the mid 60's, Westmoreland built bases and launched search and destroy missions, but it was too easy for the enemy to hide and pop up later," said Robert, who was spending more and more time with Abby. She sat beside him on the couch. "In 1970 and 71, Abrams put small units in the bushes, and everyone piled on if the enemy came by. We had the war won in '72! Now negotiations have given it all away. As much as I hated being in Vietnam, I'd be on the next plane back if they'd let us honor our commitment without micromanagement from the top."

"You wouldn't be alone," said Stan. The other veterans nodded agreement.

Carl took a swig of beer. "While we're at it, let's stop these Congressional committees and nosy newsmen covering CIA hearings. They've leaked information that got one of our Military Intelligence operatives killed in Heidelberg. I doubt he'll be the last."

Rex Top Cop, joining the group's discussion, added, "Their

hearings should be secret. We know we have men working undercover in Europe, especially along our Border and the Wall in Berlin. The other side has them too. It's a giant game of cat and mouse. But our intelligence operatives risk their necks to get us advance warning to defend our troops and our Border. They're being exposed and jeopardized every time some dummy Stateside opens his mouth or prints a newspaper."

"Of course, the newspapers didn't say the man assassinated was Military Intelligence or CIA," said John Sutton, himself in Military Intelligence, "and they keep calling it 'an accident,' but it was no accident! The commies and the Middle East terrorists send their best assassination teams across the Border to ferret out our undercover people, kill them, and neutralize their contacts wherever they can find them. They'd like to put our whole secret network out of commission, and *our* Congress is helping them do it! I'm wondering how our operative in Heidelberg got his cover blown."

"Well, they're practically shouting out names of undercover agents in Congress because one stupid newsman and one senator published 'investigative' stories," said Stan. "It's irresponsible."

"Perhaps we should change the subject, guys," said Rex, as he noticed the startled looks on Megan and Abby's faces. "We're scaring our best lady friends out of their nylons."

All eyes turned to the women. Megan said, "I wasn't sure we even *had* undercover operatives. Living here with you guys, we know the Cold War is serious, but I didn't know about these cloak and dagger things. Everyone back home thinks the world will be at peace as soon as the last helicopter is out of Saigon."

"We know you'd never talk about what you hear from us when we let off steam," said Rex. "You're under the gun with us, and you two handle it well. I hope the other gals are as closed-mouthed." His rather pointed reference was not lost on the two teachers.

Abby threw a glance at Megan, and she knew they were both thinking of Lila, and wondering where she was this night. "We don't mind letting you 'vent' with us," Abby said. "We practically feel like we're in the Army once we're here at the border."

"We're here whenever you need us. Why if the tension gets too great, I'm even good at shoulder massage," Megan added with a grin, throwing up her hands with wriggling fingers.

Stan dropped to his stomach at her feet, waiting, and they all broke into the laughter that kept tensions at bay, *most* of the time.

"I still wonder who in our government is blowing up the 'Trojan Horse' to distract the public and cover their own backsides," said Stan. It wasn't long before they knew, as news of the President's cover-ups and tapes surfaced, and impeachment discussions began.

The remainder of the school year flew by. Frequent alerts and worrisome military accidents at the Border remained constant. Between alerts, members of the large group of friends kept social life active with a variety of parties. In one of his particularly crude jokes, Luke smugly hired a 'lady friend' as a '21st birthday present' for young Lieutenant Fred Fleming. Freddy resurfaced, three days later, somewhat the worse for wear, blushing for days, and somehow everyone kept a straight face.

Megan was reminded of another fact of life overseas when several transferring teachers and officers held a moving sale of hanging plants and furnishings they couldn't take along and gave away their booze to friends in order to continue the party tradition. In the military life, everyone eventually moved on. The idea of losing friends still seemed a catastrophe to the young woman.

Megan's life was changing, or perhaps mellowing. With Carl as her guide, she had become comfortable traveling either with him, or with the group. He sometimes called after school. "Hi, Megan, what are your plans after Volleyball on Wednesday?" This was usually followed by, "I need to be saved from a life of promiscuity and non meaningful relationships. How are *you* feeling?" They could laugh over his unending and unrepentant propositions, and they'd spend comfortable time together talking over any problems.

Megan had finally come to understand that no one really *did* worry about the business of others except to help when needed. The cultural changes of the sixties and seventies had loosened up the world's value systems, and she relaxed her panic for friends who chose different roads. She was never quite sure she understood her odd friendship with Carl. But it had set her on the road back to enjoying life and being more open. For that, she was grateful. Carl summed it up with, "We're good to each other, Megan. That gives comfort and confidence to both of us."

Big Ed had returned to Bamberg frequently, and he called

Megan on her school phone every Friday afternoon. Every phone call became a guessing game as he tried to let her know where he was and when he would be back. He would say, "Remember the plan I told you about to the North? The dates have been moved back. The Southeast plan takes precedence. I might make your *Seehof* party if the 'I' job doesn't interfere. If I haven't called by your dispensary appointment, call me at the number I gave you next to last."

These clues would tell her what she needed to know in order to expect him, or not, but attempted to avoid compromising his position on the insecure phone line. But then she would have to solve the puzzles by remembering which was the North plan, which was the Southeast plan, what were the last dates he called, what was the "I " job, when was her dispensary appointment, which party had they discussed, and in which order had he given her the phone numbers? Complicated? Very! Yet Megan enjoyed the man's delightful little surprises of popping in, even though it might mean his three-hour drive for a one-hour lunch together.

They enjoyed dinners together whenever he could get away, but these visits occurred more often during alerts when everyone else was gone, so few of her male friends had met him. Ed seemed to prefer it that way. They could talk and laugh for hours about almost anything—except his job. It puzzled Megan that Ed came and went with as much secrecy as Emily's Ambassador, and sometimes she wondered if he, also, was a figment of her imagination. Though she didn't know what he really did in the Army, she feared such secrecy probably meant it was dangerous. He changed the subject smoothly, and with a smile, if her questions got too precise.

Megan had gradually become more comfortable dating, but she regarded it as merely enjoying activities with dear friends, much like activities with her girlfriends. She tended to keep men on the perimeter, not quite sure where her life would take her, or if she could feel completely secure with someone else, though she found herself thinking frequently of Ed. She wondered if she could ever again fall in love. But she was happier, more able to enjoy good times with others, and gradually growing more confident with her own decisions.

The 2/2 Cavalry Ball held at a palace downtown was magical with thousands of candles in sconces on the mirrored walls, officers resplendent in their dress blue uniforms, and elegant ladies in their formals. It was custom that a soldier follow the lead of his commander, so regardless of the growing heat in the ballroom, no one dared loosen a tie. Megan was dancing with the commander, Lt. Col. Brett Wheeler, on a particularly lively disco piece that seemed endless, and all the officers were sweating. Brett, being formal, took no notice. So, while they were dancing, Megan impetuously untied Brett's tie and flung it across the room. Immediately, ties were flying all over the ballroom. Next, Megan peeled Brett out of his jacket. This time, he grabbed it himself and sent it sailing. Within seconds, the air was filled with jackets, and the whole group enjoyed the laughter.

Afterward, Megan remarked to her friends that she had discovered Brett had a sense of humor, after all. The young officers congratulated her on getting the 'old man' to lighten up a bit. He had actually laughed and enjoyed himself once he relaxed his 'dignity.'

Soon there were two Changes of Command for Battalion Commander friends. This was a tradition where the troops of a unit all marched together and the colors were passed from the old commander to the new commander. A colleague covered her class for the couple of hours needed for Lt. Col. Sam Street's ceremony of the Infantry and she was quite impressed with his military bearing as he steered his nearly seven-foot frame around the parade ground.

The next day was Brett's Change of Command and, knowing Megan could not get a substitute teacher, Brett invited her class to come as well. They were on their best behavior and were excited when Lt. Colonel Wheeler seated them in the grandstand with the visiting dignitaries, including General Patton II, whom the children thought looked like Santa Claus. But they were *most* impressed by the Cavalry's firing of tank and artillery cannons, mortars, red, white, and blue smoke bombs surrounding the field, tanks rolling, and horses at the gallop. One of the students almost fell out of the grandstand watching rockets and, in her excitement she screamed out, "This sure is a good show!" The whole audience roared.

Afterward, Brett said with a grin, "Do you think maybe we overdid it a bit?"

But with Sam and Brett both leaving, commanders that she had first met in an effort to get their support for their Ski Club soldiers, but who had become cherished friends, it brought home to Megan again that nothing in military life would ever remain the same.

Megan's mom arrived in May to share the last month of school so they could travel a bit, then fly home together for the summer vacation. Mrs. Bent went with Megan to school daily to help out with end-of-the-year projects. She immediately became "Grandma" to these overseas children who moved so often that they rarely had a Grandma in their lives.

Sylvia, especially, latched on to Grandma right away, and Megan smiled, watching them together. Sylvia had been her heartbreak of the year, a child with brain cancer. She had hung on through early June, loving school and seeming to rally a little at times. Her father made arrangements for a compassionate retention for Sylvia, so she could remain a second year in Megan's class, though her twin sister was going on to sixth grade.

"You understand Sylvia, and she wants to stay with you," he had said. "She might as well be happy for whatever time she has left."

Watching Sylvia enjoy every moment of life that she could, Megan realized the little girl's struggle had made her own previous unhappiness seem insignificant. Her whole philosophy of life had changed perspective in only one school year with the military family of Bamberg. Her mom noticed the changes in Megan, and commented that she was much relieved.

Megan's friends also adopted Mrs. Bent as "Mom." They included her in all their plans.

"Hey," said Carl, after dancing with Megan's mom one night, "I've decided I want a James girl. I love your mom, and she won't have me. I love you, and you won't have me. Your daughters are too far away. I may have to wait to pursue a granddaughter someday."

Her mother relished the laughter with Carl when he announced, "I'm going to have to convince you to 'hustle' me, (flirt) aren't I?" It was love at first sight.

Of course, Mom's presence was comforting to Megan, since she felt that her mother approved of her caring friends, her new life, and believed her life was again productive.

The three fifth grade teachers put on an 1800's-style picnic as culmination of their year-end research units on American history. The event took place the last day of school on the terrace and in the wooded area behind the Officers' Club.

Lila came along to help with the authentic games--wheelbarrow and sack races, and she brought Klaus. Though several kids tried to include him in rolling hoops or walking on tin can stilts, he avoided the children altogether. Megan felt uncomfortable when Klaus was right behind her almost every time she turned around, yet when she asked him for help with some activity, he moved away and whispered to Lila. *How odd he is,* Megan thought.

Lila cornered Megan to ask, "When will Big Ed be coming back to see you? Hasn't it been a couple of weeks since he was here?"

"I really don't know, Lila. He'll call Friday. And right now, I don't have time to talk about it." She helped one of her boys skewer a hot dog with a stick for roasting.

"Klaus would like to meet with you when Ed comes again."

"Why is Klaus so interested? If Ed gets a day off, he just wants to do something quiet, and I don't usually know much in advance."

"I know. I told Klaus that you're the *only* one who ever knows if he's coming here or not, and I thought maybe you'd tell us."

"Us?" Megan was confused. "You and Klaus? I don't really like thinking of you two as a couple." She found herself responding irritably, "And why is anyone else interested in the comings and goings of a friend of mine, when half the time, I don't even know where he is?" She helped one of the children scoop baked beans onto her paper plate. "Lila, I don't have time for this, as you can see. I love you dearly, but right now, I just need you both to help me with kids."

Lila walked to where Klaus still hovered. Megan noted they were having an argument. Klaus stomped off alone, jumped into his black sedan and roared away, as Lila mopped her eyes with a handkerchief. Megan wondered about this sudden interest in her personal life--and in Big Ed's. What business was it of Klaus's? She resolved to discuss it with Lila after the children's event was over.

Lila went over to help Marco and Megan's mother, who had hit it off well and were watching closely as the children roasted their own hot dogs and marshmallows over an open fire. Megan saw her mother bending to conspire with young Sylvia about hiding behind Marco, whichever way he turned. Marco went along with the prank by pretending he couldn't find the little girl.

As the day ended, the children gathered their prizes and hugged the teachers goodbye for the summer. *What a remarkable year,* Megan thought. *These children are so brave.* Her good feeling dissipated as she saw Lila moving toward her.

"Can you give me a ride home? Klaus left in a huff."

Megan nodded, and walked toward the Fiat.

Her mother claimed she would wait for Megan's return at the O'Club where she'd be busy 'helping' Marco. *Mom senses that Lila and I need to talk alone. Perceptive lady!*

The teachers loaded game paraphernalia into the car, and Megan drove slowly over the cobblestone street and turned into the countryside. She was not sure how to talk to Lila.

"I've been worried about you, Lila, and I'm not the only one."

Lila looked up, startled.

"You seem to be growing closer to Klaus, even though you two fight all the time. We hardly see you anymore. He only shows up where the military officers are. Luke said he even saw Klaus hanging around the airport, alone. Are you serious about this guy?"

"Sort of." Lila seemed unconscious of the incongruity of Klaus' being at the airfield where civilians weren't supposed to be. "He's attentive. He buys me gifts. He was just being strange today. I like it that he can be here with me when Brian is out at the Border. I don't like to be lonesome. The officers are gone too much. Maybe I don't want a military man, after all."

Lila giggled nervously. "Klaus puzzles me sometimes. He hangs out at the bookstore, and with some people I don't know. I don't mind his having a life of his own, but he never introduces me to his friends. Yet he always insists on meeting mine." She sighed. "And you're right. He seems particularly interested in Ed, and whatever it is that Ed does." She patted her hair in the characteristic gesture Megan always noticed when her friend was afraid of her own questions.

"Megan, is it possible not to really know how you feel about someone or how they feel about you, even when you've spent a lot of time with them?"

"I suppose it's possible--for awhile. But, if you really feel unsure of someone, or his interest is more in our military officers than in you, *that* should tell you something, too."

Lila remained silent as she got out in front of her apartment.

It was their last conversation—a rather unfinished one--before both flew Stateside for the summer vacation.

Chapter 18

When Megan returned from her summer visit home, Carl welcomed her at Frankfurt Airport and drove her to her apartment to shower and talk a couple of hours. "Do you feel up to lunch later?"

Megan stretched and yawned. "Great! I want to see our friends and find out how their summers went. I'm so pleased with mine. My school district approved another year's leave of absence. My kids and my mom felt I was recovering my old energy and optimism. I'm here with everyone's blessing." She asked, "Do *you* think I'm okay now, too? You would know better than anyone."

Carl winked. "Why, I'd even say you're practically normal, if someone like *you* can ever achieve that state." She smacked at him as he dodged. "I missed you, though."

"I missed you too. But we've got lots of plans before you're rotated back to Fort Rucker."

"I may extend an extra year, just to take care of you through the school year. And I can think of lots of things I'd like to do." His 'Groucho' eyebrows were in play.

She smiled, reconciled to his usual banter. "At least you're always consistent and predictable, my friend, but it doesn't look like you've aged enough for me while I was gone."

"It wasn't for lack of trying. I had a hard landing on the Border that should have aged me ten years--to escape crashing into a high wire tower. They gave me a new crew chief to break in. He was green as grass—no good at all when it came to watching the terrain or reading maps. He made a major navigational error in Nap of the Earth, NOE flying at high speed and close to the ground. There's no way at that speed that I can stop and read a map—I *have* to depend on him. I'd rather have my old crew chief back!"

Megan's heart dropped. "How horrible! Was everyone okay?"

"Yeah, just bruises…no major stuff. But it aged me ten years to come screaming around a hill, look up from a quick check of my engine instruments, and see wires and orange warning balls coming at my rotors. Managed to duck the high tension wires, but then saw low telephone wires—too low to go under, too high to go over, so I over-torked the helicopter and stood it on its tail to get up and over.

Chopped off a few tree limbs with the blade before the thing stalled out. Reflexes, good eyes, and adrenalin, baby--that's all we've got to save a helicopter."

Megan squashed her feelings of panic and forced herself to smile mischievously, "I really hope you're more careful with whom you fly in the future. I still want you to have that wonderful wife and the children who'll make a long life worth living for you."

"Yeah, yeah, yeah! Luke and I *did* get in some good duty for the summer, though." He had that smirky grin she knew so well.

"What do you mean?"

"They loaned us and our helicopters to the German government to fly lifeguard duty around the lakes and watch for swimmers in trouble, or those in unauthorized areas, since many drowned last year. We just found all kinds of suspicious actions to fly low and look for."

Suddenly she got it. "The women in Germany sunbathe without their tops around the lakes, don't they? You two were out there observing..."

"You got it! Now let's go eat. There's a dance at the Club tonight."

They found their friends at the Officers' Club, as always. Stan and Charlie regaled them with stories of their July visit to Pamplona, Spain, for the traditional running of the bulls.

"It was a bad year—five people killed, and twenty-three gored," said Stan. "We spent half our time running from the bulls, and the other half trying to turn bulls away from people scrambling on the ground." He grew thoughtful. "You know, I was more scared in the streets of Pamplona than I was in Vietnam. Those bulls were so 'mindless.' At least in Vietnam, the enemy was somewhat predictable. But those bulls charged at one person then suddenly, unreasonably, they'd gore someone else. You could predict nothing!"

"He was a bloody hero, though," said Charlie. "Pulled some gored guys up onto the fence away from the bull that had other ideas. Next year's seventh month, seventh day, seventh hour, you *all* are joining us camping for a week in Pamplona. Start making plans now."

Megan wondered about that idea, and suddenly realized she was considering it—something she would not have done a year ago.

But soon she found herself absorbed in her friends' disgust at U.S. policy and the recent Department of Defense funding shortages.

"As usual," said Robert, "one of President Ford's congressional budget idiots has decided to change gears for the military--again. They bring in McNamara's 100,000 men with no skills in order to do away with an unpopular draft. Now, Congress has cut military funding, wants to cut military personnel, and has decided to get rid of the trained officers."

"We're all a bit uptight," said Big Don, "waiting to see if we'll be RIFfed or not."

At Abby's cocked eyebrow, he added, "Reduction In Force--military officers losing careers by being forced out of the service, some with only a few years until retirement. It'll leave a shortage of experienced personnel and an overabundance of the inexperienced. Best Army in the world, and we're going to lose many of our people."

"I imagine this budget tightening will hit the schools as well," said Stan. You civilian teachers will discover what it's like under the thumb of Congressional purse strings."

Stan's words were proven correct. The Department of Defense had not yet signed teaching contracts, so none of the teachers could be paid. As usual, their military friends stepped in. Stan announced, "Don't worry. You girls can fix dinner for us after the paychecks start coming again. We'll keep having parties for you until then." The new teachers were horrified of being 'beholden' to these men, but the 'old teachers' reassured them that they were now part of the Border family too. Teachers were barely hanging on, financially.

Everyone ran their usual tab at the O'Club knowing Marco would carry them until they began receiving paychecks again. At a champagne brunch, the hosts offered Megan and Abby a large bag of apples. Megan stayed up half the night teaching Abby to make apple pies. They ate pie for breakfast, lunch, and dinner until they never wanted to see another apple. Actually, Abby was becoming a really great cook, though, graduating into the gourmet category.

But DoDDS teachers were nothing if not resilient. They flew into the rush inherent in the start of school overseas, making plans for the children, helping the new crop of teachers get settled, and scrounging materials for their classrooms. Much had changed in only a year. Megan, herself now on the 'meeter-greeter' team, was amused when one homesick new teacher cried all the way from the airport to Bamberg, yet quickly spotted Charlie upon arrival, and dried her tears for good. "Charlie will never know what hit him," Megan later confided to Emily.

For their first party, Mary baked beans and meatballs. But Rex Top Cop brought his Doberman, and the dog gobbled them all. The rest of the gang laughingly resorted to "A loaf of bread, a jug of wine, and thou…" cheese, French bread, and wine, while Robert recited the Rubaiyat of Omar Khayyam to accompany their simple repast. As always, life on the Border was spontaneous chaos, and Megan felt happy she had come 'home.'

As Megan shed her own depression, she waded in to bolster others, as her friends had done for her the previous year. Officer and teacher friends tried to keep each other optimistic through troubles. Abby started her own measles epidemic, unhappily bemoaning the fact that she should get a 'kid's disease.' The teacher most critical of others fell for Rex Top Cop's 'bean strategy,' and was devastated after his usual three-day romance ended. The disadvantage was that she truly believed she was in love with Rex and was terribly hurt by his notoriously short attention span. The advantage was that she had no more narrow words about others. Bamberg was an epidemic with so many suffering from broken hearts, warts, hangnails, and diarrhea. Half the school was out with mononucleosis, 'shared' from one child in fourth grade.

"Anything else?" wrote Megan to her mom. "Oh, yes, Stan sprained his ankle jumping off a river bridging unit, and he can't keep his pants up since he lost so much weight. And Carl wants me to go to Lake Chiemsee with him for a week of sailing lessons. I can't even swim!"

Chaos in the classrooms wasn't any better. Since the government hadn't signed a contract with janitors, either, classrooms had no supplies, furniture remained stacked around the walls, and floors were neither scrubbed nor waxed. Military friends came to the rescue to whip things back into a semblance of order before the first day of school.

Also, due to government budget problems, classrooms were overcrowded. Megan was alarmed to find herself the only fifth grade teacher for 116 children, apparently a DoDDS *surprise*, almost yearly. Tim had transferred, and Kelly had resigned, but replacements had either not shown up, or had decided that life at this isolated Border Post was too rough and had gone back home. The Department of Defense based new hiring on deliberately *under*estimating their needs for the following year. So classes had to be jumbled and juggled until extra teachers could be hired and the children parceled out more evenly. Everyone took it in stride.

But the budget crunch had left no ditto paper, at least until the new fiscal year. Stan tried to fill the gap by collecting paper used on only one side by military battalions at the Post.

Gratefully, the teachers printed on the opposite sides for class work. Sometimes the plan backfired, however, and there were new 'tragedies of the day' to share. Abby passed out a science lesson to her junior high students, but was forced to pick up the papers quickly when she discovered the backside had a 'top secret' stamp on it two inches high, while a JAG paper had the name of one of her students.

A day later, a boy in Lila's class noticed the backside of his science assignment had step-by-step directions, quite graphically illustrated, on how to deliver a baby, straight from the Post's Medical Department. Naturally, he shouted out his discovery to his classmates. After a few more such fiascos, the supply man wangled some new paper from another school--where else, but Nürnberg. The women wondered what it would be like to teach on a large, well-stocked Post. Probably not nearly so much fun, they decided. This outpost near the Border called upon all the creativity one could muster. The teachers enjoyed both the challenge and the humorous snafus.

Carol, a first grade teacher, had her own moment of panic when a student at *Muna* handed her a rusty grenade he'd found while digging under some bushes on the playground. Trying to remain 'cool,' she flagged down the nearest soldier, who walked very carefully to the bomb disposal unit. The buried German 'potato masher' grenade from the Second World War was rusted, but still dangerous. On the same *Muna* campus, where mysterious trains, well-guarded and covered, brought in unmentionable cargos during each alert, a second grader decided he was the 'bionic boy' and could run out to stop such a nuke train, single-handedly. He was surprised when his teacher sprang from the classroom after him and tussled him to the ground before he could reach the tracks. Even teachers were constantly required to stay alert.

The ladies decided that teaching overseas would *never* be like teaching back in the States. But here, they'd learned to take such things in stride, laughing at each new crisis as one of the unique adventures of living. They loved their jobs, loved their children, and loved Bamberg.

Once school was safely underway, Megan had further talks with the Battalion Commanders, with whom she was now on a first name basis. They continued to encourage their young enlisted soldiers into Ski Club, and allowed posters advertising parties and trips in the barracks. The Ski Club officers began novice trips to Europe's glaciers just for the young troops from the barracks, so they'd already be advanced beginners when the *real* Club trips began.

One of the better skiers, usually Stan, Luke, Abby, or Vern-- whoever could get away, would go along to do the teaching, while Megan handled the trip planning, hotels, and *coaxing* for the new skiers. She'd become quite comfortable shepherding these young eighteen to twenty year olds. They accepted her 'big sisterly' counseling and, because of her own initial disasters in learning to ski, she was patient with those struggling down their first slope.

Before long, there were hundreds of members involved in Ski Club, and the club's parties and trips had become the hottest ticket in Bamberg. Luke was to be the new president for the year, and Megan was elected secretary. She knew it would mean keeping Luke sober and organized, at least for meetings, but Carl and Stan insisted she was up to the job.

Thus the fall went by quickly with student outings, teaching adventures, and parties, and the women knew they belonged in the Border's military community. Each had been 'adopted' into one of the military units and Megan's unit was 2/78 Artillery. This meant an initiation of 'Artillery Punch,' which she decided must have every alcoholic beverage in the world, plus turpentine, or some equally volatile liquid, included for good measure. She was surprised to find later that Abby's unit, 1/52 Infantry, had only had to endure a civilized glass of white wine. Megan loved these brave military people, all of them, and listened to the problems of each as though they were her own. She was also beginning to realize that perhaps she didn't want to stay alone for the rest of her life, and enjoyed dating more. She had crossed many new borders and was again becoming aware of the goodness in life and the joy of caring for others.

By November, the latest shake-up in President Ford's cabinet was the topic of concern.

"Schlessinger was the only voice of reason in defense spending," Charlie started one evening during dinner at the Club. "And now he's gone—just another victim of disagreement with Kissenger over this detente foolishness."

"I think the military has absorbed all the cuts it can handle *now*," said Jeff.

"Yeah," added Stan. "We're hopelessly behind on budget, and Kissinger is gambling on the 'good will' of the Soviets and China not to start anything while we're broke." He put away another couple of bites of his steak and continued. "I can't understand his rationale, certainly not after seeing examples of China's 'good will' in Vietnam, and Soviet 'good will' here at our own Border. The man needs to spend a week right here, on alert, facing Soviet tanks."

Megan was intrigued. "There you go educating us on international affairs again. I'd never even been interested before I knew you guys and got to worrying about all of you."

"We enjoy having you gals worry about us," said Charlie, with a big grin, as his girlfriend snuggled by his side. "We're also glad you're on our volleyball team for the mixed tournament next week. So let's go practice, and we'll hope old Kissinger drops into a creek."

"So much for political discussion," said Abby, already gathering her coat and gloves.

The gang won the tournament in twelve games against all challengers. Of course, that called for another party.

Worried by a young lieutenant's attempted suicide over pressure from a particularly rank-bucking commander, the Ski Club leadership conned the young man into going on the next group trip, watching him carefully. Skiing directly behind him on one of the high passes, Megan had a moment of panic when she saw him approach a cliff. Is he okay now? Will he stop? He did, and asked her to sit down beside him near the precipice. As they sat quietly, the young man finally said, "I'm so thankful I didn't miss this spectacular view today." Megan realized it was his moment to be glad his suicide attempt had been unsuccessful, and she knew what the moment meant to him. They took each other's photos to remember the day and skied together down the hill screaming, "It's great to be alive!" One of life's revelations, they had found.

The next Saturday, Robert and his roommates invited the gang for lasagna at their apartment. It was a relatively quiet group, with everyone sitting around on the floor, talking and listening to music. Yet about 2100 hours, the lights went out. Abby was terrified, with her normally secret claustrophobia kicking into high gear until Charlie found and lit several candles. But losing the stereo, endangering the refrigerator and ice supply, and having no water were definite problems. This building was old, and the German water pumps operated electrically so, 'no electricity, no flushie.' The two men went upstairs to find the landlord. The man met them at the door with a gun pointed at them. He had taken out the fuses, since he didn't want them to have any parties.

"The guy is crazy!" said Robert. It put the damper on their quiet gathering.

The guys felt so bad that the landlord had spoiled the party, but the ladies talked them out of going back up to confront the man. "No use getting someone shot over it," said Abby, "and any civilian adult who thinks he must run around pointing a gun is spooky anyway."

Megan unaccountably thought of Klaus, and the way he always kept one hand in his coat pocket. It was a startling moment of revelation. *I'll bet it's a gun he's hiding in there. I need to find a tactful way to talk to Lila about this.*

Chapter 19

A week later, an artillery captain, Vance, invited Carl and Megan to go glacier skiing with him at Hintertux. He wanted to teach his new girlfriend, an elegant blonde, to ski. On the drive to Austria, Vance persuaded Vera to room with him, though he seemed reluctant to leave Megan and Carl 'stuck' with each other, since only two rooms were available.

Once the younger couple had retired, Carl and Megan leaned against their own door and collapsed into giggles over Vance's nervousness. "You aren't shocked anymore, are you?"

"I guess I'm through being concerned about what others do or think. And as long as it's you, it's a bit too late to be concerned about us being together, isn't it? No problem."

Carl smiled. "You've grown up a lot, and we enjoy spending time together, anyway." Then he confessed, "You know, I dated Vera only last week. But that's the story of my life." He threw up his hands emphasizing his point. "Someone else always gets the girls."

When Megan looked at him with direct, honest eyes and a hint of surprise, he chuckled and revised the comment. "Don't worry. It really wasn't any good—we'd just both had far too much to drink. I knew she was a mistake immediately. I think she knew I was too."

He took Megan's hand, quite formally. "Do you want the shower first, Milady, or will you share?" He knew enough to dodge out of reach quickly.

The morning brought unbelievable beauty, with cobalt sky and brilliant sun reflecting off crystals of snow. Jackets, hats, and scarves were discarded. Carl and Vance even took off their shirts, receiving blistering sunburns. They passed an Austrian woman at the summit who had removed her top, and was lying in a half-shell of aluminum foil, attempting to get an Alpine tan while her companions went off to ski. At the end of the day, however, the story was all over the street that the woman's friends came back later to find her dead. They said it was something about how the intense rays had sort of 'cooked' her from within as she lay in the foil.

With his hair sun-bleached almost white and his fair skin,

Carl's sunburn was particularly bad. No one knew sun reflecting off snow would burn the under side of noses and ears. He was one miserable puppy, and the strange woman's death had frightened Megan. She bathed Carl's face, ears, and back in cold water every two hours, to help stop the pain, and applied burn ointment often. The following day, she insisted they wear their scarves over their faces, 'bandito' style and, though they shed their jackets, the two men no longer wanted to remove hats and shirts.

But Vera was afraid to ski, sitting down on the bunny slope, even when Vance skied backwards and bent over, holding her ski tips together in a safe snowplow. She refused to try.

Vance handed Vera some money and his car keys saying, "Do what you want. Carl, Megan, and I are skiing. See ya' around." Vera seemed almost relieved as she headed out to shop in the village. The remaining trio skied all day and thoroughly enjoyed whizzing down slopes to quaint Alpine huts perched on the sides of the valley below with their endless views of mountain upon mountain. "I get much more enjoyment skiing than I get with Vera," Vance pronounced. Just like that, the romance was over.

Carl caught Megan's eyes with a grin. "See, didn't I tell you she was a mistake?"

Two days later, Megan, Emily, and Lila were at Abby's apartment for dinner.

"You guys won't believe what our crazy Engineers did yesterday," said Megan. "I broke off a light bulb in its socket and didn't know how to get the remains out without getting zapped. I asked Charlie, figuring he would know. He, Stan, and Robert all screamed, 'don't! We'll fix it!' Between the three of them, they managed to short-circuit my stove, burn out three fuses, and eat five dozen chocolate chip cookies. They finally stuck a potato in the socket and unscrewed the innards of the broken light bulb."

When the laughter died, she added, "You guys should hear what Robert told me. He said, 'You'll never be able to manage alone if you go back to California without us.' He may be right," she added, with a faint smile.

"Does that mean you're thinking about staying permanently?" asked Emily.

"I don't know. But I'd hate to leave all you guys. I'm sort of thinking it over."

Lila seemed happy about the idea. "Then you'll quit your stateside job instead of going back after this leave of absence?"

"I've heard this is the big DoDDS dilemma for teachers every year, and I suppose I'd be silly to give up a job in the states, yet I'm reluctant to leave my life and friends here. It will probably depend on my kids and my mom."

"Surely they can see that you're more alive here," said Abby.

Emily added, "We've all seen you go from a scared, potential suicide victim to one of the most active people in Bamberg. We all rely on you." She picked up her embroidery and took a few stitches in her calm matter-of-fact manner.

Megan was startled. "I didn't think it showed...about the suicidal thoughts, I mean."

"It doesn't matter, because I think you're over it now," Emily replied. "You're needed here, Megan, permanently. Department of Defense Schools and the military are good lives."

Megan realized she should have known her friends had recognized her secret fears. Relieved at not having to hide her former depression anymore, she smiled. "I think my mom understands because she's been here and has met you all. My kids may not be so sure, though one of my daughters did say that I seemed much happier than when I left. Until she said that, I hadn't realized my family was scared for me. I guess I didn't have enough sense to be scared for myself. It's been a real journey for me here." The honesty felt good.

"You needed to get away from California—and maybe it's better for you to stay away," said Lila. "When I go home, I'm there long enough to see problems, but not long enough to fix any of them. It always just leaves me frustrated."

"Isn't your romance with Big Ed heating up these days, too?" It was Abby's question, and Megan wasn't sure how to answer it.

"He calls every Friday right after school to that phone in the hall, regular as though he were on a timer. Sometimes I think he *does* wear a timer. But the call is always from exotic places—like Amsterdam, or Morocco, or Tunis. When he's able to come see me, we barely have time for a quiet dinner someplace, and he seems to avoid the crowd. He always has this stupid time limit. I'll bet you guys think he's as elusive as the Ambassador." She chuckled. "I'm not sure this run in, run out, type of friendship qualifies as a romance, but I'm sure enjoying it."

"But you do like him?" pressed Lila.

Lila's question made Megan realize she might have said too much. She continued to feel uneasy about Lila and her penchant for telling Klaus everything. She spoke more carefully.

"Of course, I like him. He's a delightful friend, and very special. I just don't know if it's a romance. If he pushed me for a decision, I might run as hard as I do from others. I'm still afraid to love someone. It hurts too badly to lose. I don't want to go through that again...ever." For a moment she stopped and stared at the wall, trying to modulate her emotions. In thinking about her growing feelings for Ed, she had forgotten about Lila.

The others were silent, measuring the break in her voice.

"Either way," Megan resumed more firmly, "I feel like the decision between staying here or going home is closing in on me, and I still hate to make decisions alone."

Staying would mean being prepared to keep making new friends and losing them? Already Stan would be transferred in July after their group trip to Spain, and Charlie, Vern, and Big Don would be getting out of the military at the same time. In another year, Carl and Luke would rotate back to the states unless Carl got his requested extension. It could be hard.

Finally, she was able to laugh. "Would you believe the doctor wants me to take Valium? He says I'm losing too much sleep over decision-making? But Luke says the easy way is to say, '1—2—3— *now* make a decision, and live with it.' I'd like to be confident enough to make decisions like that. Of course, it's easy for him. He never has real feelings about anyone."

The next evening, Megan and Carl sat on the steps outside the Officers' Club after his day's flight, having left the others to talk more privately. She had introduced Carl to every new female who transferred in or who visited any friend. But after one date, he would tell Megan that he wasn't interested. He had an earned reputation as a flirt.

"You've got to tone down your 'lines'," she said. "You scare everybody off. I think you do it on purpose. Then if a girl actually *dates* you, she gets angry when you *deliberately* flirt with someone else while you're out with her. You can't blame the ladies."

"If you don't get serious, you can't get hurt, now can you?"

Megan gasped. "You're as scared of loving someone and then losing them, as I am," she accused. "You're supposed to be my guide to living and loving, and you're scared too."

He merely grinned.

"You're not trying very hard, Carl," Megan scolded him.

"Right now, I just want to do my job at the Border safely and well, where people depend on me, yet every girl I go out with starts talking about marriage and kids."

"You should hear my mom," said Megan. "I write and tell her all the things I do with the group, with you, Luke, Milt and Ed. Then she worries I might fall in love and marry someone *over here*. I told her that I more or less 'big sister' everyone, and she shouldn't worry."

"Everyone doesn't exactly see you as a big sister," Carl mumbled, then he laughed. "The contrast between your innocent eyes and wicked walk sort of keeps some of us on edge. The others just enjoy your counsel and your company. And I need you."

He traced large ovals on the steps with his finger, leaning forward with elbows propped on his spread knees.

"You could show attention to girls, instead of just having sex and then running like crazy." She couldn't help laughing at the stern look he gave her. "Well, you do!"

"No." His traced ovals grew smaller. "I don't feel that intimacy with just anyone. I don't think you've been trying either. Is there anyone your age—since you think age is so *damned* important?" He threw the word at her.

"Most guys my age are already married, or there's some darned good reason why they're not! Or you don't trust them. Or they disappear and reappear like Milt and colleagues tell mysterious stories about him that one never knows whether or not to believe. Or there's Big Ed, who calls weekly, and I really like him, but he can only come up here sporadically and unexpectedly."

Carl laughed gruffly. "That's true around a line base. I still haven't had a chance to see if Ed's all right for you."

"You will soon. I'll see to it." She could see Carl staring off into a distant and dark sky. "My instinct says that's not all that's on your mind tonight."

"I guess it isn't. I'm in some trouble. That new general, Jordan, grounded me today."

"Why on earth would he do that?" Megan gasped in shock. "General Horst wouldn't go *near* a helicopter unless you were flying it, and I know how seriously you take your flying."

"Well, General Horst is gone now, and the new guy doesn't like me at all. I have to say I don't like flying him around, either."

"Why not?"

"We disagree on maintenance and flight safety. He wants me to exceed safety limits on air speed, weight allowance, and rotor performance, and then yells when the bird has to be repaired. I won't exceed maximums, *except* in combat, of course. He also insists on sitting in the co-pilot's seat when he's never flown a plane."

Carl's hair slid over his forehead from his emphatic gestures. "On a power turn near the Border, and he panicked and grabbed the controls. I had to shove him away when he froze. Then I had to auto rotate until I got control of the bird again, and everyone knows autorotation has the glide ratio of a brick." Carl leaned forward, again resting his forearms on his knees. "I *yelled* at him, Megan."

"Well, if he's that stupid, or panicked, what else could you have done? You had to save the aircraft—and him too, I suppose."

"He relieved me of duty, and he wrote me up as having a 'personality conflict.'" Carl sunk his head in his hands. "If he had charged me formally and made it a court marshal for insubordination, I could have fought it and won, because I could prove he endangered the aircraft. As aircraft commander, I had to push him away from the controls. But as a general officer, he's too smart to allow an investigation that would prove him wrong, so it's a 'personality conflict.' I don't get to tell *my* side of the story, under that label."

"I'm sorry, Carl. You're such a conscientious pilot." She reached over to put an arm around his shoulder. Though Carl had acted the clown around the rest of the gang and pretended being grounded was just a 'vacation,' Megan could hear signs of strain in his voice and see it in his posture. Being relieved of duty by a general could cost him his flying career and get him a desk job, or worse. "Isn't there anything we can do to get it straightened out?"

"I don't think so. A general can have any pilot he wants, and if there's a personality conflict, he can choose one. He chose Luke."

"Luke!" She sucked in her breath. "I love Luke dearly, but he has *so* many hang ups. Can he stay sober enough to please a general?"

"He'll have to! He's usually proficient about his flying, even when he's drunk as a skunk *off* duty. I'll tell him what I learned from this experience, though. If a general tells you to do something you know will crash the helicopter, you just go ahead and do it. Never tell a general 'no.'" There was no mistaking Carl's bitter sarcasm.

"You'd think with your experience, this couldn't happen. What will you do?"

"Right now, I'm relieved of duty until further notice. If Jordan decides to let me fly again, maybe I'll be down at Katterbach with First Cav or the Armored Division. I'll still be flying the Border, or as back-up for 2nd ACR, but I'll have to move down there."

Her startled intake of breath said more than words.

Carl smiled. "Well one good thing out of this is that you'll miss me. But I'll come up every weekend for dances and for our Saturday morning trampoline training with your kids. Might not be able to make it up Wednesday nights for volleyball though. The rest of the time, we'll have to play it by ear. I'll meet the ski bus at Feucht, like the rest of the Cav pilots, and you can just save me a seat. I'll still bring the wine and you bring my cookies, right?"

"And fried chicken?"

"And fried chicken." He reached around her waist. "You can still call me anytime you're feeling lonely, and I'll be here in under two hours. You *will* call me if you need me, won't you?"

"Of course. The same goes for you." She touched his still sensitive sunburned face softly. "If you need me, I'll be there, too."

He grinned. "Great…nothing has to change, except we burn up the highway between two cities. I'll let you know when Jordan decides what to do with me."

They reentered the club to join their friends. Megan knew they both felt much relieved. *What is it about this friendship that we both seem to draw so much strength and comfort?*

On Friday, Carl drove in after school, in a breathless rush.

"Megan, can you follow me to the mechanic downtown? My car is acting up, and I just got emergency orders to clear Post today and report to Katterbach on Monday. The movers will be at my pad this evening, on overtime, yet."

"Sure. If the repair is extensive, I'll drive you out to your apartment to meet the movers."

The car problem was, indeed, a big one—a part that would not be in until the following day. So Megan drove Carl out to his apartment. Carl's landlords, *Herr* and *Frau* Berg, were devastated that Carl would have to move, but they were delighted that Megan and he agreed to have a drink with them before they went upstairs to pack.

"*Frau* James, I am so happy that you are now able to take a glass of wine with me," beamed *Herr* Berg.

Megan's German was now good enough that they could converse, and Megan was teased gently that it had taken a year for her to work up to a full wineglass. Carl reminded them he must gather things together before the packers came.

"Most important, Megan," he said as they walked up the stairs, "is that my orders, passport, and pay records do *not* get packed in a shipping box. I'll need them at Katterbach to check in, so guard my briefcase with your life. I've had friends lose papers required for their move because foreign packers are notorious for taking it all."

Megan nodded, not fully absorbing the truth of the statement.

The two packed Carl's personal belongings, wrapping his Bavarian beer mugs in newspapers, pulling dirty sheets from the bed, and gathering towels and dirty clothes into one stack. They would stop by the Laundromat on the way back to Megan's. The clean linens went into another stack to be packed by the movers. Carl stuffed two pairs of slacks and sweaters, underwear, socks, shaving kit, and an extra flight suit under the briefcase, so they wouldn't get taken.

Carl loaded the contents of his freezer and refrigerator into an ice chest to take to Megan's, knowing food could not survive until the household goods were delivered in Katterbach. It would probably take a week or so to accomplish the two-hour drive. No one could ever figure out what took packers so long to arrive at a new location.

As they sipped tea, Carl noted his plans. "I'm not looking for an apartment down there. I'll just stay in the BOQ. I'll probably be up here most of the time anyway, so I won't need a bigger place."

"I've heard they have some wild parties in the BOQ 'rubber room.' Most of the pilots drink pretty heavily, and they enjoy lots of company." Megan grinned mischievously. "Can you hold your own?"

He shook his head and smiled. "You know me far too well! If

we have a party, I'll invite you down to keep me in line. Nothing will change, Meggie, I promise. We're still best sidekicks. I'll be only a phone call away."

She nodded, comforted by the thought that he would still be nearby. She hated to admit they kept each other grounded in reality.

The packers arrived. One of the men immediately grabbed for the briefcase and chest of frozen food left unguarded by the door. Megan ran after the man and brought the items back. It wasn't more than a couple of minutes before another zeroed in on items. Megan finally sat on top of the ice chest, holding the briefcase and clothing in her arms, while packers moved everything else.

When the men left, Carl congratulated her on inventiveness. He walked into the kitchen, though, and yelped, "They packed the dirty tea cups, my garbage, and all my dirty laundry! I'll have to wash everything when I get there to get the smell out. But, then, I guess we don't have to do laundry tonight." They dissolved in laughter.

"Brenda told me that when she packed out of Japan, the packers even got her cat mixed into a box of blankets. When she missed him after the packers left, she assumed the kids down the street had taken him, because they were always playing with him."

"Did the cat survive?"

"Her shipment was in storage the whole summer. Poor kitty."

"Yuck! Bet she had to throw out the whole shipment of linens, didn't she?"

It was difficult to say goodbye downstairs. There were tears in *Herr* Berg's eyes as he said, "Our home is forever open to you both." The man somehow looked older when he turned to Megan and said, "Take care of him. He's like our only son." Megan nodded. *Frau* Berg couldn't say anything. She just cried into her apron. Carl promised they would visit, and they drove away, waving.

"That was really hard," said Carl, as he dragged up a handkerchief to mop his eyes.

"I know." Megan did know--like leaving her own family.

It was already quite late when they got to Megan's apartment to fit the frozen food into her tiny German refrigerator. All, of course, wouldn't fit in the three-inch freezer. They cooked everything left over and had a late dinner. Carl would stay over and help eat the rest of the leftovers after trampoline practice the next day.

Chapter 20

The two friends rose early next morning to meet the children and Luke at the school gym. Megan marveled that these men gave up Saturday mornings to help her class. Last year's class had low reading scores. She had found research supporting physical movement from crawling, graduating to extreme sports, as a means of improving reading in young children. Early in the previous year, she had wondered aloud how she could offer her children such an opportunity.

"Would trampoline count?" Luke had asked.

"That should be 'extreme,' all right. And there's a big one in the school gym no one uses. I've sure never tried trampoline."

"I have. So has Carl. We could do it when we aren't flying, couldn't we, Carl?"

"Guess so. Can you get a key to the gym and permission to use it on weekends?"

"I think so. The principal might like having me test this theory as a practicum."

Megan sent home permission slips and invited parents to witness the first Saturday session. The guys first demonstrated an easy move then helped each child to try it, one at a time.

The program was an instant hit, and the two pilots had as much fun as did the kids. The program was now in its second year, with a new group of fifth graders who were also doing well--another example of the joy of DoDDS academic freedom to teach in new ways to help children.

While Luke was a bit flashier as he showed off flips and twists, Carl was rock solid in technique and was the better teacher. Both turned out to have great patience, and the children loved them. The kids were taught to spot for each other, and to take the job seriously to keep anyone from falling through the outer springs. While many of the more daring were already doing flips, even chubby, timid Maureen had overcome her panic enough to do a seat drop safely. The principal was delighted when reading scores jumped a whole year's grade level during each semester. It had proven true that when the children had fun bonding and took each other's safety more seriously, they began taking their schoolwork more seriously as well. They developed confidence, and they did their homework quickly so they'd be free for Saturday's session.

Carl and Luke's commitment had continued for the whole first year and into the second. They made an unlikely pair. Alcoholic Luke, who hated kids, and flirty Carl, who loved them, both enjoyed the children's progress. Megan knew the men could only help until they were transferred back Stateside, but their trampoline coaching had proven her research correct.

This particular morning, Megan and Carl hurried over to the gym at nine, and Luke was already pacing outside waiting for them, as were several children.

"Mrs. James," said little Joel. "I was afraid you wouldn't have trampoline today. My dad got called out to the Border on alert at two in the morning. Can Mr. Carl and Mr. Luke stay?"

"That's what I was trying to tell you, Carl," said Luke quickly. We tried to reach you last night. Where were you?"

"Packing out," he said, winking at Megan for silence. "Which units are going?"

"All of them! This alert looks bad. First Cav from Katterbach is already deployed, and you're expected to join them at Hof by 1300 hours, even though you're not 'official' until Monday. I'm taking General Jordan out until noon, so you can deadhead when we go. You were right, Carl--the guy is a prick."

"Watch him, Luke. He's dangerous if he grabs your controls."

"Not to worry. I've got his number."

When the kids realized their trampoline coaches would have to leave shortly, they wanted to do all the 'hard' tricks first, and promised they could spot each other on the 'easy' ones later."

Her dear student, Sylvia, came loyally every Saturday, just to watch the other kids. Megan allowed her to keep records on a clipboard. The little girl insisted on coming to school, even though the radiation and chemotherapy treatments for her brain cancer had failed. She was clearly fading before their eyes. She wore brightly colored scarves to hide her baldness. Though her mother wanted her to die at home in her own bed while she sat by her side, her father understood that the child's happy times were at school with the other children.

Sometimes Sylvia could manage only an hour or two in class before she became weak, but since her father worked for Rex Top Cop, Megan could call Rex anytime to let the father come pick up his little girl. He was happy to approve anything Megan could do to keep Sylvia going another day, another hour, another minute. Megan struggled to put grief aside and encouraged Sylvia to do all she could manage, same as the other children. But she, Carl and Luke worried often about the little girl's fading energy and fading eyesight.

Today, however, when Sylvia arrived, she didn't take her usual place at the end of the trampoline to watch Luke bounce up to speed before demonstrating the day's first trick. Instead, she walked gingerly around to the side where Carl was lining up the kids.

"Hi Gorgeous," Carl greeted the child. "What's new?"

"I would like to jump today, Mr. Carl. Will you help me?"

Carl snapped his eyes over to Megan's and Megan shrugged. "I'm not sure," she said. She could tell Carl had the same thought. *Would the jumping increase the pain in which this child lived every day? Could it do further damage?*

"Please," Sylvia insisted, taking hold of Carl's sweatshirt to pull him down. She whispered earnestly into his ear, "I just want to do it once before I die."

Megan could see the intake of breath in Carl's body when his eyes caught hers again. She nodded to the unasked question—yes, she *knows* she's dying. Megan remembered sadly the day Sylvia had whispered that she knew she didn't have much time left, but not to tell her mother, "…because she thinks I'll get better." Sylvia's German mother thought she was keeping the child blissfully ignorant, but Sylvia already knew she would die soon.

Carl bent down, picked up the little girl in his arms. Luke braced his feet apart to halt the bouncing and stood waiting while Carl lifted Sylvia into the center of the trampoline bed and climbed up after her. "Now just sit there, Sylvia, and I'll start bouncing you easy-like until you want to stop."

"No, Mr. Carl. I want to bounce until I can stand up and jump *with* you…please."

Carl swallowed hard and said, "All right, Gorgeous. Let me know when you're ready to go from your seat to your feet, okay?"

"Okay," echoed Sylvia, as she put her hands on the tramp bed.

Carl gently started the bouncing from right behind the little girl, while Luke watched Carl's eyes for the signal as to when they'd be ready to bounce her up. Luke matched Carl's movements, jumping in front of Sylvia, facing her.

After a few soft bounces, Sylvia called out, "Harder, please."

Megan held her breath. She could see Carl and Luke were doing the same.

Carl said, "Okay, Gorgeous, on the third jump, you'll pop up. I'll be right behind you. One, two, three!" Carl and Luke both hit the screen hard and the child bounced to her feet, unsteadily. Carl grabbed her at the waist from behind while Luke held both her hands from the front, and the three moved together.

The other children gathered around the trampoline as the trio jumped up and down. Sylvia beamed. But Megan could see she was tiring, and Carl felt it too. Even before Megan could signal him, he nodded at Luke, and they took each bounce softer and softer until they could stop safely. Then Luke held up Sylvia's hand in triumph as though she were a boxer after a TKO, and the whole group cheered, "Syl-vi-a, Syl-vi-a."

Her exhaustion was apparent and, as Carl sat down, cradling her in his arms on the edge of the trampoline, Luke jumped down and reached for her over the side.

Megan hugged Sylvia, and the children told her how well she had done. All three adults were near tears with worry. But Sylvia signaled with a feeble wave that she was all right. Megan turned away to keep the children from seeing her cry, and saw Sylvia's father and Rex standing in the doorway. The father was sobbing openly.

The child leaned against Luke as he walked with her to her father. Obviously struggling with his emotions, the man asked, "Did you have enough for the day, Sylvia?"

"Oh, yes, *Vati*," she said. "It was so wonderful up in the air. I'll never forget. This is the happiest day of my life." She turned to wave at Carl and Megan, her face in a haloed smile.

Her father mouthed the words, "Thank you," before carrying her out to the car.

"I'm glad you guys could manage that," said Rex. "Her dad said the doctors think we'll lose her very soon, and we're on our way out to the Border now, too."

Carl, Luke, and Megan all nodded, too choked up to speak. They shared the heartache of knowing, with death so close, Sylvia would not jump again.

"Mr. Luke, could you show me that back flip again before you go?" young Hank mercifully interrupted.

"Sure," Luke answered, his voice much too cheerful. He clapped Carl on the shoulder and jumped up to the trampoline while Carl and Megan spotted him on a picture perfect back flip. "Okay kids, line up and we'll do the back and front flips before we go."

When time was gone, Luke waved to the kids, and Carl told them to mind their teacher and take care of her. Luke hugged Megan roughly. "Ya' done good, Babe," he said, and strode out of the gym. For Luke, that was about as much emotion as he could ever show.

Carl lifted his hand to hers, exchanging the 'my strength to you' signal, as he whispered, "I'll be in touch as soon as this is over. Make sure your gas tank is full and your suitcase is in the car. If they give the word, *don't* follow NEO evacuation plans. You girls just drive southwest as far as you can, *only* on the back roads. Stay together. Try to make Switzerland. I'll find you."

The Cold War had innumerable hot incidents at the Border for military personnel. Megan knew by now that the folks at home would never know about the danger of these alerts. Those in the States would remain blissfully 'at peace' unless one of the incidents at the Border or at the Wall escalated and became World War III. She also knew she would not be leaving.

"We'll be right here at school with the kids until their parents come get them, so contact me here. We might be able to help somehow." She blinked back tears. "Fly safe."

He squeezed her hand and was gone, joining Luke for the ride to the airfield. Megan realized she'd have to get Lila's help to drive one car home, since she'd have to pick up Carl's car and keep it for him. And her girlfriends would have to come over to help her eat all the food that wouldn't fit into the freezer before it spoiled. *It's easier to think about these mundane details than about our friends going into danger, and our special child dying.* Once again life had revealed itself as short and incomprehensible.

Sylvia couldn't come to school on Monday. She quietly slipped away in the afternoon. Her father was released from the Border long enough to bury her in a German cemetery. Classmates made a wreath of photos of Sylvia enjoying school activities and picnics. The little girl's death seemed an omen of fearful events.

Chapter 21

The exodus of troops continued until the Post was almost deserted. A few mothers kept their children home, fearful they might have to try to evacuate. But most sent them to school with notes telling where they could be reached. The teachers carried on normally, though it was hard to concentrate, knowing their friends were facing their potentially suicidal duties on the Border. Everyone seemed more serious about this particular alert. Big Don, their dear Cavalry friend, reiterated Carl's warning, as he paced through the parking lot, checking the teacher's cars and leaving notes on windshields while his sergeant fired up his Sheridan tank.

"Your gas is below a quarter of a tank," he scolded. Megan had walked out to meet him as she noticed him examining her Fiat. "You need a new tire on your right front--now!"

"I'll get a new one when I get paid next week, Don, I promise."

He reached in his wallet and unfolded a bunch of bills, jamming them into Megan's reluctant hand. "Do it now, today! In case… I have to go--hope to see you soon."

Without another word, the big guy patted her cheek in farewell and double-timed it back across the muddy field. She reentered her classroom and watched from the windows. Don jumped on his Sheridan and it moved out through the 'playground' that was supposed to be safe for the kids whenever the gates were closed. Today, the gates were wide open. Tank after tank clanked over the cobblestones, the heavier vehicles peeling off toward the railhead at *Muna*, testing their rotating turrets as they went. Sheridans would forego the trains and churn straight up the highway toward the infamous 'gaps' at Coberg or Hof and Fulda through which an enemy would attack.

One tank swung its turret around while going through the makeshift playground, and the kids tattled, "Mrs. James. They just squashed our last tetherball pole!"

"I see it," she said absent-mindedly. "Just wave at them. I'm sure they'll replace it when they get back, like they did with all the others. We'll just play dodge ball today."

It was necessary to react with control to keep the kids calm. After all, it was their fathers out there, and children worried too. One could always tell when an alert was on because most of the children arrived with peanut butter and jelly sandwiches for lunch and complained of having the same thing for dinner. Teachers volunteered to remain after school, playing games and tutoring the children until the mothers working on Post could collect them. Thus, the children were never without a responsible adult watching over them, in case the ineffective Non-combatant Evacuation Order would have to at least be tried.

When the four friends talked it over after school, all agreed they would stay until the guys came back, no matter what orders they might be given from NEO officials to evacuate.

"We might still be useful," said Abby. "My neighbor, Holt, and Robert both said to get away to the west, but there's no way I'm leaving until the kids are evacuated."

"We've seen this balance of power stuff long enough now. We know it would be our own soldiers covering our retreat, if we left," said Megan. "I'm not going anywhere."

"It's strange," added Abby. "Jonas Litzfeld came by my classroom to tell me goodbye."

"You know he's had a crush on you over a year." said Megan.

"He never even talks to me—just sort of hangs around."

"He's really sweet and shy. Probably coming to say goodbye was the best he could do."

"I didn't even get to tell Brian how much I cared for him before he left," sobbed Lila.

A little late for that thought now, thought Megan, but she comforted Lila all the same. Emily expressed her confidence in their troops, "…though I doubt one in a thousand people back home even knows about their mission here, or how often these alerts come," she added.

"It's ironic that our Border guys are considered expendable by our own government," said Abby. "I suppose the men on the Border in Korea are in the same boat. Let's face it--should the communists come across, our guys can't possibly hold them back for forty-eight hours. They'll all be killed. But then that would give our government an excuse to aim the nukes and try to clobber the Soviets. Our guys are just cannon fodder, aren't they?"

Her voice sounded so bitter, Megan looked up to see tears in Abby's eyes, and she knew her friend *never* cried. She moved over to put an arm around Abby too.

"Those people in the States who condemn the military and want us to pull out of Europe don't seem to realize that if our Border troops leave, or fail, all of Europe will fall to the communists," said Emily. "Why doesn't somebody tell them?"

What little news got back to Post was not good. An Infantry unit was hit by tragedy yet again. Two young troopers were blinded from an explosion of old WWII German ammunition while digging foxholes, yet the area had been cleared a week earlier. This unit was becoming a 'hard-luck' outfit, with low morale and frequent scrutiny. The investigators never found misconduct, only horrendous accidents, which were assumed to be the natural hazard of being on a Border base. But there were so many suspicious accidents.

The teachers agreed to go on normally, even to having dinner at the O'Club. With most all the male customers gone, Marco would be on minimal hours, and things would be quiet. All buildings and gates, as well as the Officers' Club, were surrounded by soldiers in full battle dress and armed heavily. Banjo wire decorated much of the parking lot in barbed spirals. An alert condition could go on for weeks, and even the women's credentials were scrutinized carefully each time they entered the Club.

Trying to determine cause and effect, the teachers examined the day's news headlines, which implied Cuba's intervention in Angola might bring an American invasion of Cuba. That was President Ford's latest 'loose' comment. The Soviets regarded his comments as 'saber rattling' and threatened Soviet invasion in Europe.

"I'm sure it's all precautionary," said Megan. "The Soviets would like us to divert troops elsewhere because they think we'd then be a soft target, *here*. They want us to let down our guard or be distracted. This seems a tough alert, though. The guys are all working 48 hours on and eight off, not enough time to get much rest. If you see them at all, they look like zombies."

"I know everyone is exhausted," said Abby. "Lila, has Brian had a chance to get in?"

"He came out to my apartment for about fifteen minutes and then left. He said he '...had to be able to get back to decode new orders within ten minutes--to get his Cav unit rolling within twenty,' like I care what *all that* means. This whole thing is stupid! I'll just have to spend more time with Klaus. At least, he's a civilian, though he's been out of town several times lately, too. Brian keeps giving me orders like I was one of his privates, and I don't like it one lil' bit!"

"Lila," said Megan, "*all* our friends have been giving us orders. I'm learning to follow orders even if I don't understand the reason. They're just trying to keep us safe in case this escalates into something bigger. This alert seems a bad one. If Brian gets a chance to get in from the Border again, you can meet him at my apartment. I'm within the ten-minute distance. And I don't think this is a good time for you to rely on Klaus."

"Why would you say that? You never have liked him," Lila started, indignantly.

Abby quickly changed the subject, "Did Big Don check out your tires, too, Megan?"

"I think he did everyone's. He forced money on me to replace one. Now, I don't even know when he'll be in so I can pay him back. And Luke came in last night at dinner, put a map in front of my face, jabbed at it with his finger and ordered me to 'memorize the routes and alternates to *there*,' pointing at the Swiss Border. When I finished, he headed back out with his aerial map. He didn't know if he'd be gone three days or three weeks. Carl already told me the same thing before he left, only he said I was to take you gals with me."

"They don't even say, 'please,' or 'perhaps you should,' do they?" said Abby. "Just 'do it!' and I almost feel like I should salute or something."

"Yeah, in a way it's laughable, but then it's scary too," said Megan. You can tell when things are bad because they sort of bristle with efficiency, and their voices change to 'command mode.'" She turned to Lila, "I hate to see any of our guys go out there, because we know if anything happens, they'll be buying us time at a very heavy price...their own lives. I think we need to be happy they care so much about us and not be going out behind their backs."

Lila was silent a moment, taking in Megan's rare rebuke. "I suppose you're right—I should have been nicer to Brian. He said I should find my NEO cards and my passport and start carrying them in my purse. I had to tear apart my desk to find that stupid passport. If we all go up in an atomic mushroom cloud, who is going to look at it anyway?" Lila's assessment was the prevailing thought of the seventies, so no one was surprised at her pessimism.

"In a way, we're privileged to be here and know what's going on," ventured Emily. "Our guys are sleeping in their tanks, the phones are tied up, yet those people stationed in the rear echelons probably don't even know we're on the brink of something here."

A couple of evenings later, as Megan headed for the O'Club's dining room with Abby and Emily, she was surprised to see Big Ed step into the room. His smile seemed a permanent fixture on his face whenever he looked at her. She liked the warm feeling.

"I called Marco to see if you were here. I hope my barging in isn't inconvenient."

"Not at all," she said, moving to meet him. "I'm surprised you aren't out at the Border."

"Not this time. We're actually investigating some ongoing problems in Bamberg. When I sent inspectors up from Stuttgart, I volunteered to come along. Any chance I get, I'll come to Bamberg, or have you figured that out by now?" He smiled as he took her hands in his.

"Have you eaten? Would you like to join us for dinner?"

"I'd rather hoped you wouldn't mind going downtown to that Altenberg Castle on the hill for Stroganoff." He lowered his voice and added, "I'd like to have a quiet evening with you. I don't know how much time I'll have."

Megan looked at her companions and shrugged. Both Abby and Emily motioned for her to go with Ed. "We're fine," said Emily. "We'll catch up with you tomorrow."

Ed waved a salute at the other two women and took Megan's arm. "It looks like you have permission to be seen out with this tough old soldier tonight." He grinned down at her. "Let me give Marco my time away from Post, and we'll go." He left Megan for a moment, and conferred quietly with Marco. He returned to help her with her coat.

"Why do you always do that?" she asked.

"What?"

"Tell someone where you go and what time you'll be back. It

sort of feels like checking in with my dad when I was in high school."

Ed grinned. "You never miss much, do you? I think that's one of the reasons I like you so much. You're wonderfully alert, and quite curious. Of course, that always makes it harder for me to avoid your questions, too."

"I suppose you're going to tell me that even *that* question is a military secret?"

"No, my dear." He reached out to take her hand as they went down the steps to the parking lot. "*That* question is not a problem. I let Marco or my aide know where I am because if we wander away from a secure military phone to find a moment alone, they must be able to reach me. They need to know when I'll be back."

"Oh." Megan giggled. "It really is like reporting to my father, isn't it?"

Ed stopped and turned to face her with a big grin. "I suppose it is, now that you mention it." He kissed her on the forehead and helped her into the car for their timed visit downtown.

When they returned to the O'Club three hours later, the place was deserted, Marco was alone, and Ed wasn't interested in parting company. Megan stepped behind the bar to pour them each a glass of wine while Ed signed for it, slipping the paper under the register. Ed mentioned that he might have to move quickly. Megan had already assumed that possibility and had wondered about it.

"I hope you don't mind my calling you, or dropping by whenever I get the chance? Sometimes I just need to know that you're here, and that you're real."

What does he mean that I'm real? "Actually, I've come to look forward to your calls. You always seem to be in some mysterious place, but I still don't know how you knew there was a phone in our Annex outside my classroom, or how to reach me here at the Officers' Club."

"Just call it military reconnaissance, my dear. It's something I do well." He smiled

"I'll admit you're very thorough at gathering information." She didn't ask how. Instead, she asked, "Where might you go next, since you're obviously expecting a call any minute?"

"Depends on the message I receive." He took her hand. "But wherever I am, I'll find a way to let you know, if that's all right with you. At least I can still code something that would give you an idea when I'll be back to see you."

Megan noticed that her face felt warm. *Oh my God, I'm blushing again!*

"Do you mind that I want to keep seeing you?" He looked intently, watching her eyes.

"I sort of like it." Her voice was unnaturally soft. She realized she *did* like it. Ed's quiet reserve, his patience, and his subtle approach to mere hand-holding was so different from the younger men who blatantly propositioned females daily, almost as part of their normal speech.

The Officers' Club was deadly quiet. Marco said one of Ed's men had taken Abby to a *Gasthaus* in Gardenstadt for a drink. The others would check in with Marco in an hour. Ed suggested they take their wine upstairs where they could listen to music.

"Marco knows where I am, and he'll let us know when I receive the call I'm expecting." They picked up their drinks, signaled Marco, and headed upstairs.

Megan didn't feel any uneasiness around Ed, and Marco would know where she was, after all. *Is it my imagination? Did Marco wink at me again?*

Ed's room was one Megan had not seen before. Actually, it was a suite--a living room, dining area, and bedroom with bath. Lovely, matching cherry wood furniture replaced the government-issue couches and beds that graced the single rooms she and her friends had occupied when they first arrived. "Wow! This is really elegant. How do you rate VIP treatment?"

"Marco knows I need the big table for meetings--and a secure emergency phone. The other men have rooms down the hall, but not nearly so grand."

Megan kicked off her shoes and tucked her feet under her on the couch, feeling quite luxurious. Ed moved to a drawer under the cassette player, flipped his fingers through the cassettes, and soon Keith Carradine's voice spun from the stereo.

Ed joined Megan on the couch, withdrawing a short pistol from under the back of his sweater. She was startled at the sight of it, but he quietly laid it on the table within easy reach, shrugged, and said, "It's uncomfortable against the sofa back. I still have a souvenir of Vietnam in my spine." She wanted to ask about it, but he continued as though a weapon off duty was not out of the ordinary. "If you'd like another drink, there are a variety of things in the refrigerator."

"No, I'm fine. I can only manage one." She wondered what she could ask, and what she couldn't, since Ed seemed to have some important purpose here. Finally, she said, "Why Bamberg? You seem to have some important mission here, not just inspecting."

"I can't tell you much but, if I may pick your brain on one problem, you might be able to figure things out. I already know you're observant, and Marco seems to feel you know almost everyone. And he feels you can be trusted." Ed's demeanor was suddenly businesslike, as though this were an interrogation.

Megan nodded, puzzled by the change. *Trusted to do what? And why would Ed be asking Marco?*

"We've investigated several accidents here and at the Border in the last year, yet they stopped during the summer and started up again in the fall. This winter, Reforger and alerts have produced stepped up activity. 2/78 had another accident today. We're wondering about a pattern, or if someone is hanging around the equipment that perhaps shouldn't be here. Any ideas?"

"You mean you think the accidents weren't really accidents? Are you thinking someone planned them? Like sabotage?"

He nodded, slowly. "I knew you'd ask. Actually it's still too early to tell, and we wouldn't want to call it that just yet. Do you have any idea why such events might stop during the summer? What's different around Bamberg's Post in the summer?"

"The only thing I know that's different is that school's out, teachers are in the States visiting their families, and kids are running loose. But I wouldn't suspect school kids of bothering anything on Post, unless they did something out of pure mischief."

"These acts weren't just mischief. People were maimed or killed. And probably women or children wouldn't know *how* to do these things." He looked serious. "Is there any time that foreign nationals come on Post, besides the usual employees with ID cards?"

"Sure. They come for social activities, except during alerts. But one of the ID card holders must sign them on, so someone always knows about it. Didn't you know that?"

He grinned. "Which of us is asking the questions, my dear?

Can you give me examples?"

"Well, I sign in a German couple on Wednesday nights to play volleyball with us. They're teachers in the German *Gymnasium* and excellent players. Our reading teacher has a live-in German boyfriend. They're both ballet dancers, and he comes on Post with her almost daily. Lila has a German boyfriend who comes with her sometimes to happy hour or to parties, though we don't like him much. I'm sure there are lots of others on Post who sign in friends for dinner or plays. Two teachers date German men. The single officers here date mostly American teachers, but the enlisted guys often bring in a German girlfriend for steak night or something. But then you said you didn't think a woman could cause these so-called accidents, didn't you?"

He grinned sheepishly, "Let's just say it's been my experience that troops would *notice* a woman if she were somewhere she wasn't supposed to be. They don't notice other men much. If the teachers are gone, their friends wouldn't be coming on Post in summer, would they?"

"No." Megan thought for a minute. "Then you're thinking that someone the teachers bring on Post could be dangerous to our troops. That seems pretty far-fetched."

"It may be. It's just that with terrorist activity prevalent right now, attacks on Americans, these really sticky alerts, and the bombing in Frankfurt snack bar that killed some soldiers and shut down many of our Posts, a whole string of accidents at one location seems suspicious enough for a team to come check them out, don't you think?"

"I guess so. Would you want me to ask around and see who's coming on Post with us? Should I say something to the other teachers?"

"Not yet. Let us check. You've given me some ideas, though. I hadn't thought of friends of the teachers before." He paused. "Why don't you like Lila's boyfriend?"

"Oh nothing I can put my finger on, nor anything I can prove- -just instinct, I guess."

"Instinct can be a good thing. It's saved my neck a few times. Keep me posted, okay?"

She paused, not sure she should ask the question really on her mind. "Then you're really after someone, perhaps a saboteur, this time, aren't you?"

Ed was smiling, now, and seemed less intense. His shoulders dropped from rigid to relaxed. But he gave his usual type of evasion—an abrupt question. "Do you have any idea of the weather in Thailand today?"

So, he didn't want to answer. I think I've got him sort of figured out. She smiled and changed the subject. "Then, tell me about how leadership of the Stuttgart Ski Club is structured."

"I could invite you to come down some weekend to see for yourself."

"Oh," Megan was startled, feeling she didn't know the rules of engagement for serious dating yet, and she didn't think traveling to see Ed would be quite proper. "Perhaps I should bring down our president, Luke, and you could show us both." She struggled not to laugh out loud thinking of how Luke would react to her suggesting him for a chaperone. She was sure he'd ask who was supposed to chaperone him?

Ed merely grinned, and nodded. Megan had a feeling Ed had *her* figured out, too.

The time went by quickly as they laughed and talked together, sharing beliefs and stories. Megan began to realize that Ed's job required one to handle tremendous pressure, accept the hectic pace, and thrive on responsibility. The man was running practically around the clock and napping at his desk. She wondered how long a man could keep such a pace and not age rapidly.

A knock at the door startled Megan, and Ed reached for the Beretta so smoothly she only saw the movement peripherally. When he opened the door, his hand fell loosely to his side.

Marco handed him a message. "I'm sorry to interrupt, Sir. This just came in. It's coded."

Ed read the message, and picked up the phone. "I'm sorry Megan, I need to reach my contact now." He dialed, and Megan could make little of the conversation. When he finished, he said to Marco, "Tell the others we're executing code Taurus." Marco nodded and disappeared.

Megan knew not to ask about what she had just witnessed.

Ed returned to Megan and said, "Isn't Marco something? He arranges everything so smoothly and effortlessly. He sees all, knows all, and is quite protective of what he seems to believe are *his* people here, *you* included. He made that quite clear to me."

Megan smiled shyly. "No one can ever figure him out, but he's wonderful."

"Should you ever need help in an emergency, Marco would know how to reach me."

Another mystery, Megan thought. But before she could ask why Marco would know where to reach him, or why she should ever need help, he continued.

"I'm really sorry. They have a helicopter waiting for me, taking off at 0400 hours to catch a C-12 from Stuttgart. That's only half an hour away. I hadn't realized we'd talked so long. The time spent with you goes by far too fast. We'll do this again," he said.

"I didn't notice it was so late." A fleeting thought made her wonder why Marco should even be in the building at this hour. "Can I help you get ready in some way?"

Ed replaced his Beretta behind his belt. He reached for his bag, and started throwing his civilian clothes into it. Megan grabbed the remaining hangar bag from his closet, saw that it contained uniforms and zipped it up. Ed stacked both for his personal aide to take down to the staff car. Megan gathered up her shoes and handbag, and Ed took her hand as they walked down the steps to her car. Somehow, it felt quite natural. From the curb, a uniformed guard strode toward them with gun at the ready.

"My ID." said Ed, flipping open his wallet. The young man saluted smartly, slinging his rifle over one shoulder. "At ease, Soldier. You don't need to see the lady's ID, do you?"

"Oh, no Sir."

"Thank you, Son." Ed recaptured Megan's hand, walked her across the parking lot, and took her keys to open the car door. Then, before she could quite expect it, he slowly kissed the palm of her hand that he'd been holding.

"Thank you for a wonderful evening, Megan," He looked into her eyes so directly, still holding the hand he'd kissed between his two larger ones. "You've made this evening quite memorable, and I'll want to see you again as soon as this mission is over."

Megan asked it straight out. "Whenever there's a code name, you disappear. It's like living from one crisis to another, and you seem to thrive on it. You come and go like a phantom, or like Emily's

'Ambassador.' You have to do something dangerous, don't you?"

"Probably not as dangerous as your young officers out at the Border." He paused, seeing a glimmer of anxiety in her eyes, so he answered more honestly, "I won't know until I get to the crisis area and decide how best to handle it. And if you overhear a code name, you must forget it. Coded events may stay classified for many years."

Perhaps sensing her silent curiosity, he said. "I'm sorry I can't tell you more for now. Try to think of me as a prevention expert. My team answers only to the Secretary of Defense. We try to either prevent international terrorist, assassination, or commando emergencies, or at least squash them before they become an excuse for war. If you ever read about such a crisis in the newspaper, you'll know I failed."

Megan nodded. "I think I understand--sort of."

"If you do, you'll also know our conversations must be kept completely private. You're so darned perceptive, and you pick up on so many details, that I worry about you. I need you to understand this secrecy idea, though I know it's foreign to your open nature. I'm afraid your association with me could put you in danger if the wrong people should jump to conclusions. If anyone asks, just stick to the inspector story. Do you understand?"

She nodded again. "Just the friendly old inspector, here on TDY, on temporary duty."

"That's my darling girl. Now go home safely, continue taking care of all your fifth graders, and I'll call you again Friday." He kissed her on the top of the head, brushing his face against her hair. Then he pushed himself away and tucked her gently into the car.

As she pulled out of the driveway, she saw him stride across the parking lot. He patted the young guard on the shoulder before he joined his team and disappeared into the staff car that had glided silently to the curb.

Chapter 22

The alert went on for three additional weeks. During that time, it didn't improve, nor, thankfully, did it worsen. At least, no call came to evacuate the children, though all dependents remained on fifteen-minute evacuation orders. Units came back to Post to refit equipment, do temporary maintenance, and then returned to the Border. The Bamberg, Katterbach, and Stuttgart pilots sometimes came in for helicopter maintenance needs, but after catching a much-needed hot dinner, they flew right back out. The women adopted two jobs—the official one to carry on as normally as possible to reassure the children's fear for their fathers' safety, and the unofficial and voluntary job to bake lots of cookies to be handed to whoever got a temporary return. They included enough for their friends to share when they returned to the Border.

Marco kept hot food available at the O'Club, and the elderly waitress worked overtime to feed whoever could get in, no matter what the hour. Luke came in unexpectedly one night, joined the ladies, and said he'd have two days off before returning.

"How'd you manage that?" asked Abby. She was lounging, her feet up on a low bench after a tense day.

"Had an engine failure today and sat down fast and hard."

"Oh, Luke! Are you all right? Was anyone hurt?" Megan worried about everyone.

"Just some bad bumps, but my skids and tail boom took a beating, and the engine needs changing. I can't figure how anything could go wrong so suddenly. The bird was fine on the previous flight, and there was no indication of anything abnormal on pre-flight."

Luke couldn't resist a sudden grin. "General Asshole was happy with my quick reaction time, though. I headed for the ground at the first odd engine sound instead of waiting to see if I could get a clue as to what was wrong! By the time it gave up completely, we were almost down. But, while my bird is crippled, I can't fly."

"You probably needed the rest anyway," said Abby. "When Bill was in, he said the snake and scout pilots have been putting in some unbelievable hours out there."

"It's bad on pilots and machinery, obviously even on my

command bird. But the guys on Nap of the Earth flying have it worse. NOE is nothing but low-level hedgehopping at high speeds, sometimes around trees instead of over them. It takes its toll on concentration. When you also get the additional strain on the engines, a split second can be disastrous. Carl's bird is fairly dependable, but he and the other guys are putting far too many hours on the machines, *and* on themselves." Luke sat back and gulped his beer.

"Carl said he would try to call tomorrow to let us know if he can make the weekend ski trip or not," said Megan.

"Not! He and Bill are both already committed through the weekend, unless one of them has a breakdown or an accident."

"I don't really want to think about *that*. We'll cancel the trip if none of you can go. Maybe Abby and I will check out a French ski slope on our own, instead."

Luke offered to take the girls out to a special restaurant. True to his own philosophy, he said, "We go first class, or nothing. We'll celebrate my survival."

Luke had news of most of their circle of friends, and shared it during dinner conversation.

"What are the engineers doing out there?" asked Emily, thinking of her nephew.

"Blowing up stuff," said Luke. "They keep equipment within sight of the Border...probably to intimidate the enemy who observes every move we make. They dig anti-tank ditches to keep enemy forces away from us. Bridges near the Border are mined, just in case the constant Soviet buildups and threats melt into a war."

He scratched his head in thought. "They build bunkers, tank emplacements, and airplane revetments to help NATO forces survive the effects of enemy fire." He laughed gruffly. "Of course, should the Soviets come over that Border, you'd better believe Engineers are quite prepared to pick up their rifles and act like infantry."

The women laughed, trying to picture Stan Lang, for instance, carrying a rifle instead of a bottle of beer, or growling at an enemy instead of flashing his famous friendly smile.

"I know our soldiers face an enemy superior in numbers," said Emily. "I'll never understand why communists think they need to threaten us. We mean them no harm. They should tear down these fences, let their people go where they like, and try to get along."

Though no one could disagree with Emily's idealistic assessment, Luke said, "That would be great, but I don't think they're going to change their attitude toward the West anytime soon. And as long as they threaten, we have to be here to meet their threats."

Lila asked about Cav. "Well, half the time both they, and we, sleep in tanks and our helicopters, and it can get darned cold." He glanced at Megan. Oh, yeah, I happened to see Milt taking his helicopter down the 'elevator bunker' near the Border. I'd heard of it, but I didn't know he was hauling clandestine stuff."

"Neither did I," said Megan, a bit puzzled. "He doesn't talk about that, and I suppose that means we shouldn't either." Luke nodded. Megan wondered what she'd be told next time she saw the 'gentle giant.' He seemed to have a new explanation for every event—an unusual friend.

She knew lower ranking Military Intelligence people were sifting through daily situation reports and providing briefings for Generals. She wondered where Ed would be, or if he was even in MI. Was he CIA? Special Ops? Or something else entirely? She wasn't sure, but he was the only friend of whom they'd had no news.

Luke described a terrible incident near 1/54's sector. "An East German guard tried to defect by climbing across the Border fencing. He got caught up on the razor wire, which triggered the scatterguns the Soviets have mounted in the fence posts. I'm sure you gals remember those guns from your Border tour with Cav." They nodded.

"The poor guy hung in the wire while the Soviet guards shot at him with rifles and machine guns." Luke painted the picture for them as he sat sprawled out after dinner, already with his third drink. "It was awful. And you never know if the whole thing is a decoy to make us fire on them first, or to distract us at one point while they try to get across someplace else."

"My Gosh," said Lila, her eyes round and scared. "What happened to the East German?"

"The Soviets stopped firing when the man was dead. But the brutality of the incident wasn't lost on the troops, of either side."

Megan was startled by another thought. "If they'd do that to their own man, imagine what they'd do if they caught one of ours."

"I did think about that, actually," admitted Luke, who was usually the brash risk taker. "The whole Border is so twisted and convoluted, sometimes it's difficult from the air to be sure if you're on the right side and not violating communist airspace. Our pilots sure don't want to get on the wrong side and be captured. I knew one high-ranking pilot who messed up on a stretch of Border where the only signs were rearranged boulders. He landed, realized his mistake, and got out of there fast, but he wasn't so high-ranking after that, and he was cashiered out shortly thereafter. We especially have to be ready if we're carrying any of our special weapons, or any of our intelligence people--to *see to it* they never get captured. I need another drink just *thinking* about that!"

"Why? What could you do to be sure no one got captured?" Abby sounded alarmed.

"Nothing...forget I said that!" Luke hurriedly sipped his beer.

Megan didn't understand his reference. Could he mean they would have to shoot each other to keep from being captured, or what? She was revolted by his fearful slip of the tongue, but resolved to ask Ed or Milt later. She was also curious about the risk of pilots getting lost. She knew from discussions with other aviators that, with both armies facing each other in a standoff, no American wanted to be the one to trigger World War III by inadvertently missing navigational checkpoints. "Don't you have instruments to tell you where the Border actually is?"

"What instruments?" Luke said, surprised by the question. "We only have the topographical map I showed you. We memorize the Border from fence post to fence post, and get constantly tested on our knowledge of each of four sectors along it. Carl's unit flies it randomly, three times a day, almost with one skid on the ground, so they practically recognize the cows on both sides by name, but there isn't really a reliable instrument. I've heard the military is working on a new positioning system, but until we get it, we just have to rely on our eyes and 'gut' feelings. It's hard to consult a map at high speeds." He paused with a thoughtful look on his face. "I know the pilots on the Fulda Gap are doing the same. Fulda's a wider gap; so Soviet tanks would have an easier time advancing there. That's why Milt's unit has specially modified helicopters to lay mines."

"What do you do if you think you may have crossed over accidentally?" asked Abby.

Luke gestured with his hands, in the manner of pilots of all aircraft, everywhere. "If we hear the 'Brass Monkey' go off, from one of our three radio stations, we take a 240 heading, squawk our identification, so hopefully our own troops won't shoot at us, and light out of there."

Even though Luke was obviously quite aware of the dangers of the Border, he was still in a hurry to get his helicopter fixed and get back out to his fellow pilots.

"Carl's been 'painted' twice today," he said to a startled Megan. "He's a bit on edge."

"What does that mean?" asked Abby.

Luke was becoming more expansive with each drink, and Megan became aware of Lila, listening quietly. *Will Lila keep her mouth shut? Will she think it's okay to talk to Klaus?*

Luke explained, "If the Soviets lock their radar on one of our aircraft, an alarm rings in the cockpit. Basically, the alarm's saying, 'You're dead!' If the commies fire, the missiles follow the heat of our engine, and there's no way to escape. But sometimes they're only targeting our aircraft hoping they can make us fire first, or get us so rattled we sit down dangerously, or accidentally cross over the line."

"Is Carl okay?" Megan's voice quavered. She ignored Lila.

"He was when I left, but twice in one day is quite enough. He was able to take escape and evasion maneuvers, but it's not been the first day he's gone through this. Everyone's edgy."

Megan wanted to cry, but instead, she opened the school bag she toted everywhere and drew out the special cookies. "Give these to him for me and tell him 'my hand' is on them."

Luke, of course, didn't know what a 'hand' might mean, so he just shrugged and said, I'll tell him you made them by hand, right? But where's mine?" His mustache flicked with his smile.

Megan handed him a package of chocolate chip cookies. "Now you remember to share with the other guys, won't you?"

Luke's smirky grin surfaced. "Sure, if the cookies make it back out that far once my bird is fixed." With hugs for everyone, he was off to check on his helicopter.

When finally it was Carl's turn to come in for maintenance on his helicopter, he had only a short time while the mechanics worked feverishly. He bummed a lift over to Megan's classroom, entered, and greeted the excited children, fielding their hugs and smiles with, "I'm stinky. You don't want to hug me, do you?" The children, of course, didn't care. He whispered to Megan that he only had a few minutes. "Are you doing okay?" he asked. He would know she was still distraught over losing Sylvia, and she knew that was his meaning.

She nodded. "We're doing our best to cope. But I've been worried about you, too. What's all this about getting painted?" When he looked surprised, she added, "Luke told us."

"Luke should keep his mouth shut," Carl said with resignation in his voice. "Well, I can tell you it's unnerving to hear that alarm go off, and they're doing it to us daily. You have to check and recheck your own navigation to see if you are where you think you are and haven't missed a fence post or slipped over the Border in the dark."

He paused to hug a child who had missed out in the first round. "Then, even when you *know* you're right, by the time you get back to base, the communists have filed a complaint with the U.N. that you flew over one of their positions. It's crazy. Then our pilots must file mountains of paperwork to prove those U.N. charges false."

He shook his head, frustration evident in his expression. "They're playing a mind game to see if they can trick us into attacking, or making a stupid mistake." He ran his fingers through his tousled blonde hair.

"If they should decide to actually fire on the target they've locked radar on, there wouldn't be time to get out. But I don't think they'll do it. I'm hoping they're just testing their radar or trying to scare me to death." He grinned to reassure her. "They do a pretty good job of that!

She nodded, hiding her anxiety. She didn't want the children to see it...or Carl.

"Did you get your special cookies?"

Carl nodded, and stuck out his palm across the children's heads, wiping it first on the side of his flight suit. She met it with her own and smiled. "Luke told me you 'made them by hand,' but I got the message, and I really needed the strength that day."

"I have some more for you," she said, as she dug deeply into her 'magic cookie bag' as the kids called it. "Go get 'em, my friend. We'll see you when you get back."

Carl pulled away from the children, telling them to mind their teacher and only do seat drops on the trampoline until he and Mr. Luke got back, and to say a special prayer for Sylvia. Then he walked out to where his ride was waiting to take him back to his helicopter.

"Okay children, Mr. Carl will be back soon. In the meantime, you have math to finish."

The call came just as the bell rang, and Mindy, phone girl of the week, answered.

"It's for you again, Mrs. James," she called from the hall.

"Tell them I'm coming," said Megan as she supervised the children's exit for the day, reminding them of their homework and meeting their hugs. Then she went to the phone.

"This is Major Henderson, Ma'am. I'm calling on orders from Colonel O'Brian. He says to tell you...I'm reading this exactly here, Ma'am, 'I'll be in Bamberg when Marco serves the special meal at the O'Club again.' He said you would understand, Ma'am."

Megan paused in confusion for a moment and then remembered--prime rib was their first 'special meal' at the Club. And Marco had mentioned he would have it Thursday for whoever could make it in to Post. "Yes, I understand, Major. Thank you."

"Do you have a message for the Colonel, Ma'am?"

"Tell him I'll be there to talk about--skiing."

"I'll tell him, Ma'am."

As Megan went back into her room to clean up and prepare lesson plans for the next day, she thought about Ed. His gravelly laughter warmed her heart, and he was good fun. She teased him unmercifully about the stodgy views in his "military mind," when he also had occasional lapses into humanitarian views that somehow didn't mix together. He said he liked relaxing with her and forgetting his tense job for a little while each time he came to visit. "You restore me," he'd say, taking her hand in his big ones. Ed's attention to her was far more subtle than the other men around Bamberg—a low-key contrast to their more blatant flirtations.

Of course, he was frequently missing, with no explanation, though he usually managed to call her on Friday afternoons--from where? He rarely said. He could only give her coded messages about when he might be back. But later, when he came to talk, over lunch or dinner, she'd find out he'd been to Tunisia for an earthquake, or to Turkey where the Cypress conflict brewed hot again. It was a warm friendship with a man frequently missing. Thursday was two days away. Where could he have been for this week that I've heard nothing, and what has he been doing? Will he be able to tell me?

Next day, the alert ended, and units filtered back to Post. The O'Club filled as each unit returned, cleaned their equipment, and came joyfully to their 'community living room' to be with friends. The maintenance battalion came first. Their captain said the Soviets had finally turned away and withdrawn their combat forces, leaving only their cavalry at the rim of the Border. So the NATO forces and Americans could come back, too, except Bamberg's Second Cavalry soldiers, who would start rotating guard again, unless the Soviets made a further threat.

"It'll go like it usually does," the captain said. "Our Cavalry and the Soviets will sit there facing each other for a few more days, then we'll wake up one morning and their tanks will be behind the death strip, and ours can back up 200 yards as well. It just took them a lot longer to decide to retreat this time than it usually does."

"Then why do they do it?" asked Abby. "It's a ridiculous cat and mouse game."

"Partly to see if we're still here with forces large enough to slow or stop them. If we didn't go out to face them, they'd just keep on coming. Even the folks stationed in Frankfurt am Main know exactly how many hours it would take Soviet tanks to reach them, if we weren't right here trying to hold the Border."

"You said 'partly.'" Emily wanted to understand. "What else could there be?"

"Well, it's for the Soviets to gather intelligence, too. They want to know how big our force is and any of its problems. If they can threaten the Border enough that we all turn out, they'll determine with their own surveillance, plus any informers here at the Post, just how much firepower we have at any given time. Their intelligence operatives always want to find our intelligence people, too, and wipe them out, if they can, making it look like an accident, of course. And we have to watch out for their sabotaging our equipment or causing accidents. They probably also would like to keep us 'trigger-happy' and nervous, so perhaps one of us fires on them. They'd consider that an excuse to attack all the way to the Rhine River."

"What's that you said about informers *here*?" asked Lila, incredulous. "How would they get on Post? We couldn't have any spies here on Post, could we?"

"They'd try to come with one of our own people, naturally. We let guests come on Post if they're with someone holding an ID card, except when we're on alert, of course."

Lila didn't ask any more questions. Instead, she left early.

"Wonder what's on her mind," said Megan.

"Perhaps she's wondering about Klaus," said Abby. "That man still makes me jumpy. And she's seeing him so often she has little time for anyone else."

"Do you think she understands it's important not to tell him what our guys tell us?"

Abby shrugged. "I don't think our guys talk as freely around Lila lately, except for Luke that night when he'd been drinking. Do you know a tactful way we can discuss it with her?"

"I've tried," said Megan. "It didn't go well. She worries me."

The aviators were late because they'd been covering the returning forces all the way back to Post. The Katterbach people didn't need to report back down to their base until the next day, so most were staying with Bamberg friends. By ten, all were on hand for a mini-celebration at the O'Club—lots of talk, a bit of bragging, and a free-flowing bar. Even the brand spanking new Brigade Commander joined the celebration. Some of the aviators lined up tables in a long row and challenged everyone to 'carrier qualifications.'

Luke pulled Megan and Abby up to one end of the tables and pointed down to the other end to explain. He asked a volunteer to be Landing Control Officer, or LCO, and one to be Fire Control Officer, or FCO. Two engineers quickly took places, one in front of the first table and one standing on the table at the far end. "Now, all you do is get a good run, watch the LCO for a signal that the carrier deck is clear, and that you are straight and level, then you land on it and slide down to the far end. Should you crash and burn, the FCO will douse all flames. Ready?"

Abby said, "I've seen it done in the Philippines. I'd have to drink a lot more first."

"I'll go first so you'll see how it works," said Luke. He stepped back, as the crowd circled around. He got into a launch stance, and started running toward the tables. Everyone shouted, "Luke, Luke, Luke." The LCO tipped his arms as though to indicate he should straighten up his left wing, then swung his arms through in the signal for landing. Luke took off, sliding almost the full length of the tables on his stomach before he came to a halt.

There was applause, but the Fire Control Officer, said, "Shucks, I didn't get to douse any flames. Who's next?"

One by one, the aviators challenged the artillery, the infantry, and the engineer officers, and even the teachers took turns at LCO and FCO. At some point, it was the new Brigade Commander's turn, and he gamely lined up toward the 'runway.' Jean, his wife, squealed out, "Hey let me up there, I want to be Fire-Control Officer for this one." There was a roar of approval as the current FCO stepped down and helped her up in his place. Megan was thankful Luke's nasty General was not present, but then he rarely socialized with anyone.

"Whoa. I'm not so sure but what she'd just let me burn," said the Brigade Commander." Jean grinned wickedly at him.

The rhythmic chant began, "Go, go, go, go…"

He launched himself toward the tables, slid faster than anyone had anticipated, and barely stayed on the table at the end. Jean immediately said, "He looks on fire, doesn't he?" The crowd roared, "Fire, fire." Jean doused her husband soundly with her beer.

After that, everyone took turns, while Emily begged off, due to her 'advanced age.' She was allowed a reprieve.

Lila didn't come in until late, and she had Klaus with her.

The festivities more or less shut down upon his entrance, and everyone had one last drink. As usual, Megan's first drink might be Mosel wine, as Carl had coached her, but anything after that was Tab. It had taken her a long time to drink one of something. A second drink was still disastrous and unpredictable.

Carl caught Megan's eye and raised his eyebrows--asking if he could stay at her place, or if she would prefer he stay at Luke's BOQ. She nodded. She had worried during alerts. Everyone knew an alert could escalate to a war at any time, and the pilots would have been some of the first 'gone,' as everyone so euphemistically called it. Megan hated even the day-to-day danger of flying a helicopter, which conventional wisdom said was not supposed to be able to fly. The guys would joke about it being unnatural to try to fly anything that 'screws itself into the sky.' But, there were accidents or near accidents just from normal flight operations.

The pilots tried to make light of it by sharing their latest helicopter jokes. This time it was, "You can always tell a helicopter pilot by his intensity. He's 'spring loaded,' listening for the next piece of his ship to fall off." Another time it had been the fighter jet pilot's prayer—"Lord, give me the eyes of an eagle, the heart of a lion, and the balls of a combat helicopter pilot." These jokes didn't necessarily convince Megan not to worry under normal circumstances. Being on alert status with heightened tensions and greater fatigue was worse.

But now, she couldn't avoid thinking about Ed's suspicion that a saboteur might be trying to *cause* these frequent accidents. Then there was the matter of the 'painting' of Carl's aircraft on so many occasions. That was scary. Though he kept up the role of 'clown and chief flirt' in public, when they were alone, his genuine side appeared, and Megan knew he would share the emotions he never showed to others. They talked all night, since they had lots to catch up on.

Megan wanted to ask Carl about Ed. "He seems more interested in me, at least he keeps saying he *needs* to come back to know I'm *real*, whatever that means. Any suggestions about him?"

"Oh?" Carl looked up. "Do I need to worry about you?"

Megan measured the anxiety she sensed in his voice. "Not really. He's older and settled."

"What does he do for the Army in Stuttgart, anyway?"

"I'm not really sure. Something to do with inspections, but he travels a lot." Megan wasn't sure how much she should tell Carl, but she wouldn't lie to him either. "Marco introduced us the first night Ed and his team members were at the O'Club. I'm not sure what Marco knows about him, but he must think he's okay. Ed has visited several times since, but you were always gone some place, so I haven't had a chance to introduce you. I told you about him."

"I didn't realize he'd been back so often."

"Pretty often. I've had dinner with him, and showed him around downtown. We can talk easily. But then he always has to leave suddenly. He calls me after school on Fridays."

Carl raised his eyebrows. "He sounds serious. Where does he go when he leaves so suddenly?" Carl seemed a bit skeptical of every man's motives, except his own, of course.

"I don't have any idea. He wears civilian clothes when I see him, but he carries a gun, too. He always says he'll *find* a way to contact me to say when he can visit Bamberg again."

"I find it hard to imagine you hanging around with someone who wears a gun off duty. He didn't try anything, did he?" Carl's voice sounded gruff.

Megan detected his usual concerns and smiled. "Not at all. He's tall, older, about forty-three or so, and gentlemanly. He didn't do anything wrong." She paused to think. "Well he does kiss my hand or my hair, of all things, when he walks me to my car, but he says he just enjoys our time talking. I don't think he means anything by it."

"You never think anybody means anything by it, even after all this time." Carl shook his head and grinned. "You still believe the best of everyone and smile at them all. I still have to worry about you. But, then, I don't really want you to change, either." He sobered suddenly. "Why is forty-three okay for a guy to be older than you, but your being older than me is not okay?"

"I don't know. I guess just tradition that the man should be older. Knowing you, I don't quite understand why, since I rely on you for everything. But my daughters are traditional. They'd never understand my caring about you." She felt some kind of sadness."

Carl looked away. "I do understand. It's okay, Meggie. We knew this would happen sometime." He straightened his shoulders with a sigh. "So Ed keeps wanting to see you again?"

"Yes. He contacted me today, or rather his aide did, to say he would be here Thursday evening--at least I think he meant Thursday."

"Why do I have the feeling you're a bit shaky about what you know about this guy and what you don't?" Carl walked to the kitchen and returned with cookies for both of them, flopping on the divan next to her. He munched contentedly as he listened.

"Well, except that he has a quirky sense of humor, and he's patient and sweet, I guess I really don't know much. He's awfully idealistic and dedicated, and feels quite strongly about the Duty, Honor Country thing of the Army, the nation, the world, the universe…" I think what I want to know from you is if it's all right to keep seeing him or not because he has a weird job?"

"Do you want to?" He grasped her arms, turning her so he could look closely at her face.

"I think I'd like to know him even better. He's a fun person, a fine man. I think you'd like him, too, and you know friendship is probably all it can ever be for me."

"You don't usually ask my opinion of just friends. This must have the possibility of becoming more serious than that. Do you think you might want him—the way you want me, I mean?" Carl threw his arms around her and wrapped one leg over her lap, pinning her to the couch, flashing his best leer, and grinning wildly.

She laughed huskily; relieved he seemed back to his old joking self. "It will never go *that* far, and he never leers at me like you do. He's quite dignified—and much more subtle--just always on the run. I'm not sure how I feel about him. I *know* how I feel about you," she said, tickling him until he squeaked, "Uncle."

They quieted their teasing and relaxed for a time before Carl spoke again. She could feel his thoughts moving and waited patiently for him to put them together.

"Meggie," he almost whispered. "If you really like this guy, I want you to be happy. I'll encourage you, if you think this is the real thing. I just don't want you to be hurt if he isn't the person you think he is."

She hugged Carl and said softly, "I know. You'll wish me well should I ever want to go, and I'll do the same for you." She thought it over. "I don't know right now. I'm beginning to feel something new with Ed. But I won't know what it is unless I see more of him. He's so darned mysterious. But when he comes Thursday, I want you to be there too. Perhaps you can sense something I don't, like you always seem to sense something about others. You know I'm still pretty skitzy about guys who seem interested in me."

He chuckled softly, "Yeah, I know. I've seen you run like hell, practically sit in my lap to get away, or make up an excuse to go straight home often enough."

"You know I'm still a bit afraid of personal closeness, with everyone but you, anyway. I want you to tell me honestly what you think about him, and if I should continue to accept his attention."

"Okay, Megan. I'll drive up Thursday evening after I put the bird to bed. Will he want you to dine with him alone, do you think? Will he mind if I'm there?"

"I really don't care if he minds. I'll just tell him I want you to be there so my potential boyfriend can meet my best friend. If he balks, that will tell me something important about him too, won't it?"

Chapter 23

Thursday evening came, and Megan found the whole gang expected to join her for dinner at the O'Club. It would be even more obvious to them that Ed had come to see her privately should she refuse them. *Hardly discreet enough.* Thus, not only Carl, but also Stan, Luke, Abby, Lila, and Emily announced they were coming.

She arranged with Marco to save the large round table for them. "Are you sure that's what you want when the Colonel comes tonight?" he asked.

"Yes, Marco. I think perhaps there's safety for him in numbers, and I want him to know my friends sooner or later, anyway. Don't you think that's a good idea?"

"If that's what you want, I'll arrange it." Marco left to attend to her wishes.

Though she could tell Ed wanted to talk to her alone when he arrived a few minutes later, he was a good sport about the crowd that followed them into the dining room. He responded jovially to all the ski talk. 'Major America,' Gary and his wife, joined the group after dinner in the bar. Outspoken Gary asked Ed, "Are you married?" Ed shook his head and added that he was divorced and had teenaged girls who lived with their mother in the States.

"What's your MOS—your job classification?" asked Stan and, though he didn't ask rank, Megan could tell Stan was sizing up Ed as though he were under a microscope.

"I'm in weapons inspection," said Ed with a straight face, blank as a card shark holding a fist full of aces. *Boy, he is cool under pressure,* Megan thought. By the time the talk had lightened to everybody's favorite topic of skiing, Gary had invited Ed on the next Ski Club trip. Stan was insisting Ed needed to come up from Stuttgart to attend the next Ski Club party at his house, *Seehof.* Megan knew Ed would prefer not to go with a crowd because the more people who knew about him, the greater would be his security risk.

But he answered diplomatically, "You know, I'd like that. Your Bamberg group has fun together. I'll have to let you know later when I know my schedule of inspections, but I'll try to make it."

Toward the end of a delightful evening with the guys

questioning Ed non-stop, he finally said he'd have to get back down to Stuttgart that night, a two hour drive, and he asked Megan to walk him out to his car.

"That was quite a third degree your friends gave me. They seemed to sense I enjoy your company. I hope they can be discreet." He took her hand while walking to the parking lot. "Do you think I passed inspection?"

"With flying colors, I think. You charmed them all. I'm really sorry though, and a little embarrassed. I wanted Carl to meet you. I had no idea it would get so public, or so personal." She couldn't help laughing. Her friends had been terribly obvious.

"Oh, it's quite all right. I can tell they care about you. I'm glad you have such protective friends. It speaks well of your character, young lady." He kissed her on the forehead. "But I do have an ulterior motive tonight. How would you like to go to London with me this weekend?"

"Oh, I couldn't do that, Ed." She shook her head quickly. "I've never traveled with anyone except that gang in there and, if it would mean missing school, I can't leave my kids."

"First, so you and your friends will know I'm on the up and up, I promise I'll have a hotel room reserved just for you, and second, your children might be impressed if you got a chance to meet Kissinger, don't you think?"

"What kind of trip is this?" Her startled eyes opened wide.

"We'll be doing some diplomatic negotiating and fence mending with a NATO ally whose leadership is in some hot water these days. This nation may have become a security risk, which might kick them out of NATO entirely. It's a real flap at European Command Headquarters with calls coming fast and furious from the Pentagon. EUCOM HQ is not sure yet if the U.N., or NATO Security Council will handle it, or if we'll have to. They chose London as neutral ground. The only boss to whom I report will be there, too. That's the Secretary of Defense, so you'll meet him too." Ed paused to let her catch her breath. "There'll be the usual formal dinner and lots of handshaking between delegations. I'd be proud to have you on my arm as I work the protocol. I'd like you to see what my more quiet negotiations are like, if you're interested. I'll even wear my uniform for you." He smiled down at her, waiting.

"It certainly sounds intriguing, and I'd love to know more of what you do, but…"

When she hesitated, he hurried to add, "I've never taken along a date before, but I don't want to miss the opportunity to spend the whole weekend with you."

"When would you have to know? At the very least, I'd have to arrange for a substitute for one day. When will you be leaving, and when are you coming back?"

"Sounds like you would like to meet Kissinger." Ed chuckled. "He's a strange egg, but you might like him. My plane will leave Stuttgart Friday night and return probably on Monday night, if all goes well. At least, consider it, will you? Even your thinking about it will make me feel better, after that grilling I took inside."

His smile was almost pleading, and Megan found herself considering the idea. There was one problem. "You aren't sure when you'll be back? Does that mean there could be a delay in getting back to my classroom?"

"I can never actually *guarantee* when I'll be coming or going. It will depend if the 'gentlemanly approach' works, or if my group will have to handle it."

Megan wanted to ask if that meant his group's approach might be 'ungentlemanly,' but she restrained herself.

"Then I don't know, Ed, though I must admit it sounds exciting, and I'd like to know what you do when you're off gallivanting." She thought of another question. "How do you get all these trips and rooms scheduled so quickly, anyway? Every time I go somewhere on military orders, it takes weeks to get visas, clearances, schedules, flights, and such. You seem to just pick up and go."

"This is something I don't show anyone, but it might help you understand." He unfolded a somewhat rumpled piece of paper from his wallet and handed it to her.

As she glanced at the usual letters and numbers that appear on all military orders, she skimmed down until she saw the more pertinent part of Ed's orders. She gasped in surprise.

"These orders don't have the usual formal limitations of anyone else's. My gosh! I've never seen any orders like these. Why, if I'm interpreting this right, these say you can go anywhere, anytime, commandeer any means of transportation, and everyone is supposed to do whatever you want them to do and give you immediate access to all top secret documents without question. It's not even dated—it's good indefinitely. My orders are always quite specific. Yours almost sound like you could start WW III single-handedly."

"I hope not, but I'll let you know first, if that's ever necessary." He laughed softly as he refolded the document into his wallet. "Of course, you realize you mustn't talk about my standing orders, either, don't you?"

"I sure wouldn't tell anyone. They'd think I was crazy! Your orders are scary!" She felt a shudder of apprehension in her spine, and her hands shook. *What was Ed into?*

"Suppose we leave it this way. I'll call you tomorrow at three, and find out if you can go with me. Perhaps I'll know by then exactly when we're due to return. If your answer is 'yes,' you can drive down to meet me at the Patch O'Club by six in the evening. Bring along something formal. The plane leaves at eight, so we'll have time for a quick dinner. If the answer is 'no,' I'll call you to make plans when I get back from a speedy mission juggling people in the Netherlands, Lebanon, Tunis, and Berlin--probably Wednesday afternoon. We'll go skiing at Garmisch next weekend, after I get back."

His smile was a bit sheepish as he added, "Do you think we can go alone for that one? I'll happily go along with the gang another time, if I can." Megan laughed and nodded, noting that it was unusual to see a 'full-bird' Colonel blush.

As he waited for her answer, he added something else. "Don't worry. I always sleep in the camper I keep parked at Garmisch. I'll get you a room at the Abrams military hotel for the weekend. I'm afraid we're of a generation that's pretty old-fashioned. Is that okay?"

"I understand." She smiled, letting out a relieved breath. "That sounds like fun. You did guarantee you could nurse me along to parallel ski, didn't you? I'd like that. It'll give us time to talk, which of course, we didn't get much of tonight."

"Okay, it's a plan. I'll call tomorrow to see about our date in London. Whether that works out or not, plan on next weekend skiing with me." He took her hands in his. "You know, Megan, it wasn't as bad being on the mission this time because I kept thinking of spending time with you when I returned. I'll call you tomorrow."

He started to go, then turned to add, "Something else, Megan, obviously we are not a secret anymore. I told you once that I feared my affection could bring you danger. I don't want that to ever happen.

Please be careful what you say to anyone. We'll make our friendship seem as casual as we can and hope your friends aren't too talkative." He grinned down at her, kissed her hair, climbed in his car, and drove away.

Megan slowly walked back into the Club. She knew there would be a haze of questions, and she didn't know any answers, at least none she could tell. Being discreet might be hard.

"You should have told him you'd go to London," announced Luke loudly, after she had relayed Ed's invitation. "How often does one get to meet that SOB Kissinger?"

"Well it wouldn't be just for that. I remember that you don't like him."

"Why, we were behind the eight ball almost from the start in Vietnam," said Stan, "because Johnson ignored his trained Army leaders and tried to micromanage the war himself. I'll never forgive our leaders for agreeing to a cease-fire for a year, supposedly to get our guys out. His negotiations agreed to look the other way while the North Vietnamese resumed their attacks on the South. That was the 'chicken' bargain to buy so-called peace at the expense of the South Vietnamese. President Ford is carrying it out right now."

"And," added Robert, "though maybe we shouldn't have been in Vietnam at all, once we were there, we had an obligation to the Vietnamese who fought on our side, who trusted us. We have a good idea how they'll be treated from how the Cong treated our Prisoners of War."

There were deep shadows in Stan's eyes as he added, "Our government leaders were oblivious to what it cost us to fight that war. They all listened to Hanoi Jane and the draft dodgers who spit on us, instead of to our own commanders. They hung us out to dry with all our friendly forces, our equipment, and even our own men. It was unforgivable!"

Looking into the stony eyes of her friend, Stan, who normally was always smiling, Megan said, "I don't think I want to meet that man after all, even in a social setting."

It was not in the cards for Megan to go to London, anyway, because Ed could give no definite return date. By late Friday night, however, she regretted not going, since her other military friends were on flying duty for the weekend, and her colleagues were traveling. She had a small relapse of depression, just being alone. But a surprise phone call cheered her on Saturday at the O' Club—from London.

"Wish you were here with me, Megan, but you can watch for me in the newspapers," Ed said. "If nothing surfaces about 'Scorpio' you'll know we were successful. Keep your fingers crossed for me." She could hear disappointment in his voice, but he came back immediately with, "I'll look forward to our ski trip next weekend." She felt warm as she hung up the phone.

Later, Carl's private comment was simply, "I liked him, Megan. Let me know how it goes, and whether or not you'll want all my propositions to become pure and platonic."

His super-innocent look to the heavens dissolved her in giggles. "I'm not sure you know *how* to be pure, Carl." She couldn't help laughing, yet she almost felt a strange urge to cry as well. Something was changing in her life. She felt a momentary shiver of apprehension.

"Oh well," Carl said, with a big sigh. "My kid sister is coming to visit me soon for her eighteenth birthday. It was my graduation present to her. I'll probably have my hands full anyway. She plans to stay for a year. Guess I'll have to be all celibate and lonely while she's here, to set a good example—like I really know anything about an eighteen-year-old redhead!"

"I'll help you, should you get in trouble." Megan realized Carl was telling her they wouldn't have as much time together. This young girl wouldn't understand their strange bond. "And I know what you're thinking, my dear. I understand."

"I don't," he said. "I invited her long ago. Thought it might be fun to have my baby sister here when she turned of age. Now I wish I hadn't. It'll put a crimp in my love life, won't it?"

Megan smiled at her friend, her head bowed. "You'll be okay, Carl. We'll work something out, and we're always trusted sidekicks—no matter what."

Carl nodded, but he looked miserable. Megan realized it was time for their comfortable relationship to change. "Don't worry. I certainly don't expect a friendship with Ed to be demanding anything more of me than it already does. So I'll be okay too." When he pursed his lips and looked away, she added, " Is that all you wanted to say?"

"It's all I'd better say, because I want you to be completely free to make your own decisions. I think you're ready now to be more independent. Remember, you're no longer *a woman alone*. You are now *a woman on her own*. There's a *big* difference. Think about it. You know I love you either way, and I want you to do what is best for your own future."

Megan kissed him on the cheek and said, "Thank you. I'll do nothing until I talk it over with you. It helps to know you think I'm ready to be free, though I'll admit to some uneasiness as to whether I'm ready for freedom, or even if I *want* it."

Carl simply put his hand up to hers in their usual 'my strength to you' handshake, saying, "We'll always have this openness and honesty between us. So don't worry about anything. Be happy, Megan." Then he suddenly threw both arms around her and hugged her tightly, rubbing his cheek on hers. She *felt*, rather than heard the goodbye. He fled to his car for the drive back to Katterbach.

She stood watching him go until he waved from the corner. She moved slowly back inside. That night she had a private chat with her Andy, wherever he was up in Heaven. Was it really all right to date Ed--to perhaps let herself care about him? Should she go skiing with him? He had arranged for her to have her own room--no pressure. She did want to ski better, and he promised he could change her intermediate Stem Christie turns to a nice Parallel.

Carl had given his blessing to do as she chose, but she detected reluctance, too. Would she be hurting their friendship if she became closer to Ed? She didn't want to do that. But Carl had said that Ed might turn into the 'big love of her life,' and that he approved. This crazy young friend had brought her a long way toward self-confidence and understanding the realities of modern life, when she'd apparently been living in the Dark Ages. At least that's what everyone told her. If she were honest with herself, she also knew he had saved her from suicide. How could she ever repay that?

"By being happy," Carl had said.

Megan sighed. "Learning to live life alone is really tough, Andy." She spoke out loud to the flowers and walls and windows of her apartment, wishing Andy could give her guidance.

Then she decided. She would go skiing with Ed. They were, after all, getting to know each other better. What could it hurt? It would all be in good, clean fun, and she would learn to ski better. He had even joked that he could teach her "How to Parallel Ski in 25,000 easy lessons." Ed was a fine man, with a great sense of humor, and even older than she was. That was quite rare, already.

Friday was a school holiday, so Megan drove down to Stuttgart early to visit with a former student from her teaching days in California. Tony, his girlfriend, Robin, and a third friend, were now Army privates stationed at Patch Barracks. Megan took them to see Ludwigsburg Palace with its fairy tale garden before returning to meet Ed at the main gate as planned. Ed rode with them up the hill to the Officers' Club and Guest House.

Since they were crowded in her little Fiat, Ed invited Robin to sit on his lap in the front passenger seat. He chatted amiably with the young people. Megan noticed with amusement that it was a one-sided conversation. The young soldiers were quite tongue-tied, and Robin, with much embarrassment, was trying valiantly to sit 'lightly.'

As Ed retrieved Megan's bag and carried it into the Guest House, Tony whispered to her, "My God, Mrs. James, do you know who he *is*? How'd you get to know *him*?"

Their friend was equally excited. "He even asked how we were, and everything!"

"He was so nice to us," said Robin in some wonderment. "I can't believe he actually *talked* to us. He only talks to Haig and God. He's really big brass, and we're only privates."

Megan hugged the kids goodbye and stifled her giggles all the way to dinner with Ed. She was glad he was kind and comfortable with young soldiers. It said volumes about his character, she thought—that he could be completely at ease with everyone. She decided to relax, though she knew it would be difficult. She would simply enjoy Ed's company for one of the few weekends he had off. After all, what could possibly happen?

Chapter 24

Late Sunday night, Megan slammed on the Fiat's brakes, jumped out, and ran into the Katterbach BOQ without even locking her car. She glided quickly down the familiar hallway to Carl's room and knocked. There was no answer, so she let herself in, knowing he always kept it unlocked. She assumed if he were out flying, or out with a girlfriend, she would simply wait for him. There was nowhere else she could go for advice on the problem weighing her down.

She heard him mumble from the bed, "Is that you, Megan? What time is it?"

"About eleven. You must have gone to bed pretty early. I'm sorry if I disturbed you."

"You know that's okay, Megan. Come on over here and get in where it's warm. You'll freeze to death out there."

She obeyed, sliding out of her boots, coat, and outer clothing quickly, still shivering. He lifted the covers, she climbed in next to him, and he tucked the blankets around her. "What happened? I didn't expect you'd come here after spending the weekend with Ed. But I was feeling kinda' down. I'm glad you came."

She could not at first get the words out, but he could apparently feel her anxiety.

"Tell me what happened. Did he hurt you?"

"No, nothing like that. It was something else that happened, and I don't even know where to begin to tell you." The tears she had thus far held back began to fall. "I don't know how I get into these complicated situations, and I always come running to you for help."

"Don't cry Megan," he said, wrapping her closely to him. "And I'm happy that you come to me...always. Just slow down and start at the beginning. You drove down to Stuttgart to meet him Friday, right? And..." He reached to his bedside table and handed her a clean handkerchief.

She mopped her eyes and took a moment to calm herself. "He met me and we went to Patch's Ski Club meeting. I met the club officers and compared notes. That part was fun. Then we went for dinner at the Patch O'Club with some more Brass. They were in some kind of flap expecting calls from the Pentagon, the NATO

226 M.J. Brett

Commander, and General Haig. "Ed had simply cut himself orders for a weekend off, but he was still on call for an emergency. We'd just started dinner, when his aide brought him a strange-looking telephone and Ed got really quiet when he listened to the message. He apologized and said he'd have to leave me for a couple of hours because he had to go to HQ to clear up a problem. He introduced me to this Colonel, a charming man named Warren, who I felt had been pressed into duty to take care of me. Ed said he'd be back in time to walk me to my room at the Guesthouse. Then he left, and his friend acted like nothing unusual had happened."

"Did Ed come back later?"

"At about 2100 hours, after Warren and I had finished dinner. Ed walked me over to the guesthouse, up the stairs to my door, and said, 'Our crisis has heated up faster than we thought it would, Megan. I'm really sorry. I'll probably be up most of the night making phone calls and writing a briefing for General Haig but, with any luck at all, I'll be able to pick you up here at 0730 so we can go skiing as planned.' He kissed me on the top of my head and didn't explain further. He just left. I didn't know what to think."

"Hm, that is strange. And...?"

"He came in the morning as though nothing had spoiled our dinner date, loaded my skis into his van, and we drove to Garmisch and took the cog train up to the Zugspitze."

"Did he talk on the trip?"

"Oh yes, about Civil War history and everything *except* the night before and what the problem was. It would have been a lovely trip if I hadn't felt so much in the dark."

"How was the skiing?" At least Carl felt comfortable talking about skiing because she felt his body relax. Even through her own anxiety, she had a fleeting thought about how much the two of them had learned to read each other's moods.

"Beautiful. He really did help my Stem Christie turns change to a Parallel." She giggled. "It was like having private lessons. Just wait, I'll have some tricks to show you. We had a wonderful day, except for a sudden 'white out' when the fog and snow made every landmark disappear. I somehow got lost over on the opposite side of a ridge. I couldn't tell if I was moving up or down, or even moving at all. It was scary. I ran into a man who had done the same thing, and we stuck together until we finally figured out which way was 'up' and sidestepped to get back on the right side of the ridge.

"Once we reached the ridge, other people could hear our shouts in the fog and came to help. I could hear Ed out there calling my name. When he found me, he practically crushed my ribs and said that one minute I was right behind him, and the next, I had disappeared." Unconsciously, Megan held Carl's hand as she talked. "But Ed was frightened. He said if we had kept going down the wrong side, there was a huge drop off we wouldn't have seen."

"Megan, *only you* could get yourself into something like that. Didn't I tell you to be careful?" Carl scolded. Obviously he worried it was the getting lost that had scared her so much.

"Carl, I was fine once we got back on the right side of the ridge. We skied awhile longer until it was too socked in to see. About three, we headed down, and he dropped me off at my hotel so I could shower and change while he went back to do the same at his campground. We met in the lobby at 1800 hours and went to dinner.

"So what was the big deal?" Carl obviously didn't see what was wrong.

"Same thing as the previous night," she slapped the bed firmly. "Right in the middle of a marvelous dinner, here comes his Aide with the funny phone again. And again, Ed excused himself to go 'try to solve the problem.' This time, the young officer stayed with me until I finished dinner, and walked me back to my hotel. About 2200, Ed called, apologized, and said he'd again be working most of the night, making seventeen calls to put NATO forces on alert status and collect situation reports." Megan came up on her elbow. "Were you guys called on alert Saturday?" At David's nod, she continued. "That sounds like he's deep into something, doesn't it? I really don't understand what he does, but I do know there is a tremendous amount of responsibility weighing on him, and he keeps saying he needs me to 'restore him,' whatever that means. He takes everything so seriously. Why would *he* be the one to put everyone on alert? What have I gotten myself into?"

Carl shook his head. "I'm not sure, Meggie. I'm assuming there's more—tell me."

Megan bit her lower lip. "Well, anyway, he said he'd still try to pick me up in the morning for skiing. By this time, I was a bit miffed, and I asked him if he was *sure* he'd be coming. He apologized all over again and said it was really an important crisis that needed instantaneous solutions, and he would see me in the morning--that I should please try to understand. I fibbed and said I did."

"Did he show up in the morning?"

"Yes, but when I asked if the problem was solved, he said, 'Not entirely. I'm hoping the people I sent to solve it will have fixed things, and I won't have to go. I think we're clear for skiing though. I've made some emergency arrangements, just in case, so let's try.' Then he was full of fun and mischief as always, on the trip up the mountain and on the slopes, until..."

"It sounds as though he was simply trying take care of his military business at night to keep it from getting in the way of showing you a good time. I hate to admit it, because I don't *want* to like him, but I do. He seems genuinely to care about you."

"But, Carl, you haven't heard the worst. About 1400 hours, this helicopter circled slowly around the mountain above the ski slope. When we noticed it, he said, 'Oh damn,' and started waving his ski poles at the helicopter, and we skied up to this ridge. He gave some kind of signal to them. Everyone on the slope was staring at us. Then he said, 'Follow me...quickly,' and headed for the gondola. When we got down, the helicopter was hovering over the parking lot. Ed turned to me and said, 'Can you drive a stick shift?' When I said 'yes,' he handed me his keys and said, 'You'll need to drive my van back to Stuttgart to pick up your car to get home. Just leave my van at the O'Club and give the keys to the manager.'"

Carl shifted to hold her closer, sensing her agitation.

"I felt completely bewildered. Ed's aide was in the back of the helicopter with his gear. Ed handed his skis to the aide and says to me, 'I'm more sorry than you'll ever know. They need me after all. I'll call you Friday, after school.' Then he kissed me, really hard, and rubbed his face in my hair--my hair again. He climbed up on the skid and into the helicopter. He waved as they flew away, as though nothing unusual had happened at all. People were staring."

"He just left you there?"

"Yes! I felt like some kind of fool, so I got his van, gathered up my belongings at the hotel, and drove to Stuttgart to pick up my car and drop his off. Then I came here because...I don't know why...I guess I needed you..." Megan began to cry. "I don't understand any of this at all."

Carl absent-mindedly rubbed the back of her neck as she cried. He seemed to be thinking, trying to analyze the whole story. Finally he said, "Megan, I could be wrong, but I think Ed is a spook."

"What's that?" She raised up on her elbow to face him fully.

"It's someone so deeply into secret military intelligence operations that he comes and goes without telling anyone. Spooks do all types of clandestine stuff, usually the most dangerous missions out there. If one disappears or is killed, no one would even be notified, and there would be no records left behind with our government or any chain of command to tell anyone what happened to him."

Megan drew in her breath sharply. "You mean he's a spy."

"He must have had a really sticky problem for the helicopter to go to such extremes to come get him. It would have to have been something no one else could do, because flying over the Zugspitze Mountain is totally against regulations."

"So it's something really bad when he keeps disappearing?"

"I think so, Megan. If you guys were having a good time while he was with you, he wouldn't have left you during dinners, or from the ski slope either, unless he had to go."

"I'm telling you something he told me not to talk about, but maybe you'll know what it means. He carries his gun hidden in the back of his belt, even while skiing. When he takes it out, he keeps it right next to him. And his orders say he can go anywhere and do anything he wants. I saw them." She took a deep breath, realizing she was saying more than she should, but she needed this to make sense.

"I think it's safe to tell you he once said to think of him as going anywhere on a minute's notice to try to keep an international problem from erupting into an incident of war. He said if I ever read about it in the paper, he'd failed. And he answers only to Haig. Does that make any sense to you in light of this latest disappearing act?"

Carl spoke slowly. "The gun by itself may not mean too much. We all carry them in the cockpit, though not usually loaded unless on alert. Bill sleeps with a knife under his pillow. Some of that's left over in all Vietnam vets. But, if Ed is keeping it close by, even when not wearing it—that could only mean he's expecting someone to be coming after him. I don't think I like the idea of your being with him at all, if he's expecting *that* kind of trouble."

"He did say once that my association with him could be

dangerous for me, and he worried about that. He also worried about too many people knowing he cares about me."

Carl paused, again thinking. "Yeah, Megan. I'm afraid it does make sense. He's a spook!" He sighed audibly. "He's into something deep. I know this will scare you, but you'll just have to hope he gets through whatever it is, and *can* call you Friday, like he said."

"You mean if he can't call Friday..." She felt tears again.

"That's it, Meggie. You'll just have to wait to hear from him."

"Will he be able to tell me what happened, afterward?"

"I'm sure he will, if he can, but if it's an ongoing threat..."

"I don't think I'm cut out for all this mystery and 'derring-do.' How did I get myself into this situation? It was Marco that got us together, and he seems to know all about Ed."

"That sort of surprises me, yet maybe not, since Marco seems to be on top of everything. He may know more about Ed than you do. I think you have the choice of learning to live with Ed's disappearances and silences, supporting him, and understanding his job, or of not seeing him anymore."

Megan was silent as she mopped her eyes again.

"Put the 'derring-do' out of your mind a moment, would you want to see him again, otherwise?"

"When he was with me, Carl, he was wonderful. He's smart, witty, easy-going, and we tease each other and laugh constantly. He relaxes his identity with me and seems just to be himself. His smile makes me feel wriggly all over. But this top secret stuff scares me."

"Almost everyone here is into secrets, but I'll admit his dwarfs the rest of us. You'll have to decide, Meggie." He whispered in her ear, "I can tell you want to see him again. You're just frightened. I'll make it easy for you. I won't even *tease* about my propositions until you decide if he's the right guy for you. You're only confused about your feelings right now. Just let me hold you tonight until all the fear goes away, and you can look at it more rationally. You'll know what you feel when you see Ed again."

"Thank you for understanding. I don't ever want to lose you."

Carl chuckled. "Ed may not understand that, but I appreciate the vote of confidence. Put it this way. Would you have wanted to make love to Ed if all this odd stuff hadn't happened?"

"I admit I'm attracted to the man. I don't know how I feel. I'm a little scared of caring so much. But I sort of find myself thinking about him pretty often."

"If you're anxious about his safety, Megan, and you seem to be, then you may want to have a deeper relationship with him. Remember, we agreed that if either of us ever found the right person, we'd be supportive friends through a lifetime. Perhaps Ed is the right person for you--old geezer that he is." Carl grinned wickedly.

"I'm not sure of my feelings. You already know I'm still afraid of loving someone and then losing them. And loving Ed seems *particularly* risky. Look, I'll call you after he calls me, and you can help me figure out how I feel then. Is that all right?"

"I'm supposed to help *you* figure out how *you* feel about another man. That's rich!"

She could hear an element of amused sarcasm in his voice. "I guess that does sound pretty strange, doesn't it? But you know I don't listen to anyone except you and Abby."

"It's a deal, Meggie. I'll be waiting to hear you're okay with it. But you know, sooner or later, you must make the decision for yourself. I'll help you all I can, but you're ready for the next step. You're falling in love with him." Carl said in a more muted voice, "You understand, if he doesn't call..."

She sobered. "Yes..."

"He'll call if he's in one piece, Meggie. But if you don't hear from him, it will mean he isn't capable of calling, not that he didn't want to. It's like Andy didn't want to leave you—but he had no choice. You need time to digest that fact, and to decide if you can live with it or not." Carl smoothed her hair and kissed her on the ear. "Now, try not to think about it for now. I'll make you think of another topic. You're coming down here for my promotion party, aren't you?"

"Of course I will, though if it's just going to be all guys, perhaps you'd rather I didn't."

"I want you there." He sighed. "Now turn over and don't take up all the room. Let me just snuggle against your back, and we'll both get some sleep. The alarm is set for 0500 for an early flight. That'll give you time to get back to Bamberg in time for your kidlets. I know you're scared, Meggie, but we'll take this one baby step at a time."

She felt protected in Carl's arms and, in spite of the quiet tears of fear and confusion that ran down her cheeks, she finally fell asleep.

But her nightmares were of someone else dying.

Chapter 25

The week seemed endless, but finally Friday came. As the children gathered up their things and hugged their teacher on leaving the classroom, little Deirdre stuck her head in to say there was a call for Mrs. James. Megan hurried out to the hall and picked up the receiver, breathlessly. "Is that you, Ed?"

"It's me, but I'm not sure how long I've got, so I'll tell you the important thing first. I'll try to be with you on the evening after your prescription runs out. Think about it, and you'll understand. I'll meet you at the O'Club."

"Okay, but what's all that noise in the background?" She could hear what sounded like the staccato of machine gun bullets hitting something solid, accompanied by other explosions and single shots. "Where are you? It sounds like you're in a phone booth outside the Beirut Hilton. We've been hearing bad things in the news…"

The line went dead. Megan's hand flew to her mouth. A shot might as well have pierced her body. She couldn't breathe. What could have happened? She hung up the phone and stayed at the desk, trying to concentrate on correcting papers. Ed would get back through to her, if he could. The 'if' made her heart constrict in her chest.

"Stay calm," she told herself sternly. It may have been just a bad connection. But the sounds she had heard frightened her. She forced herself to push thoughts of the latest headlines out of her mind. Beirut, Lebanon had only come from her mouth when she heard gunfire, because it had jumped into the forefront of violence and bombings worldwide. Between highly publicized problems with the Palestinian groups, the PLO, and Syria, poor Lebanon was being overrun by terrorist organizations. But surely Americans wouldn't be there, would they? Confused, Megan tried to concentrate only on her math corrections. Twenty interminable minutes went by before the phone rang again. She caught it on the first ring.

"Ed?"

"It's me. Sorry, the line went dead. I had to find another working phone. Sorry for the noise. Damn! You're sharp, my dear! You're close. Now be a good girl and wait for me the day I said. If I make it out of here, I'll be coming back to you. I promise."

"Are you in danger there, Ed? Please hang up and get inside someplace where it's safer." She surprised herself by crying out when she heard the next volley of bullets. "Ed...Ed...are you there?"

"I'm here--needed a moment to duck. I'm coming back to you—back to *you*, my dear..."

With that, the line went dead again and Megan was suddenly crying with her head in her arms on the telephone table. The children's math papers became a sodden mass.

Fellow Annex teachers, Les and Frank, came through the hall on their way out. Les said, "Hey, Megan. Are you all right?"

Megan straightened up, pulled a tissue from her pocket and dabbed at her eyes. "Sure, I'm fine--a momentary lapse. I'll be fine."

"Are you meeting the gang over at the Club for happy hour?"

"Sure, just let me get finished here. I'll be over later. Go ahead without me for now."

The two walked out, meeting two other teachers, and they all went on together. Frank kept looking back at her, so she waved encouragingly to show she was okay.

She went back to her classroom to think about Ed's code words...what prescription? When would it run out? *How would Ed know about my prescriptions anyway? Oh, I do remember.* She had dropped her purse in the Abrams Hotel lobby, and Ed had helped her pick up the contents. He'd looked at a prescription bottle and asked if she were sick. It was a prescription for a minor lung problem and the label had specified two pills per day. *My God, he is much too observant for me to keep up. I suppose that's part of his training too.*

She dumped the contents of her purse onto her desk and fumbled for the plastic bottle. There were five pills left, one for tonight and two each for Saturday and Sunday, so that meant Ed would try to be back in two days...probably not counting Sunday, he'd said "...after the pills run out," so perhaps Monday. That must have been what he meant.

He'd be back Monday, or perhaps not at all, if things went badly. In spite of Carl's explanations, that was the idea Megan couldn't accept. She couldn't help crying again. Did she care about him that much, or was she just so softhearted about the danger her friends were in that she worried about them all? No, he must be special. Perhaps Carl was right, and she liked Ed more than she wanted to like anyone. Raw, edgy emotions gnawed at her thoughts. She quickly dialed Carl's number. The phone at the Katterbach BOQ was in the hall, so there was no telling who would answer. Finally someone did, and they went to check Carl's room. "He must still be out flying. Maybe you can catch him at the airfield."

She dialed the airfield's tower. "He's just landing now," said the air traffic controller. "He'll be here in a few minutes—has to post flight the bird. Do you want him to call you back?"

"Yes, please," and she left her number, though she knew Carl could dial it by heart.

A few minutes later, she was sobbing to her friend, her confidante, her would-be lover, about the dangerous situation with her 'boyfriend,' a man of forty-three. "This whole thing is so upside down," she said, not understanding her own feelings at all.

"I'll be right there, Megan. Hold on and don't discuss it with anyone until I get there. Can you manage that? Give me a couple of hours to clean up and drive. I'll meet you at the Club."

By the time Megan filed away her papers for grading and lesson plans, Lila and Abby had walked over from the main building, and the three headed over to the O'Club. On the way, Abby asked, "What do you hear from your mysterious colonel?"

"Oh, yes, Megan," added Lila. "I just think he's a charmer...and sooo sexy," she giggled, "like Yul Brunner."

Megan spoke slowly, carefully choosing her words. "He called today. He's hoping to visit Monday, if he gets back on time."

"Where was he this time?"

"I didn't ask." Megan didn't want to say anything, even to her best friends, until she could talk to Carl about what might be classified as secret. "I'll have to wait until he calls." She forced a smile, as though Ed were only slaving away in his Stuttgart office.

Lila said, "Y'know, Megan, Klaus still asks me about Ed."

Megan stopped walking, then realized she shouldn't give any sign she was distressed.

"I told him how Ed sort of comes and goes. He thinks Ed is doing something important, and asks about him almost every day. He wants to know when Ed will be back for one of our group activities, and he suggested we have a double date. Wouldn't that be fun?"

Megan was slow to answer, trying to think what she could say that wouldn't hurt Lila's feelings but also wouldn't compromise Ed. Knowing how uncomfortable she felt about Ed's situation, whatever it was, she now searched for a way to avoid any contact with Klaus.

"Well, Lila, it's hard to say just when Ed can get away from his office. He can only come up here when there are inspections to be done, and it's usually with little advance notice. And he works so much with people in Stuttgart that he feels more comfortable if we can just ski, or go on a picnic by ourselves to relax the tension. Besides, he sort of seems to want to have a little more time alone…to get better acquainted, I mean…just the two of us…" She finished lamely; somehow sorry she had made it sound more of a romantic thing than it was as yet. She could feel herself blushing. On the other hand, that seemed to be an argument Lila could understand.

"Oh, sure, Honey. That's right, more romantic. I'll bet he'll especially want you all to himself Monday when he's coming from another exciting mission. Where are you meeting him?"

"I'm…I'm not sure. He said he'd call first. And it's probably not all that 'exciting' just to inspect weapons over at Heidelberg or Augsberg." Megan hated the need to fib to her friends, but she had a vague and probably totally unfounded feeling Ed's safety might depend on it. She tried changing the subject. "Are you and Klaus getting to be that close *again*, then?"

"I don't know." She sighed, and pouted. "He's still really interested in coming to all our parties and dances on Post, and he has questions about everything then, but he rarely calls me in between events, unless he wants to come on Post. I don't think he wants to see me alone. Of course, I like being alone with Brian, so I don't *really* need Klaus." She giggled. "Brian has asked me to go steady again."

"What did you say?" Abby was more verbal. "You know Brian's really upset by your continuing to see Klaus."

"Well, he'll just have to get over it and be less jealous. I don't want to go steady with anyone until I've dated everyone. Otherwise, how will I know that Brian is *the* one?"

"But you like Brian. It's written all over your face when you're with him," said Megan.

"Yes, but I don't want him to be so possessive, and I want him to wait a little while."

"Lila," said Abby slowly, stressing her words, "I understand what you're saying, but don't make him wait so long, while you're playing around, that he gets tired of your game and leaves. Especially, not if you truly like him."

"Y'all are depressing me. Brian wouldn't leave me. He loves me."

"Then you'd better figure out why you're still seeing Klaus," cautioned Abby. "Brian needs to see light at the end of the tunnel."

"Abby's right, Lila. I feel like you're taking Brian for granted." Megan suddenly felt a sick feeling in her stomach that she might soon have to choose between loyal friends, too? *No, probably not, since the arrival of Carl's sister's will settle that for us anyway, and we've never taken our friendship for granted.*

As they entered the Club, the gang was settling in at the bar for a round of Happy Hour drinks before dinner. Megan knew Carl wouldn't arrive until dinnertime, so she chatted and joked with everyone else, knowing her heart wasn't in the cheerful banter. Was this ability to play the actress going to become a required part of her life should she become closer to Ed?

"Don't look so glum, Megan," teased Carl. "Everyone knows you're happier than *that* to see me." Whenever he entered, amid jovial handshakes and greetings, there was a lighter feeling in the air.

She felt instant relief, knowing she could turn the problem over to Carl. She realized she'd relied heavily on his presence, almost from the beginning of their friendship.

Robert asked, "Megan, I heard you were looking for another apartment. Is that true?"

"Yes," she nodded emphatically. "Last time I took off for the weekend, my landlady went in, and she changed my freezer setting. Everything thawed and had to be thrown out."

"Yeah, they think we keep the temperatures down too low," said Stan, "but then they have time to shop fresh every day, and we don't. Did you lose a lot of food?"

"A turkey I'd sliced up to make it fit in that tiny freezer, and ice cream was running all over the floor, that sort of thing." She went on. "Of course, there was something worse. She got into my hamper of dirty laundry and refolded everything and put it right back into the drawers. I had to take the whole works to the Laundromat before I could wear *anything* again. I just want her to stay out of my things!"

"They can enter by German law," added Mary. "Wish they'd change that, though your landlady does sound strangely obsessed. We'll all help you look for another apartment."

"You and Carl and Luke should team up to rent *Seehof* when Charlie and I leave in July?" Stan said, "It has three bedrooms—rare in Germany. At least it would keep the digs in the family for future parties, and you guys know where the booze is kept."

The crowd urged the trio to commit themselves, but Carl said, "We've given it some thought. Megan could keep Luke and me in line and see that we eat plenty of cookies." He patted his tummy jovially. "But, it would be a two hour commute for me every night, and I wouldn't trust Dirtball Luke to watch out for Megan, if I didn't make it home from Katterbach. Besides the rent is pretty high and heating bills are even worse. We'll keep talking about it."

As always, Carl was able to deflect difficult questions. In the general hubbub, he steered Megan over to a quiet table and pulled out her chair. "What's up? You sounded bad on the phone. Where is he?"

"I made a wild guess, based on the shouting and gunfire I could hear in the background. We were cut off, so he had to call back. He said I was 'close' to being right."

"Where'd you guess?"

"The Beirut Hilton."

"Ouch! There's been far too much terrorist action there lately. It's been all over the news."

"That's what scared me. He said he'd try to come Monday--at least I think it's Monday. He codes his statements so his movements can't be tracked as easily on an insecure phone line." She made sure no one could overhear. "Carl, it sounded really bad over the phone."

"The fact that it worries you tells me you've become rather interested in the old guy." He grinned at her. "I never thought you'd go for the bald look before, or I'd have shown you this sooner." He bent and tousled his hair, revealing a thinning spot on top. "See, how's that for a 26 year old to be going bald just for you?"

Megan smiled then, and followed his more relaxed lead. "Do you think, after all the time we've spent together, I never noticed you were destined for a monk-like coiffure in a few years? And of course, *I* don't feel that's a handicap." She wanted to tell Carl how confused she felt, but the words wouldn't come. The tears came instead.

"Don't Meggie, I know what you're trying to say." He stretched out his palm to her. She dropped her head as she met his hand with her own.

"I *do* need your strength, Carl. I don't know what I'd do without you. I don't even know how I feel, but I think Ed is feeling a lot more than I thought. He sounded on the phone like he really was 'coming back to me.' That's the way he said it. Not back to Stuttgart, or back to work, or even back from danger. He said he was trying hard to get back to *me*. What does that mean?"

Carl took her hand and said softly, "It means he needs you, and he cares about you. And, that puts me out of a job--that of protecting you and constantly petitioning to take care of your sexual needs. I still expect to take care of your emotional ones, and keep you out of trouble." He tried to laugh.

But Megan could sense his feelings as well, and she ached inside. "I'm sorry. I don't know what to think about when he gets back...if...he gets back."

"I do! And it's okay, Megan." Carl looked candidly in her eyes and said it plain. "I can't even imagine that he wouldn't want you all to himself when he gets out of this mess. And if you care for him, you'll want him too." He took a deep breath and whispered, "You'll know for sure how you feel *the minute* you see him."

He folded his free hand over both of hers. "It's all right, Meggie. You're ready to love someone again. I'd like to believe I had something to do with your being ready. We'll always be a team. Perhaps not the way you want it to be, with me completely bald and losing my teeth." He made her laugh by banging his lips together as though he were toothless. "But since you're pining for an older man, I'll wait while you decide. Follow your *own* heart and your *own* feelings, Megan. You always worry about what everyone *else* needs. It's your biggest asset in the camaraderie of Bamberg, but it's also your biggest liability, and it gets you in trouble. Go after what *you* need this time." He paused. "I guess I can always hope it doesn't work out and you'll come back to try out my expert sexual prowess. I'll try to age a lot by then."

He pulled out a handkerchief, dried her tears, and stuffed it back into his pocket. "We've got to stop weeping like this. People will think you're telling me you're pregnant or something." He grinned and stroked her cheek with his palm. "Actually, I sure wouldn't be unhappy if you would have my baby."

"Carl!" She gasped.

"I'm waiting right here as long as it takes for you to smile," he said, folding his arms and sitting staunchly with stern expression. "It's all going to work out. We'll just wait and see how it goes."

She could never hold anything back from Carl, and he could only maintain a straight face just so long. Her smile finally came, as his stoicism exploded in laughter. She *did* feel better.

"I need advice about something else. Lila said Klaus keeps saying Ed is doing something important. He wants us to double date. I told Lila again that Ed isn't important—that he only does inspections for EUCOM. But she insists Klaus thinks differently. Am I being paranoid if Klaus' being so interested worries me?"

"Klaus bothers me in a lot of ways…the other guys too. He's too concerned about things that *shouldn't* concern him. Yet, when we ask questions about his background, he's vague. We only tolerate him around because we all love Lila, but we try not to say anything in front of him, or her, that could be used against us."

He paused, biting his lip. "I've dropped phony information to Lila, wondering how long it would take to get to Klaus. You know where it turned up again? At the bookstore, when Ilse mentioned the departure of the phony unit I'd invented. I've told all the officers not to tell Lila anything important because I'm *sure* it gets to Klaus, and then to Ilse. I don't know why Ilse would even be interested, but that's weird, isn't it? Ilse has worked on Post for years."

Carl took a drink of his beer and leaned forward to whisper, "I'm afraid Klaus' interest in Ed puts him more in the dangerous category than I already thought. I hope I'm wrong, but if I were you, I'd not tell Lila anything. Klaus can wheedle it out of her."

"Should I tell Ed we're worried about Klaus?" They both knew and skirted the unspoken words that if Ed couldn't make it back on Monday, there would be no way to tell him anything.

"Tell him. Intelligence people exist on both sides of the Border, and they're frequently targeted if someone thinks they know too much or have accomplished counter-intelligence goals too well. Only Ed knows what his covert undercover level needs to be.

By that time, Abby and Robert had walked over with their drinks and they all went in to dinner. Still, nothing felt resolved.

Chapter 26

Carl spent the weekend with Megan, quite platonically and without his usual leering propositions. He said he was practicing his big brotherly skills for when Laura arrived. But he kept her busy with other enjoyable activities. They drove down to Katterbach for his promotion party, then came back to Bamberg, went to the movies, ate *Schnitzel* at Rudi's, bowled, went hiking in the late April snowy countryside near his old home in Litzendorf, and of course, they dropped in to visit with the Bergs.

He hadn't given Megan any time to worry. They had joked and laughed together. "We'll give you time to follow your heart Megan," he had explained. "You know I'll always be here if you need me." He smiled broadly. "Of course, it would be nice if…." She smacked him as usual.

It was heart wrenching for Megan when Carl left at 0500 Monday morning to go back down to Katterbach. "Let whatever happens, *happen*, Meggie," he'd said, slowly and succinctly. "Ed may or may not be the one, but you'll never know unless you allow him to become closer to you and know who you really are. You'll feel it for sure, *you'll know*, when you see him. You have my blessing." Out came the hand she so much relied on, locking her fingers in his own.

God, what would I do without him!

Monday seemed endless, though the needs of her children kept her worry at bay most of the day. What if Ed hadn't gotten away safely? She resigned herself to waiting all evening, alone in the O'Club that was always closed on Monday nights, and perhaps being stood up for her trouble. Everyone else would be at Steak Night at the snack bar, as was usual when the Club was closed. She had lied to Lila. Ed hadn't said he would call first, just that he would come directly to the O'Club. After school, she realized she didn't want to be found by other friends coming by her classroom, so she packed up her ungraded papers and decided she could grade them just as easily in a deserted Officers' Club hall, at the phone table, in case Ed called or arrived there.

About five, the door opened and she looked up, startled. The O'Club was eerily quiet when closed and empty on Monday nights, but Marco kept the halls open for anyone billeted upstairs. The footsteps were those of Klaus and Lila.

"I told Klaus this might be the place, Megan." As always, Lila sort of bubbled into a room, making Megan smile in spite of her anxiety. "Klaus wanted to come see if Ed got here."

"Ed won't be coming tonight, after all, Lila." She said it with a straight face, looking directly at Klaus. It was easier to keep a stoic expression to him than it was to lie to her friend. "He called a few minutes ago and postponed. He had to stay in Stuttgart tonight."

"Then why are *you* here?" The question came from Klaus in a flatly accusing tone. He didn't seem to have bought her story. He made a move toward her saying, "I think you're lying."

Lila gasped and grabbed his arm, "Megan doesn't lie. What a terrible thing for you to say."

Megan decided her best bet was to ignore the implied threat, somehow more blatant than Klaus' usual cold stance. She would try to smile and keep the encounter under control. "I got started on my test grading before his call, and didn't want to quit and lug these papers around until I finished. This is a quiet place to work. I'll join you guys after Steak Night. You two go on ahead. I'll catch up with you inside the movie theater." She rustled the test papers.

Klaus just stood there, staring at her, his steely eyes making her uncomfortable, as usual.

"Unless, of course, you two want to *help* me correct all the math tests and science essays?" Megan held up a stack of papers she hadn't yet touched.

Klaus shuffled his feet and looked angry. He grabbed Lila's arm and dragged her out without a word further. Lila seemed accustomed to his rough treatment, as she waved cheerfully, and Megan returned the wave. She prayed fervently that if Ed were coming, he wouldn't happen to enter just as they were leaving. Klaus would be even more suspicious if he caught her in an outright lie. Silently, she crept to the tiny window in the darkened ladies room and peeked out to watch them leave the parking lot.

Another two hours went by, the phone had not rung, and her papers were done. *Where was he? Would he really come? Had he made it out safely?* She read over her lesson plans, made some changes, and finally dropped all the completed work into her bag.

She checked her watch again--five 'til eight. *I think he'd be here by now, if he were able to make it.* She fought back the thought that maybe the strange phone call might be the last she would ever hear from him. Tears rolled down her cheeks. *I don't think he's coming.* But she scolded herself into the mundane task of gathering her belongings. There was nothing further to do. She could avoid leaving no longer.

It had snowed lightly all day, so she wrapped her hooded *Loden* coat around her shoulders. As she turned toward the door, it opened, and Ed walked in, dressed all in black and stomping snow from his boots. She stood stunned for a moment as he met her tearful gaze with that huge 'Big Ed' grin.

Carl had said, 'You'll know what to do the minute you see him.' And suddenly she *did* know. They both dropped their bags and ran to greet each other.

Ed slid his arms around her waist under her coat and swung her around gleefully before stopping to hold her close. He pulled back to see her face, and bent to kiss her long and hard.

She surprised herself by responding with joy. "You're here," she said, as she caught her breath. "But--that cut over your eye. It's all purple, and it hasn't even been cleaned yet."

"I told you I'd get back to you--somehow. I had to work at it a bit." He kissed her hair, her eyes, hugged her tightly, and then kissed her deeply again. "God, I've tried to wait patiently until you were ready, but I've wanted to kiss you this way for so long."

They both began laughing, as they realized the snow from his overcoat was puddling at their feet. Ed yanked off his coat and his black knitted cap, and dropped them on the chair, lifted her coat from her shoulders and tossed it in the same direction. Then he took her hand to lead her into the darkened bar. Before they sat down, he hugged her again, and she realized she was crying in relief.

"Don't cry, my darling, Ed said, as he nuzzled her hair and neck, breathing in deeply. "I kept thinking about the wonderful smell of you, the way your hair shines and the way it feels when I kiss the top of it--so touchable. I was thinking about you through the whole mission. And now that I'm here, I'll not let you go, ever again!"

He pulled her onto his lap in a nearby chair. "Let me look at you." He held out her arms and said, "I love that pink angora sweater. It looks marvelously huggable." He wrapped his arms around her. "See, I was right."

"Was it bad?" In spite of her effort to remain calm, she sounded choked.

"Bad enough that I feel intensely lucky to be holding you right now." His voice was husky.

"Can you tell me anything about it?"

Ed took her slender hands into his big ones. "Only that you were right about my location, and the shooting. The whole area is a hotbed of rebel groups bent on terrorizing the population and picking off foreigners--legitimate travelers, business people, and our operatives trying to get information. We don't completely know who is behind all this ferment yet. One of our teams trying to find out had been kidnapped, and our intelligence people believed the Syrian or PLO rebels had them. The operative I sent in to find them and get them out was killed execution style, by PLO, we're pretty sure. Early Sunday morning, his body was found in an alley. Somehow his cover story was blown. Someone leaked information. That's why I had to go... I realize that helicopter incident was frightening for you and quite dramatic, but I had to get there immediately. I hope you can forgive me for leaving you like that."

Megan put her arms around him and buried her tears in his neck. He held her quietly for a moment until she could speak again. "Were you successful?"

"Did you read about either a kidnapping, an execution, or a rescue in the papers?"

She shook her head.

"Remember what I told you. If you read about it in the papers, I failed. That's all I can tell you for now. But I lost one of my men, so it doesn't *feel* much like a successful mission." Ed sighed, his sagging shoulders registering his grief. She hugged him instinctively.

"But, of course, you know even that can't be discussed. I'm not supposed to tell anyone, even the one I care about, but I do so much want you to understand why I had to leave you."

"If someone asks, where should I say you were?"

"As far as anyone else in the world knows, I never left Germany. I was on an inspection tour of the Augsberg communication complex, and no one disappeared at all. There will be no word of my lost agent, ever. Do you understand?"

Megan said softly, "Augsberg isn't all that exciting. So I guess I shouldn't have worried."

Ed searched her face in the dim light. "Were you worried?"

"I was more confused at first when you kept leaving me stranded. But when you called and I could hear the gunfire, I realized it was serious. I sort of panicked when we got cut off."

He held her tightly, whispering in her ear, "I figured you'd want me to take cover." She nodded, and he continued. "In a way I can't explain, this mission was more difficult than others. I wanted to come back to you, and always before I didn't care--no reason to worry if I made it or not, because *only* the mission mattered." He kissed her cheek. "Knowing I cared about you may have made me less effective. I got the job done, but I didn't jump into the line of fire as easily as I usually do. I'm not sure that's good thing."

He smiled at her. "There, I guess I've laid my feelings on the line. Now, if you tell me that you feel nothing for this old man, I can go back to being full of confidence when I run through machine-gun fire--but I'm hoping you can't tell me that you feel nothing."

His smile melted her confusion, but not her fear. "I wouldn't want to make you less effective in your job, but I'm afraid I *do* care, more than I ever thought I could."

"Afraid?"

"I don't know how to accept your risks. I'm afraid to learn to love you and then lose you. It was so hard when I lost Andy. I couldn't survive another... Yes, I'm afraid."

"We'll talk about it, Megan. I do understand. Life with me would not be without risk. Life with *anyone*, anywhere would never really be without risk. I'll tell you all I can. Let me try to ease your fear. Give yourself a chance to love again. Please give me that chance as well. I've been alone a long time, too. I know that weekend was terrible for you. Not being able to tell you what was happening scared me too, but I couldn't risk blowing our team's cover. I just had to pray you'd understand." She heard the hope in his voice.

"I understand now." She nestled into his arms and tried to relax the knot in the pit of her stomach. "Just promise you'll always come back to me."

"Always," he said, nuzzling her cheek, and her neck.

After a few minutes of snuggling, during which Ed found Megan's angora sweater a tremendous source of interest, he said softly, "Can we please go upstairs? I'm too old to be caught necking in the O'Club, but I can't keep my hands or my heart to myself a moment longer. I need to hold you, just to convince myself you are real, and not my fantasy. I'll tell you all I can. I want to be truly alone with you. Will you come with me and give me your trust?"

Carl's words rang in her ears, "You'll *know* when the time is right, Meggie."

She could only nod, since the words choked at the back of her throat.

Silently they rose, and Ed stepped behind the bar, slid his hand under the cash register, and pulled out an envelope. "Marco always leaves a key for me." They gathered their things to leave no trace and, hand in hand, walked up the stairs. Ed turned the key in the door. Then he tossed all bundles inside, lifted Megan into his arms, kicked the door shut behind them, and strode to the suite's sofa. Dropping her again into his lap as he sat down, he kissed her while stroking her face, her arms, and finally, her sweater. "May I?" he whispered.

Megan felt a flood of warmth as he gently touched her breasts through the sweater, and then kissed her again and again. "If you only knew how often I've thought about holding you like this," he murmured. "It's the *only* thing that got me out of Beirut."

"I'm glad," she said softly laying her head on his shoulder.

"Do you want this as much as I do?"

"Yes, I…I think I do."

"Then come with me while I get cleaned up, and we can have this whole wonderful night together." When Megan hesitated, he explained. "I flew straight from the fight in Beirut, found a Stuttgart helicopter crew heading for Hof, and bummed a ride, having them drop me off here. I need a shower, *badly*. But I don't want to let you out of my sight again for even an instant, so please, come with me. You can scrub my back." He laughed, and pulled her gently to her feet.

As Ed started the hot water, and as it steamed up the room, he peeled off his clothes, laying the Beretta close by on the countertop. He reached for Megan's sweater. She started to protest, but he kissed her gently as he pulled the sweater over her shoulders. The nearness of him made her dizzy. By the time she had kissed him back, they were leaning together in the shower, kissing fervently with the hot water running down both of their bodies.

"You feel wonderful," he whispered. "As wonderful as in my fantasies."

She smiled and said softly, "You said I should scrub your back, so turn around while I can still think clearly." He turned, and she gasped. "Where did you get all those cuts and welts? Were you beaten?" She touched them gingerly, and he winced.

"Don't ask, my darling, because I can't explain. Just wash gently, okay?"

She barely touched the damaged skin of his back and buttocks with the soap, fearful of hurting him further. But her touch soon brought him around to face her again. "I can't stand it when you touch me so softly, Megan. Let's get out of here." He lifted her out of the shower, grabbing nearby towels and wrapping her in a big one. He led her to the bed, toweled himself off, and lay down beside her, carefully unfolding the bath towel from around her. She didn't feel shy with him. Afraid of hurting him by putting her arms around his tortured back, they made love slowly, carefully at first, as she touched his face, and only the front of his shoulders. After awhile, neither remembered the carefulness, or the pain.

Later, Ed pulled back the covers and tucked her carefully next to him for the night. After he dozed off with his arms still around her, Megan laid awake, calm, serene, thinking. *I'm surprised at myself that my emotions have finally let me love someone again. How far I've come—from wanting to die, to looking forward to living and loving again—and Ed feels so right. Somehow I know Andy understands. It's as Carl and Darlene have told me--Andy wouldn't want me to be alone for the rest of my life.* A weight melted away and a sense of peace took its place. She snuggled against Ed's lanky body and drifted to dreamless sleep.

"Caring about me will not be easy, Megan. You understand that, don't you?" They had stirred during their sleep and wakened to talk, lying in each other's arms.

"I know. You'll disappear a lot and I won't always know

where you are."

"Most women can't handle that, and I don't want to put you through it unless you're sure you want to be with me." He searched her face for clues. "It will be hard sometimes."

"The hardest part may be not being able to tell anyone about you," said Megan quietly, "or how I feel about you."

"Yes, I'm afraid that's part of it too, my dear. If people realize how close we've become, they could try to hurt you in order to get to me."

"I don't understand why."

"Counter intelligence people come on *both* sides of a war, Darling—even a Cold War. Our enemies don't want us to have a functioning spy network. They'd like our soldiers to be more vulnerable to attack, sabotage, and murder. What I'm doing to try to find their people in order to protect our forces is an operation our enemies would like to shut down. To accomplish that goal, they're always watching for a chance to shut *me* down."

He seemed intense, trying to explain what his job meant to him. She could hear the 'duty, honor, country' echo in every word.

"We must protect our international operations, even while our Congressional hearings are making our covert plans more open and exposing our agents as more vulnerable. I need to play the happy-go-lucky Big Irish Ed, inspector of weapons, until we track down those who would do us harm. And they will keep trying to get rid of me, and those like me." He paused as though waiting for her to understand. She could barely nod. Her throat constricted.

"What scares me now, is that they might try watching you too, if anyone figures out how much I love you. They'll be trying to get information about what I'm doing, or who I really am, and I'm not willing to risk your safety. So we'll need to be careful not to be seen as a couple. Do you think we can see each other discreetly? Can we hope most of your friends have not yet suspected, or at least that they will say nothing about our being together."

"I guess so…for as long as we can. How long before you're finished with this mission?"

"I don't know. There's always *another* mission. I could tell you it would end soon, but I'd be lying if I did. I'll probably be with it as long as I can be effective, as long as my cover isn't blown, or as long as I come back from missions in one piece. So, getting tangled up with me will be difficult." He traced her cheek with his finger, slowly approaching her lips before kissing them. "I'm very much hoping you'll allow me the privilege of coming home to you."

"I understand." She was thoughtful for a long time. "I'm frightened of my own feelings. For a long time I've been quite sure I could never love anyone again. Certainly I didn't want to love anyone who might die and leave me to face such grief. I wanted someone who would be quite safe, and who could love me for a hundred years." She touched the slash on his forehead gingerly. "But no one is really safe here. I…I'm very frightened of your job, but I know you must continue doing it. It's not for me to ask that you give up what you feel you must do." She took a deep breath and added, "Your job is as much a part of you as teaching is a part of me. I…I want you to come back to me, too." She buried her face in his neck and whispered, "Just understand that you'll have to help me with the fear."

He kissed her tenderly and said, "I somehow knew you'd be tough enough to handle it. I lost my first marriage over my job. My first wife assumed my military career was a normal one, until I came home injured and couldn't tell her how I got that way. She suddenly became 'The War Department' and made her disapproval *quite* apparent. She vowed she'd never again leave her house with the crystal chandelier for someone in my line of business. She never did."

Megan knew he had parted from his first wife years before, and that he sometimes brought his teen-aged daughters over to visit, but she hadn't known the cause of the break-up.

"Actually, she still has the final papers. We separated ten years ago, forever. It was more or less amicable, with the understanding that if either of us ever wanted to marry again, she'd send the papers quickly. I called her and told her to send them after the night I got the third degree from all your friends. I'm sure they'll be waiting for me when I get back to Stuttgart." He laughed out loud. "I think I knew I wanted to be with you from the first night I asked Marco to introduce us. It was something in your eyes. Isn't that crazy?"

"Maybe. But it's nice." Smiling at him made her warm inside. *So he had asked Marco…*

When he continued, however, the warmth inside took on a chill.

"There's more you need to understand, Megan. If I ever don't make it out of a mission, you'll not be able to inquire about me or make any public statement about where someone should start looking. Will you be strong enough to live with that? The government will deny any knowledge of me, or my mission. Do you understand?"

"Carl explained it to me. Our life together will be living from crisis to crisis, won't it?"

"I'm afraid so, Megan. But after each crisis where I must be alert to the bad guys, I'll be able to come home to you and let you restore my faith in my fellow man."

Ed held her closely and assured her again with kisses and promises that he would always find a way to get back to her.

Through their shared warmth, Megan suddenly remembered she needed to warn Ed.

"Carl said I should warn you about one person. It's that boyfriend of Lila's. He's German, but of indeterminate background. He never answers questions about himself--that bearded guy named Klaus. You met him once. Remember, I told you about him when you wanted to know if teachers might be bringing anyone on Post."

"Why did Carl think I'd need warning? What was his take on this guy?"

"Klaus asks a lot of questions about you, personally, and he wanted us to double date with Lila and him, so he could get to know you better. Carl planted false information with Lila, and it went straight to Klaus, and then to Ilse at the bookstore. Klaus has been hanging around the airfield and around *Muna*. The officers try not to discuss their work whenever he's around. The guys only tolerate him because Lila likes him. Do you think he could be any threat to you?"

"Does he know about *us*?" Ed's voice sounded tense again.

"Yes. Lila told him she knew you would call me, and come to see me."

"What did you say?"

"Earlier I told them you hadn't called, so I didn't think you could get away from Stuttgart. Then when they came here about five, I told you had called and said you'd be staying in Stuttgart. He moved toward me as though he wanted to hit me because I said you weren't coming. He seemed to know I was fibbing. Then he sort of got control of himself."

"They came here?"

"Yes. But I checked to be sure they really left."

He chuckled softly, "You're going to be good at this, my darling."

"But I hate lying to Lila. She's one of my best friends."

"It'll only be until she breaks it off with this Klaus, or until I can investigate him further to see if he's any real threat. I think your friends are right that he's not to be trusted--not if he continues to ask tactical questions. Does anyone else know we're seeing each other?"

"Just Carl, of course. I have no secrets from Carl."

"Yes, you said Carl had explained my disappearance to you. Can Carl be trusted?"

"With my life, *and* with yours, since he knows I was…I was concerned about you."

"Did he know I was coming tonight?"

"Yes, I needed to talk to someone about my confusion after your last disappearing act from the ski slope. He's been my best friend and my protector ever since I arrived in Bamberg."

"Why were you so confused?"

"I didn't realize I cared for you as much as I did, even though he *did* realize it." Embarrassed by her tears, she added, "I care deeply for him, too, in a different way."

"Did he understand your confusion?" Ed whispered the words, looking into her eyes.

"He always understands, and he gave me his blessing. He said to let my own feelings guide me, and that as soon as I saw you again, I would know what to do. He said 'to let whatever happens, happen.'" She took a deep breath and caressed Ed's cheek as she spoke, "Tonight, when I saw you come in the door, and you were safe, I knew I would let *this* happen, and I knew I loved you, more than I thought I could ever love someone again."

Ed breathed softly, "I'm glad, my Darling. This old soldier loves you, and he wants to make love to you again and again, starting right now." He smiled down at her as he caressed her face and folded her into his arms, full length, body to body, and she relaxed against him.

Chapter 27

After an early morning departure to the airfield in time to catch the helicopter picking him up on its way back to Stuttgart, Ed had kissed her fervently before he left the car, but had only smiled and waved in front of his air crew, so she realized he was beginning the *discreet* part of their relationship. It was, of course, impossible to know who was watching in the shadows and tree lines of the airfield. Megan had expressed her hope he could still go skiing with the gang the next weekend.

"I'll try, Megan. It will depend on events between now and then. I'll call at our usual time, if it's at all possible, just to let you know. I'm sorry to be so undependable." They waved goodbye and she stood still, watching as the helicopter blew snow over the airfield, whisked up into the sky, and turned to the southwest.

"Y'all didn't show up at the movies, Megan?" It was almost an accusation from Lila.

"By the time I finished the test papers, I was really tired. I didn't think you two would miss me anyway." It sickened Megan to have to tell fibs. Was this the way it would always be to love and protect a spook?

Lila said quietly, "May I ask you something--something private?"

Megan dreaded the next question, but she could only nod.

"Do you think there's something funny about Klaus?"

Megan could think of no way to side-step the question, and she was relieved it was about Klaus and not about Ed. "Lila, I don't know why we're *still* discussing his strange behavior. You *know* how we all feel—you just haven't wanted to see it. We have other German friends who come play volleyball with us, or come to some of our parties, and they never ask questions about our guys' military missions like Klaus does. Don't you think that's unusual?"

"You think he's a spy or something, don't you?" She turned partially away.

"I didn't say that, Lila. That's a big accusation. I can only say that his actions make me uncomfortable. I've seen him hanging around field trips and the school, and I fear he carries a gun in that pocket he always keeps his hand in. Am I right?"

At Lila's barely perceptible nod, Megan added. "It must be *you* that trusts him--or not--not me. You know, we've had this discussion before." She bit her lip, wondering if she should continue. "You've noticed something odd, yourself, haven't you?"

"I'm beginning to have funny feelings when he's around, and I don't know what to make of them." Lila seemed a bit confused. "He does carry a revolver, and he seems preoccupied with it. He takes it out and plays with it, turning it around in his hands, slipping a silencer on and off of it. Not like a threat or anything, but he knows it makes me nervous. He asks me a lot of questions too--about things I don't even know about. He gets really mad if I don't know the answers, and he tells me I'll have to find the answers for him, if I care about him." She shrugged and sighed.

"He seemed really determined to come find you last night. I thought we should have left you alone with Ed, *whenever* he came. But Klaus insisted that we come, practically dragging me along. He even drove by after the movie and noticed your car was still parked at the Club. He was angry at *me*, and I didn't know what to tell him."

"What kind of questions did Klaus ask that you didn't know, Lila?" Megan was feeling a prickly burning sensation up her spine, but she needed to know.

"Oh, lots of things. About the Air Force guys in *Muna*, for instance. I told him we didn't have any Air Force guys here, only Army, and he laughed weirdly, like he thought I was dumb. He said I should go check it out myself." She looked sideways at Megan. "*Do* we have Air Force guys, six of them, that do something dangerous?"

"Lila, even if we know, or don't know, such things, we shouldn't be answering those kinds of questions from *anyone*. Don't you know that? We've told you again and again."

"I guess I sort of thought that if I liked someone, it would be rude not to answer whatever they asked. It never occurred to me that we--the U.S. I mean--should have any secrets. We're the good guys, aren't we? Besides, I sort of let all that security mumbo jumbo the guys talk about just go in one ear and out the other. It seems so silly to me--like little boys playing cops and robbers. I still like Klaus because he's more mature, and he can be real sweet. But I almost feel a little afraid of him at times."

She swallowed hard, collecting her thoughts before she

continued. "Like the other day we were over at the bookstore, and he got into a big argument with Ilse. It was a real scene and it embarrassed me, so I moved away. I couldn't hear what they were saying very well, but he gave Ilse a piece of paper he said had the name of a book he wanted, and she screamed at him that the paper didn't give enough information about the book for her to find it on the shelves. Later, he acted angry with me, as though *I* had done something wrong."

"That's funny. Any other questions, about any of our friends, or their jobs, or anything?"

"He's always curious about people *you* know, like your meetings with the Battalion Commanders, and about that tall commander who asks your advice, and he thought it interesting that pilot, Milt, hovered his helicopter by your classroom. He said he knew Milt flew 'clandestine missions,' whatever that means, and he wanted me to get you to introduce him. But he really got *aggressive* about your relationship with Ed. He thinks *you're* some kind of spy, since you seem to know everyone, and they talk to you all the time." She snickered. "I told him that was dumb--that you just worry about everyone and watch out for all of us. But he says you '...know too much not to be involved in some kind of intrigue.'"

"How does he know about any of these things?"

Lila shrugged, looking at the floor, "I think I might have told him some amusing tales from time to time when Abby and I were trying to get you to date—and about some of the crazy things that always seem to happen to you--sort of pillow talk."

Megan felt her heart sink. Klaus knew too much about her friends and her activities. Lila, in her chatty innocence, and disregarding security, had apparently aroused his curiosity about her and Ed, and about her friends among the commanders, too. "Perhaps you should reconsider inviting him to the party next week. You did plan to invite him, didn't you?"

"I'm afraid I already invited him. He asked about the party, and it seemed natural to invite him. But when he asked if Ed was going with you, I began to feel uncomfortable that he seems more interested in Ed than he does in me." She pouted for a moment, then grinned mischievously. "I just wanted Brian to feel the teensiest bit jealous of Klaus, so he'd ask me to go steady again."

"I thought he did that before."

"Oh, lots of times, but I always said no." She smiled and leaned her blonde head closer to whisper, "Don't tell this to anyone, Megan, but I'm ready to say 'yes' to Brian now, so I need for him to ask me once again."

"Then, I really think you should go directly to him and tell him so. Don't fool around with his feelings by trotting out Klaus every time you want Brian. That's not fair to either of them. Besides, you never know when an alert could go bad. Go tell Brian *now*."

"I suppose you're right, but I'll have to tell Klaus about my decision first. I wonder if he'll get mad. But even if he does, I think he wants to come to this party, really. He's asked me about it again and again—exactly where we'd be meeting, what time, and if Ed was coming. Why do you think he's so dad-blamed interested in Ed, anyway?"

"Lila," Megan interrupted, wondering how she should say what she needed to say without making an open accusation, "As my friend, do me the favor of keeping Ed and I private. Please don't tell everything you think you know to Klaus, please. We're a long way from being ready to make anything public, and it's taken me a long time to care. Do you understand?"

"Yes, I guess so." Lila obviously felt the secrecy was about Megan's love life, not about any danger to Ed, because she grinned wickedly before continuing on about her own love life. "And don't worry. I'm not hurting Klaus any by asking him to tag along. He really wants to go to the party."

Megan threw up her hands in frustration. "This whole thing is wrong, Lila. I wish you'd just leave Klaus out of it and talk directly to Brian. If you love him, you love him...go tell him!"

"Oh, Megan, you and Abby are so 'out of it!' One should never show a guy exactly how one feels about him. He'll lose interest. Y'all need to keep men guessing."

"Perhaps I'm not knowledgeable enough about men, but I think they all appreciate honesty. I'm scared you're getting into a mess here, Lila, and the results might not be exactly what you want them to be. Are you positive now, about your feelings for Brian?"

Lila beamed, still oblivious of Megan's concern. "Oh, yes, I am. I want to marry him and have lots of babies."

"Then do us all a favor and go tell him. Get rid of Klaus,

now."

Thursday, several of the gang had planned to eat lunch at the O'Club, even though the teachers had a relatively short lunch hour. But just as they were seated, Megan saw Marco point around the corner to their large table, and Ed entered. He paused to greet several of the officers he now knew, and leaned over Megan to whisper that he needed to talk to her, before moving to an empty seat by Stan. As the others drifted into conversation, Ed returned to her, pulled up a chair near hers, and whispered, "Sorry for the lack of a warning call. I tried the hall phone, but Frank said you were already over here, so I came. Something essential has come up. I won't be able to go skiing with your club this weekend. The helicopter will be picking me up tomorrow morning and I don't know when I'll be back or able to phone."

"You're staying here tonight, then?"

"Ed nodded, his face split into a grin. "I ordered an inspection of 6/10's weapons for this afternoon to give me an excuse to come up here. They'll be surprised! Can you meet me for dinner? I'd like us to have some time together before I go on this mission?"

"Dinner will probably include the others too. Do you mind terribly?"

"No, I like them, and I love the fact that they look after you so well. Sooner or later, they'll have to go home, won't they?" She felt her face grow warm in answer to his smile. He moved back to his seat and finished his sandwich, chatting amiably with Robert and Stan.

When Megan entered the O'Club bar later that evening with Lila and Abby, Ed was in animated conversation with 'Major America,' Gary, and his wife. Gary waved the girls over, and all had drinks, then walked to the dining room together for dinner.

Afterward, it seemed an inordinately long time before some of the activities around the Club began to wind down and people waved goodbye and started clearing out the place. Perhaps it was Megan's own impatience that made it seem that way.

Ed, Megan, Gary and Loretta were enjoying the last drink of the evening, just the four of them. Megan noticed that Gary kept

looking back and forth from her face to Ed's, and finally said to
Loretta, "Come on, old girl, we're going home."

"I'm not ready yet," Loretta answered, looking rather miffed.

"Oh, yes, you are," insisted Gary, taking her arm to lift her to
her feet.

"I should be getting home too," said Megan. "It's getting
late." But she lingered to say goodbye, as Gary hurried Loretta out
the door.

Ed was chuckling softly as Megan turned to him.

"What's so funny?"

"Gary knows." He pulled her to him. "And I can tell, he
approves."

"Oh, goodness. Will that be a danger for you?"

"I don't think so. The guy doesn't know my MOS and he
seems like a straight shooter. He won't say anything—probably not
even to Loretta."

"Do you know your mission for the morning?" She said it
tentatively, quite prepared for his answer, a shake of his head. "Do
you think it will be a bad one?

"I can't tell you now, and perhaps not even later. But it will
mean so much to me knowing you'll be here waiting when I come
back to you, no matter how bad the mission gets. If you can forgive
me for not making the ski trip with the gang this weekend, I'll try to
make it back to you in time for the party."

She smiled, and he took her in his arms. "That's my darling!"
He pushed back to look in her face. "I love calling you my darling,
since that's the way I think of you?"

She couldn't hold back her own smile as she nodded,
squeezing his hand.

"Then, is the rest of your evening free, my darling, or do you
have someplace important to go right now?"

"I think I have someplace important to be--right *here*, if that's
okay with you."

The big man's grin warmed her clear through. They climbed
the stairs arm in arm.

Friday's Ski bus ride was a wild one. Megan had to take over
as Trip Captain when Luke was called to flying duty at the last
minute. The pick-up of Carl and the other pilots at Feucht gas station

went smoothly. After eating his chicken, Carl joined several of the guys in the back of the bus and left the girls to 'chatter,' as he called it, up front. Abby joined Megan and they talked of their plans. Abby seemed to have found Robert of more interest lately, and discussed their latest dates with more animation than she had in the past.

From the rising noise level, Megan could tell there was some heavy drinking going on in the rear of the bus, and she wondered what had prompted Carl to take part. He didn't usually. But toward the end of the trip, he apparently decided he wanted to come forward, and there were too many 'bodies' asleep in the aisle to make much headway. To the chant of "Go, Carl, Go," Megan turned to see Carl crawling across the tops of the seat backs on his elbows and knees, straddling the aisle, and balancing a wine bottle in one hand and two paper cups in the other.

Abby noticed his progress and said to Megan, "I'll go talk to Patti. It looks like Carl has something on his mind, and he's coming here to you." She rose and moved away, just as Carl slid over the top of the seat, head first, and landed scrunched up next to Megan.

"Hi, Carl. We're an uneven number this trip, so I gave you a room by yourself. Are you okay with that?" She noticed his fuzzy eyes and peered closer. "In fact, are you okay at all?"

"Sure, I am. I am! If I have a room alone, maybe someone will come visit me." He grinned a crooked grin at her. His usual leer was sort of sideways, and she laughed. Then he apparently remembered the reason for his precarious journey from the back of the bus. "I brought you a drink, Meggie," he stammered. "Here, hold your cup and I'll pour."

"You seem to have had enough, and I don't really need anything just now."

"Nonsense! We need to toast the love of your life, Big Ed."

"Carl, let's talk about this later?" She took the cup he thrust in her hands and tried to steady his hand as he poured. Only a little sloshed out as he 'clinked' his paper cup to hers.

"Meggie, I want you to be happy. You know that, don't you?"

"I know. And I want you to be happy too. Are you dating again now?"

"Yeah, but I'm back to those one-night stands that disgust me so. Don't feel anything drawing me to any of them--tried 'em all, probably every one on Post and all those out in the German economy, too." He swept his arm in a gigantic arc, as though including the whole feminine world into his experience. None of 'em has any character, and they never understand me. I wanna ask ya sompun. Do ya think it's normal for me not to want any of them? I'm supposed to have this big ol' reputation, and I don't even like it when some of these gorgeous creatures fall at my feet. What's wrong with me?"

To Megan's horror, tears were rolling down his cheeks. She hugged him to her and said, "Why don't you just sleep a little now, Dear, and we'll talk all this out later."

He clunked his head into her lap, and she was able to grab his sagging paper cup with her free hand before he dropped it. He snored softly the rest of the way to the hotel at Kitzbuhel, as she held him to keep him from falling off the seat.

As Trip Captain, Megan eventually had to lay Carl's head on the seat and slide out from under him to give everyone their room numbers as they exited the bus. When someone woke him, he lurched up the aisle to the door, staggered suddenly and, before anyone could grab him, he fell out the door and hit the ground on his back.

"Oh, Carl, you fell out of the bus!" Megan scrambled down the bus steps to reach him.

"Was I hurt?" he asked, surprised.

"I sure don't think so," said Top Cop Rex. "You're totally sloshed." He helped Carl to his feet. Megan handed her clipboard to Abby to finish assigning rooms, and got on the other side so she and Rex could support Carl into the building, and up to his room.

"Rex, I've seen you and Luke like this, but never Carl."

"He's been pretty out of it lately. Don't know what's bothering him."

"He has this room to himself. Do you think he'll be all right alone?"

"Sure," said Rex. "He just needs to sleep it off." They pulled him out of his jacket and boots and pants, leaving him in sweat pants, covered him with the thick Austrian down comforter, closed the door quietly, and went to their own rooms.

When Megan got to her room, she found Abby was already asleep. Her own sleep was troubled, as she was worried about Ed, wondering about this latest mission, and about Carl, who was acting very little like his normally happy-go-lucky self.

At dawn, it fell to the trip captain to run around the pension knocking on doors to wake the hung-over sleepers for breakfast. As Megan made her rounds, nearing Carl's room, she picked up his sweat pants from the floor. Puzzled, she walked to his door, only to find it wide open. There he lay on his stomach, naked as the day he was born, with even the down comforter lying on the floor.

Megan glanced up and down the hall to be sure no one else had seen him like that, then entered, shut the door, grabbed up the comforter and covered him with it. Then, she touched his shoulder gently to wake him.

"Hm, Megan?"

"How did you know it was me?"

"You could touch my body anywhere, anytime, and I'd always know it was you, even if I was already dead. *Am I?*" He rolled over to face her and reached out his hand, palm up.

She lifted her own palm to meet his, and sat on the bed. "You're not dead, Carl. But are you all right?"

"Don't mind me, I just had a rough night."

"So I gathered." She held up his sweat pants where he could see them. He immediately felt under the covers and, sure enough, they were not where he thought he'd left them last.

"Oh, Crumb!" he said. "Sorry, Meggie." He slapped his hand to his forehead. "Then it wasn't a dream, it was all real."

"Do you want to tell me about it?" Megan could barely suppress her giggles.

"I got up in the night to go to the john, and I had trouble finding it down some hall or other. When I got back to my room, a woman sat up in my bed. I thought someone had come to visit me, after all, so I took off my sweat pants to join her, but then a man sat up right on the other side of her. I remember he said, *"Was ist los!"* and was kind of excited. I figured I'd better get out of there *fast.* I rolled out of bed and tried to get my pants back on, but I tripped over one leg and ran out into the hall, dragging the other one. I don't know how it came off too, but I *think* I got back into my own room...didn't I?" He asked plaintively, looking around in confusion.

"Well, Carl, I guess you made it to your own room because this is where Rex and I left you last night, but you lost your britches in the hall, the door was wide open, and you were naked when I came to wake you up this morning."

He cautiously lifted the comforter corner, "Then you covered me up?"

"Sure didn't want the rest of the world to see your family jewels."

"Are you sure you wouldn't like to join me for just a little while. I'm not so sure any of the jewels are even working anymore. I've had a hard time lately."

Megan couldn't help smiling. "My Dear, I'm sure all your parts are working just fine. And there must be lots of gorgeous girls on whom you can try them...girls your own age."

"Meggie, forgive me, but I have to ask. Are you happy with Ed? Is he good to you."

She paused a moment, trying to say it right. "He's very good to me, Carl, and he knows how close you and I are. He understands, and he likes you for having taken such good care of me." She chuckled at Carl's question. "If you're asking if he's good in bed, I would have to say that no one can possibly be as good as you keep telling me *you* are. But Ed is sweet, kind, considerate, and his smile melts me all over. When we do make love, it's lovely and tender and warm." She smiled. "I *know* he loves me Carl. That's a good thing, isn't it? Please say you understand, and that you approve."

Carl nodded. "I understand, and I do approve. He's a good man." He looked outside at the sunrise, heaved an enormous sigh, and said, "My sister arrives next weekend, changing my life forever, and you're in love with Ed. Can I at least have one last hug now?"

Megan bent swiftly and threw her arms around his neck in a big bear hug. There were tears in his eyes, and she felt her own tears too. "You'll always be my best friend, and my favorite ski buddy. You know that, don't you? No one will ever come between us."

Carl put his two fingers together, kissed them, and reached out to touch her breast where the old scar should be. "Forever mine, remember? No matter what?"

"I'll remember, no matter what."

Chapter 28

The Soviets had lost a submarine! Newspapers reported that they proclaimed loudly it was not nuclear, but there were hints from the U.S. State Department that intelligence operatives were suspicious. Of course, loose nuclear warheads or nuclear fuel on the bottom of the ocean could be hazardous to the health of the whole world, so the U.S. was understandably upset by the habitual delay in information coming from the Soviets. Both sides were spreading the war of words--threats, denials, and more threats, while the search went on for the submarine.

The Soviets claimed they had no idea where it had sunk. But American officers speculated that they only made this claim to give themselves time to find and retrieve the nuclear reactors and warheads everyone felt sure were on board, in spite of their denials. The Soviets claimed they were never near the most logical spot, the spot where U.S. intelligence lost contact with the sub, since, by treaty, they should *not* have been there--it would have been an act of war against the U.S. It seemed the communists would rather lose their whole crew with no rescue effort, than give away the places they had been spying. No doubt, they believed the American operatives were looking for the sub also. But Megan's military friends speculated there were, possibly, operatives from rogue nations, anxious to get their hands on nuclear devices as well.

Megan had a funny feeling about all the rhetoric, and the searches. She had been back from the ski trip for over a week, and still had heard nothing from Ed. Nor had she read anything in the papers about "Dawn Patrol," so she hoped he was all right.

But she and the other teachers of the stable Annex soon had something *else* to worry about.

Just after lunch on Tuesday, the principal strode into Megan's room, the first on the end of the long Annex building, and whispered to her, "Get the kids down to JFK gym on main Post, now. Don't let anyone stay behind, and don't let anyone slam doors." With that, he stepped out to the hall and hurried on to the next room.

Six classrooms, two exits, no explanations--Megan tried to keep her voice calm and commanding. "Boys and girls, please stand up and put on your coats...quickly. Take your math folder, and follow me. Don't drag your feet, Patrick, but please hold the outside door open until the last person is out. Let's see how fast we can get down to JFK gym, without running. We'll finish our math down there."

Megan gathered her own coat and her book bag, into which she dumped a box of pencils and crayons, a stack of drawing paper, and *Wrinkle in Time,* a book she'd been reading to the group every day after lunch. She led the children out of the room, across the hall, and past little Patrick. He dutifully counted people until the last class was out, and then ran to catch up to his class. They walked at double quick time to the street and turned toward the Post gymnasium.

Megan tried to keep her mind only on getting the children there fast, which was hard enough on the slippery iced-over cobblestones. But she couldn't help wondering what emergency would send them out into the frosty air in such a hurry.

"Why do we have to go so fast?" called out Patrick, as he caught up to Megan?"

"Think of it as a speed run, Patrick," Megan answered. The children picked up the pace as best they could without falling. She silently blessed the confidence with which military children learned to obey orders quickly and skip most questions, when they sensed it was an emergency.

She could see the other five classes following along behind hers, but the others carried nothing with them. She knew if they had to stay for any length of time in the gym, she would be thankful she had brought something for the children to do.

It turned out to be a wise move. The other boisterous classes couldn't sit still on the bleachers at JFK and created headaches for the teachers trying to keep them under control. Megan's children finished their math with no complaint, bringing her their completed folders. They loved her individualized math program in which they could each work at their own pace. The growth was more than twice as much as they had learned under the old lock-step program. Megan and the children's parents had been more than pleased with their progress, and she relished her academic freedom in DoDDS

As each child finished his math, Megan passed out art paper from her bag and let each choose one crayon to do a monotone portrait of the child next to him. Except for an occasional giggle when a pair collaborated over a green eye or purple nose, the kids were fairly quiet. She felt sure they would be going back to their classroom soon, whatever the problem. *No such luck!* So, Megan pulled out her copy of Madeleine L'Engle's children's masterpiece of space travel, held it up high, and her children piled their other things on the bleachers and gathered closely around her as she read to them.

Finally, a few parents began to appear at the gym door, and one by one, the children were sent home with them.

"It was sabotage," said Mr. Essex, their principal, as he gathered the Annex teachers around him after the children left the gym. "We don't know who did it, or why, but the POL tanks of high-octane fuel on the hill behind the Annex building ruptured. It wouldn't have taken much to start the fuel flowing--the cold weather could have cracked the rest of it. The fuel was pouring down the hill to engulf the Annex school building. I'm sorry for the rush, but we had to evacuate all the children from the building before it was completely encircled. The MP's were standing knee deep in 23,000 gallons of fuel, holding their breath and waiting for the kids to get clear of the main street before they dared try to stop the flow. Had they used a wrench or any other tool, it could have caused a spark and the whole thing would have become flaming napalm." He wiped the sweat from his brow and said, "Thank you all for being so quick to move with no questions asked. There was no time for explanation."

The event was the talk of the O'Club that night as bewildered officers and teachers gathered for dinner.

"Who could have done such a thing?" Stan was indignant.

Luke was quick to look for logic. "Who, besides our folks, have been seen up that hill?"

"Who would be dumb enough to be seen?" asked Charlie.

Rex and some of his MP's walked through, questioning everyone to see if anyone had seen any unauthorized persons or suspicious behavior.

No one had, but one of the MP's related his fear as they had stood knee deep in fuel, waiting for the last kid to clear the area before they dared move. "Man, I thought Rex and I were goners," one said. "I know the teachers were hurrying the kids, but that was the longest eight minutes I've ever lived through."

"Was that all it took us, eight minutes to get the kids across

Post to JFK, snow and all?" Les was surprised.

"Believe me," said Rex, "We were watching the clock. You were super. And one kid kept the door open for all the classes before he closed it and caught up with his own class. Believe me, had that metal door been banging against its metal frame after each kid, a spark would have ignited the fuel for sure!"

"That was my Patrick," said Megan. "He needs really clear instructions, but he'll follow them as soon as he understands."

"Would you mind if we make up a little certificate for him?"

Megan was amazed to see Top Cop Rex considering a little kid. "Sure, I think Patrick would be pleased to know he helped."

Talk quickly turned to finding the person or persons responsible and preventing such a thing from happening again. Everyone had ideas and suggestions, but no one had a clear suspect or motive. Rex felt it should be called 'an accident' until they caught the culprit, to keep him from escaping. "We'll let everyone think we're only looking for the *cause* of the accident, not any particular person. Maybe, if they think they're safe, they'll give themselves away."

"I just don't understand why anyone would target the Annex," said Abby. "If they're mad at someone, they could just go after that individual. And there are plenty of military targets around."

"They might have been trying to make a statement--sort of like the Bader-Meinhoff gangs targeting Americans around Germany right now," said Mary. "Have we had an incident like this before?"

"Not since I've been Provost Marshall," said Rex. "But that doesn't mean an act of terror couldn't happen here too. We've had civilian and military casualties at several other Posts. Everybody, think hard. Has anyone seen anyone, other than our own people, hanging around, asking questions, or loitering around the Post?"

"And," added his MP, "is there anyone who might be a target, if an enemy wanted to say--get back at someone, or draw out someone who has a high security clearance, or some such thing?"

Megan felt a sudden cramp in her side. *What had Ed said, that if anyone knew he loved me, they might try to attack me to get to him?* She gripped her hands together tightly and tried to think. Surely, even if someone wanted to try to get to Ed, through her, if they even knew they *could*, since so few knew they were in love, why wouldn't they simply target her, and not endanger all the children? There were too many 'ifs.' There had to be a better explanation.

Not enough people even knew about Ed and her to be a threat. Carl knew, and Abby and Emily had figured it out. 'Major America' and Luke had guessed, but they knew nothing about Ed's job, and Gary had a high security clearance himself. Besides, Gary had already told Megan that he realized Ed needed someone, and he wished them well. Everyone else simply assumed she and Ed were casual friends. She wracked her brain to think if she'd been 'discreet.' But Lila knew, or thought she did, and by extension, that meant Klaus knew. Megan shuddered to think of that sleazy man making assumptions about her private business.

But truly, Megan thought, there would be no reason for anyone *else* to think Ed was any more important than her other friends. Everyone knew people came to her with their problems. Bill would show up on her doorstep with his guitar to 'sing for his supper' when he really wanted to talk. Colin, Charlie, or Robert often dropped by to be 'mothered' a bit, bringing her flowers, eating her cookies, or talking over problems about their young troopers, or their girlfriends.

She and a professor at the college, both being Literature majors, enjoyed discussing poetry. And she enjoyed Milt's company, though she still felt he kept something about himself secret, and he seemed to be missing lately—at least no one had seen him since the last time he'd dropped by, talked only a few minutes while they listened to a Barry Manilow tape. He'd given her a hug and simply said, "Someday…" as he turned and walked away, not looking in her eyes at all. She knew he was hiding something, but had no idea what.

Luke was another friend often at her side, always with heavy burdens. He wanted her to go with him to symphonies, or to let him into the school music room at night so he could work off his frustrations against his parents by pounding out classical music on the piano. No one but Megan knew he could play beautifully, but with such angry emotion, or that he always tore up his mom's letters without reading them. Recently, he had 'seen death' when his motorcycle was involved in a tragic accident, and Megan and Carl worried about his mood swings. He slept in his clothes, drank far too heavily, and 'disappeared' along the Border. Carl had gone looking for him during *that* crisis, even volunteering to fly extra Border duty. They knew Luke was too depressed to fly a helicopter. After three weeks, Luke had resurfaced jovially playing magic tricks on his friends, as though nothing had happened, apparently having exorcised his personal demons. Megan and Carl were sure Luke's mind bordered on schizophrenia, but he relied on them both for stability and to preserve his 'public image.'

Even Top Cop Rex liked to sit around and talk about history, politics, or his police work, since no one else ever took his ideas seriously. Big Don was protective toward Megan, full of fatherly advice, even though he was younger than she was.

After any party, there would always be two or three people crashed on her floor or couch for an overnight, especially if they had drunk too much, or the weather was violent. No one thought anything about people staying over wherever they happened to be, and Megan had long since stopped worrying about what people thought. It was all family. Of course, it was a good thing when a few people stayed over. The understanding was that if you stayed after a party, you helped clean up in the morning while the host or hostess fixed breakfast.

Cavalry commander Wheeler, she could make laugh, and they would talk for hours in the O'Club on Saturday nights.

With no phones at apartments, drop-in guests were common among Megan's friends. And, of course, Carl had been her constant sidekick for almost two years, sharing all their activities and practically living at her apartment whenever he was up from Katterbach.

No, Megan thought. No one could say she had played favorites. Both male and female friends knew they could pop in whenever they needed to talk. No one should suspect Ed was any different, so no one would have reason to think much about Ed being around to talk to her at odd intervals too...*except* Lila. Megan shuddered.

Lila knew, or at least thought she knew, that Megan and Ed were serious. And, by extension, that meant Klaus knew. But even Klaus, if he really liked Lila, wouldn't endanger Lila's friend, or those children he must know teachers love, even if he was trying to get at Ed...*would he*? She had a sudden moment of intuition. Perhaps Klaus was only using Lila to get to the other military people here. With growing dread, Megan found that idea somehow was beginning to make more sense, given some of Lila's latest remarks.

Should she mention this to Rex, or would it set off a hullabaloo that couldn't be stopped once it got started? She wished

Carl weren't flying today, or that Ed would call so she could ask him. She didn't want to put Lila or her friendships under scrutiny when there was probably no connection, and an easy explanation. Perhaps she could at least determine if Klaus had been on Post with her that day.

Megan drove straight out to Lila's apartment, climbed the stairs, and knocked on the door. She hoped Lila was home, and alone, since it was a school night.

Lila answered the door with her usual delight and invited Megan in.

"Something important has come up, Lila. I need your input."

Lila immediately put hot water on to brew tea, and they sat down at the kitchen table.

"What's going on?"

"Lila, was Klaus on Post with you today?"

"Sure, why? He often meets me at the gate so I can get him on Post with my ID card. He can get things done while I'm at school, and we often meet for dinner."

"What sorts of things?"

"Oh, lots of things…he likes to go to the Bookstore. I think he's known Ilse for a long time, and she gets books for him, though they argue a lot. He likes to browse through the library and play pickup basketball with some of the Engineers over at JFK gym. I don't know what all. Sometimes he meets me at the O'Club or at school, or he doesn't, if he has something else to do." She picked up two packages of hair color. "I just get him on Post in the morning and then, he's on his own." She looked thoughtful for a moment. "He didn't meet me after school today, though, so I came on home to do my hair." She held up two boxes and asked, "Do you think I should go to an even lighter blonde this time?"

Megan ignored the hair color. She didn't know how to question further without implying something she was not quite sure she should touch. "He met you to come on Post this morning, though, then you heard nothing further from him today. Is that right?"

"Sure, but what's all this about?"

"I'm going to ask you some questions I'm not sure you'll like. If you didn't go by the Club tonight, you mightn't have heard about our accident at the Annex. It's all okay now, but somehow a fuel tank ruptured and we had to evacuate the children."

"There was just something on the radio news about that a few minutes ago, and I was surprised I hadn't heard anything. Being in the main building, we never know what happens in the Annex until y'all tell us. Was it really serious?"

"It could have been, but fortunately Rex and the MP's came soon enough, and we all got out safely."

"Thank God. The newsman said it was a terrible accident. Does anyone know how it happened?"

"So far, they're just looking for ideas about what caused the accident." Megan felt it necessary to keep reiterating the 'accident' idea, in case she couldn't ask further questions about Klaus.

"Lila, I need you to tell me what you think about Ed and me?"

"Why, honey, it's as plain as the nose on your face that you two are in love, and I'm just so happy for y'all." She threw her fists in the air for emphasis. "He's such a fun person, and its so exciting that he just appears and disappears like a phantom." Lila just wriggled all over when something made her happy, and Megan, with a steadily sinking heart, was positive Lila was so happy about the two being together, that she wouldn't have been able to keep it a secret.

"I felt sure you knew about us, Lila, but it's supposed to be a secret for now. Have you told anyone else that we're serious?"

"I've talked about it to Abby and Emily and Carol, and Carl already knows, doesn't he? And Brian, and perhaps Stan--just our closest friends. Why is it such a secret?"

Megan ignored that question. "Have you discussed it with Klaus?"

"Why, of course, Honey. He's as pleased for you as I am. He can hardly wait to see how it all comes out. He has speculations about what Ed really does, and they all sound *so* exciting."

"Like what?"

"What do you mean?"

"I mean like what kind of speculations has he had about Ed's job? Ed simply does weapons inspections."

Lila giggled. "Klaus says that's what they *all* say when they're big in CIA or Military Intelligence or Special Ops. It gives them an excuse to roam around freely with no one asking questions."

Megan felt an icy chill wrap around her spine and creep up her neck. What should she say now? "Well, Klaus is wrong about that. Ed really *is* a weapons inspector, artillery MOS, does War Planning, and that's *all* he does. And even if Klaus were right, which he isn't, I wouldn't want you to discuss Ed or me, or our relationship, or Ed's job, or anything, with Klaus, or anyone else for that matter. It really is private, Lila. Don't you understand?"

Lila backed up sharply, and her eyes narrowed. "You do think Klaus is a spy, don't you?"

"I didn't say that, Lila, exactly, but we shouldn't be talking about any military person's job, whether we know about it or we don't, with someone outside the military. There are too many terrorists, activists, and those who would like to harm us out there right now, and we're not exactly in the safest place in Europe. We don't know who comes across that Border, who could threaten our guys, and perhaps even our school children. I don't know how to say this kindly, because I love you to pieces and one of the reasons why is your generous and bubbly nature, but you mustn't talk so much about important things!"

Megan's forceful statement must have finally registered because Lila's eyes grew large. "Does this have something to do with our conversation of the other day? Do you think Klaus tells someone else whatever I tell him?"

"Yes, I do. Carl thinks so, and Luke has seen him lurking around the airport where he's not supposed to be. I certainly hope I'm wrong, because a lot is at stake here. But I think we'd better tell Rex that Klaus was on Post today."

"I don't want to get him in some kind of trouble. I *know* he wouldn't do anything to hurt us. He's one of my best boyfriends."

"I still think we'd better tell Rex. Will you come with me back to the Club, or do you want me to go tell him?"

"I'll come, but this is ridiculous, and I intend to tell Klaus so."

"Please, no, Lila. That's the whole point!" Megan was emphatic and frustrated by how an intelligent person like Lila could be so clueless.

By the time they returned to the O'Club, Carl was in, had heard about the fuel incident, and he and Rex were muddling over what clues they had about the rupture. When Carl saw Lila and Megan come in, he rose and came to hug Megan. "Are you all right?"

She nodded, taking his hand for support. "We have something to tell Rex."

Turning to Rex, Lila said, "Megan thinks I should tell y'all that I brought Klaus on Post this morning. He wanted to go see Ilse at the bookstore." She looked a bit huffy as she said, "This whole thing is silly, but Megan gets an idea in her head and just won't let go of it."

Rex looked at Megan, then at Carl, and tried to speak carefully. "Lila, it's all speculative at this point. We just need to know everyone who was on Post today because perhaps someone saw how the accident happened. We must find the cause so it won't happen again. You understand, don't you?" When Lila remained silent, he added, "Perhaps Klaus would be willing to come tell me if he saw anything peculiar about the way the tanks looked today."

"I doubt he was even on that end of Post, but I'll ask him for y'all, if you're sure it's important. I may not see him until the party."

"Do you think you could call his apartment and have him drop by to help me with this?"

"I suppose so. But he may think that I think he had something to do with the accident."

"I'll be really careful not to give him that impression, Lila." Rex was doing his best to be diplomatic, quite a feat for his big, tough guy image. His nervousness was evident in the way he twisted his mustache between his fingers as he spoke.

Carl cornered Megan for a talk. "Megan, I really think Klaus may be sending information from Lila through Ilse to someone. It would appear after this fuel tank mess that he might be from the other side of the Border. That would explain his vagueness on background information, and his lack of a job. We need to be really careful with you, until we get to the bottom of this whole thing. One of us will be with you, or near your classroom at all times. We'll take turns, just in case you're the target." He took both of her hands in his and said, "I don't want you to act any differently, just don't be surprised for one of us to be near by. And, I think we need to warn Ed somehow, in case this fuel tank thing is related to whatever he's doing. Do you know where he is, or is there an emergency number where you can reach him?"

Chapter 29

Late that night, from Top Cop Rex's secure phone, Megan dialed the emergency number she carried in her wallet. It was Ed's 'hot line' that only he could answer, and it still had the 'scrambler' on it, so she knew he was not in Germany. She tried instead the number Marco had given her and left a message with the Warrant who answered. "Urgent message for Col. Ed O'Brien. Please call Bamberg office at #69703. Sincerely, Ms James"

"Oh, Ms James," said a pleasant young officer, when he called back within minutes. Colonel O'Brien is out of his office right now. Can you tell me the urgent business?"

"If you can reach the Colonel, please tell him the person about whom we had concerns may have tried to target the school, perhaps to persuade him to return here sooner to investigate. Tell him he should avoid coming here for any further inspections. He'll understand."

"I'll get this message to him right away, Ms James. You'll hear as soon as the Colonel can break free to call."

"Thank you." Megan's voice broke. "Don't let him come here without backup, Captain. It would be better if he didn't come at all. And…and please tell him to be careful."

The young man's voice softened. "Understood, Ma'am."

Wednesday the phone outside Megan's classroom rang right after school. During that time, she had not been alone. Two of Rex's MP's patrolled outside the school Annex, checking ID's, while two more watched the workmen repairing the damaged fuel tanks up on the hill. Megan believed the security was an overreaction. "This is taking up a lot of you and your MP's time, Rex, and it still could have been just an accident, couldn't it?"

"The precautions are only until the Colonel tells us how he wants to handle this, or until we can complete our investigation of the tank spill to see if there is any connection at all."

Megan now ran to the phone, feeling guilty that she had perhaps called Ed over nothing.

"Megan?" Ed's voice sounded strained. She could tell he was

tired.

"Yes, it's me, and I'm so sorry to contact you this way. I told myself I never would, but Rex thought this was important enough that you needed to know."

"What's happened with the person about whom we were concerned?"

Megan took her cue from his caution over the unsecured phone line. "We've had an accident involving a fuel tank spill that forced us to evacuate our school Annex. Rex feels the party may know something about it, especially since it was my wing."

"Are you all right?" His anxiety rang through the wires.

"Yes, and someone is with me at all times. Don't worry. Are you okay where you are?"

"Tricky business, but we're trying to get it wrapped up as quickly as possible." There was a pause. "Do you know if there are further plans concerning the person in question?"

"We have that Ski Club party planned for Friday night. I don't want you to come, especially since he seems to know things he shouldn't. It could be a trap…"

"I won't leave you alone to deal with this. I'll be there somehow."

"Just in case he really did threaten our kids in order to get you to return, your coming would play right into his hands, wouldn't it? Let's break off contact until this issue is resolved."

"Negative. We need to resolve it now. There's no need to worry about security any longer. I won't take chances with the kids or you. If he's connected to an organization, he'll already know anyway, from their surveillance, from insecure phone lines, even coded, and he'll be waiting for me to surface. Might as well get him to make his move and get it over with. I'll try to be there before the party. If I don't make it, keep Carl, or Stan, or one of the other officers with you at all times, understood?"

"Yes. What about my female friend? You know who."

"Don't change any plans, but Top Cop could arrange some coverage for her, too."

"I think he already has, but do you think she's in any danger? She called in sick and hasn't been to school the last two days, but when we drove to her house, she wasn't there. We've not seen her."

"She's so open and unaware, he could be using her,

unwittingly."

"I know. That's what scares me. Anything else I should do?"

He chuckled softly. "Pray for me. I don't swim as well as I used to when I was a young tight-body lifeguard chasing girls. And remember what I told you the last moment I saw you?"

She said, "I remember. Same here. And don't forget to duck."

"Good bye, my Darling. Be careful."

Megan held the phone a moment more before placing it carefully back in its cradle with both hands. She gathered up her school bag just as Colin stepped into the hall.

"We're going to the Laundromat together, aren't we?" He took her arm and escorted her out to his car. "I brought my laundry too, so we'll have time to talk about my latest girlfriend problems while we do your laundry and mine."

Megan pressed the arm of her volunteer bodyguard with affection. "I'll be happy to listen, Colin. Which one is it this time, Stacy or Lynn?"

After dinner at the Club the next evening, Thursday, Marco came to Megan, Rex, and Carl, whispering that they should go to the suite upstairs. Each of the three excused themselves, individually, so they wouldn't be seen leaving together. Megan went first, her high heels clicking down the upstairs hall. Before she could knock, the door opened, a hand grabbed her arm, and pulled her inside. Suddenly, she was in Ed's fierce embrace, and he was nuzzling his face in her hair.

"Did I remember last time to tell you I love you, and I love the smell of your hair?"

She couldn't help laughing. "You told me about the hair, and I couldn't see what the big deal was—it's only baby shampoo—I hate perfume." She looked up into his eyes. "You did say you loved me then, but I think I'd like to hear it again."

"You need to be told again and again. I love you. That's just in case I can't say it in front of someone else, or in case you forget. God, you feel so good in my arms—so wonderful."

She stood on tiptoe to kiss him, her arms reaching up around his neck. "Was it bad?"

"I imagine you've surmised the mission. Can't confirm

anything. Navy has dive ships. We ran into renegades we weren't sure would be there, and there was a turncoat involved. It was touch and go, but our job is more or less done. My team is still there now, mopping up."

"If Klaus had anything to do with these accidents, your coming back would be exactly what he'd want you to do. I feel uneasy about your being here."

"We have to find out, don't we?"

At the next knock, Ed quickly opened the door to Carl. Rex followed. Ed laid his Beretta on the coffee table and faced the trio. "What do we know about this Klaus character?"

"We know he's not who he claims to be, Sir," said Rex. "Our investigation shows no 'Klaus Blick' registered in Bamberg, and all Germans must register, so now German authorities are helping—for observation only. They've agreed not to interfere until we complete our investigation. Klaus also gives a phony address. We can find no evidence that he has a job. He comes on Post frequently with Lila. Ilse, the bookstore's manager, is his most frequent daily contact. We have Ilse under surveillance." Rex shuffled through sheets on his clipboard, and continued.

"Klaus asks questions of everyone—soldiers playing basketball, the Post librarian, asking her about officers or units coming and going from the Border, and he makes himself a general nuisance. But, he's also asked folks about *you*, Sir, by name and rank. Since the only people who know you are Megan's friends, he could have gotten information about you from only one place—Lila."

"But we all know Lila," said Megan, defending her friend. "She's too naïve about the military to understand when she should keep quiet, and her personality is so bubbly that she never knows a stranger, nor can she be suspicious of anyone."

"That's probably why Klaus latched on to her that first night on the Rhine cruise," said Carl. "He could have approached anyone he thought might be vulnerable, and he obviously *chose* Lila. Do we think she's in danger, or Megan, or both?"

"I'm sure it's the Colonel he's after," said Rex, "I think Klaus only uses Lila as the weak link for gathering information. The uncharacteristically high accident rates here and at the Border were to lure the Colonel up to Bamberg with the investigation team--to pull him from undercover out into the open, so to speak. Bamberg makes the perfect site because we're isolated. They probably figured you, Sir, wouldn't have as much support here without your Stuttgart team, so maybe they could make an attack on you look like an accident, just like those in Heidelberg and Frankfurt. Of course, Klaus lucked out when you became interested in Megan because that brought you back here even more frequently. Now he and his group have connected you two, and they are apparently ready to move against you, Sir."

Rex paused, then blurted it out. "Sir--I think Klaus wants to take you down. I don't know what you're doing, and I don't *want* to know, but you must be well known to some of our enemies. I feel sure Klaus was given an assassination mission. It's *you* we need to protect."

"That's why I told you not to come," said Megan, with a note of desperation evident in her voice. "We've played right into his hands."

Ed smiled slowly, already moving into 'Spook mode,' Megan thought—that in-between territory of training and duty taking over, and regard for his own safety departing.

"Or he's playing right into *our* hands. We'll smoke him out." Ed reached for Megan's hand. "At least I know what to expect now, since it sounds like he's a professional, too."

"Who knows you're here right now, Sir?" asked Rex.

Ed ran his hand over the smooth top of his head. "My aide in the hall, the helicopter pilots from EUCOM Flight Detachment. They have high security clearance. CW 4 Carlson from your airfield drove my aide and me over. Only Marco knows we're up here now."

Rex shifted his position, and Ed added, "Before you even ask, Marco is trusted."

"We've always assumed that, Colonel," said Rex. "I just didn't know he was in so deep."

"You still don't." Ed winked. "What precautions are you taking for Megan and Lila?"

Rex outlined the rotating volunteers from among friends who were watching over Megan, and the detail of MP's, in plain clothes, who had been following Lila and Klaus. "Lila may think she's safe with Klaus. He may not show his true colors until she leads him to you, Sir. My men tailing them say Klaus has barely let her out of his sight. One MP followed Klaus downtown where he picked up packages at an apartment registered to Ilse. He's been seen there so often, we think he's living there."

"That's curious," said Megan, "since we've thought he was courting Lila."

"We've been tracking counter-intelligence cells of Soviets and East Germans working near the Border," said Ed. "We've strongly suspected they were responsible for the rash of accidents, but we've assumed their objective was to bog down our operations and demoralize our troops. What we haven't known is who's in charge of the teams, and who all the members are. We need to know where Klaus fits into this picture, if he does. I need to talk to the man." Ed paused, his voice controlled. "What's the next event at which Klaus may be present?"

"I guess just the Ski Club party tomorrow night at Stan's," said Carl.

Ed nodded as he sat down on the sofa and signaled everyone else to relax as well. "We can put the word out that I'm taking Megan to the party. It might tell us whether or not Klaus is suspect, because he'll either come to circulate with other guests, or come to confront me. Of course, I won't really take Megan in case it gets ugly." He turned to Carl. "Will you keep all the ladies safely here until we see how Klaus' arrival goes?"

Carl nodded. "No problem, Sir."

"Hey, wait a minute," said Megan. "I don't want you going off acting like bait. If Klaus follows you, you'd be alone to fight him off. We'll go with you."

"And what do you think you could do to stop him, young lady?" A soft smile played around Ed's lips. "My dear, I've been taking care of these kinds of things, alone, for many years now. You're safer here."

Megan was angry at both Ed for suggesting she should be left behind, and at Carl for agreeing to it. "But if Klaus comes with Lila to go to the party and doesn't see me there," she insisted, "he'll suspect something. He might think Lila lied to him, and he could hurt her."

"That's possible, Megan," said Ed, slowly reevaluating her presence. "Let's look at the whole picture and try to assess his intentions, and therefore, his moves, so we can counteract." Ed had turned all business and Megan could see the methodical way he prepared for a crisis.

"The way I see it," Ed ticked off his fast-running ideas as Rex took frantic notes on his clipboard, "we need to know if Klaus is really our saboteur? Is he a professional operative, or merely a lone discontented terrorist, or some star-struck swain of Lila's? If he's professional, who is in his chain of command so we can be sure no one gets away? Does he have complete control of Lila, which would make confrontation more difficult, especially should he try to use her as some kind of hostage or shield? What does he know about me and is it really me he's after? Is he a trained sniper, or will he try a confrontation? If it's me he's been sent to find, I'll need to talk him into meeting outside, away from other guests. We don't want to endanger Lila, or any other bystanders. What scenario do you see as best to protect your people?"

The question caught Rex by surprise since he'd been scribbling so fast. "I'd like to pick up Klaus for questioning. Lila said she'd ask him to come in to help with the accident investigation, but he hasn't come voluntarily."

Ed intervened, "But if you pick him up, he'll know we're suspicious, and anyone working with him will vanish. We need to get the *whole* cell, hopefully all at once."

"What if we simply allow Lila to bring him to the party," Rex suggested. We'll see his reaction when he sees you there, Sir. That should tell us if we need to subdue him, or isolate him, or take him down. If so, we can get him to talk and pick up any accomplices."

"I don't know if Lila's still bringing Klaus to the party," interrupted Megan. "Lila has decided she wants to marry Brian. She said she was going to try to stop Klaus from coming."

"Does Brian know that bit of news?" asked Carl, with a dry chuckle.

"I don't know. I told her to go tell him before she messed their relationship up, again."

"Then we don't know if Klaus is coming or not?" asked Ed.

"If he knows there's any activity involving the officers," said Rex, "he'll come." He's been a pain in our ...excuse me, Sir...but he's been a pain. And if we let it be known you are coming... He's been acting just too strange to ignore. We'll check back here after I brief my men, tomorrow about 1600 hours, to finalize plans and brainstorm ideas for isolating Klaus." Rex bid the group goodnight, adding to Ed, "Will you please stay here, Sir, unless you notify me? My men feel you and Megan weren't seen arriving upstairs, and few people know this suite exists, so this is probably the safest place." Ed nodded. "Even if you don't see me, or my men, Sir, we'll be here." Rex checked the hall for an all clear signal from Ed's aide and sauntered out.

Carl leaned over to put his palm against Megan's in the 'strength' signal. "I agree with Rex. You're safest to stay here tonight, Meggie. The Colonel and his aide will be your bodyguards. I'll be with you at school tomorrow. Wieder night, night." He started for the door.

"Carl," called Ed. He rose and reached his huge right hand out to shake Carl's. "If ever I don't make it back from one of my…'inspection tours,' I'll trust you to watch out for Megan."

"It goes without saying, Sir." Carl smiled at Megan, touched two fingers to his lips and waved them in the air at her as he left.

"I guess this is our little hide-out until the party, Megan." Ed's chuckle was low and guttural, as he took her hand and led her to the couch. "Think we can handle being alone for awhile?"

"Maybe," she said. "I guess it depends on what you can tell me and what you can't."

"Not much, at present. But you're good! I'll bet you already have it figured out."

"I think so, but do you think the Soviets lost it on purpose just to see who'd come out of the woodwork, or was it an accident?"

"I'm glad you have such an inquiring mind, my Darling. Did you know you look ravishing in that jump suit?"

"You always change the subject when my inquiring mind gets a little too close to fact. I accept that. I'd rather get back to just how much you love me…that's nice to hear, you know."

"I wouldn't be here, if I didn't love you, my Darling. I've assigned myself to clear up this mission first--both for your sake, and for all these so-called training accidents that are taking a toll on morale and unit stability. Klaus and his co-workers may account for some of our losses of life and limb."

"And I can see your brain cells already churning, planning how you'll defuse the trouble. You must think Klaus is important."

"Wish I knew. He may be a harmless idiot, or playing that part. Or maybe he's as much of a threat as the killer who shot our operative in Heidelberg, the rocket attack on the general's staff car in Karlsruhe, those who bombed the snack bar in Wiesbaden, or the Bader Meinhof terrorists. He could also be the 70's counterpart of an old-time 'hit man,' if it's me he's after."

Megan flinched at the idea of a hit man stalking Ed, but she maintained control enough to ask, "How are we going to bring him out in the open?"

"Not *we*, my dear, *me*. I don't want you nearby. I can tell his intentions from the questions he asks, if I can isolate him from the other guests…that will be a necessity. I don't want anyone else endangered." Ed took a deep breath. "Of course, if he knows what I'm doing and who I am, we must find out who else he's told, or my effectiveness, and that of my team, will have been compromised."

"Does that mean you'd be able to quit?" Megan tried not to show the quickening of hope.

"Most likely reassigned Stateside. They've been trying to get me to the 'Pentagon Puzzle Palace' for a long time, and I've always managed to convince them I'm more useful to them in the field." He grinned. "Besides, I want to stay here now, closer to you."

He saw her tears and added, "Are you going to ask me to quit my current assignment?"

She examined the veins on the top of his hand, silent for a moment. "It's ironic that if I ask you to stay here with me, your mission will put your life in danger, and I'd risk losing you. Yet if we could be together safely at the Pentagon, I might lose you because you would hate not having the excitement of your missions anymore, and I'd feel at fault." She sighed sadly at the dilemma. *I'm about to say I can accept a risk, and I don't even know if I'm strong enough. Is this the step my friends have been training me for?*

She took a deep breath and plunged ahead. "No, I'll not ask. Your job is a part of who you are, and I love you, just as you are. I have no way to ask you to quit. But I won't lie and say I'm not scared every minute you're gone."

"It's been a long, lonely life with no one to understood my mission, or the military life, or me. I'm glad you understand. I need you, my darling. I'm also glad that you can usually figure out what is happening, so I don't have to guard my words. You tease me when I'm too stubborn, and you make me laugh when I'm particularly tense. It's peaceful to be with you when the rest of the world comes crashing down." He kissed her on the forehead, looked into her eyes, and said, "You restore me."

Megan could feel the man's need, and she realized she again wanted to be a part of another human life—to belong to another—and she also knew it could have happened nowhere else but Bamberg. She owed it all to the Border. Megan took Ed's big hand in hers.

"Being here on a line base, I've learned to live again by watching my friends. They do their jobs under the worst possible circumstances, yet they always find spare moments to make the rest of us feel safe, support us, and have fun, too. I don't hear about that kind of shared experience happening at HQ or rear echelon bases like Stuttgart or Mannheim." She fought back tears for some unknown reason. Was this night the end of something--or the beginning?

"Border bases are unique," Ed agreed. "Americans tend to take the military for granted and don't want to know what soldiers actually do. In Washington right now, the current administration is cutting necessary military spending and weakening our force structure. Don't get me started..." He sighed. "I'm sorry, but sometimes... Actually, I'm glad you were assigned to Bamberg. The Border's camaraderie been a healing experience for you."

"Everyone has been wonderful. I didn't realize it when I came here, but I was suicidal. Carl and my other friends saw it, and they pushed me to stay busy, active, and to become someone they could depend upon. Carl forced me to face myself so I could get back to caring about others. I believe that prepared me to love you, as well."

"I'm grateful, my Darling. I hope they'll all be at our wedding. If we have it here in Bamberg, that would be the best way, don't you think?"

"When did we start talking about weddings?" She couldn't help laughing at the quick way their conversations evolved into new surprises.

"Now—though I think I won't propose formally until we see how things go at the party."

"Do you have some kind of bad feeling about this?"

"Sometimes my gut tells me when something may be wrong with a situation."

"Please hold me tonight. We'll pretend the party's over."

Chapter 30

Friday morning, Stan swung by the O'Club to take Megan to school, while Ed watched from the upstairs window.

"I wasn't sure who would come to get me today, Stan," Megan said with a smile. "I'm glad it's you, but I don't like to be so much trouble for everyone. Thank you."

"We don't mind, Megan. We all just want to keep you safe, and that big guy who obviously loves you. Top Cop fears Klaus might try to nab you to force the Colonel's hand, so he wants you protected a little longer. Carl and Big Don will be in your Annex today. Carl will be bringing you to the O'Club after school and to my house at *Seehof* later for the party."

"Are you sure this operation can be done safely for everyone? What if Klaus realizes he's being watched? I sure don't want anyone hurt."

"Stop worrying. Mary will come help me set up for the party, and we'll find a way to warn everyone when they enter that we'll want them to stay out of the way if Klaus starts going haywire. We know he's armed, so one must assume he's also dangerous--or deranged." Stan paused for a moment. "I'm assuming Top Cop or the Colonel will let me know if there are changes to the plan."

"It seems like everyone else knows what's happening, whether I do or not. Rex is meeting with Ed to make plans now."

"Rex told me neither the Colonel nor Carl wants you there, but Rex and I think Klaus and Lila would be tipped off right away if you weren't helping to set up for one of *my* parties." He laughed and tried to get her to smile. "This will all be over soon, my Dear. Chin up."

"Thank you for everything, Stan," Megan said, as she grabbed her school bag and hurried to meet her school children for the day.

Carl and Big Don were in the hall, greeting children. They merely waved at Megan and went on being invisible.

As Megan finished up after school, Carl told her, "Big Don said he'll see us at the party. He had to go check on his unit. It seems they have an Inspector General, or IG inspection so everything must be perfect. But they painted their offices, and big patches of ceiling plaster kept falling off, leaving holes. They've plastered and painted the ceiling four times. Now Don thinks they'll just paint it thirty minutes before the IG team arrives, hide the paint cans, and pray the ceiling stays up until the inspectors leave."

The two were able to laugh over one more of the usual military snafus.

"So, let's go on over to the O'Club and wait. Maybe Ed or Rex has heard something."

They quickly drove the short distance, and were met by Marco. "They're waiting for you," was all he said, but both Megan and Carl knew he was referring to Ed and Rex. Just as they started up the stairs, Marco stopped Carl and said quietly, "Ilse was arrested this afternoon, for passing information we didn't even know was missing. She and another accomplice are in custody. We don't know if Klaus knows this yet. Be careful."

Carl took Megan's hand and they walked up the stairs. "Megan, whatever happens, I want you to know we can always count on each other, right?"

"Of course. You know you'll always be part of my life."

He kissed her on the left cheek and then knocked at the suite's door. It immediately opened, and the two were rushed inside. Ed was smiling as he shook hands with Carl and kissed Megan on the right cheek, leading her to a chair.

Megan couldn't stifle a giggle, thinking of the two men she had learned to love in such different ways, both being by her side in a crisis.

"What's new?" asked Carl. "Marco said Ilse had been arrested."

Rex pulled up a desk chair and sat in it backward. "Yeah, we hadn't wanted to tip our hand this early. But one of our MI guys, Sutton, caught her trying to hand off information and materials to another guy, and they couldn't wait any longer to arrest them both. We hope Klaus hasn't gotten word of their arrest yet, and that he'll still get to the party. It may be too much to hope that he won't hear something by tonight. We'll have to set up the trap at Stan's anyway."

"Even if he hears about the arrests," said Ed, "being a professional, he'll still want to wait around long enough to complete his mission. He'll try to think of a way to get me, and still get away afterward. I'll bet he'll try to hang out with Lila until the party, figuring that even if we know about him, we won't risk Lila's safety by confronting him."

"Do we know how close he's hovering around her?" asked Megan. We haven't seen her. I heard she came to school today, but there was a 'guest' in her room. I'm betting it was Klaus."

"Colin said that he tried to talk to her," answered Rex, but Klaus was standing right beside her. Klaus just interrupted and said he'd bring her by the O'Club for a drink, and then take her to the party, so apparently we can look for Klaus to be downstairs at some point."

"What happens if Klaus knows Ilse was arrested?" asked Carl.

"Then," said Rex, "Klaus might assume Lila or Megan turned her in, and it could be necessary to intervene *before* the party to protect Lila. We're hoping he hasn't heard. Of course, there's no way to be sure. He may already know, and he's just holding on to Lila as insurance."

Ed broke in. "Perhaps we should go to *Seehof* earlier, so if Klaus has people watching, they'll get the word and show up before the other guests. If he has heard about Ilse, he may already be there, lying in wait."

"We can do that," said Megan. "Everyone, even Klaus, knows I help set up for parties at Stan's. If either Lila or Klaus sees us, they'll just assume we're on the decorating committee."

"I want Klaus to know I'm there," said Ed. "If it's me he's after, I'd rather not have others in the line of fire."

Rex thought through a scenario. "This might work. If you are inside with Stan, we can set up in the woods on the perimeter. We'll see Klaus arrive and hope he can be provoked to make a move earlier rather than later when he sees you. My men can block off the road to further visitors after Klaus has passed to keep the exposed number of people small. We can close in at the first sign of trouble, or catch him outside if he tries to run. I wish we could just shoot him on sight, but we have no proof until he tries something."

"I assume your MP's are armed," said Ed, looking at Rex.

"All of them, Sir."

Ed picked up his own weapon, checked it carefully and repositioned it in the holster behind his belt. He pulled up his pants leg to reveal where a knife was fitted into his right boot. "Just so you'll know where this is in case of emergency." His glance was at Carl, who nodded.

"Okay, let's go," said Rex. "Colonel, you and Megan stay here and wait for my signal. We'll hope he's out there now to see you leave?" My men will be watching in case he attacks you directly, but I think he'll feel *Seehof* and its terrain is more advantageous to his getting away into the forest. There's *no* chance of his getting away here on Post, so I think he'll wait. But we'll be covering you without revealing to Klaus that we are there. He'll be more willing to come out in the open if he thinks you're unguarded at the party."

Less than ten minutes went by as the two watched from the suite window. "Megan," said Ed, in a serious tone. "All this may be for nothing, but it's beginning to look as though Klaus is at least part of the same group as Ilse and this other man, if not something more. If there's any trouble, I want you to drop to the floor immediately and stay there, no matter what."

She lifted her face to his and kissed him, long and softly. "I'll be where you are."

He shook his head, smiling. "You're quite a girl, my darling. I seem to have gotten lucky in my middle age. No matter what happens, I want you to know these months I've been drifting in and out of your life have been the happiest times of my life. When all this is settled, we'll be making some big-time plans."

"I never thought I'd even want to love anyone again, but I do love you. Both Carl and Abby told me that some day I'd want to feel like this again, and that it would be a *different* experience. I didn't believe them." She smiled up at him and leaned into his embrace.

"Just stand there a minute, my Darling, and let me hold you…"

Then they saw the signal, descended the staircase, and Megan got behind the wheel of her Fiat. Ed sat up front, quite visible, hoping whoever was watching would get word to Klaus. Carl climbed in the back, surveying the perimeter as though admiring the spring foliage peeping through the trees. Megan assumed Rex and his MP's would be taking up positions somewhere in the woods so they could see who arrived down the dirt road leading from *Seehof* palace to Stan's familiar carriage house. But she never saw them.

Stan and Charlie weren't surprised when Megan, Carl, and Ed

showed up at their door early. "Hey, I'm glad you found a way to come help us set up, after all." Stan hugged Megan.

"What's our latest plan?" asked Charlie, as soon as everyone was inside. "I saw one of Rex's men lying camouflaged in the woods when I came in the back way, and he put his finger over his lips, so I ignored him. So, Rex has the woods covered already."

"I suppose we wait to see who shows up first, and why," said Carl. "Do we have any personal weapons around here, Stan, just in case?"

Stan went to his bedroom, returning with two handguns, one of which he handed to Charlie. He had a baseball bat, which he placed behind a screen near the door. "Megan, I suggest you and Mary go stay in my bedroom for awhile." The men realigned themselves around the room, not exactly as casually as they were trying to appear.

Megan said, "You are all laughably obvious. Anyone entering this room and not seeing Mary and me would immediately know something was wrong. We'll finish setting tables and you guys can at least look busy putting out food, firing up the grill, and setting up the bar."

Within moments, Abby arrived with Robert. Both were laughing as Robert playfully chased her in the door. "Thought you might need some extra help," said Robert. "Abby said she thought you all might be here." He gently pushed Abby over toward Mary and Megan as they placed flowers on the trestle tables that would soon bear food.

Abby whispered to Megan, "I had to tell him. I didn't want you out here alone."

Megan squeezed her hand and the three women continued to work near windows where they could be seen from the outside, as normally as possible.

The party was due to start at 1900 hours, but at 1830, they heard yet another car coming along the path. All took their places, but it was Brian who burst in. "Marco sent me speeding over here to warn you Klaus and Lila were at the O'Club. Klaus told him they'd come to have a drink before coming out here to the party. But Klaus ordered drinks, kept looking around like he was expecting someone to come in, and he didn't take his hand out of his pocket or let loose of Lila's arm, even to sip his drink. Marco said to tell you that he didn't think Lila was there by choice. She looked terrified. Marco felt she was trying to tell him something with her eyes."

Ed said, "Wasn't there any chance to get Lila away from the man?"

"Marco said he tried, but short of grabbing her and risking Klaus's shooting at her, he couldn't seem to do it. He caught me in the hall and said he'd try to delay them as long as he could, but he wanted you to know Lila might be in the way should you try to take out Klaus. I came as fast as I could. Do you think he'd really harm her?" His face contorted with concern as he asked the question.

"We hope not, Brian," said Ed. "Rex's men will let Klaus' car go by, then put a sign at the entry gate so everyone else will wait. They'll close in to try to arrest Klaus after he and Lila are inside the house. I know you care about Lila, and we'll do everything we can to protect her."

"And Brian, you should know right now that Lila has already decided to marry you." Carl couldn't help grinning as he added, "I know that may be a hell of a surprise to you, but it's true."

At Brian's sharp intake of breath, Megan said, "...and she wants to have lots of babies, Bri. Can you handle that? We just all have to get through tonight successfully, and maybe we'll have a wedding..." She looked at Ed, and he grinned.

"Or two," he added.

Stan said suddenly, "Girls, stand where you can dive behind something if anything happens. I hear a car coming down the path."

Chapter 31

Everyone tensed. "We'll not act surprised they came early," said Ed, "and we won't do anything until we get Lila away from him."

"It's my job to take him out, Sir," said Brian.

"You're unarmed, Son," said Ed softly. "Just try to get Lila to walk away from Klaus so we can get a clear shot if we need to. Call her calmly to come help you put food out. Can you do that, slowly?" In a louder voice, he added, "Don't anyone make any sudden moves or get between we who are armed and Klaus. Understand? I'm going to try to talk him into going outside with me first, so don't anyone move too fast." Everyone in the small group nodded.

"Do we look casual enough?" asked Mary, actually picking up a broom.

"You look quite domestic, Dear," answered Stan. "That could be a good thing, right?"

She stuck out her tongue at him, and he smirked at her.

The car door slammed, and Stan's front door swung open without the usual knock. No one expected it. They tried to maintain the usual conversation with mixed results as Lila was shoved through the door ahead of Klaus. Megan recognized the fear in her eyes and started toward her, but Robert reached out and grabbed her arm to stop her from moving.

"Now," said Klaus, holding Lila in front of his body and making no pretense. "Where is your undercover operative, the Colonel, and where is the young pup that wants Lila?"

Brian moved closer, ignoring Klaus, telling Lila to come help him put out food on the table, as Ed had requested. Lila motioned Brian to move away with her eyes.

"I believe you already know where I am, Klaus," said Ed in a low, steady voice. "And if it's me you want, you can let Lila go help the other girls prepare for the party, now."

Klaus' lip curled in an ugly sneer. "And you also know I'm not going to do that until I get what I came for."

Megan glanced around the room, realizing that someone was

missing. Then she knew. It was Carl and Charlie. They had moved behind an Asian screen when the car drove up. She could see Charlie ducking his lanky height behind the room divider as Carl carefully peeked one eye around it. She knew Carl so well she knew immediately what he wanted her to do. She needed to distract Klaus to get him turned where the two could tackle him from behind.

"Of course, you don't want to let Lila go, Klaus." Megan smiled innocently at the man as though she thought everything in the room was normal. "She's our most beautiful blonde, and no one can blame you for wanting to keep her." She touched Abby's hand as she strolled casually toward the left past her friend, knowing Abby would sense her signal and follow.

Their movement forced Klaus to watch both of them. He turned, ever so slightly, enough to allow Carl to slip around the screen as stealthily as though he were dancing the latest fad dance steps. He had the baseball bat behind his back.

Lila's eyes also followed Megan and Abby, as though pleading with them to make no sudden move. They didn't. They could both see from their new position that Klaus' arm held Lila pinned against him.

"In fact," said Megan, "Abby and I heard a rumor that you were really in love with her, didn't we?" Abby took her cue and nodded. As the two walked further to the left, they could see Charlie also slip out from behind the screen into a position behind the frightened Lila and stoic Klaus. Megan assumed they'd try to pull Lila away to give Ed an open shot at Klaus. But Charlie was not so agile as Carl, and his foot caught the edge of the screen, bringing it down with a crash.

Klaus immediately grabbed Lila tighter to his chest and pulled the revolver he had in his hand from his pocket, putting it to her head. "You Americans think you're so smart, don't you?" he snarled. "Sending your spies out to find all our operatives and foil our missions. Sending your men to circle around behind me is the oldest trick in the book."

"Easy, Klaus," said Ed quietly. "Let's talk this through. No one will rush us."

Lila started crying, and Ed could see Brian ready to make a dive for her. Ed put out his hand and motioned Brian back, while he stepped in front of him. He motioned Carl and Charlie to back away, now that they had been discovered.

"Klaus, go easy now. There's no need for you to hurt Lila, or any of these people who love her. Obviously, your quarrel is with me. What do you say the two of us step outside and settle this like gentlemen?" Ed moved slowly and deliberately a few steps closer to the door, holding out his hand.

But Klaus' voice rose in pitch and volume. "Stand still, you, or I'll shoot her."

"Please," said Lila. Any further words were lost in her cry as Klaus pushed the revolver harder against her temple and tightened his grip on her body.

"All right, Klaus," said Ed. "No surprises. Just tell me what you want to happen here, so we can all expedite the process and release the damsel in distress quickly." He spoke to the wild-eyed man, as casually as though they had been ordering a beer, and deliberately avoided bringing out his Beretta, which Megan thought was odd. Perhaps Ed felt Klaus was too near hysteria to be trusted in an open gun battle. Ed was putting himself in the open, apparently unarmed, to try to protect Lila. "Ladies," he added, in a slow voice. "I'd like you all to go in the bedroom and be very quiet for awhile."

Megan knew from his subdued tone that he meant for them to obey. He had always said his job was easier if there were fewer people, so she motioned to Abby and Mary, and the three started moving slowly across the floor. Ed could actually smile at them as they passed. His cool attitude kept Megan thinking perhaps he could talk his way through the whole thing.

They were almost to the bedroom door when Klaus suddenly saw his advantage slipping away and shouted, "No! Stop where you are!"

Carl said, "Klaus, the ladies can't do you any harm. Let them go."

Stan, from across the room, added, "They don't need to witness this, now do they?"

Brian walked forward a few steps to a position in front of Mary. "Let them go, Klaus."

Ed motioned them with his eyes to keep walking toward the door. But Klaus panicked and fired in front of Megan's foot, waving the gun wildly before immediately putting it again at the side of Lila's head. Megan yelped and jumped back to Abby.

"I see what you're doing, O'Brien," screamed Klaus. "Don't move or the women die first." Immediately Carl poised to jump at Klaus, but Ed held up his hand to wait.

"Klaus," Ed said, still in a calm, slow voice, trying to get the man to focus directly on his face instead of jerking Lila's head around as he bobbed from side to side trying to watch everyone at once.

Megan wondered how Ed used such a calm voice when she couldn't trust her own to speak a word without screaming. Was she getting a glimpse of Ed's professional ability in action, even as this drama unfolded?

"Klaus," Ed said again. The German's gaze ranged frantically around the room from person to person. The steady voice finally had the desired outcome as Klaus focused his eyes on Ed's. "Tell me who you are, Klaus. What has your cell sent you to do? Talk to me."

"I'll tell you nothing, and I'm not letting you live, O'Brian." Klaus almost spat out the words. "You've been working against our intelligence operatives too long. You're dangerous to our operations."

"Why is that, Klaus?" Ed walked slowly toward one of the room's couches and sat down at the one nearest Klaus and facing the door. "Why don't we two professionals just sit down and talk about your job and mine?"

"I'm not sitting down with you, O'Brian." Klaus aimed his weapon around the room, threatening all those present, but as Carl poised to jump Klaus while his revolver was not on Lila, Klaus sensed his movement and immediately put it back to Lila's head. She whimpered, looking beseechingly into Brian's eyes. "Please," she finally was able to say, "Don't try anything, please." Brian held up his hand to Carl, then both hands fell helplessly to his sides.

"We seem to be in a standoff, Klaus," said Ed. "What is it you think I've done? Or I should ask what you've been sent to do?"

"You know what I've been sent here to do, O'Brian. To take you out for our assassin squad, to take you out the way you took out our operatives in Heidelberg and in Beirut."

"Your men killed one of ours in Heidelberg, Klaus, and your operatives kidnapped six of our people and killed one in Beirut, didn't they? I would call that self-defense. Let me see. Are you aligned more with the communists in the Soviet Union, East Germany, or the Islamic Jihads in the Middle East?"

"Oh, yes, you know about all of those cells, don't you O'Brian? So you know why I've been sent to get you." Ed lounged casually on the couch, leaning one arm half under the cushions while moving his right hand back as though to settle more comfortably on the sofa. "Then, if we've been doing the same job for different causes and different sides, that makes the two of us enemies, but I see no quarrel that you might have with my friends here. Why can't we let them all go to the other room, and you and I can come to an agreement, or finish this, one way or the other."

"Can't do that." Klaus' steely eyes searched the room as he said, "These people are either involved or know about this in some way, and they'd never let me kill you and get away clean." He looked at Megan and said, "You, O'Brien will never fire at me as long as you know I can kill Megan. I knew you'd come back from your 'sea-going' mission when her precious Annex was threatened. Your same American fatal and phony sense of chivalry will not let any of you fire on me as long as I have Lila in my arms, dumb little flirt that she is." He looked straight at Brian and added with a smirk, "And how does that make you feel, Brian, for me to be holding her hostage?"

Brian tensed, but he knew he didn't dare move toward the man, or Klaus would shoot Lila in the head immediately. Forcing himself to follow Ed's lead, he answered calmly, "Lila is smarter than you think, Klaus, and I love her, flirty nature and all." Lila opened her eyes to look into Brian's. "Because you took advantage of her friendliness and her closeness to the people in this room, that doesn't mean you can change my feelings for her...or hers for me."

Lila looked at Brian as long as she could before Klaus jerked her neck sideways by pushing the revolver tighter against the smooth flesh on the side of her face. Klaus laughed. "Hurts you all to see her like this, doesn't it?" He leered out at the people in the room. "Then I have a deal for you all. Let me take out the Colonel, nice and tidy like, right here, right now, one shot to the head, and I'll take Lila to the end of the dirt road in my car and I'll dump her out there for you to pick her up. Guaranteed."

Brian said, "I don't believe you."

Trying again to distract Klaus's attention, Ed said, "Sounds like a good deal to me, Klaus. You kill me, and get away with Lila's help. How do you plan to get out of West Germany and back to your own country? By the way, what country did you say you worked for?" Ed casually moved the pillow at his side to a seemingly more comfortable position behind him, as though settling down for a long, leisurely talk.

Megan could see Carl brace his feet for a spring since he knew where Ed's gun was now. She wanted to shake her head at him, but it would have drawn attention toward his movement. Instead, she fixed her eyes on his, knowing he would feel them and look at her so she could signal. But before she could catch his eye, something shifted in her peripheral vision. She watched the next moment in a horrible slow motion.

Lila made a sudden diving lunge, screaming Brian's name. Klaus fired into her back as she fell into Brian's open arms. Ed immediately fired his Beretta at Klaus, hitting him full in the stomach. Klaus clutched one hand over the gaping hole, as though surprised, and stretched out his right hand, firing at Ed with a muzzle flash. Ed fired again, bringing Klaus to his knees. Carl, Charlie, and Stan quickly surrounded the man, yanking him from his knees to the ground and holding him down. Carl kicked away Klaus' revolver while Charlie and Stan tied his hands.

As soon as they realized Klaus was down, the remaining friends rushed to Lila where she lay bleeding. Brian cradled her head in his lap as he sat on the floor. He put his ear down to hear her whisper, "I love you Brian. I shouldn't have played games...to get you to love me." Tears ran down her face as she choked back gasps. "It hurts...bad."

Brian kissed her face, mingling their tears, as blood now gushed out onto the hardwood floor. "Shh, Lila. We'll get you to the hospital, and we'll have all those babies after you're better."

She attempted a wan smile. "I'm glad...you know...about the babies..." Her words were interrupted by fits of coughing, and Megan could hear blood gurgling around in her throat when no more words would come. She was unconscious.

Brian looked up helplessly to Mary, "Do something, please." She applied pressure by staunching the wound with a sofa pillow.

Megan grasped the limp hand and whispered, "Lila, please hang on. We all love you." Abby rushed to the door to let in Rex Top Cop's men who had already heard the shots and radioed for an air evacuation, fearing the worst.

The MP's rushed in to take charge of the prisoner, who was also badly wounded. Carl came and took Megan's hand. "I think you'd better come over here, Meggie," he said softly.

Megan turned to see Ed still lying where he had fired his Beretta twice, one arm crushing the sofa pillow tightly to his body. She could see a slowly enlarging blood pool soaking the sofa.

"Oh, my God," she cried, and rushed to remove the pillow. "Where were you hit?" The big man looked at her with cloudy eyes, and she and Carl started feeling around for where the blood might be coming from. "Can you move, Dear?" she begged plaintively. "Can you tell us where the bullet hit?"

Carl tried to lift Ed to get him into a more upright position.

"No…" Ed said slowly, feebly waving Carl's hand away. "Can't move…got me low…is Lila okay?"

"They're taking care of her now," said Megan, glancing to the right where her friend was being loaded onto a stretcher by the medics. Brian held Lila's hand to his lips and cried.

"What can we do for you, Dear?" Megan didn't trust her voice to remain calm.

Carl pointed out to the medics there was yet another shooting victim, and they radioed for another helicopter and medical team.

"Bring a back board over here," Carl shouted. "And forget about that guy on the floor. He's the cause of all this. Let him wait for the next medical evacuation. Take the Colonel with Lila in the first bird, or I'll fly it myself!"

The medics moved away from Klaus and hurried to the couch.

As Carl returned to Ed and Megan, she looked into his eyes with thanks, pleading for him to do something. He put an arm around her shoulders. "Hang on, Meggie. It'll be okay."

Megan clasped Ed's hand in both of hers and nuzzled his close-cropped head and ran by his side as the medics carefully loaded him onto the stretcher and carried him to the waiting helicopter. "Carl says it's going to be okay, Darling. Don't give up on me. I love you."

"Put your head down here…by my face, where I can…smell your hair."

Reluctantly, Carl pulled Megan back from Ed, and the medics jumped on board. Everyone ducked back as the helicopter rotors groaned, flexed, and lifted off into the darkness.

Chapter 32

Carl drove Megan's Fiat to the military hospital at Nürnberg, with Megan holding tightly to his arm for her own reassurance, and with Brian in frozen silence in the back seat. The others followed in several cars of those who were arriving for a party, and encountered a crime scene instead. Rex Top Cop had allowed his friends to postpone their depositions until they could discern the conditions of Lila and Big Ed. German police had secured the crime scene.

It was dark when the convoy of autos pulled into the hospital's parking lot and spilled out several worried teachers and military officers. Brian and Megan were shuttled off to a private waiting room, but both agreed their friends should be brought in, too. And the waiting began. Both Lila and Ed were in surgery, as was Klaus, so there was nothing else to do.

Abby had called her landlord to get word to Emily. The older woman reached the hospital before any of the doctors came out, the fenders of her VW bug flapping all the way to Nürnberg. And so the gang waited together…for some word…any word.

Brian was not holding up well at all. He sat in one of the ugly, green plastic chairs in the waiting room asking of everyone who came near, "They had a deal worked out. Why did she lunge to me like that? Klaus said he would have dropped her off at the end of the road after he killed the Colonel. We'd hate to lose the Colonel, but at least Lila could have had a chance." He cried out again, "Why didn't she stay still and wait?"

Robert made the situation more clear to him. "Lila may be our lovable dumb blonde, but she's smart, Bri. Think about it. Lila knew Klaus had no intention of letting her go. She could testify to everything she knew against him. He would have dropped her off at the end of the road, all right--dead."

When Brian raised his head to look at Robert and consider his logical words, Robert added, "Lila knew that gun in Klaus's pocket was aimed at her all the way to Stan's. She was his ticket to get close enough to the Colonel to take him down. She knew Klaus wouldn't let her go, alive. She lunged to you because she wanted to be in your arms--that's all. She simply wanted you to *know*..." Robert's voice curled away as Brian nodded and sank his head in his hands.

"Ed never even cried out," said Megan to Carl and Abby, who sat on either side of her while Emily, Stan, and Mary hunched in the chairs across the aisle. "We didn't even know Klaus' shot had hit him because we heard him shoot Klaus twice after Klaus shot Lila in the back. I lost track of the number of shots fired. Why didn't he say something? I should have been with him. We were all rushing to see what we could do for Lila. But then we couldn't have left Lila either." She mopped at her tears with the handkerchief Carl provided. "You always keep a handkerchief just for me, don't you?"

He put one arm around her protectively while pressing the other hand to hers. "My strength...as always, Meggie."

After what seemed an eternity, one of the doctors entered the waiting room. "The young lady is semi-conscious and wants to see Brian first, and then Megan, Emily, and Abby. Are they all here?"

The four rose, but the doctor placed himself in front of them. "I must warn you that she's very weak, and we'll only be able to let you look in on her. She's being taken by helicopter to Ramstein where she'll be medically evacuated to Walter Reed Military Hospital back in the States. We're hoping they'll be able to do more for her. We've done all we can to stabilize her here." He removed his glasses and wiped his eyes with his bloodstained jacket sleeve. "You can see her for only a moment, please."

Brian gasped, "Are you saying...?"

"We don't know, Lieutenant. It's too early to tell if the surgery we did will be sufficient, or if she can get through this emergency free of massive infection. We just don't know yet. Gunshot wounds are often unpredictable." The four followed the doctor down the hall, Abby and Emily holding Brian's hands while Megan looked back beseechingly at the others to tell her if any news came of Ed.

Stan rose suddenly and went for the phone. "We have to get Brian an emergency leave to accompany Lila." He rang up a number and waited for someone to answer, tapping his foot on the floor impatiently. Soon everyone in the room was listening to his one-sided conversation.

"Yes, I know emergency leave is granted only for the spouse.

These two are engaged." He stamped angrily. "Yes, I know, but we're all witnesses tonight that she and Brian are betrothed. How do I know when they'll marry? Soon as she recovers, but she may not recover at all, if we can't get Lt. Brian Cox there to help her."

"When? Now! Never mind his unit chain of command...I'll vouch for all of them. Believe me, they'll sign this...just get him on that plane. No, he won't need baggage. We'll send him whatever he needs. Just take a set of blank orders by helicopter to the Ramstein Medivac flight terminal. Luke's with you there? Great, get him in the air to Ramstein. He'll sign those orders himself if he has to. That's right...do it now...we'll figure it all out later."

The three women stumbled back to the group. Emily was crying softly, while both Abby and Megan looked stricken. "She wants us to help ourselves to anything we want and send everything else to her parents in Kentucky," said Abby. "She makes it sound as though she won't be back. She was talking so slowly, and was so pale...not our usual bubbly Lila. She said to thank you all for the friendship and to keep having parties for her."

Abby put one arm around the weeping Emily and steadied Megan with the other. "I keep thinking about her comments about us 'four musketeers' all the time. How will we manage without her?"

"She'll get well," said Megan, as though to convince herself. "She finally made a decision about men...she finally realized what she wanted out of life. God wouldn't let her die after such an important choice. She must live to commit to Brian. He loves her."

The waiting friends joined hands in a circle and silently bowed their heads.

Brian returned, massively shaken.

Stan grabbed his arm and gave him instructions to get in the helicopter with Lila, and Luke would meet them in Ramstein with orders...of a sort.

"What does that mean?" asked the young man.

"Not to worry, Brian. This is me, and I'm ordering you. I outrank you! At least I do until your promotion to Captain in a couple of months. Just obey as you're told and stick by Lila. You'll fly with her to D.C. We'll send you whatever clothes or paperwork you need."

"Better still," said Big Don, reaching for his wallet and handing Brian a stack of bills. "Buy what you need."

"But I..."

"Forget it, Bri. You'll be back when Lila is better, and we'll take it out of your hide then," said Don. "Just go, and take care of her. Tell her we all love her."

The young man ran back down the hall to Lila's room and disappeared. Stan said quietly, "You all are witnesses that I ordered him to go, *against his will*, aren't you?" Everyone nodded.

"Okay, Megan," continued Stan. "What can we do for you and the Colonel now?"

"I don't know. I don't know how bad his injury is. He said he couldn't move." She put her hands over her face to stop their shaking. "I wish the doctor would come tell us what is happening to him."

Another two hours went by, with Don and Stan bringing back coffee and sandwiches from the snack bar. Finally, a doctor entered the waiting room. "Who is the next of kin for Colonel O'Brian?"

The group looked at each other and then Carl said, "Megan is his fiancé. You can talk to her, but we all want to be with her." He reached out and took Megan's hand. "She's ready."

"Well, said the doctor. The Colonel will live, but..."

There was a noticeable rustle of relief in the room.

"But," the doctor continued more forcefully, "he's paralyzed."

Megan gasped. "How bad is it, Doctor? May I see him?"

"You may see him for a moment, but you must understand. He won't be able to move. He's sedated and immobilized. We found an old piece of shrapnel left over from Vietnam that had been too close to his spine to remove. This new gunshot injury blasted through the front of his body into the spine and clipped the metal. It shifted, and it has paralyzed the nerve. I don't know how he's managed to stay on active duty with that shrapnel remaining in his spine, but for now, it's impossible to say if this will be permanent or not."

"May I see him now?"

"Yes, but I must make sure you are clear about this. You mustn't mention the paralysis. Act hopeful, for the sake of his mental attitude and rehabilitation."

"Nothing else matters. I just want to see him." She reached unconsciously for Carl's hand, and he escorted her down the hall.

"Of all the tough luck," said Robert. He held Abby's arm in his. Everyone merely nodded and waited.

No one moved to go home.

Chapter 33

The normally hectic patterns of the end of a school year were a jumble of hazy events for Megan as she waited for her flight to Washington D.C. Ed was improving, and even working part-time at the Pentagon, in a wheelchair, when he didn't have to stay in Walter Reed Army Hospital for physical therapy. He had insisted that Megan wait to come until after school was out. Since they were not yet married, she wouldn't be granted emergency leave. Even Stan couldn't manipulate orders for a Department of Defense civilian instead of a military member. Of course, she never said so, but she hesitated to quit her job just in case it would be the only employment to sustain the two of them should Ed not recover the use of his legs.

And Ed felt it would be easier for him to tolerate his physical therapy and long recuperation in the hospital by himself. He was determined to *walk* to her when she arrived. They agreed she would be with him when he found out from the neurologists if his condition would be permanent or not, a rendezvous for July 13th.

The first weeks were difficult, as Ed struggled to accept his paralysis, and Megan yearned to be with him, but Carl kept reminding her, "You're in love with a proud man, Megan. Grant him his pride to do this alone, in case it turns out that's all he has left."

As the weeks went by, however, she found Ed's sense of humor was intact. His frequent phone calls were full of hope, jokes, and anticipation of the big day when they would find out the news. Megan could almost hear his smile through the telephone wires. When he received her letters, he was delighted. "Darling," he'd say, chuckling over the phone, "You can make starting a lawn mower sound like a national symphony. What a jewel you are." His confidence and hope sustained her.

Megan knew if the paralysis were permanent, he would be medically discharged from the Army. Twenty-four years of service were on the line plus his promotion to general. She knew how much Ed wanted to remain on active duty. The Army was his life.

On July 12th, Megan watched the clouds outside the jet chase each other, changing shapes even as she gazed. As the plane banked to land in Washington D.C., she prayed silently that the news would be good. Her fear of flying could not have deterred her from being at Ed's side, whatever the outcome.

The sterile hall seemed endless as Megan walked beside Ed's wheelchair to the neurologist's office deep in the catacomb of Walter Reed Hospital. They were holding hands tightly as though each could give the other strength. Her steps slowed outside the door. "I know you wanted to walk to me, Darling, but this wheelchair is probably just for your physical therapy, just for a little while longer--nothing for us to worry about. No matter what happens, you know that I love you, and I want to be with you."

"I know, darling. And you know I'll love you forever. It all is riding on what the doctor says," he answered. Megan felt an ominous chill. She sensed Ed was not saying all that he was thinking.

"Are you ready?"

He steadied his hand in hers, and pulled her down to kiss her. "You're the light of my life, darling...don't ever forget that."

The warmth of his kiss could not quite touch the coldness that suddenly gripped her heart.

I know what he's thinking. If the news is bad, he'll try to send me away. Oh God, don't let that happen!

Ed's hands were shaking, and Megan sat down in the waiting room next to him and hugged him to her...whispering, "Darling, it's going to turn out all right. You'll be back on active duty and up for that General's Board before you know it." She hoped her voice sounded suitably optimistic, but when she looked into his eyes, she saw the doubt there, and it scared her.

"The doctor will see you now," said the buxom nurse, ushering them into the office.

"Are you sure, Doctor?" Ed's hands clasped on Megan's so tightly she feared they'd break, but she made no sound. She didn't even bother to hide the tears that rained down her cheeks.

"Yes, Colonel. This is not the prognosis you wanted to hear, but I'm trying to be as honest as I can so you can make your plans for the future. I know you wanted to remain on active duty, but your medical discharge will be in the mail by tomorrow. Even with more surgery, unless there is some monumental new discovery for nerve damage, you'll not get back the use of your legs. I'm sorry."

Seeing Megan's tears, and Ed's pale, stoic face with teeth clenched to hold in his emotion, the doctor brought the interview mercifully to a close.

The taxi ride to Ed's hotel was quiet, each of them holding tightly to the other, and thoughts of their future decisions intimidating conversation.

Ed seemed embarrassed for Megan to help him transfer his lanky, 180-pound body from the chair to the bed and roll him over to make room for herself beside him when they reached his ground floor hotel suite to rest awhile. She immediately wrapped her arms around his prone body and kissed him. "Darling, you mustn't mind my helping you. I love you. Why would I feel badly about helping?"

"You know, Megan, don't you?" His eyes focused on the ceiling, and he seemed to be choosing his words carefully.

Megan's throat tightened.

"You know that your love has been the best thing I've ever had in my life. Our time together has been pure joy to me. I know I've always joked around about having had a million 'little honeys,' but you know that was all B.S. Only you have ever mattered to me."

"I knew that." She smiled at him and touched his face softly. "It's been a joyful time for me too, Ed…you know it…I…"

"But I can't let you stay." The words tumbled out fast.

"What?" Megan jerked up to her elbow to stare at his face.

"I can't allow you to take care of me." He took a sharp breath and rushed on as though he needed to say it all before he couldn't say it any longer. "You know I wanted to marry you before…before this all happened. But you must know it's now impossible."

"Why would you say that?" Her tears choked into sobs. "I love you too much to leave you. I would never leave you just because of this…this temporary setback."

"I know you wouldn't, darling. That's why I must send you away *now*…while I still have enough strength. I love you too much to let you watch another man you love die. It's been your greatest fear. It almost destroyed you once--I won't let it destroy you again."

"But I won't let you die. No matter what happens, we can still do things together, go places together. A wheelchair is no big deal-- millions of people have them. Do you think I'm so weak that I can't handle helping you?"

"I don't want to be helped, darling. I want you to go on with your life, and someday meet a man who can carry you over the threshold, make love to you all night, and hold you forever—one who can give you a secure life. I'm no longer that man, my darling, and I want you to live, for *both* of us."

"But, doesn't it matter that I want to be with you, that I don't mind any of those things?" Her tears were now a flood, and her words were scarcely intelligible. "Don't I get a choice in this decision? It affects us both, you know. I love you, and you love me, and that's all that matters to me. I don't care about any of the rest."

Ed's cheeks were also wet with tears as he pulled her body over his and hugged her to his chest. "You know, darling, I still love the scent of your hair, and it's what I will remember forever--that once a beautiful, stately, long-legged brunette loved me, and she had the most remarkable hair." When Megan was sobbing and could not respond, he added, "No darling, this isn't your choice. I'm the one who must make this decision. I want you to go live your life and be happy. It's the one thing you can still do for me."

When Megan snuggled her face into his neck, crying, he whispered, "My darling, you must allow me to make this decision final, because I wouldn't be able to stand watching you change your life in order to take care of me. I've made plans just in case this was the outcome. I'll be all right. But I want you to go bravely out there and be all right, too."

"And do you think making another life out there without you will be any easier for me than at least being *with* you?"

"Darling, I wanted to take care of you forever, but I won't allow you to take care of me."

"This is all your silly pride talking, Ed. Why does it matter who takes care of whom? You know you want me with you."

He sighed. "Yes, my dear, I will always want you with me, and I suppose some of it is my silly pride, but...I want to think of you out there living as vibrantly and enthusiastically as the night I met you. If you love me, you'll do as I ask. "

"And what if I *won't* leave you?"

"This will be our last night together, my love. We'll hold each other tonight, and I'll make you understand."

Chapter 34

"Father Harry said I'd find you here." Carl mopped sweat from his forehead.

Megan reached out her hand to her friend and pulled him down to sit beside her on the late summer grass. No other greeting was necessary. "I guess I've climbed up here almost every day since Harry invited me here my first day back in Germany. He suggested I needed a safe place to just 'be.'

They quietly surveyed the valley below from their perch at the top of the Kneifelspitze, a mountain brooding over the strenuous Maria Gern trail of Berchtesgaden.

Carl finally broke the silence. "They tell me that valley below is where they filmed those incredible opening scenes of *The Sound of Music*. Is that true?"

"That's what Father Harry says."

She seemed regally calm to Carl...almost supernaturally so. "Have you made any decisions yet?" he asked quietly. "Are you ready to go back to your classroom for a new year or have you decided to pack out and go home to California?"

"I've spent the week since I returned from the States at Harry's dormitory, and hiking these hills. I feel as though I know each mountain intimately. He told me he'd 'saved a mountain for me.' One from which I'd be able to see my way more clearly and feel my faith again. Harry said that God doesn't leave us in decisions to flounder alone."

She sighed. "I've watched the hawks and mountain sheep with Harry's binoculars, and I've sketched the peak's pastel in water colors and chalk. The Alps are self-contained and serene, in a way I'd *like* to be. You know, I always loved that Psalm, 'I will lift up mine eyes unto the hills from whence cometh my help.' But I think I know what it means now. We sort of felt that before too, the first time we skied together from the top of the mountain. Do you remember?"

Carl nodded. The companionable silence endured a long time.

"Did your sister, Laura, get here after I left for the summer?"

"She came back with me after my leave, so I haven't been in much mischief this summer." He tried, as always, to make Megan laugh. "Except, of course, for during my week's leave back to the states for Lila and Brian's wedding."

Her grin erupted, finally, as she remembered the scene. "Carl, you'll never change! And I'd never want you to." She paused a moment. "But, I'll bet you never saw that cute little blonde you brought to the wedding again either, did you?"

"How did you know?"

"You were dreadful. When I came in, you ran all the way across the ballroom shouting, 'Here comes the only woman I've ever loved!' The guests about fell out of their chairs. That was tacky, my dear. How many beers had you had already before I arrived?"

"Oh, is that what I did? I sort of wondered when the blonde left the hotel immediately. But I didn't care. You never know what you'll say with a few beers. Did I embarrass you?"

"I just tried to get you off the hook by laughing and proclaiming it was one of your jokes. You were too sloshed to notice." She laughed at him and shook her head in sympathy.

"And you also know that it might not have been a joke, don't you?" He threw up his hands in the air and looked helpless.

"You never learn, do you? I guess strangers were mostly surprised by the age difference. Our friends just laughed. They know you." She looked away to the valley beyond. "But tell me about Laura." Megan's eyes showed him she was not ready to talk about the hard things yet.

Carl tried to be enthusiastic about his new foray into surrogate fatherhood. "She's a neat kid, but she turned out to be too pretty of a redhead, and I'm having trouble keeping all those pilots in Katterbach away from her. She scares me to death—she likes them all!"

Megan smiled again, arching her eyebrows in mock surprise. "Gee whiz, Carl! Where do you think she got *that* trait? She's grown up since you left her a cute little twelve-year-old. You've not been around a teen-ager before, and you don't remember what it was like to be one."

"Maybe that's it, but it does seem like it's dangerous to leave her alone with all those guys around, so I can't come up to see you in Bamberg unless I bring her, and I can't have you down to stay with me when we need to talk. I'm already tired of setting a good example. And what on earth would I tell my folks if that little girl got into trouble with one of my friends or something?" Sheer panic at the potential catastrophe was written all over his face. "And HQ gave me an additional job, too. Now they have me swamped prosecuting court marshals and dishonorable discharges—in court all day, preparing cases all night, and playing back tapes of testimony. I haven't been near an airplane in a week, and I'm not around enough to watch her."

"Send her to stay with me in Bamberg, especially while you're up to your ears in this extra assignment. I've raised teen-agers, so it won't be a problem. Then you'll be free to go out in Katterbach."

"But then, I won't be able to come stay with you either, will I? This is a real dilemma."

"You can come up anytime you want, Carl. The couch or the Flocati rug will always be there." She cushioned the statement with a smile. "It's time for you to seriously look for a nice young lady, and you won't do it while you're spending all your free time with me. As for Laura, I can take her along on ski trips, or any traveling I do. She'll see more of Europe than you'll have time to show her."

"You're planning on staying on another year, then?" He sighed. "I was afraid you might decide to go home after all the disappointment, and after Ed."

"That's why I've been here, searching for answers, alone. I think I've decided to stay, only in these few days since I've been on the mountain to think it all through. I couldn't seem to decide at home. I love Bamberg, and I'm needed there. That's a big part of it. I've learned that I need to be needed. Ed needed me for awhile, and I'm sure that's what let me love him."

She ducked her head, then arched it strongly. "There are other reasons, too. DoDDS has a great educational program for children, and it's a marvelous chance to have the academic freedom to really teach. I love our military officers, I believe in their mission, and I want to support them in their jobs at the Border too. I guess that motto of 'duty, honor, and country' rubs off on those of us who see you guys in action. I'll just grow old as a DoDDS dolly like Emily, I suppose."

She grew pensive again, holding Carl's hand in her lap, absent-mindedly stroking it.

He waited quietly, knowing she was drawing strength to tell him the painful part. "Do you want to tell me about your trip to D.C. before Lila's wedding? There was little time for us to talk with so many people around, and I could tell you weren't ready yet..."

Megan stared off into the clouds slowly gathering toward twilight. "He sent me away, Carl. He didn't want me to take care of him." There were tears coming to her eyes.

"Did he say why? I know he loved you."

"Actually, his loving me was the reason he gave. He said he loved me too much to watch me grow old trying to take care of him." She alternately smoothed and crinkled the Bavarian dirndl skirt she wore with one hand while holding Carl's hand tightly with her other.

"You knew he wanted me there with him when he found out from the doctor whether the paralysis would be permanent or not. We were so glad to be together, and I was so relieved to see that big Irish smile again. He kept saying he needed to hold my hand to reassure himself I was really there, still his 'anchor to life and warmth,' as he calls me." She dropped her head and sighed. "Then there is always that crazy thing with my hair.

"But, I think I began to realize what he was thinking when he kept stressing the idea that we'd get married *after* the hospital had released him to go back to active duty, *after* he had recovered, *after* he could hold me again, as soon as he could *walk* with me, and as soon as he could make love to me..." Her voice broke.

"The news was negative, then?"

"Yes. The medical specialists agreed the damage was permanent, the shrapnel couldn't be removed, and that nothing could reverse his paralysis from the waist down. He held tightly to my hand through the consultation." Her tears were streaming down her cheeks, now. "He told me his plans that night—but his plans weren't for me."

"What was he planning?"

"He'd hired a crusty old sergeant who had served under him in Vietnam and Cambodia to be a sort of 'British batman,' whom he could pay to take care of bathing and dressing and such. I met the man—a huge, warm bruiser who certainly was able to lift even 'Big Ed' in and out of a wheelchair. Sgt. Middlefield was kind to Ed, and to me. He told me he had confidently followed the Colonel's lead through many missions, and since he, too, was alone, he had nothing better to do than to follow him to the end. We understood each other. He said he knew I'd be visiting the Colonel from time to time—to keep up morale, of course. The sergeant is a good man.

"Ed plans to just fade away into the backwoods of North

Carolina and fish from his lake cabin. Sgt Middlefield had already enlarged and strengthened a lakeside platform to accommodate the wheelchair. He said that if I loved him, I'd let him go, alone."

"He's trying to spare you grief. I'd feel the same way. Ed's proud and independent."

Megan nodded, then lay back on the grass to watch the clouds darken in the sky. "I know," she said, wiping her tears. "He wouldn't even discuss it. He had already made up his mind that if the news were good, he'd marry me. And if it were bad—he'd send me away." Megan paused to control her voice. Carl waited in silence, always able to feel her pain.

"It was something more, too. He didn't want me to see him die, like I had Andy. He believed it would be too much for me, and he wanted me to find someone who could be a real husband, to 'make me a life,' as he called it. I felt *he* was that person. In the end, I wasn't the one who got to make the choice."

"Life doesn't always give us choices, Megan. You loved Andy, but you had no choice when it was time to let him go. You love me in some special way, but I had no choice that you feel I'm too young for anything permanent." He grinned for a moment. "But, you'll have to admit we've made a hell-of-a team!"

She smiled softly, and put her hand over his on the grass. "You'll always be my best friend and knight in shining armor, Carl. We know and understand each other so well."

He squeezed her hand. "And now you've finally learned to love again, and a bullet takes away Ed's mobility. Again, you didn't have the choice. It was his choice, Meggie."

"I'm sure you, of all people, will see the irony in this, Carl. Ed said I was 'too young' to be tied down to an 'old man.'"

"There's that crazy age thing again, isn't it?" He grinned at her revelation, and then took her hand again to say the hard things. "He doesn't want to put you through another crisis by your watching him struggle, Megan. He wants to spare you that, and I like the man even better for it. It's *your* job, now, to support his decision."

"I know, Carl. Good old 'stiff upper lip' and all that. I had to push all the pain under, again, and keep smiling, *for him*. He was determined to give me my freedom, whether I wanted it or not. Why do all you men think you know best?" Her wan smile focused on her companion of the mountaintop. "I love to watch the colors as the sun goes down." They watched painted trails of reflected pinks and purples on the surrounding mountaintops in silent communication.

"You know, Carl, I've pretty much accepted these new changes in my life while I've been sitting on the top of these mountains watching God perform miracles in the sky. This was Ed's choice. I was always teasing him about his intense dedication to 'duty, honor, and country.' Now, I see that our love was not meant to be easy, or even possible. I'll have to see where my own duty lies."

She brushed back her hair to feel the breeze. "I wish he hadn't been doing the job he was, but had he not been doing those missions, we might never have met. I'm certainly not sorry we met. Our love was, in its own way, a healing experience for both of us. I guess we're both stronger now. I hope so, as we're both going to *need* to be. Now, once again, I must just accept that life is not always fair, and start over. Ed says he'll always keep in touch, and that he'll call me every February 14, wherever I happen to be."

"Why February 14? Because it's Valentine's Day?"

"No. It's both Ed's birthday, and the day my girls and I buried Andy. The date was significant to us both—a good day to reach out to each other. I asked him how he'd know where to find me--I might transfer or move. He just said, 'I'm still good at intelligence gathering. Don't ever think I won't find you, that I won't know should you ever be in trouble, or that I won't be watching over you.'"

She smiled softly, remembering. "He also said the same thing he'd said about his secret missions—that if February 14th ever came, and I didn't hear from him, I'd know he was gone. They would deny his existence, just as though he'd been lost on a military mission."

They watched the sun drift down the sky in silence. Long shadows brought a chill to the air. Megan shivered, and Carl moved closer to put an arm around her for warmth. "I was glad to see you 'Four Musketeers' together again at Lila and Brian's wedding."

"More will change. Abby accepted a job in Wisconsin. She'll be packing out in a couple of weeks. Robert is helping her. Emily will stay in Bamberg until she decides to move on with another transfer. And I know you'll be going too, in another year." Her eyes grew quiet…trying to accept what she couldn't change.

"And you'll stick by me through all that departure trauma I'll have, won't you?"

She nodded, knowing he didn't doubt she would.

"In thinking of Lila, she's fought a great deal of infection, but she definitely seemed on the way back to recovery, didn't she? It's a miracle, since she was shot at such close range. She feels she was spared for a reason, and Brian says it must have been the only way to make her see she should marry him and have all those babies."

"She's in some pain still, but I've never seen her so radiant."

Megan smiled. "It's funny that when Brian transferred Stateside to be near her hospital in Kentucky, he still didn't know how he'd gotten those orders to accompany her on the Medivac plane. I didn't tell him how far out on a limb Stan had climbed to procure them. We've always said Stan could do anything, haven't we?"

The two smiled, remembering all the things Stan had done for the friends at the Post. "I had so hoped he and Mary would go home together," she mused. "But once Mary became ill in Pamplona and her diagnosis came through as Multiple Sclerosis, she was as stubbornly proud as Ed."

"Things don't always work out the way we plan them. You know Rex was determined to get to the bottom of the whole mess regarding Klaus and Lila."

"Klaus was still in a coma when I left."

"He died in late July...no great loss. But MI and CID hadn't had much luck interrogating him. The other accomplice, the one usually with Klaus in the dark car, committed suicide in custody rather than talk to our people. But Ilse broke down and told it all. The authorities were able to get the whole ring."

"But of course, we know there will always be more rings. The Border attracts intrigue like honey, it seems. What did they decide about all those so-called accidents?"

It was pretty much as Rex had figured. The accidents were especially designed to draw Ed out into the open. Klaus stalked Lila because she was the weakest link in the Bamberg group for getting information. Ed's obvious attraction to you gave them the opportunity to track his whereabouts because Ed kept checking in with you. They apparently meant to take Ed out of operation from the first."

"And I guess they did, didn't they? And once more, I feel partially responsible. Yet we had something good between us, and Ed said I 'restored' him after each mission and 'made him able to keep doing his job.' And Ed took them out, too, so it wasn't all lost."

Megan looked out at the darkening hills. "We'd better start down. The trail gets harder to follow in pitch blackness." Carl rose and pulled Megan to her feet. They stood still, taking one last look at the panorama below, now deep in shadow.

"You know, I'm sort of feeling my way back to my faith and even a sliver of the old optimism that I had before Andy...and Ed. The experience between Ed and me turned out all wrong, but I wouldn't have changed our time together."

Megan smiled at Carl. "You knew I came to Bamberg to get away, to be alone, to end my life. Yet it was the people here, you and Abby, and Ed, who've dragged me kicking and screaming back into the mainstream." She held out her arms and breathed in deeply. "My folks at home believed the Border was too dangerous, too isolated, too backward for anyone to enjoy being there. But now, I think it is exactly because of the danger, the isolation, and the backwardness, that I have seen so much beauty in each Bamberg friend.

"Sitting here these last few days and thinking about it, one feels a bit bewitched, as though we were each of us a chip in a giant Kaleidoscope, constantly moving and shifting, an insignificant splash of color alone, yet buoying each other up with mutual love and strength--folding, changing, moving through shared crisis and heartbreak, staying long enough until the next person is strong enough to move on. Somehow we've all become part of the whole, a beautifully moving panorama. I truly don't feel this group experience could have occurred elsewhere but in the shadow of the Border. Whatever happens, one must go on--looking for the next miracle, and perhaps learning to accept the inevitable more gracefully."

"That's more or less what I've been trying to tell you for the last two years—that we're always meant for something more. But your words say it better. You must believe that, and keep on surviving for another day—both for yourself, and for those who love you." He offered his hand. "Are you ready to go back with me, now?"

They descended the mountain trail, stepping carefully in the darkness. Their trek was to Bamberg to start life over again, believing that they and their friends were strengthened because they cared about each other. Even the continuous threat of a brutal Iron Curtain Border could not stand against that kind of strength.

Epilogue – 2002 – The Return

The woman had saved the most important building for last, knowing the difficulty of confronting old ghosts. By force of habit, she swung her rental car into the empty parking lot, into the spot she'd always occupied, despite the passage of many years. She sat still a moment, thinking of other days, gathering courage.

The base itself had been disappointing, but in a post 9/11 world, she had not been surprised. Since the fall of the communist occupation in 1989, the Army had closed many Western European bases no longer needed and consolidated them into this one. Bamberg was no longer the tiny corner of expendable Hell facing the dreaded Border--the end of the line for supplies and creature comforts. It was now an actual 'city' she barely recognized.

The muddy field of tracked vehicles was now a paved parking lot for a new Headquarters and a Commissary the size of Wal-Mart. She remembered with a smile when Rex's hijacking activities had brought them needed food and long underwear. Only the HQ of 82nd Engineers had retained its original spot on post, complete with its mascot out front. And *Seehof* remained, though it was now broken into several smaller German apartments-no party hall or dance floor. She'd tell Stan when she saw him at next year's Vietnam Helicopter Pilot's reunion, since her husband was also a member.

Her first classroom in Germany, the Annex renovated from cavalry horse stables, was now derelict, used only for storing junk, if anyone noticed it at all. Tufts of grass had overcome the makeshift playground's cobblestones. In her heart, she could still hear the laughter of children and the growling of tanks outside her windows, the ones that always had to be open when artillery was firing. Now, an enormous new school for 1500 children graced the top of the hill, looking just like Stateside. *Folks stationed in Bamberg now will never know what it was like for us then, she thought. They will never understand.*

She walked up the familiar steps to the ornate building from the time of Bismarck, their beloved Officer's Club, their 'family living room,' and found the door locked. Not believing it could truly be closed, she headed immediately to the alternate door. The side door was open, but her footsteps echoed down the empty hall.

She peeked into the Red Room, once center of quiet, romantic candle-lit dinners, and found a lone cleaning lady who looked up, questioningly. She nodded at the woman and turned away, recognizing storage lockers standing in front of the graceful old marble fireplace.

The main dining room, where all political discussion and ski trip planning had taken place over nightly family dinners had been converted to a beauty shop. Any current activity seemed represented by two middle-aged ladies under dryers while the beautician smacked her gum and filed her own nails. Cosmopolitan Marco would be horrified, but he now had a restaurant in Spain.

The woman stuck her head into the Club's bar, almost expecting to hear a lively game of Liar's Dice, or Luke's magic tricks causing consternation among the Happy Hour crowd. But the room was silent. The burnished paneling had been torn out and a counter stretched across the floor where the bar used to be. A sign proclaimed this was now ITT, International Tours and Travel, where GI's could book recreational trips. She remembered that no one in the seventies had such free time. The soldiers had been lucky to get away for an occasional Ski Club weekend, and then only with special permission, since the Border alerts had taken all their time.

Now there was no Border to "alert". She wondered what soldiers stationed here now actually *did*. No one was at the counter. There was only a sign-up sheet where one could list his destination and phone number to be called when the clerk decided to show up.

Pausing at the Ballroom's wide leather doors, she wanted to plunge into a Ski Club party with a live band and all her friends waiting there to dance once she arrived. But the silence made her turn away from the desecration of what time and the demise of military Service Clubs had wrought. She felt suddenly older.

She glanced at the wide staircase leading up to the second floor, and immediately was flooded with warmth and longing. She knew seeing the VIP suite that, for a time, had been so very important to her, would only bring heart-wrenching memories. But then, why else had she come?

No, the Officer's Club was gone-with many of its regulars vanished, or dead. Outside, she returned again to the original locked door, and sat down abruptly on the steps. Closing her eyes, she thought of all the times she had sat in this very spot, listening to the hopes and fears of one friend or another--the teacher having boyfriend troubles, the young officer distraught over loss of one of his men, the pilot worried he might be grounded before his next convoluted flight along the Communist Border, the commander concerned about breaches of military secrecy, her beloved spook worried about a plague of mysterious accidents, the young child dying of cancer...

Yes, she knew the Cold War was over, and that the Iron Curtain had collapsed under the weight of communism's fall in 1989. In fact, she had been among the first joyful carloads of people driving through the recently de-mined mud path between the East German Border and the Free world. Once the Soviets had run away, soldiers from *both* sides, who had opposed each other fearlessly for over forty years, joined together to eliminate mines, tear down razor wire fences and machine gun nests so people could cross back and forth freely. She and her husband had immediately driven to Berlin with her little hammer to help knock down the hateful Wall, talking and smiling through its ever-widening gaps to the East German families hacking at the Wall from the opposite side. What a marvelous thing had happened!

With the fall of communism, however, a way of life had ended for military officers and teachers stationed in Bamberg. Far from being the spot at the end of the road where no one came unless ordered, Bamberg now had freeways, *Autobahns,* running all the way to Berlin. Most Americans in the States had considered The Cold War no war at all, even while the people stationed at that Border were threatened and conspiracies flared back and forth from both sides. Bamberg was now a huge, impersonal Post--no longer the place where so much of her life, and that of many others, had changed.

She shuddered, thinking how the end of the Cold War had brought delight, shock, disbelief, suspicion, doubt, all mixed up in the realization that their soldiers had previously been tasked to hold this Border at all costs. Perhaps that danger was over--forever? Who could know? Could they now relax their guard? But then, something even worse would come along--and of course, it had on 9/11, when suicidal terrorists had destroyed friends and buildings *on U.S. soil*, something unheard of in the dangerous days of Cold War when the goal was to keep enemies away from U.S. or Western European soil. It had been a different kind of threat, then. Had it all been for nothing?

The woman sat quietly, remembering. She had found camaraderie, help to live again, a job with children she treasured among people she regarded as best friends. She had found love here, and lost it again in a torrent of bullets. But it had prepared her to believe she still *could* love, that she was still alive and *could* feel again. Eventually, once she transferred to Stuttgart, she had found a lovely pilot, also from the Vietnam era, who treasured her as well. She knew her husband would soon be wondering where she was and come looking for her.

Her friend, Carl, had married late, had a couple of beautiful children, and become a pilot for a national airline. They were still sidekicks and best friends, a bond not breakable through many years. When she had considered marrying, he had flown to her side to check out whether or not her proposed husband would be good to her. She, on the other hand, had flown to be with him when his first child was born, since he was nervous about such a large change in his life. The two families still met to ski together.

Through 21 years at overseas bases, Megan had seen many friends come and go. Abby had gone to teach in Wisconsin, but she seemed happy in her single life, and her poise was still a source of admiration to the woman sitting on the O'Club steps. Emily had finally retired from DoDDS and chose to live in California near her children. Her friends never did meet the 'Ambassador,' but Emily's sense of mystery and humor stayed with her into retirement.

Lila and Brian raised two of the most beautiful little girls imaginable, and remained happy, appreciating each day together.

Milt disappeared one day from both Bamberg and Stuttgart, and colleagues said he had 'gone black,' meaning all his tracks across Germany and Vietnam had to be cancelled out as he began flying for the CIA. So that had been the secret he kept, and why he couldn't establish the permanent relationships he kept trying to predict. He resurfaced again in the new century, looking back on friendships that 'might have been,' but which could have existed nowhere else but a Border base. Rusty, his co-pilot dog for many years, which had surely helped keep him alive in a blizzard, was buried on his farm in 1991.

Mary died of MS. Luke eventually drank and smoked himself to an early death, his bipolar problems and silent schizophrenic moods never allowing him to create a happy life either for himself, for his eventual wife, or for their children.

Big Ed remained paralyzed, but active on the computer as a consultant with a top-secret firm who called upon him for still-needed expertise and knowledge of the secrets game. His phone calls still carried the message of "Hello, my Darling," but Megan's husband understood the bond, as he had understood her special bond with Carl.

Megan realized she had lived on this military Post during a unique time, and had learned to live and love again with people who cared in the way only a Border Base could care--as family. They had supported each other no matter what problems emerged. The danger and intrigue of the Border had forged friendships that could never be broken. And that kind of camaraderie would never come again on this huge, grotesquely urban military base with no discernable mission that had replaced her tiny, beloved Bamberg Kaserne. That special time would never come again.

When a young soldier strolled by and glanced at her curiously, Megan became aware that seeing an older lady sitting on the now-defunct Officer's Club steps with tears flowing down her cheeks, he would probably think her crazy. Perhaps, in a way, she was. But she couldn't move away at that moment. After all, one of her lives had ended, and a new one had begun, right here on these steps. And now their Officer's Club and its beloved people were gone, and even the door from these steps was locked. The Cold War Border that cast shadows on the Iron Curtain for many years, and the warm-hearted people who pledged their lives and loves to defend it, were no more.

She rose, walked briskly to her car, and drove away to meet her husband and catch a plane home to the United States.

Acknowledgements

Though writing is normally a solitary endeavor, this novel came about through the involvement of many friends who freely offered their stories and support. Taken altogether they helped create the untold story of life on the Cold War Border. Many e:mails arrived starting, "Do you remember…?"

Special thanks go to my husband, Eric, and our family, who have been instrumental in encouragement, and to my critique group, Sue, Cindi, Marcella, and Joan, who kept me on task. Thanks to Ron Hosie for interpreting the Border for cover art.

Perhaps most of all, I must thank my Mom, Mary Jean Brant, who kept every letter ever written home from Germany and gave them back to me for reference, when I began writing this novel. Where normally, documenting names, dates, events, times and concerns for an accurate historical novel of an era thirty years gone would be daunting, Mom made it easy by keeping all the records. Those old letters brought back both laughter and tears.

Special credit is due friends who helped me track down factual events and technical data which were top secret until the Soviet Empire fell and Border secrets were no longer classified. These include, but are by no means limited to: Jed Brown, Darlene Bryda, Tom Butz, David Casady, Mike Gray, Ruth McCampbell, Matt and Kay Miller, Al Murphy, Matt Quinlan, and Roger Winslow. These are listed safely in alphabetical order, and I sincerely hope I didn't miss anyone. Generals, Colonels, Warrants, Majors, Captains, and DoDDS teachers, but friends most of all.

Finally, I would be remiss if I didn't acknowledge the Border itself, with a capital "B." By dominating the lives and choices of every person who lived and worked near it's barbed wire, mine fields, and the ugly guard towers erected by the Soviet Union and its Satellite States, the Cold War Border lent its impetus, danger, and its intrigue to this story.

About the Author

M. J. Brett (a.k.a. Margaret Brettschneider) spent twenty-one years teaching literature and journalism on U.S. military bases in Germany for the Department of Defense, or DoDDS. Seven of those years were served on a post where the Infantry, Cavalry, Aviation, Artillery, and Engineering units were tasked to defend the volatile East/West Border that stretched across Europe.

From this vantage point, Ms Brett saw first hand the courage and dedication of the soldiers who manned the front line of a Cold War--whose daily fate depended on the whims of Soviet dictators. She also observed that the story of the Border was relegated to last place, *after* the famed Berlin Wall. Out of that observation came this novel.

Her fascination with both the intrigue *and* the camaraderie of the Border made her feel someone should at least try to tell the Border story—not only the story of the military mission, but also the story of life in a foreign country, and the warm friendships between all who become *family* under the shadow of barbed wire.

Research for *Shadows on an Iron Curtain* came from letters and interviews with many who lived and understood the special challenges of the Border life.

This is Ms Brett's second historical novel. The first, *Mutti's War*, tells of a mother forced to walk her three little boys across WWII to save them and to find her missing husband. The story won the prestigious Paul Gillette Award for Historical Fiction in 2003. It seemed a natural progression from WWII to the Cold War. A third novel is well underway and will be released in 2006.

Ms Brett and her husband retired from their overseas military lifestyle to live in Colorado Springs, where she enjoys her family of children and grandchildren, e:mail from former students, writing and speaking, skiing, and watching wildlife in the back yard from a deck overlooking Cheyenne Mountain.